TINSEL IN A TANGLE

LAURIE GERMAINE

May all your Christmas seasons be joyous and blessed!

Laurie

www.cleanreads.com

Tinsel in a Tangle
by Laurie Germaine
Published by Clean Reads
www.cleanreads.com

ISBN 978-1-62135-716-2
Cover Art Designed by AM DESIGNS

To Leah Schwabauer, who has rooted for Tinsel and Niklas since their humble beginnings at a Christmas party.

And to my Heavenly Father. This is my first fruits. May its aroma be pleasing, and may You be glorified.

OOPS

Crumbling candy canes! Why won't this stuff melt?

Beads of sweat trickle down my spine despite the icy draft seeping around the windowpanes, and I fidget on my knees beside the miniature lab bench. A mound of multicolored Gummy Bears smiles up from the tabletop. I glower in return, for the chewy candies sizzle and burn with success at every lab around Herr Chemie's classroom but mine.

I adjust the Bunsen burner under the test tube, turn it up a notch, and wait.

The potassium chlorate remains a powder.

Blowing out a breath, I drum my fingers on the table. Across the aisle, Niklas crouches at his own mini lab, blond locks falling over his forehead, his eyes gleaming with delight as he detonates his Gummy Bears one by one. Perfection, as usual.

In his accomplishments, I mean. Not his looks.

He glances up to catch me staring, and heat stings my cheeks. Okay, his looks, too. His gaze flits to my untouched candy then back to me, and he whispers, "No blunders this time. Remember?"

"I'm capable of melting a simple compound, thanks."

The corner of his mouth lifts. "That's debatable."

I make a face. I may be far from perfect, but he won't be the only one to ace this—

Glass shatters in front of me.

I yelp and tumble backward, wind-milling my arms and landing on my rear. My eyes flare wide at the remnants of test tube and potassium chlorate littering the tabletop.

Not. Again.

Waving aside the smell of burned sugar, I search the immediate area for the Bunsen burner. Where did it—

Something pops and crackles to my left as Pix Betriebs jabs a dainty finger in my direction. "Fire! Tinsel's set the cabinet on fire!"

Found it.

Fine time for Herr Chemie to leave the cabinet doors open.

My classmates shriek, Herr Chemie shouts, and I yank the hose to the Bunsen burner. It zooms from the shelf, clattering on the tiled floor, but though Niklas shuts off the gas valve at my bench, the damage is done. Flames already swallow piles of papers and books, and some of the stored chemicals bubble, hiss, and foam. One changes color.

A battery of sparks explodes into the room.

Silent night! I scramble to my feet and race for the fire extinguisher. Clutching it to my chest, I whirl about, pull the trigger, and a cloud of CO2 jets across the cabinet shelf. Debris shoots in every direction, chemical flasks topple and smash on the floor, and a fireball of sunset colors erupts amid the mess. My jaw drops.

Students flee the room in a screaming tsunami.

"But...but..." The extinguisher falls limp at my side.

"Forget it, Tinsel." Niklas tugs my elbow as the monstrous inferno spreads. "Time to get out of here."

We dash into the hallway behind our pint-sized, chaotic classmates and make for the exit on the first floor. As we reach the stairwell, a rumble sounds from Herr Chemie's room and the building shakes.

Flashing me a lopsided grin, Niklas shouts above the din, "I have a feeling you just *bombed* your final exam."

WE ALL FLEE THE SCHOOL TOWARD MAIN STREET, RACING AND slipping across the snow-covered yard, the acrid stench of scorched chemicals hanging overhead. I glance back once and let out a moan.

I've done some coal-worthy things in my life, but this blunder takes the fruitcake.

Smoke pours from the third-floor windows of Flitterndorf's School of Talents. Flames dance along the sills to bake the frosty air. "Tinsel was here!" they taunt. In the distance, sirens wail as another *KA-BOOM* vibrates the ground and puckers the roofline.

I compress my lips. This is going to tank my chances for the managerial internship at the Workshop.

Once I reach the sidewalk, classmates cram around me, their little bodies shivering in school-issued *lederhosen* and *dirndls*. Main Street becomes a sea of red and green as townsfolk dash from nearby businesses and homes. With wild gestures, they exclaim alongside students and school faculty members. Gazes slant in my direction; mittens cover heated whispers. I brush nonexistent lint from my dirndl apron. Were I not hemmed in on all sides by the expanding mob, I'd be tempted to slip away unnoticed.

Okay, so the unnoticed part is an exaggeration. When you tower over everyone at sixty-five-and-one-quarter inches (the Red and Green Clans consider forty inches the ideal height), there's no going anywhere unseen.

Believe me, I've tried.

The firefighters have maneuvered into position and are

blasting the flames with water when my father materializes through the frenzied crowd. His face sags in relief when he sees me, and he wraps a floured arm around my middle. He must have come straight from the bakery's kitchen. "Tinsel, *mein Schatz,* are you all right?"

I rub my arms through my wool sweater to stem the chill. "I'm fine, *Vati*."

"Any..." He clears his throat and adjusts his green cap before looking up at me. "Anything I should know about before I talk to Meister K?"

I snort. "You mean, did I have a hand in this?"

The one positive in this situation is knowing that at seventeen, I stand at the lowest point I will ever get in life. I can only go up from here, right?

Please tell me I'm right.

I chop at the crusty snow with the curled toe of my boot. "It was supposed to be a simple lab experiment. 'Even you can't mess this up,' Herr Chemie told me. Unfortunately, I believed him." Bet he'll never again forget to close those cabinet doors.

Vati nods, brows furrowed, and gives me another squeeze. "You're a good kid, Tinsel. One day we'll discover what you're good at." He tilts his head back to toss me a bright smile. "I'll speak with Meister K, *ja?* Maybe he'll...maybe he'll give you a different Penalty this time."

I don't dare to hope. Herding sheep (my most recent Penalty when I exploded the oven in Baking 305 two months ago) was the one job I didn't bungle. Since common sense says to keep me where I do the least amount of damage, I might find myself tripping over wool well beyond graduation in May.

As my father disappears into the crowd, I yank on the brim of my beanie, crimping my ears. The next time something's on fire, remind me *not* to reach for the extinguisher.

A few yards away, dressed in a resplendent green overcoat and cap (with matching badges as a visual reminder he holds the second-most powerful job in Flitterndorf), the COE stops to talk with a few teachers. He nods, listens, nods again, then clasps his hands behind his back and scans the area. As his gaze rises to meet mine, his mouth turns down at the corners.

When *I* become the COE, I won't look like I swallowed a stocking-full of lemons.

"Tinsel Kuchler, I'd swear on Frosty's hat you're trying to destroy Christmas."

I turn at the nasally voice by my elbow. Classmates Jopper and Pix unite in a glare, but since they come to the middle of my ribcage, peaked hats included, their intimidation falls...short.

Pix crosses her arms. "Figures you'd blast the production wing to smithereens with only three weeks to go. How are the Toy Makers supposed to meet quota now?"

"We could always pit the clans against each other in a competition for 'most gifts completed.'" I force a smile, my gaze flicking over her cherry red *dirndl*. "Nothing like the threat of losing to spur the Red Clan into productivity."

Pix's eyes narrow as a hand claps me on my shoulder. A strong, confident hand, and I steel myself for another encounter with the only classmate I look up to (literally; *so* not figuratively).

"Should you ever wonder if you'll make it into the history books"—Niklas gestures with his perfect chin toward the school, green eyes twinkling—"wonder no more. They're gonna write your name on the pages with a jumbo-sized marker."

Shrugging off his hold before his warmth can seep through my sweater, I glance at the building spewing smoke. The red and green timbers have taken on a charred quality, but at least the flames are gone. "I didn't mean to knock the burner into the chemical cabinet. My hand must have caught the hose when I jerked away, and its trajectory did the rest."

Niklas's lips spread into a dimpled grin. "Still, next time you want to go out with a bang, stick to the Crafters' rooms."

"Tangled lights!" Jopper flaps his arms. "One-fifth of our

school is destroyed, one-fourth of the Christmas presents gone, and you two crack jokes?"

Niklas waves his comment aside. "Look on the bright side, Jipper—"

"Jipper's over there." I point to the twin down the street. "This one's Jopper."

Niklas's grin widens as he catches my gaze. "Look on the bright side, *Jopper*. Thanks to Kuchler's impromptu school renovations, I'll be a shoo-in for the managerial internship."

My stomach drops, but I mask my nerves with a serene smile. "Don't count your candy canes before they're striped. Meister K might be so wowed by such spontaneous creativity, he could convince Herr Referat to skip all interviews and outright hand me the internship."

"Not a chance." Pix clenches her little hands into fists. "He can't afford your kind of creativity at the Workshop."

Niklas taps the bell atop her hat, making it jingle. "I'm sure Grandpop will take many things into account, my friend."

Pix beams up at him. Probably because he referred to her as "friend." (She must not realize it's his cover whenever he can't remember a name.)

"But setbacks and internships aside"—he skims his hands along his leather suspenders—"let's not forget the blessing in disguise."

I arch my eyebrows. "And that would be?"

Niklas turns to address the crowd. "Fellow students, it would seem our winter break has come a day early. For those wishing to stand around and sulk"—he winks in my direction—"carry on. But anyone in the mood for a little celebratory fun, follow me!" With a whoop, he tears off down Main Street, and on his heels scamper a dozen classmates, starry-eyed and smitten. I bet a pound of my mother's chocolates he calls only two of them by name.

There was a time (back when I was naïve and Niklas wasn't so puffed up) when my heart would have melted at the fact he knows both my first *and* last names. Now all it does is—

I grimace. Never mind. The point is, Niklas remembers my name because I'm the one classmate who can (almost) look him in the eye, and I tolerate Niklas for the same reason others fawn over him. His lineage.

And the fact that someday I'll have to call him "Boss."

A shoulder nudges mine. "You know you want to join them."

My gaze slides to Kristof. "I'd rather eat coal for breakfast." At sixteen, Kristof is not as tall as his brother and has yet to surpass me in height, but I definitely look up to him in the figurative sense. "I'm still searching the books for some loophole that would allow you to usurp Niklas when the time comes."

Eyes twinkling (it's a family trait), Kristof shakes his head. "I don't want the job. I take orders better than I give them, like most everyone else." With a sweep of his hand, he indicates the dispersing students trailing after Niklas without question, without thought.

"Exactly the problem. Niklas cares more about having fun and racing his SnoMo than learning the family trade. And if he leads for fifteen, twenty, thirty years or more, imagine the state of this place when he's done."

Down the street, a snowmobile chugs to life, and Niklas pulls on his helmet. I scowl. "Mischievous, spoiled, doesn't-appreciate-how-blessed-he-is grandson of a Kringle."

Which Kringle? Kris, of course, though we call him Meister K around here. And since their family's mantle usually passes to the oldest son, it's likely that one day that boy zooming away on his souped-up SnoMo will be the one delivering toys to believing children on Christmas Eve.

I'd fear for our holiday's continued success, except when Niklas reaches Santa Claus status, I plan to have already established myself as the new COE. This will allow me to counteract any foolhardy decisions he makes in not taking his job seriously.

But first I must nab that managerial internship, the next logical step on the Workshop's corporate ladder.

And though today's hiccup might have broken the rung preceding the internship, I'm not about to let that bother me. I have a long reach.

For an elf.

A LITTLE UNEXPECTED

The next afternoon, clad in an old green *dirndl* and sturdy snowshoes, I race up Huff 'n Puff Hill, almost a half hour behind schedule. One of my brothers changed the time on my alarm clock, so now I'm late for a meeting with Herr Stricker at the Lower Stables. I don't suppose a retired elf who works part-time to keep his mind from going numb has anything better to do than wait for his assistant to show up?

That's my year-long Penalty for damaging the school's west wing: aiding Herr Stricker in his duties involving Niklas's reindeer, the Third String. Not as exciting as working with Meister K's Big Eight in the Upper Stables, but it's better than herding sheep. And if I can prove my competence in this area, then maybe another mishap or two will land me some Penalties at the Workshop across Huff 'n Puff Hill. Penalties like...detailing the interior wood trim or, uh...scrubbing toilets.

I bite my lip. Getting a position at the Workshop through less embarrassing means is preferred, of course. And thanks to Meister K's penchant for second chances, I still have my interview for the managerial internship next week.

Nearing the hill's midway point, I'm tempted to linger at my favorite switchback, where a crumbling stone wall has yielded to a grove of evergreens. It's a great place to pause and catch one's breath, but today I pass the wall without slowing down.

Off to my right, Flitterndorf unfurls in an alcove of the Clandy-Stein Mountains. It's a haven of Christmas-colored timber-framed buildings that reflect the Red and Green Clans' homes and businesses. While it's true squabbles break out over which color best offsets white and which one, as a candy, offers the mintiest flavor (hint: it's the color of the *dirndl* I'm wearing), we clans know we're nothing without the other.

On the east side of the Town Square, the roofline to my parents' bakery, The Flaky Crust, rises higher than the others. Unconventional in height, sure, but it boasts the best pastries and cocoa concoctions for a thousand miles in any direction. To either side sits Herr Lanny's Post Office and Frau Rutschig's Skate 'n Ski Shoppe (where, for different Penalties, I once sorted mail and waxed skis respectively). Frau Leben's Vittles Mart takes up the west side of the Town Square (I mopped the floors there to work off another Penalty), and the library lies to the north, where I…

My smile wavers, and I trip on a clump of crusted snow. Have I really—over the years and for one Penalty or another—worked a temporary job in most shops downtown? That's a lot of Penalties.

And a lot of bungling.

My mother blames my colossal frame on the decisions my great-grandmother made, but I wish I could blame Great Oma Fay for a few other things, as well.

Gritting my teeth, I increase my pace. "Let me nab that internship, and I'll prove I'm not a total mistake."

The hum of a snowmobile drifts on the air, and in another minute, Niklas's neon green and blue SnoMo rounds the switchback I cut across a moment ago. When he passes on my right, I'm braced for his usual spray of snow, but then he skids to a stop in the path ahead. Snowflakes whirl in a frenzy, coating me in a layer of white dust. My eyes narrow. He's up to something.

Niklas flashes that dimpled grin over his apple-red and pine-green scarf. "Off to see Herr Stricker today?"

"How did you—"

"Pa told me."

Of course. Being next in line as Santa Claus, Meister Nico *would* have the inside scoop.

Niklas's grin broadens. "Plus, I convinced Grandpop he should give you a Penalty in the Lower Stables this time."

"Versus what?"

"Darning socks at Frau Kleider's Boutique."

A shudder passes through me. "Thanks."

Niklas revs the SnoMo's engine. "Hop on."

I shake my head. "I've come this far on my own, and I only have a few more switchbacks to go."

"The steepest ones yet."

Lifting my chin, I try to edge around him on the path. "I'm fine, *danke*."

Niklas heaves a sigh. "If it were up to me, I'd leave you to your mulish tendencies, but my mother is probably watching from the tower room right now, and you know she's old school. I'll never hear the end of it if I don't give you a ride."

I glance to where the upper part of the Workshop's southern tower pokes above the hill. While I don't believe Madam Marie stands behind the lattice window—she's got better things to do than monitor her son—a ride sounds tempting. I am late, after all. My gaze slides to Niklas in his garnet sweater and brown *lederhosen*. But must the offer come from Mr. Perfect himself?

In the end, the issue of time overrides my stubbornness, and I strap my snowshoes to the SnoMo's luggage rack. Wedging myself sideways behind Niklas, I tug my skirt down to my knees.

"Okay, I'm ready."

His blond hair curls over the brim of his beanie. It looks soft to the touch, not straggly like my long, copper-colored hair. If I run my fingertips through it, would the curls bounce back or would I encounter tangles?

Frosted windowpanes, what am I *thinking*?

Niklas peers over his shoulder, and my gaze darts away. "You need to hang on to me, Kuchler, otherwise you'll fall off."

Oh. Right. Um… Chewing on my lower lip, I place a hand at his waist. It's not like I've never ridden a snowmobile before, but this is the first time I've ridden with Niklas. That makes things different for reasons I don't care to fathom right now.

Chuckling, he grabs my hand and pulls it across his middle. I smack into his back. Then we're off, and I clap my green hat to my head before it gets whipped away.

Snow flies behind us and the wind numbs my cheeks. As we round the last few bends, the Workshop's gabled roofs and Tudor architecture rise into view. Four cylindrical towers form the corners, two of which house the Kringles' living quarters, one serves as a lookout, and the fourth has been inaccessible for years. At the ground level, a cranberry red, double-door entryway welcomes both workers and visitors alike, over which a rudimentary sign with rotating numbers counts down the days until Christmas Eve.

We have seventeen days left.

Cresting Huff 'n Puff Hill, Niklas aims for the Lower Stables connected to the Upper Stables by the Flight Training Arena, or FTA. He skids to a stop at the west entrance, sending up another mini snow shower, and as the flakes fall back upon us, I duck my head against his shoulder. The fibers in his sweater graze my cheek. Mmm, he smells like cloves.

When the snow subsides, I straighten away, but Niklas traps my hand at his waist. He nods toward the horizon. "Look."

Most of the sun has slipped behind the southern valley between Mount Gnade and Mount Frieden, swathing Flittern-dorf-proper in shadow. For a moment, a splice of golden brilliance prevails above the horizon before disappearing in a flush of rusted orange.

Niklas expels a breath. "We won't see the sun again for another month."

I don't know why—maybe it's the melancholy tone in his voice—but I give his waist a squeeze. "Personally, I like this time of year. And it has nothing to do with our month-long break from school." The lights twinkle in the village below, and I smile. "Think of the way the street lamps bathe us in a warm glow as we pass underneath, even at midday. And that extra cup of drinking chocolate each afternoon that keeps the pep in one's step. The stars shine their brightest, and *Vati's Lebkuchen* tastes its sweetest."

Niklas angles his head in my direction, but my gaze drifts over to the Workshop. "Then there's the last-minute frenzy on Christmas Eve before your grandfather flies off with a toy-filled sleigh, followed by a long week of relaxation. Before you know it, we're celebrating the Sunrise Festival."

"You would put a positive spin on the darkest days."

I can't tell if that's a compliment or complaint, and I meet his gaze with a frown. His face is closer than I anticipate, and for the first time I notice the freckle on his right cheekbone. The flecks in his eyes shimmer emerald in the waning light and hint at... admiration? A zing shoots through me.

I yank away and hop off the SnoMo, my eyebrows pinching together at this most recent shift in Niklas's ribbing, this softening. It picks at the barricade I built long ago, but I know better than to let it undermine the years of mockery I've endured. Besides, a crush won't do me any good, for romance between elves and Kringles is *verboten*. It says so in the books lining the shelves in Meister K's office.

"Thanks for the ride." I straighten my skirt. "I trust we showed Madam Marie you're chivalrous. When you need to be."

He grins. "Today's chivalry ends here. Wish me luck."

A hunched elf wearing burgundy *lederhosen* emerges from the stables, but before acknowledging Herr Stricker, I ask Niklas, "Luck for what?"

"I'm meeting Herr Referat to interview for the managerial internship. Have fun with my reindeer." Eyes twinkling, Niklas speeds away toward the Workshop.

I glare after him. He might think he's got this internship nailed, but I plan to wow Herr Referat next week with a competence and fortitude my peers don't know I possess.

My elfin future depends on it.

THE LOWER STABLES

Herr Stricker sizes me up, squinting beneath bushy white eyebrows and tugging at his waist-length, scraggly beard. "You're late." Then he grunts, turns, and with a lopsided gait, shuffles back into the stables.

Swallowing my excuse, I follow him through the eight-foot doorway. The pungent stench of animal, hay, and leather invade my senses, along with the realization the Third String have better living conditions than I do.

The Lower Stables' spacious interior is a masterful blend of cherry oak and wrought iron. From the European-style, open-grillwork stalls to the heavy rafters in the vaulted ceiling; from the curved, iron hooks dotting the walls to the asymmetrical benches on the flagstone floor, everything compliments each other in a stunning, cohesive arrangement.

Aside from my future office at the Workshop as Chief Operations Elf, this might be the best working environment I'll ever experience!

"You're the one they've sent to replace me, eh?" Herr Stricker fritters about inside a closet off to the left. He flings his beard over his shoulder. "Couldn't have chosen someone with more…skill?"

I sidestep his veiled insult. "Did you say 'replace'?"

"I do believe that's wha' Stricker said, didna he, Choc'late?"

"S'right, Chip. The gel's height must've depleted her elf-hearin'."

I whirl about at the guttural Scottish accents, but no one's there. Hmm. With knitted brow, I turn back to Herr Stricker. "Meister K said I was to help you. He said nothing about replacing you."

"Was decided this morning." Herr Stricker hefts a bucket of myriad combs and brushes from the closet. "With the school's production wing gone, all retired elves are required at the Workshop to ease the burden on the Toy Makers. As of tomorrow, you're on your own in here."

"On my own. As in alone?" My heart ramps up its beating. "After training me for one day—"

"Two hours."

Gulp. "—you're trusting me to take care of the Third String by myself?"

Herr Stricker cuts me a look. "Your job is to feed them and muck out their stalls. Frau Hüter claims you handled the sheep all right, so you shouldn't find this difficult. Besides, if you get into a bind and it's late enough in the morning, someone'll be working in the FTA who can help you."

My mind loops around the words "muck out their stalls." I'm to scoop poop for the next three-hundred and sixty-five days? Snowman, this keeps getting better and better. No wonder why Niklas suggested such a Penalty.

Herr Stricker reaches up to wag a finger in my face. "That said, if you mess up in here"—he points the same finger toward the side entrance—"then you've got no future out there."

"And we've haird all kinds o' stories about her messes, havna we, lads and lassies?" comes a new voice followed by a chuckle.

Bristling at the dig, I spin around again. "I beg your—"

But nobody's there. Nobody except the eight reindeer, whose antlered heads poke out over the sloped stall doors. A vague memory from a field trip when I was in Sixth Level seeps into my mind: strange voices murmuring in the background that hadn't matched my classmates or teacher. It didn't faze me at the time with all the commotion, but now...

I glance at Herr Stricker. "Did you hear something?"

He smooths a gnarled hand over his beard and purses his lips. "Maybe I should ask Meister K for a different replacement. Pix Betriebs is a quick learner. She's applying for that managerial internship, but she could handle both."

The elf's name sets my teeth on edge, and I straighten to my full sixty-five-and-a-quarter-inches. Not that I wouldn't love to see Pix work a pooper-scooper, but if Herr Stricker thinks someone half my height can do this job, then I can do it twice as good. "Show me where to start."

He stares from beneath those bushy brows then heaves a sigh. "All right. Come meet your charges." He limps down the stone-paved aisle between the stalls, four on each side. The reindeer tower above him, powerful muscles rippling beneath their tan hides, broad antlers branching out atop their heads.

"On normal days, the Third String would be outside right now, but I brought them in for introductions." Herr Stricker gestures to the first reindeer on the left. "This one is Butterscotch, the group's natural leader. Next to him we have Cinnamon, and opposite them are Cocoa and Licorice. Then there are the twins: Chocolate and Chip"—I toss those two a suspicious glance, but they blink back with their simple, chestnut eyes —"followed by Peppermint over there and lastly, Eggnog."

Recalling three are female, I repeat the names to myself with a grin. "Why not 'Slapjack,' or 'Buffalo Jerky,' or 'Mincemeat'? Now those names would have packed a punch."

Chocolate gums the bell atop Herr Stricker's pointy red hat, and he gives the animal's nose an absentminded swat. "Madam Marie named this lot when she was pregnant with Niklas. Her cravings weren't what you'd call healthy."

"The name 'Tinsel' isna exactly a gem among stones, lass," a voice twitters to my left. I jerk around again to find—no one.

"And if rumors are true, Tinsel the elf isna the pick o' the clan, either," yet another voice chimes in further down the aisle.

"What d'ye expect from a gel named after the bothersome plastic strips that static-cling to everythin', and that, after servin' their unnecessary purpose o' clutterin' up a Christmas tree, are thrown away?"

I mash my lips together at this last comment, which comes from Licorice's stall beside me. Though her head towers above my own, I edge closer and peer inside. Empty, save for Licorice, who snorts into my face.

I cough, waving away the hot breath, and look around the room. "All right, whoever you are, show yourself. And if this is someone's idea of a joke, it isn't funny."

Silence follows, but I think a significant look passes across the aisle between Cocoa and Butterscotch. Then Herr Stricker clears his throat and rubs the back of his neck. "Look, Tinsel, perhaps Meister K wasn't fully aware of your, ahem, limitations—"

"You didn't hear that?"

"Hear what?"

I jam my hands on my hips. "The barbed remarks flying about like ping-pong balls!"

Herr Stricker's blank stare matches the reindeer's, and I have my answer. My shoulders slump. If he can't hear who spoke and I can't see who spoke, are the voices real…or trapped inside my head?

THERE ARE NO MORE GHOSTLY COMMENTS FOR THE NEXT TWO

hours, but as Herr Stricker gives me a tour and explains my duties, I feel eight pairs of eyes studying my every move.

"The Minor Flight Team trains the Third String five days a week," the aging elf says. "When they arrive, stay out of their way. Your job is to muck the stalls, feed and groom the reindeer, and keep the general area clean. Understand?"

After I've barraged him with countless questions (yet assured him I will manage on my own tomorrow), Herr Stricker shuffles me back to the west entrance. "Between you and me, despite the trouble you've caused, I'm excited to get out of retirement for a while." He cracks his knuckles. "I'm itching to pick up my knitting needles again."

"You used to knit?"

"Sweaters, bags, hats, mittens, socks. You name it, I knitted it." He puffs out his chest. "Best knitter in the whole Red Clan."

"Then the Workshop is lucky to get you back for a few weeks." I grip the door latch, but Herr Stricker puts a tiny hand on my arm.

"Er, one more thing."

"Yes?"

His fingers tighten on my coat sleeve. "Promise you won't blow up the stables while I'm gone."

A CRUSTY ENCOUNTER

It's not until I emerge from the stables into the frigid alpine air that I remember strapping my snowshoes to Niklas's snowmobile. Ah, well. Walking downhill no matter the footwear takes minimal effort. That said… I squint into the growing darkness beyond the stable's lamplight. Huff 'n Puff Hill has no streetlights. If I had skis, I could whizz down and emerge into the illuminated town below before the dark caught up to me.

Okay, I'd attempt to ski.

I reenter the stables. It takes me a full ten minutes to convince Herr Stricker to let me borrow Meister K's extra skis. "I promise I'll bring them back tomorrow."

"That's not what concerns me." The elf wrings his beard between his hands. "Think about the last time you tried skiing."

I wave aside the memory of broken skis and a sprained ankle. "That was seven months ago. And the skiing conditions weren't good. I'll be fine this time."

He mutters in the background as I fasten the old-fashioned buckles around my curly-toed boots. Meister K's skis are longer than I am tall, and that's saying something. I take the poles in hand, the grips a full six inches higher than my shoulders, and give Herr Stricker a nod. "Wish me luck."

He places a hand over his eyes. "I can't watch."

I bend at the waist and knees, and the skis slide over the snow. Gravity pulls me downward, and I grin. Then the slope sharpens.

My speed increases, and I wobble on the uneven terrain. Do these things come with brakes? I aim for the trail, but the skis take me into the trees. Another wobble throws me off balance, and I flail my arms windmill-style. Trees whizz past. Rocks and debris clip the skis. A passing branch catches a pole and rips it from my hand.

Roasted chestnuts! It's going to take me hours to find that pole again.

The skis zoom over a steep, but short, incline, and I'm tossed into the air. Stars spin in the sky and switch places with the trees. I might enjoy this if I knew how to land.

Too soon, I drop and plow backwards into something crunchy yet forgiving, the air whooshing from my lungs.

Quiet settles around me, and I take a moment to assess any damage. No sharp pains when I move, just an overall ache. I try to right myself, but I've landed upside-down on a snowbank, and my skis got crisscrossed, the ends wedged in the snow. A ski pole strap holds one hand hostage, two fingers on my other hand poke through a new hole in my mitten, and judging from the cool air on my head, I've misplaced my hat along with Meister K's pole. The more I wrestle to extract myself from the snowbank, the deeper my backside sinks and the colder I get.

I don't suppose Herr Stricker knows I crashed.

A SnoMo purrs in the distance, growing louder until its headlights reflect off the nearby snow-dappled tree trunk. I wave with my free arm. Surely whoever it is will see me and pull me out. Unless...unless I've fallen some distance away. In this darkness, no one will notice a disturbed snow pile off the beaten path, and it's useless to scream over the engine. Once again, I strain to sit up or turn over, but I'm stuck like a cookie in caramel.

And since caramel breaks when frozen, you can guess what that will make me a few hours from now.

The SnoMo draws closer until it's almost on top of me and then someone cuts the engine. A deep, rumbling laugh replaces the drone of the motor. A belly laugh that will someday grow into that famous "ho, ho, ho" children love to hear.

I love to hear it from Meister K. I love to hear it from Meister Nico.

I do not like to hear it from Niklas. It means something strikes him as hilarious, and given the present circumstances, I can guess what that "something" is. I squeeze my eyes shut. Why must it always be Niklas who bails me out of a jam?

His footfalls crunch in the snow, and a flashlight beam shines on my face. I shield my eyes with a hand. In a voice bubbling with mirth, Niklas asks, "What in the winter wonderland are you doing, Kuchler?"

"It's not obvious?" I feign contentment while lying upside-down, the snow soaking into my clothes. "I'm tanning."

Niklas cups a hand around his mouth. "I found her, Herr Stickler! All pieces intact. I'll see her safely home."

"His name is Stricker, genius."

"He comes off more as a stickler to me."

I snort. "Admit you didn't remember his name."

"Why would I do that?"

"Oh, right. Admitting you forgot something would mean you're less-than-perfect, and we can't have that, can we?"

Niklas leans in close. "Are you saying I'm flawed?"

I push him away with my free hand. "Implying it, maybe."

"Hmm. Imperfection. Something to ponder in a few weeks when I'm studying the A's on my report card."

"Before your inflated ego whisks you down the road to greatness, help me from this snow bank." I try to wriggle free. "The blood is congealing in my head."

"Stay still for a second. Let's get these skis off first." His gloved hand cups my lower leg, and he tugs on my boot. He grunts. "The old elf must be going daft to have let you strap these on."

"In his defense, I had to beg and plead quite a bit before he relented."

"Then you're the daft one. Everyone knows you're helpless standing on anything besides your God-given feet or snowshoes." Another jerk on my boot, followed by a sigh. "The buckles are caked with snow and ice crystals. Hold these." Niklas slaps his gloves into my hand. "I don't know how you get yourself into these scrapes."

"It's not like I go searching for them." Upside-down, I consider the proximity of the surrounding trees, grateful I didn't smash into them. "Maybe it's the aura of excellence I radiate that attracts trouble. It finds me a challenge and can't resist going up against me."

Niklas gives a snort. "You radiate an aura, all right, but it's not excellence."

I kick with the leg he's holding—

"Ow!"

—and smile in perverse satisfaction. "That's for convincing your grandfather I should muck stalls for a year."

"Hey, that wasn't my fault. I convinced him to give you a Penalty involving the Third String. How he carried that out was up to him." Finally, my boot pops free, and I stretch my leg as Niklas begins on the other one. "I never want to see you wearing skis again."

"I'll get it right the next time."

"That's what you said the last time."

"Yes, but this time, I made it halfway down the hill."

"Think again." With my second foot liberated, Niklas works the ski pole loose from the snow and slips my hand from the strap before hauling me to my feet. He gestures up the hill. "You made it less than eighty yards."

"That's ten more yards than last time. I must be getting better."

He chuckles. "You never know when to give up."

My smile disappears. "If I gave up after my second or third try, I'd have run out of things to do a long time ago." Teeth clenched, I move away to pick up the skis and pole. After a moment, I manage to grind out, "Thank you for helping me. I hope it wasn't too inconvenient."

"Not at all." Niklas takes the equipment from me and stows it in the luggage rack beside—

"My snowshoes. I wondered when I'd see them again."

"I was on my way back to the stables to return them when Herr Stricker hailed me down and said he heard you crash." He takes a seat on his SnoMo and pulls a pair of dry gloves from a saddlebag. "Come here." I step forward and he proceeds to remove my sodden mittens. His own fingers, bare but warm, graze my palm, and goosebumps prickle along my arms.

I pull away with a mumbled, "I've got it, *danke*," but my hands shake as I tug on the gloves. Interactions with this Kringle leave me agitated lately, though I can't explain why. Crankiness tightens my gut. "Do you have a flashlight I can borrow? I need to find Meister K's pole."

Niklas flings a leg over the SnoMo and starts the engine. "Search tomorrow when it's not as dark. Let's go."

"Go where?"

"I told Herr Stricker I'd see you safely home."

"You know I won't hold you to that." Spending more time with him is the last thing I need right now. "Thanks for the rescue, thanks for returning my snowshoes, and thanks for offering to bring me home, but—"

"It's not an offer. It's a statement."

"No. Thank. You."

"You don't have a flashlight, and Huff 'n Puff Hill doesn't have street lamps."

"Then maybe you could suggest to your grandfather we have some installed. In the meantime, I'll ask again. Do you have a flashlight I can use?"

"Great lords a'leaping." Niklas tips his head back, and I imagine him glaring at the darkened sky. "Are you going to be mulish about this again?"

My eyes narrow. "How was your interview with Herr Referat?"

"Perfect."

"Exactly." I hold out my hand. "I'll take my snowshoes now."

Niklas laughs, and I grit my teeth. "You can have them back when I drop you off at home." Grabbing my outstretched hand, he yanks me onto the seat behind him. "Hold on, Kuchler. Going down is way more fun than going up!"

NOT ENTIRELY AN ELF

I try hard not to enjoy the ride. That's twice in less than twelve hours Niklas has disregarded my wishes. But he zooms along faster than last time, and with the wind whipping my hair and the ground rushing beneath my feet, the exhilaration building inside me pushes away my irritability.

His speed slows when we enter the town proper, and the two-story Tudor homes close in around us. Metal and plastic holiday yard art and 3D light sculptures spill across front lawns, twinkling lights adorn every façade, and I point out the more lavish Christmas trees brightening several living room windows. He turns down another street, where the houses disperse to make room for the expansive, outdoor ice skating rink. (Contrary to popular opinion, Meister K's headquarters are not located at the North Pole, but rather in northern North America, and its half-pint workers adore ice hockey.) Floodlights circle the area as couples skate hand-in-hand, singles pirouette, and...yep, there's Kristof at one end, honing his hockey skills with a puck, a net, and half a dozen elves. I wave as we pass.

Approaching the Town Square, Niklas slows further. Swags of pre-lit garland arch across the street, and huge plastic candy canes hang from the lampposts. Here, the buildings huddle against each other and light pools from the windows onto the snow-covered sidewalks. The Flaky Crust faces us from the opposite side of the Square with its towering roof, tree-stamped shutters, and wide, lattice windows.

The shop is closed for the day. Though my older brother, Chorley, moves about inside, tidying up the dining area for tomorrow's customers, Niklas drives around to the back entrance before coming to a stop. He looks over his shoulder with a smug grin. "Now, aren't you glad I strong-armed you into accepting a ride home?"

I let out half a laugh. "I should know by now you don't like to be told 'no.'"

"I'm a Kringle. Who says 'no' to Santa?"

"Santa's mother."

"You're telling me you'd have rather walked all the way home?"

I hop off the snowmobile and remove my snowshoes from the luggage rack. "What if I wanted some exercise?"

"You're thin enough as it is, Kuchler."

I reach for Meister K's skis. "My mother says I eat more than my three brothers combined."

"Leave the skis. I'll take them back to Grandpop, myself. And naturally you'd have a bigger appetite when compared to an elf."

I straighten and meet his gaze. "I *am* an elf."

He smirks, looking me up and down. "Not entirely."

I've dealt with jokes and snide remarks for so long, few continue to rile me, except this one comes with a bite. I hug my snowshoes to my chest. "I don't need a reminder I'm different. I see it every day when I look in the mirror."

"Tinsel, you mis—"

"Good night. Thank you for the ride." I spin on my heel and stomp toward the bakery's back door, hoping to make a dramatic exit. Instead, I smack my head on the low crossbeam while plowing through the doorway. Niklas's chuckle follows me into the dimly lit mudroom. Had roles been reversed, I might've laughed, too (seriously, you'd think I've learned to duck by now), but I slam the door to cut off the sound.

With a sigh, I scrub a mittened hand over the sore spot on my forehead and drop my snowshoes near the base of the staircase leading up to my family's living quarters.

"Tinsel, is that you?" my mother's voice calls from the bakery's kitchen to my right.

I step through the doorway, this time avoiding the crossbeam. "*Hallo, Mutti.*"

The savory notes of chocolate mixed with yeast and cinnamon waft in the air, and I take an instinctive breath as I remove my hat and mittens. Delicious magic happens in this room when my parents work, *Vati* with his pastries and *Mutti* with her chocolates. Even now, *Mutti* stands at a worktable large enough to be my bed, surrounded by bowls of tempered chocolate, plastic sheet molds, and flavored fillings as she prepares chocolates for tomorrow's customers.

Unbuttoning my coat, damp from the snow, I plop onto a tiny stool close to where she "paints" the sides of her leaf-shaped molds with dark chocolate. I sit sideways since my knees won't fit under the tabletop and glance around the empty kitchen while loosening my scarf. "I saw Chorley out front. Are Tinder and Mash upstairs helping *Vati* with dinner again?"

Mutti abandons her brush and flits to the stove, where she always has a pot of warm milk waiting. "He's making lasagna tonight. Oma Fay's recipe."

"Mmm. Can't wait." My tone oozes sarcasm.

Mutti chastises me with a look over her shoulder. An enormous brick oven dominates the wall beside the stove, emanating warmth into the room. It stands empty now, but in the wee hours of the mornings, six days a week, its heat transforms *Vati's* raw dough into delicate pastries and golden bread loaves.

With a few practiced movements, *Mutti* mixes some drinking chocolate in an oversized mug. It's her signature creation, which the elves have dubbed the "Kandi Cup" in her honor. She places the liquid chocolate before me and fetches a blueberry scone from the day's leftovers. "You know you're going to have to make peace with Great Oma Fay at some point."

I shrug off my coat and fold it across my lap. "The decisions she made cause me grief on a daily basis. Where's the peace in that?"

Pursing her lips, *Mutti* returns to her molds. "It wasn't personal, Tinsel."

"*Nein,* but more than half a century later, I'm the one who has to live with the consequences."

As the story goes, Fay Grünenbaum, graduation cap in hand, left Flitterndorf to seek a more adventurous future. With a traveling circus. Seventeen months later, she returned home, alone, disillusioned, and pregnant. Three months after that, she had my Opa Denny. Though several of Opa Denny's descendants stand almost six inches taller than your average elf, no one gave thought to the human quality in his genes. Until I came along.

You wouldn't know it to look at me, but I'm only one-eighth human. My father and his siblings have more human genes in them than me, yet the height chromosome skipped over them all. It skipped over my cousins. It skipped over my brothers. It chose, instead, to sink its teeth into *my* DNA strand.

Still, I think the clans would forgive me my height and look upon me as a fellow elf if I had a knack for concocting distinctive goodies like my parents (or if I exhibited any knack at all). But an oversized elf without a talent? Who leaves a trail of mishaps in her wake? Doesn't sound like much of an elf.

I recall Niklas's cheeky reminder I'm not "entirely" an elf and let out an exaggerated sigh.

Mutti peeks up at the sound. "How did it go at the stables?"

I sip some cocoa before answering. "All right. If you overlook

Herr Stricker's doubt in my abilities." And the voices inside my head.

"Don't let it bother you, *Schatz*." She slides the sheet of leaf molds into the freezer to set and withdraws a sheet of jingle bell molds ready for filling. "Someday you will prove them all wrong."

"I need to win that internship." I rub my throbbing forehead. "While I learned the finer points of scooping poop, Niklas had his interview with Herr Referat."

"Mmm." *Mutti* squeezes strawberry filling into the white chocolate bells.

"He said it went perfectly." I pull off a piece of scone and pop it into my mouth. Its sweet, buttery flavor dances on my tongue before I add in a more acidic tone, "I'd love to know how it feels to do anything perfectly."

"He's a Kringle. And under pressure to perform well."

"So? Must his achievements hinge on my failures?" I mash another piece of scone between my thumb and forefinger. "Must he flaunt his successes in my face? He might have a cute, dimpled grin, but must he use it to tease me when I've botched yet another assignment?"

"A cute, dimpled grin?"

I squirm at my faux pas. "You're missing the point."

"What is the point? Don't waste time focusing on your shortcomings, Tinsel. You have many beautiful qualities, and someday they will all come together to shine." She taps the candy mold against the tabletop to even out the filling. "Who knows? Niklas might be the initial spark that sets the whole aflame."

"Ugh." I wrinkle my nose. "It won't ever be like that between us. The ancient edicts prevent it, remember?"

"I don't mean it in a romantic way. Although"—she chuckles—"where else are you going to find someone to suit your height?"

"If I had to, I'd start by looking beyond Flitterndorf's borders."

Mutti glances up, her eyebrows rising toward her hairline. "You would leave home?"

I shake my head. "You know I won't. If Great Oma Fay didn't find her happiness in the world beyond, the least I can do is learn from her mistakes and stay put." Balancing my snack in one hand, I push away from the table and gather my things with the other. "Besides, I have my parents' love. I don't need it from anyone else, especially not Santa's heir."

"What *do* you need, *mein Schatz?*"

Her words stop me at the back door. I give her a small smile over my shoulder. "What I've lacked since I broke Pix's bike when we were five." Then I gesture to my soggy state. "I'm going to change before dinner. I smell like reindeer."

ANOTHER BLUNDER

I wake earlier than usual for a Saturday. After washing up, I change into my green wool *dirndl* paired with black stockings and weave my hair into a hasty braid. Yanking a black sweater over my head, I hurry downstairs to the kitchen where my father and Chorley will have already made several rounds of breads and pastries for today's customers.

The luscious smells intoxicate me while I peruse the choices laid out on half a dozen trays. Chorley slips two trays from the table and carries them to the shop's display case. My gaze flicks to my father kneading dough. "Morning, *Vati*."

"Off to see to the Big Eight this morning?" He has flour dust up to his elbows and smeared along one cheek.

I choose a huckleberry bear claw before Chorley snatches that tray, too, and give *Vati* a quick kiss on his clean cheek. "*Nein,* the Third String."

"When will you be back?"

"Not sure." I retreat into the hallway to gather my belongings. Holding the pastry in my mouth to free my hands, I shrug into my wool coat and fling a scarf about my neck.

Vati pokes his head around the doorjamb. "If you ring me

from the stable phone when you finish, I'll have a Kandi Cup waiting for you by the time you return."

I give him a thumbs up then tug a green stocking cap over my hair.

"But be sure to work slow, think things through, and—"

Chorley pokes his head out from beneath *Vati's*. "And for the love of gingerbread, don't botch anything!"

I shoo them away with my pastry, grab my snowshoes, and head outside. My breath fogs in the frozen morning air, and as soon as I've donned my shoes, I begin a slow jog to keep warm. I'm completely winded by the time I reach the top of Huff 'n Puff Hill. If nothing else comes from this Penalty, I'll be in tip-top shape by the time I've served it. Three hundred and sixty-four days from now.

I enter the Lower Stables, set my snowshoes against the wall inside the door, and fumble for the light switch. The lanterns overhead and along the walls flare to life, and eight pairs of sleepy eyes blink at me from the stalls.

"*Guten Morgen*," I say in a singsong voice. Not that they can understand me, but it's better than going about my business in silence.

"There's nuthin' good 'bout mornins," somebody grumbles in that same Scottish brogue as yesterday.

Taking a lead rope and halter from a nearby hook, I glance over my shoulder. No one's there. Same as yesterday. I swallow and grip the rope tighter.

"Are ye daft?" comes another voice. "Mornins mean food, and there's nuthin' I like more than food."

I peer down the row of stalls. "I-is someone there?" I don't think the Minor Flight Team comes in until nine, but I could be wrong.

"Wish she'd get on with it," a voice complains near Cocoa's stall. "I'm starvin'."

I approach Cocoa and inspect his stall. Empty, save for the

reindeer. I study his face, but his dark eyes give nothing away. I don't know what's going on, but I do know I won't survive a whole year hearing voices inside—outside?—my head.

Determined to ignore the oddity for now, I fit the halter over Cocoa's antlered head and lead him through the east entrance into the corral. I repeat the process for the other seven and afterward toss hay biscuits fortified with lichen and seed plants into a long trough. Then I turn to the metal basin, as wide as I am tall and filled with water, and break through the icy surface with a pickax.

Satisfied the Third String have enough sustenance, I return to the stables' warmth—and escape the random mutterings of disembodied voices.

I'm starting to suspect the reindeer can talk.

A little detail the teachers left out in school.

I stow my coat in the closet, grab the pitchfork, and survey the vacant stalls. Time to get mucking.

Two hours later, hot and dusty, I push the wheelbarrow over to the muck heap one final time and dump it out. Parking it behind the stables along with the pitchfork and shovel, I allow myself a small smile. I did a decent job for my first morning. I completed my chores without any further ghostly voices, and I didn't mess up once.

I MESSED UP.

The pandemonium I find upon reentering the stables is my biggest clue.

At the far end of the aisle run amok with reindeer (how did the beasts get back in here?), three elves struggle to contain a single reindeer who is carrying on a full-fledged temper tantrum. One elf, Leif (I recognize him from the Minor Flight Team), has the reindeer's lead rope in a death grip, a second elf holds Leif around the middle, and a third elf (I think that's Jangles) holds another rope that's tangled in the reindeer's antlers. They get air each time the reindeer tries to rear and break away.

And there are far too many voices ricocheting around in here for three wee elves!

"Chip! Easy, fella."

"Ye look like a yearlin' throwin' a fit. Is that what yer goin' fer?"

"Whoa, there. Steady, boy."

"Ye'll be put on the Naughty List fer sure."

"Settle down, now, you spoiled beast."

"Want ta be welcomed inta the Upper Stables? Lairn ta control yer temper."

Dodging around the momentarily-liberated animals (and praying I don't get poked in the eye by an antler), I shout above the bedlam, "What's going on?"

"That's what we'd like to know," Leif hollers back, looking like he might get pummeled any moment by a wayward hoof. "You're supposed to put these guys in the corral *before* you muck their stalls."

"I did!"

"Then explain this." The second elf releases Leif's waist to motion at the other reindeer.

"We're flyin' reindeer," a voice scoffs behind me. "Use yer imagination."

"And explain why Chip is going berserk," Jangles demands.

Chip's head turns in my direction, and I swear his eyes narrow.

"H-how should I know? I was gone for a few minutes to empty the wheelbarrow—"

"Ye tealeaf," a voice says with a low growl. "Where'd ye stash it?"

Righting a bench that's been knocked on its side, I glance around for the source. "Tealeaf?"

"He means thief, lass."

I raise my hands in surrender and take a step back. "I didn't steal anything."

The second elf scowls at me over his shoulder. "Don't be so dramatic. Nobody said anything about stealing."

"But—"

"We can't hold him much longer," Leif says through gritted teeth.

"Ye nicked me chew toy."

I still can't locate my accuser. "Chew toy? What chew toy?"

"Meister K should give ye a time-out," someone mumbles.

I whirl about. "I should get a time-out?"

"Snowflakes and frostbite, Tinsel!" Jangles yanks on the rope. "I don't know what you're prattling on about, but—"

At that moment, Chip shakes his head, and the elves lose their grips and tumble to the floor like chocolates from a stocking.

"Time to retreat, boys," Leif shouts, scrambling to his feet. First one, then two, then three elves dash past me and disappear through the west entrance faster than you can tear into a present.

I stand alone in the stables with several unfettered reindeer, one of which is crazy.

My chances for the internship are starting to look like that muck heap outside.

Rope dangling from his antlers, the crazy reindeer lowers his head, paws the floor, then charges down the aisle.

My heart drops to my knees. "No, wait. Stop!"

Blocked on all sides by antlered beasts, I shield my head and brace for the impact.

TALKING REINDEER

Something solid shoves me aside. I sprawl on the cold flagstones as pain flares in my elbow and curl into a fetal position. Antlers clatter overhead and someone grunts, "Back off, Chip."

When the anticipated gouging from an antler tine doesn't come, I chance a peek, opening first one eye then the second. Where I used to stand, two reindeer now stand, heads down, their bodies forming a barrier between me and Chip, their antlers locked with his. Struggling against the temporary imprisonment, Chip breathes hard and his eyeballs rotate to glare at me.

"Why'd ye nick it?" comes the angry question.

"Ye dinna ken fer a fact the lass nicked it," a calming voice replies.

"Kristof will get ye another one," a different voice suggests.

"He canna, Cocoa. Nik gave it ta me. One of a kind, he said. And 'twas the last time we saw the lad."

"Aww, now ain't that sweet. Chip kept it as a memento."

"'Twas me favorite toy. So's I repeat"—Chip's gaze hardens

and my breath hitches in my throat at the intelligence lying within those brown depths—"why'd ye nick it?"

"Okay, okay, okay." Standing, I put my hands out in a placating gesture, then wince and rub my sore elbow. My fingers encounter a hole in the sleeve. "Forgetting for the moment that you guys can talk, what is this toy you keep referring to? I didn't steal any toy."

One of the tangled reindeer—it might be Cocoa—tries to raise his head but can do little more than rotate slightly in my direction. "How is it ye ken reindeer speech?"

Ken? Oh, right—Scottish for *know*. "No idea, but if it means I'm not going insane, I'm good with it." I scowl at my ruined sweater then cross my arms. "Now, the toy."

"It didna look like a normal toy," my second champion (Butterscotch?) says with another grunt, trying to disentangle himself. "Nik gave them to us years ago. Said sumthin' 'bout them bein' petrified cookies a classmate had baked and botched, but they made the perfect chew toys. O'er the years, most of us have either lost them or lost interest in them, but no' Chip. The petrified cookie is ta Chip what the thumb is to a wee bairn."

"Shut yer geggy, Butterball," Chip mutters.

"Hold the mistletoe." I fist a hand in my hair. "Are you talking about that hockey puck-look-alike I threw out with the soiled straw an hour ago?"

"Ye threw it away?" Chip tries to ram me again and drives the other two reindeer backward a few paces.

I fling out my arms to ward off an attack. "Before you skewer me, hear me out. I think I can solve this dilemma." When Chip remains still, I drag over a bench and climb on top to reach their antlers. "Now, you say Niklas gave you these so-called cookies years ago?" I work to separate the beasts. "How many years ago?"

"Five? Six? Seven?" Butterscotch tries to shake his head. "I dinna ken."

"'Twas seven," Chip answers, a bitter edge to his voice.

I avoid a random antler tine and purse my lips. "That would put Niklas at eleven years old in Fifth Level, which was the year we had to take that introductory course to baking."

"Whoop. Dee. Doo." Chip's sour tone matches his expression.

"Here's the thing—" I duck away as Cocoa springs free.

"Thank ye," he says.

"You're welcome." I resume my efforts to free the other two. "As far as I know, I'm the only one who burned several batches of cookies that year. I threw them away, but maybe Niklas salvaged some and gave them to you? If that's the case…" I dislodge the remaining tines and Butterscotch gracefully backs away. Praying Chip doesn't knock me flat, I smile. "I can burn you a whole new batch of chew toys."

The side door smacks open, and I whip about on the bench. Too fast. Off balance, I topple backward as Meister K and Meister Nico charge into the stables. Before I hit the floor, a warm, broad muzzle catches me under the arm and lifts me back to a standing position. I meet Chip's gaze, and in the silence, we call a truce.

"Was geht hier vor?" Meister K demands in his booming voice, no doubt ready to go toe to hoof with one feisty reindeer. The COE, Herr Geier, hovers at his elbow.

"Nothing's going on, sir." I feed the rope through Chip's antlers to untangle it. "We had a little issue, but I fixed it."

Meister K frowns at the other brawny animals shuffling about, guilty looks on their faces. "What are they doing in here?"

I glance at Butterscotch, who ducks his head and mumbles something incoherent. I suppress a grin. "I think they were trying to make me look bad."

"Is that so?" Meister K smooths a hand over his beard and eyes me in quiet speculation.

Herr Geier points at Chip. "What's this we hear about him giving the Minor Flight Team a hard time?"

The three half-pints cower by the door, caps in their hands, their eyes wide with apprehension. And is that Niklas backing out the doorway?

My gaze shifts to the older Kringles. "With all due respect, sirs, if you found out your prized possession had been pooper-scooped, you might have made a little fuss, too. But no worries." I give Chip a reassuring pat on his neck. "It's nothing a little baking won't cure."

"Baking?" Meister Nico exchanges a glance with Meister K, and I scratch Chip beneath his chin. His eyes roll back into his head with pleasure.

SHORTLY THEREAFTER, WITH VISIONS OF COCOA AND A HOT SHOWER dancing in my head, I tromp down Huff 'n Puff Hill in the deep morning twilight. My woolen cap dangles from one mittened hand and my coat droops in the other. I had a task or two to finish in the Lower Stables, but the Kringles insisted on doing them for me, and I am not one to argue with two Santas. Personally, I think they want to verify Chip hasn't gone off the deep end. And I'm guessing they figure after I witnessed such a scene as the elves described, I might be a bit shaken and want the excuse to retreat and compose myself.

Shaken? Bah. My pace increases, and I give a little hop in my snowshoes. The reindeer talk—and I can understand them.

Why, again, did we not learn about their communicative abilities in school?

Unless... I bite back a grin. Unless nobody else knows about it because nobody else can communicate with them.

My fingers tighten around my coat. Perhaps I'm the only one who can.

I contemplate this theory all the way down the hill and am nearing the ice rink before I remember there's a lone ski pole in the woods I must find. But instead of turning around, I let the high-pitched shouts, clashing sticks, and the *shish, shish* of ice skates draw me from the sidewalk. An elf-sized fence surrounds the rink, and I drift over to it, squinting until my eyes adjust to the floodlights that give the illusion of daytime. The Tiny Tyke's game must start soon. Kristof, the team's assistant coach, kneels before several Second Level students, presumably giving them instructions.

I crouch to lay my coat over the top railing of the fence (it only comes to my mid-thighs) then lean my arms on the rail. Between helping with the Tiny Tykes and playing in the Junior League game, Kristof won't leave the rink again until late this afternoon. And he'll be back on the ice tomorrow after the Sunday morning service. If I had half his passion, Herr Referat would've already offered me that internship.

"What's with the dreamy look?"

I slap a hand to my chest as Niklas crouches beside me. "Don't *do* that."

He takes a sip from The Flaky Crust's red, green, and white striped to-go cup. "Mooning over my brother, are you?"

My gaze narrows. Today Niklas pairs his *lederhosen* with a slate-gray sweater and black scarf. The dark colors offset his pale hair and eyes.

Not that I notice in an admiring way. I'm merely stating a fact. And if my tummy goes a little squirrelly, it's because he won't break eye contact.

Mooning over Kristof, indeed.

"What are you doing here?" I hitch my chin at his SnoMo purring in the street behind us. "I thought you'd be off racing by now."

"I'm on my way. But first"—he hoists his to-go cup, steam escaping through the lid—"I stopped to get a peppermint Kandi Cup." His mouth spreads into that cocky grin. "And then I was detained by the sight of a pretty elf all alone at the ice rink."

I make a face. "Please. That false charm could put you on the

Naughty List."

"Naughty Lists don't apply to Santa's offspring."

With a skeptical snort, I turn back to watch the pre-game practice.

"But maybe it should apply to reindeer." Niklas plucks at the hole in my sleeve. "What was going on in the stables?"

So, I did see him scurry out the door, after all. Not yet wanting to reveal I discovered the reindeer's chatty side, I shrug a shoulder. "I tossed out Chip's favorite chew toy this morning by accident. But I've promised to bake more, so it's all good."

"You're going to bake Chip a new chew toy?" He says the words slowly, eyebrows drawn in confusion.

"'Burn' is closer to the truth." I give him a light punch on the shoulder. "It's your fault, you know. You never should have given them my cookies in the first place."

Niklas's eyes widen in sudden understanding. "You mean those things? Who told you I was the one..." His voice trails off as he rests his arms atop the railing. "Someone on the flight team must have seen—"

"Who cares how I found out? It's sweet. Probably your one kind act for that entire year. And the reindeer were thrilled. But I gotta ask"—I study his profile as he takes another sip of chocolate —"my burnt cookies, Niklas? That was the best you could do?"

He chuckles. "You didn't burn them. You petrified them."

"All the more reason not to have given them away as gifts. They were useless and you should have left them in the trashcan where I dumped them."

"Few things are one-hundred percent useless." He nudges me with his shoulder. "You need to think outside the box."

I nudge back. "Then I'd love to hear what you would have done with the fruitcake I made in Baking 203. Remember that assignment? It was supposed to have been edible."

"Half the class failed that one."

"But mine was the one that chipped Herr Mudge's front

tooth."

"Which made it match his other front tooth." Niklas fiddles with the lid of his cup. "And I got myself a great doorstop."

The warmth of his arm alongside mine seeps through my sweater. "You used my fruitcake for a doorstop?"

"Still do. Mostly to keep my bedroom door shut when I'm in there so the house elves don't bother me. They're a pesky lot, but that fruitcake weighs a ton, and they can't push their way inside." Our gazes meet. His dimples have come out to play, and his eyes twinkle in the lamplight. I'll allow he will make a decent Santa someday, with friendly eyes like that. Have they always looked so friendly?

Elves pass by behind us, some on SnoMos, some on snowshoes. One of us should acknowledge them, but I'm busy contemplating the different green hues in Niklas's eyes. Then his gaze drifts to my lips, making my stomach do funny things again. Our shoulders still touch, an innocent gesture at first that now seems to suggest something...more.

Niklas's eyes intensify. An electric sizzle pulsates the air between us. "You know something, Tinsel—"

"Yep, you should get going." Swiping my coat from the rail, I rise from my crouched position to flounder in my snowshoes. "And I need to locate a missing ski pole."

Niklas catches me by the elbow, a smile curling one side of his mouth as he leads me back to the sidewalk. "Right. Good luck." At his SnoMo, he stows his to-go cup in a holder then reaches for his helmet. "See you around, Kuchler." His dimples disappear behind the visor, and in the next instant, he peels away from the curb.

I hug my coat as the snowflakes created in his parting fall about me.

Romance between elves and Kringles is verboten.

I use the words to shore up the barricade around my heart, even as a teensy part wants to stomp them into oblivion.

PAST, PRESENT, AND FUTURE

Niklas hasn't always been a burr under my woolen cap. During our younger years in school, I thought we were BFFs. Looking back, I wonder if perhaps he just liked the fact we could play at the same level—as in *eye* level. But Pix Betriebs has never forgiven me for breaking her tricycle (technically, I bent its frame), and by the end of our Third Level she had almost every student convinced I was a bumbling, misguided elf who would never amount to much. By the end of Fourth Level, she had Niklas convinced, as well.

I remember the exact moment our friendship disintegrated. One minute it pulsated bright and lively; the next, it lay cold and broken. Dynamics between us have been a barb-fest ever since.

It happened on one of those springtime days when colors gleam so vivid your eyes hurt, and the sun's warmth seeps into the marrow of your bones. A perfect day to explore Figgy Forest and poke along Candy Floss Stream, fat from the runoff of winter's snow. With Niklas leading the way, several classmates and I scampered along the water's edge until we discovered a massive tree that had fallen across the streambed earlier that winter. We made bets to see who could cross it the fastest.

I was the last one across. Niklas had gone first and held the record for the fastest time. No surprise, there. When Pix went, she pretended to lose her balance, and Niklas reached out to pull her to safety. That didn't come as a shocker, either. Ever since First Level, Pix has contrived numerous ways to get Niklas to notice her, regardless of the edict prohibiting a romance.

When it was my turn, I got partway across the trunk when I began to teeter. Then totter. Until in classic form, I toppled into the stream, its numbing waters swallowing me whole.

Another elf with more sense would have given up right then. Me? Soaked and shivering, I schlepped my way back onto the bank and tried it again. And again. And again.

By this time, the elves had collapsed on the forest floor in fits of laughter, but having survived a year of their teasing by then, I didn't let it bother me. Much. To see Niklas bent over double as he wiped tears from his own eyes, however, struck me like a physical punch. Never had he joined in their teasing, yet there he stood, telling me between laughs I was the most ridiculous elf he had ever seen and I needed to quit before I damaged something.

"Pix is right about you," he wheezed. "You can't do anything right. That log is a foot wide"—he let out another round of giggles—"and you can't get across it? What an oaf!" He shared a high-five with the elves and something inside me snapped like a fisted candy cane.

Training my sights on Niklas, I marched across that tree trunk like it was ten feet wide, hopped to the ground, and gave him the hardest shove of my young life. He stumbled backward, tripped over a root, and landed—*smack*—on his rear. (In an ideal world, he would have fallen into the stream.) I crossed my arms and smiled.

One beat later, the collective gasp from the others jarred the smugness right out of me. I pushed the future Santa Claus! Their faces contorted, their hands clenched, but before they could converge on me, I raced away as fast as my too-long legs would carry me.

I received my first Penalty for that stunt, but so did the others. Knowing Niklas suffered penance elsewhere in Flitterndorf while I got saddled with garbage duty at The Flaky Crust helped ease the sting of losing his friendship.

On Sunday afternoon, I petrify a batch of cookies (much to my father's horror) and present them to the reindeer Monday morning. The new chew toys are met with hoof stomps and heads tossed in approval, and Chip apologizes for how he behaved on Saturday. After I let them outside, sans the halter—can't exactly lead them around like run-of-the-mill animals now that I know they can talk—and give them fresh food and water, I return inside to muck the stalls.

I'm separating clean and soiled hay with a pitchfork in Cinnamon's stall when the hair pricks at the nape of my neck. I turn. Chip stands in the aisle beyond the wheelbarrow.

Mouth twitching, I toss the load of questionable hay into the wheelbarrow. "Okay, I know you can fly over the fencing, but how did you get past the door with no hands?"

Chip tilts his antlered head. "Long ago, we mastered the art o' depressin' a latch with a hoof and pushin' against a door with our antlers."

I grin. "What about pulling open a door?"

His antlers wobble. "No' so much, though with a bit o' jigglin', we can sometimes manage it."

I laugh and pitch the good hay into a pile against one stall wall. "If you're here to supervise me, you don't have to. I know enough now not to throw away the hockey pucks."

Chip studies me in silence, and my hands grow clammy at the

scrutiny of a four-legged creature. "For not bein' good at much," he says after a while, "ye do a fair job cleanin' stalls."

I snort. "Thank you. I think."

"Is it true what the other elves say abou' ye? Ye have no talent?"

My fingers dig into the pitchfork's handle. "So it would appear, but I haven't given up hope in finding it."

"Herr Stricker is quite the talented knitter. And the Kringles, o' course, they're good at everythin'."

I clench my teeth. "Yes, they are."

"Kristof—have ye seen him on the ice? The things he can do in a pair o' skates. And Niklas? Sometimes durin' me flight lessons o'er the woods, I catch sight o' him racin' his SnoMo through the trees. 'Tis magic, that. I dinna ken much else abou' him, though." His gaze follows the trajectory of soiled hay as I toss a forkful into the wheelbarrow. "I imagine, bein' a Kringle, he's good at everythin', too."

My smile feels as brittle as candy ribbon. "I imagine he is."

"Do ye see him much?"

"Too much." I glance at the clock above the side door and curl my lip. "I see him in a little over an hour, as a matter of fact."

"'Tis no' a good thing?"

"Encounters with Niklas are rarely a good thing, especially when"—I stack my hands atop the pitchfork handle and rest my chin on them—"I have to meet him and my other classmates at the school to practice the Festival Dance." Every year at the Christmas Eve Ceremony before Meister K flies off in his sleigh, the elves in Letztes Niveau (Last Level) perform the Festival Dance for the whole Flitterndorf community.

This year, unlike all years prior, will be the first time a human-sized elf performs.

Should be interesting.

If the dance were similar to a country jig, where everyone fans out in a long line, no partners needed, I wouldn't be so worried. But the Festival Dance involves partners and twirls and boys flipping girls at their sides. Like another elf could twirl a giant like me. And even if I could execute this dance on my knees, there's no way my partner could flip me anywhere. Unless he's flipping me off.

The phrase "sticking out like a mint among chocolates" is going to take on a whole new meaning at this year's ceremony. I think I'd prefer to scoop poop for a decade than perform the dance.

I think.

"But Niklas isna an elf," Chip says, reminding me I'm not alone in the stables. "Why would he have ta practice the dance?"

"He might not be an elf, but he is in Letztes Niveau." I jab a finger toward the ceiling and proclaim in a twangy bellow, "Each student must perform at the ceremony. There are no exceptions!" In my normal voice, I add, "Thus saith Frau Tanz. I believe she's preparing a solo for Niklas, though." Lucky Kringle.

Chip paws at the tiled floor with a hoof. "So, could ye give him a message from the Third String, perchance?"

"Ugh! Why does everyone have a fixation with this guy? He pops up in every conversation I have, whether it's with my parents or a classmate—or a reindeer! Did you know there's not one school-age female elf who hasn't had a crush on him at some point in the last decade? Not one." And yes, that (unfortunately) includes me.

Chip's eyes flare wide, and I cringe. "Um. Not that you're school-age. Or female. Or…obsessed." I rub a hand over my face as Butterscotch nudges open the door with his antler tines. "Sorry. It's hard enough handling my shortcomings without the constant reminder that the only other classmate my size is perfect at everything he does."

Butterscotch props his chin atop the wall of the last stall, his front half inside the stables, his back half out in the cold. "He isna our preferred Kringle, either. Hard ta build a relationship wi' someone you havna seen in seven years, 'cept in passin'."

"Seven years? Don't you see him on a weekly basis?" I stab at the hay with the pitchfork. "I thought Sundays were 'Kringle days' for you all." (And my one day of reprieve from mucking stalls.)

"Kristof comes on Sundays. Never Niklas."

Chip nods his head. "We saw him lots as a wee tyke. Him and his bruider. They'd come in with Meister Nico and feed us carrots and ride on our backs. But after Niklas turned six, well, we didna see him again 'til that day he gave us the chew toys. Seven years ago."

I put my hands on my hips. "What Kringle neglects his reindeer? Does Meister K know about this?" Then I straighten. "Does *Herr Referat* know about this?"

A negligent Kringle is bad enough, but a negligent Kringle vying for the managerial internship is even worse...unless you happen to be standing in my position. A crafty grin tugs at my lips. I wonder what Herr Referat would think, if word ever leaked out about Niklas's lax behavior.

DANCE PRACTICE

After I clean up from mucking stalls, I snowshoe it to the Flitterndorf School of Talent before I'm officially late. I haven't dared look at the school up close since it exploded four days ago. On the bright side (if that exists), it happened just before our month-long winter break started. Enough time to patch any holes with plywood before the students return in January. All students, that is, except those in Letztes Niveau. *We* should be up to our bell-topped caps in internships.

My stomach dips and dives. I have my interview tomorrow.

As I near the school, my pace slows. In the morning twilight, the blurred lines of the charred west wing emerge. A jagged hole of twisted metal and blackened rubble now marks the spot where Herr Chemie's classroom once stood.

Uh, that's going to require a lot more work than plywood.

Snowman, did I screw up or what? Sure, it was Herr Chemie's glass tube that broke, and his chemicals that caught fire, but I was the one who freaked out and sent the Bunsen burner flying.

Outside the gymnasium, I lean my snowshoes against the wall beside several tiny ones that look like toys in comparison. In the neighboring parking lot, a monstrous SnoMo with a flashy paint job has the same effect on the dozen or so elf-sized SnoMos crowded around it. No need to guess if Niklas has already arrived.

Chewing on my lower lip, I enter through the gym's main doors. Surrounded by a sloppy circle of students, Frau Tanz paces and lectures on the importance of the Festival Dance and how it must be perfectly executed. A switch in her hand punctuates the air every few words. Herr Geier sits in the bleachers, his gaze panning over the group. I slink my way into the circle, but Frau Tanz zeroes in on me with narrowed eyes.

"*Some* students might have more difficulty than others in learning the steps, but I will not let anyone"—she waggles the switch in my direction—"make this year's Festival Dance less than magnificent."

Her words are met with grumbling and sidelong glances. I put on my poker face as she comes to stand before me like a mini drill sergeant. "Speaking of you, Tinsel, I received a message that Meister K would like to see you in his office following practice."

An "ooo-you're-in-trouble-now" murmur sweeps among my classmates, and Niklas smirks from across the circle.

Frau Tanz holds up her hand for silence before addressing Niklas. "Meister K would like to see you, as well."

"Of course he does. We missed our weekly chat over eggnog yesterday. Tinsel, on the other hand"—Niklas gets that smug look on his face I'm all too familiar with—"I can't imagine what she's done this time to warrant another meeting with Grandpop."

I tap my chin. "I suppose it's too soon for word to have reached him about what I accidentally did to your SnoMo outside?"

Though Niklas schools his features into carefree confidence, his eyes twitch—which tells me he's *almost* positive I'm joking. Satisfied at his discomfort in not knowing for sure, I match his carefree expression before looking away.

My pleasure erodes when Frau Tanz pairs us up—boy-girl,

boy-girl—and announces upon reaching me, "You will be dancing the boy's steps. And Pix Betriebs will be your partner."

"What!" Pix and I blurt at the same time.

"I'm not dancing with that clumsy oaf," Pix whines as I complain, "I'm not dancing the boy's part."

We glare at each other, and I cross my arms. "I'll sit this one out, thanks."

Frau Tanz shrugs her tiny shoulders draped in a red woolen capelet. "First of all, Tinsel, it's impossible for you to perform the girl's steps. You're too tall. How is your partner supposed to flip you, let alone twirl you?"

I grind my teeth at her verbal affirmation of my earlier concerns.

"Second"—she slaps the switch in her palm—"if you don't dance, you flunk the course."

Flunking the course means I wouldn't graduate in the spring, thanks to another ancient edict scrawled in Meister K's books. And if I were slated not to graduate, then goodbye internship. My gaze darts to Niklas and an idea forms. "What if…" I bite my lip then blurt before I lose my nerve, "What if you paired me with Niklas?"

Mouths drop and gasps rise from the students. I fiddle with the edges of my apron as my stomach hardens.

Frau Tanz emits a patronizing laugh. "Oh, no, no, no, no, no. I will not let the likes of you interfere with Niklas's solo performance. You either dance with Pix or you flunk. Your choice."

Resigned to my fate, I throw back my shoulders and form a line with the boys. I sense Niklas's stare but refuse to meet his eyes.

I don't want to see the arrogance that's probably plastered all over his face.

PRACTICE GOES ABOUT AS WELL AS I EXPECT IT TO. WHICH IS TO say, I bumble my way through it, stumbling over my two left feet and dropping Pix twice when I'm supposed to flip her (she's not as dainty as she looks). The derisive glances cast my way rake me like sharp fingernails, and the snide comments fan the heat in my face.

"I told you she has a crush on Niklas."

"My dad said she was draped all over him the other morning at the rink."

"Whatever attention Niklas gives her stems from pity."

"She knows better than to defy an edict."

"I heard he has a European girlfriend."

"I heard he's betrothed."

This last bit almost makes me laugh out loud. It takes a special woman to become Santa's wife—but to become *Niklas's* wife? No woman in her right mind would willingly fill those shoes. Besides, if Niklas had a significant other, Kristof would have told me.

By the end of practice, I have half a mind to pull a Great Oma Fay and leave Flitterndorf for the outside world. Unlike her, I'd blend right in with the humans aside from my ears, and I can hide those.

Trekking up Huff 'n Puff Hill on my way to the Workshop, I gaze over the twinkling lights of Flitterndorf. Pride and love swell inside my chest, rejecting thoughts of escape. I could never leave this place, no matter how much the elves tease me. And what about my goals? I won't forsake Christmas's future to the likes of Niklas. No, I need to stay and prove my capabilities. Otherwise, I remain "the clumsy oaf" in everyone's minds.

As I pass the last switchback, a SnoMo chugs in the distance, and a moment later, Niklas zooms by in a neon blur. He cuts across my path before swerving to a stop at the Workshop. Sighing beneath the mini snow shower, I walk through the stinging flakes and take a seat on the bench beside the double-door entrance.

Elves bustle in and out of the four-foot tall entry cut into one of the nine-foot tall oak doors. Most bypass me, but they all acknowledge Niklas with cheery waves and smiles. Hopping off his SnoMo, he responds to them with distracted greetings as his gaze catches mine. I duck my head and concentrate on unbuckling my snowshoes.

The toes of his boots come into view. "So you want to be my dance partner, huh?" He rocks back on his heels. "I suppose the rumors are true, then."

"Rumors?"

"Haven't you heard? You've got a crush on me."

I pretend to be flustered and fan my face with a mittened hand. "Well, you *are* the future Santa." I bat my eyelashes at Niklas for extra sarcasm. "Makes a girl positively giddy in the presence of such a celebrity."

His mouth lifts at one corner. "Flattered as I am—and as much as I'd like to make your dancing dreams a reality—I don't think I could keep up with that fancy footwork you displayed during practice." He takes a seat next to me. "Although I wouldn't have to worry about you dropping me."

"No, I'd have to worry about *you* dropping *me*."

"Tsk, tsk. You're too hard on yourself, Tinsel." He drapes an arm about my shoulders and gives me a squeeze. "You might be the heaviest elf in Flitterndorf, but I think I could manage to flip you a time or two."

"Oh, I wasn't concerned about my weight." I pat him on the leg. "I was concerned about your strength. But it's a moot point since Frau Tanz has forbidden us to dance together."

"Probably for the best." Niklas angles his head close, and I ignore the way my stomach flops about. "Over time, it might have made the other elves wonder if I'm crushing on you, and we can't have that."

"True. You've worked hard over the years to convince everyone you can barely tolerate me. With that in mind"—I pluck his gloved hand off my shoulder, toss it back onto his lap, and dig my elbow into his side—"this PDA-stuff could send the wrong message should someone walk by. Think what your betrothed would say."

Niklas rubs his side with a grimace. "Good point." Then he blinks. "What betrothed?"

"Haven't *you* heard? You're engaged to a European beauty."

"I'm not engaged." The words fly from his mouth with a cutting edge.

Standing, I shrug a shoulder and prop my shoes against the wall. "Whether you are or aren't, it's all the same to me." The fact my insides unclench at his denial has nothing to do with relief. I reach for the thick iron handle, and the door groans open on its foot-long hinges. Giving an exaggerated flourish with my arm, I say to Niklas, "After you."

He gets to his feet and mimics my gesture, his eyes twinkling. "Please. Ladies first."

But I shake my head. "Ever since Seventh Level, I have made it a rule never to precede you into any building, whatsoever."

A smile plays on his lips. "And what happened in Seventh Level?"

"You opened the door for me at school. No sooner had I taken three steps inside when some elves in the lobby balcony dumped a bucketful of coal on me."

He snorts on a laugh. "You blame me for that?"

"In." Taking Niklas by the arm, I push him through the doorway. Warmth blankets me as I enter the octagonal lobby and peel off my mittens. Strains of "Silent Night" drift on the air.

"Tinsel, I had no—"

"Shhh." I clap my hand over his mouth. Gazing about the grand timber-framed room, I breathe deep of cinnamon and pine. "You'll ruin the magic."

"What magic?" he mumbles through my fingers.

I sweep my arm to indicate our surroundings. "Christmas magic."

MEISTER KRINGLE

Though I've passed through here oodles of times over the years, I'm as enthralled now as I was at age four when I saw it for the first time.

Curlicue wall sconces dot the perimeter, their glow reflecting off the honey-toned timber to create the inviting ambiance. Centered in the room stands a two-and-a-half-story Christmas tree, its boughs graced with thousands of tiny white lights like a lacy filigree. They glint off gilded ornaments swaying among the needles, while gold-flecked red ribbon and pinecones add to the sparkle. At the very top presides an old-world angel, swathed in burgundy and faux-furs.

Hugging the curve of the outer lobby walls, two wide staircases rise to meet the second-floor balcony, its oak railings looped in garland. Secured to the third-floor balcony railing hangs a hand-hewed cross backlit with rope lights. Sure, the two Christmas icons clash in the outside world, but here in Flitterndorf, the Son of Man is the reason the jolly fat man delivers free gifts to thousands of believing children every year.

Niklas touches my elbow. "I had nothing to do with the coal in Seventh Level, I promise."

"Like you had nothing to do with the toothpaste-filled, Double Stuffed Oreo?"

A pleased-as-rumberry-punch smile flits across his mouth. "No, that was me. But the coal? My pranks are more original than that."

I shake my head. "And I'm supposed to believe you've never made the Naughty List."

As I unbutton my coat, my gaze falls to the wrapped gifts mounded beneath the tree's bottom branches. A shiny sea of reds and greens, blues and whites, ivory and gold reflecting today's work before they're collected and sent to Assembly. "There must be a few hundred of them."

Niklas shoves his hands into his front pockets. "I've heard the numbers are low in Assembly. The mounds don't reach as high as they should for the second week in December."

My fingers stall on the last button at his unspoken words: *because of the explosion last Thursday.*

Slipping my scarf from around my neck, I recall the stockpile of finished gifts that awaited transfer to the Workshop in the teacher's lounge—which sat directly beneath Herr Chemie's classroom.

My stomach bucks. Suddenly each tiny pinpoint of light stings like the prick of a needle. The angel atop the tree glares, and the pungent air chokes my throat. I force myself to draw slow breaths then blow them out again through pursed lips.

"Ah, Miss Kuchler. Meister Niklas." A lady elf with wire-rimmed glasses and a clipboard approaches, her shoes tap-tapping on the wooden floorboards. The closer she gets, the more she must tilt her head back to look at us. She wears a white blouse with ruffled collar, neatly pressed. Her hunter green, wrinkle-free *dirndl* skirt swishes about her knees, and her black hair is pulled into a tidy bun below her matching, fur-trimmed hat.

I smooth the wrinkles in my own *dirndl* as "clumsy oaf" prattles inside my head.

"Good morning, Frau Bericht." Niklas bobs his head. "How goes the Workshop today?"

"As well as can be expected." The assistant slides a pointed glance in my direction. "Meister K is waiting for you. If you'll follow me, please."

I ascend the right-hand staircase, staying two risers behind her, my fingers trailing along the polished oak banister. After several steps, Frau Bericht glances over her shoulder and gasps. "Meister Niklas! Where are you going?"

I turn to look. Niklas has jetted off in the opposite direction, gaining the halfway point of the left-hand staircase before he halts and swivels around. "To my room, of course. When Grandpop is finished with Tinsel, someone can send for me."

Frau Bericht compresses her lips and folds her arms over her clipboard. "Meister K wants to see you both at the same time."

The surprise crossing Niklas's face is unmistakable, and I chew the inside of my cheek to hide my smirk. After a brief hesitation, he jogs down one staircase then up the other. Once he's joined us, Frau Bericht resumes her ascent to the second floor.

When we reach a wide oak door sporting a red-and-white striped wreath with a spray of mistletoe pinned at the top, she holds up a slender hand. "If you'll wait here, I'll announce you." She disappears behind the door, and muffled voices carry from within. At length, she reappears with Herr Referat, who gives a curt nod before standing aside to usher us in.

Niklas ignores his reindeer!

The words fight for release on my tongues as I pass the elf, but I mash my lips together. I want the truth to leak; I don't need to be the leak*er*.

The door shuts behind me.

I've been inside Meister K's office countless times to receive countless Penalties; I know it almost as well as I know my family's apartment. At the moment, Meister K stands at the far end with his back to us, gazing through the wall-to-wall picture window at the view of Mount Trost to the east. A mahogany craft table, twice the size of the bakery's kitchen table, stretches the distance between us. Its distressed surface spills over with myriad pieces of wood, metal, hardware, and tools. Fabric bolts, paint bottles, miscellaneous jars, and books by the hundreds clutter the deep shelves and cubbies lining the walls. From a set of hidden speakers, Michael Bublé croons "Ave Maria" in his swoon-worthy voice.

I sink into one of the two upholstered wingback chairs that flank the office door—and squeak when I land in Niklas's lap. Meister K turns from the window as I spring to my feet.

"Alles in Ordnung?" he asks in his deep, captivating voice.

"Everything is fine, sir." Moving to the other chair, I scowl at Niklas. He winks.

"Good. Good." Meister K claps his broad hands together then rubs them vigorously as he steps toward a small, round table in the far corner, upon which rests a plate of cookies and a glass of...well, it's probably pumpkin spiced eggnog, knowing Meister K. He lifts the plate and skirts the craft table as he approaches us, his blue gaze ping-ponging between Niklas and me. "I'm sure you're wondering why I called you here. Cookie?"

"Nein, danke," I whisper.

He offers the plate to Niklas, who takes two. "Nik, you may have a better idea than Tinsel, so to get you on even ground, I'll come right out with it." Setting the plate aside, Meister K leans against the table's edge and levels me a penetrating look over the rim of his half-spectacles. "You know that a few times each year Meister Nico, Niklas, and I head to Waldheim to gather supplies for the Christmas toys. Typically, we've completed our travels by late September, but with the unfortunate explosion on Thursday, we need Niklas to make one last trip. I'm sending you along to help him bring back the supplies."

"What?" Niklas and I say in unison. Meister K is taking a chance on *me*?

Niklas leans forward, hands clenching the arm rests. "Grandpop, you can't be serious. Why are you breaking with tradition?"

"If we're to meet quota by Christmas Eve, your father and I can't leave Flitterndorf right now."

"Then send Herr Geier or Frau Bericht along to help me."

"You know what kind of commotion an elf-sighting among humans would create."

"Yet you're willing to send Tinsel?"

Raising an eyebrow, Meister K sticks his thumbs behind his red-and-green suspenders. "Hide her ears and she'll blend right in."

Unwittingly, I finger my pointy ears to assure myself they're working right. This conversation sounds surreal.

Niklas rams a hand through his hair. "Why not send Kristof?"

"He's running another errand for me."

"Doing what?"

"Enough, Niklas. This decision is final."

Niklas slaps his thighs on a growl. "Can you blame me for doubting her capabilities in this matter? She has a history of botching almost every job she undertakes."

My eyes sting but I blink the sensation away.

"The problem is not in her abilities." Meister K turns his kind gaze on me. "The problem, Tinsel, is lacking faith in your abilities and lacking opportunities in which to exercise that faith."

I spread my hands. "How much more faith do I need?"

"And how many more opportunities?" Niklas rubs his forehead. "At some point she's got to accept that, talent-wise, she's not the brightest candle on the tree."

There's an audible gasp and I realize it came from me, but Meister K winks, skimming a hand over his beard. "A tiny flame is all one needs to dispel the darkness, *nicht wahr?*"

My lips spread into a grateful smile. If Santa Claus himself believes in me, I've got all the faith I need.

"Can you operate a snowmobile, Tinsel?"

"Yes, sir."

Niklas snorts.

I lift my chin. "Kristof gave me some lessons last year. Although, it's true I might be a little rusty."

Niklas shoots me a dubious look. "When did you guys ever sneak off together?"

"There was no 'sneaking' involved. What is your deal, anyway? Why are you such a Grinch?"

"I don't want you going to Waldheim. An elf's place is in Flitterndorf and—"

I jump to my feet. "Of all the audacious, highhanded things to say!"

Meister K's perceptive eyes narrow at Niklas, and his face darkens to match his rosy cheeks. "I think you would do well to give Tinsel a refresher course with a SnoMo following this meeting. Along with an apology."

Niklas slouches in his chair, arms crossed over his chest.

"Allow me to reiterate." Meister K clasps his hands behind his back. "Tomorrow after dance practice, you two will meet me outside the Workshop's back entrance where I will have SnoMos waiting, hitched to cargo sleds. You will return in the evening with those sleds loaded, your mission a success, and I will not hear one more complaint against it. Is that clear?"

I grip my elbows across my middle. "Tomorrow, sir? I have an interview with Herr Referat after lunch."

"Already handled, my dear." Meister K's eyes twinkle. "We've postponed it for another day. Herr Referat will let you know the rescheduled time once he's checked his calendar."

I blow out a relaxed breath. "*Danke.*"

He picks up a half-finished toy car from the craft table and brings it close to his face to examine it. "You may take your leave,

Tinsel. Enjoy your evening, and we'll see you tomorrow. Niklas," he adds as his grandson stands, "you are to remain. I have a few more things to discuss with you."

"I thought you wanted me to help Tinsel with the SnoMo."

"You can find her when you're done."

On a muffled groan, Niklas drops back into his chair.

LESSONS

Reality sinks in once I'm outside. Wringing my mittened hands, I pace beside the Workshop entrance. Some elf must have slipped a shot of bourbon into Meister K's eggnog for him to choose me to accompany Niklas on this über-critical venture, straddling a vehicle with which I've had little prior experience. No one in his or her right mind would recommend me for anything more than a glorified pooper-scooper, let alone a gas-guzzling machine with speeds reaching 150 mph!

I stop pacing. Good garland, what a perfect way to show Herr Referat my capabilities. When I return a success, *I'll* be the shoo-in for the internship.

Biting back a grin, I sidle over to Niklas's racing SnoMo. The dashboard instruments look more complicated than those on the elves' snowmobiles. While its body has all the normal parts, like wind deflectors and bumpers and a windshield, it flaunts ungainly shock absorbers, and what's with the extra girth at the back end? My smile fades. The SnoMo I used with Kristof wasn't so complex.

We better not use this one for the practice lesson.

I rub at the ache in my temple only a triple fudge Kandi Cup can alleviate. But as I plop my snowshoes on the ground and take a seat on the bench, a door slams open and Niklas stomps outside.

My eyebrows rise. "That was a quick chat."

He plows a hand through his hair with a scowl. "And quite unpleasant." He glances across Huff 'n Puff Hill toward the Lower Stables and gulps. Santa's grandson…nervous? Then he straddles his SnoMo and fixes his glare on me. "Ready?"

"For what?"

"The refresher course."

I nudge the snowshoe with my foot. "I don't know if that's a good idea. You don't want to, and I don't want you to, so—"

"I'm sorry for how I acted in Grandpop's office, okay?" Niklas straps on his helmet. "I'm fine with helping you. Honest."

I purse my lips. "What's with the sudden change of heart?" When his attention flits once more to the stables, a thin shoot of suspicion unfurls in my head. "You're hoping to avoid something else by helping me."

His gaze snaps back to mine. I've guessed correctly—and he's about to deny it.

"That's a load of charcoal."

Called it.

"C'mon, Kuchler." He waves an extra helmet in my direction. "You want my help or not?"

AFTER I REASSURE HIM I KNOW THE DIFFERENT PARTS OF A snowmobile, Niklas gives me a few pointers, like I should verify the vehicle's in proper working condition (duh), always use a tether kill switch (no kidding), never drive side-saddle—

"Time out. Why not?"

"You have less control that way."

I huff. "You're lucky I wore thick leggings beneath my *dirndl.*"

He laughs. "No, *you're* lucky."

At last he shifts backward on the seat, and I slip in front of him. On his cue, I squeeze the throttle. We jerk forward at a fast clip, and Niklas snags his arm about my waist in a death grip.

"I almost flew off," he shouts, his voice muffled by the helmet.

I shrug, then head northeast around Huff 'n Puff Hill toward the woods. Okay, so my takeoff was a little iffy, but once we reach the woods, I've gotten the hang of it.

If you ask me.

"Not so fast!" Niklas hollers.

Not if you ask him.

"I thought you liked going fast."

A tree slices by to our right. I swing out a little. Another zips by on our left. I swing back again. Two more on our right *and* left. I squeeze my eyes shut.

Oops—I'm driving.

"Slow down!" His grip tightens, crushing my ribs.

"Relax, will you? You're making me nervous."

"*I'm* making *you* nervous?" He taps my right arm. "Use the brake. Slow down a little."

I swerve around more trees, and Niklas's hand comes forward to correct my steering. "Don't turn too quickly. You'll flip us over. Didn't Kris teach you anything?"

I elbow him hard in the stomach. To his credit, he backs off.

After a few successful minutes weaving between tree trunks and boulders and following the curves of Candy Floss Stream, I turn my head to shout, "I forgot how much fun this can be. And the best part is I haven't fumbled—"

"Watch out!"

I whip around. Tree dead ahead.

Wrenching the handlebars, I miss the trunk by a scant few inches, but veer onto a downward slope. The momentum in the sudden turn combined with the slope causes the SnoMo to roll, and it pitches us into the snow in a tangle of arms and legs.

I hate it when Niklas is right.

I hate it even more when I'm the one who's proved him right.

"You're on my arm." His helmet makes his growl sound deeper and more menacing. Either that, or he's ticked at me. "Get off."

"Hold your reindeer." I twist onto my side and try to leverage my legs beneath me. "My boot's caught." I give my foot a tug.

"That's *my* boot."

"Ugh, I can't see in this frostbitten thing." I wrench off my helmet and manage to sit up. After peeling off my mittens, I work to untangle our boots where the straps got caught on each other. Niklas groans to a sitting position beside me.

"You had to turn too fast, didn't you? What'd I say about turning too fast?"

Freeing my boot, I give him a shove before pushing to my feet. "You're the one who insisted on doing this in the forest." I reach for the handlebars of the SnoMo, where it landed on its side, and pull. Holy frankincense, this thing's heavy. "I suggested a nice, wide-open field"—I grunt as I strive to right the metal contraption—"like the one where Kristof taught me, but nooo"—another grunt—"you had to take us into a tree-infested forest."

"Name one forest that isn't tree-infested."

"Not my point."

Niklas heaves a sigh then joins me where I struggle with the SnoMo. "We'll be driving through a tree-infested forest tomorrow. How will you successfully maneuver around tree trunks if all you can do is drive in a straight line without obstruction?"

My gaze narrows as he rights the SnoMo. "I hate it when you make better arguments than me."

He laughs. "I'm full of better arguments, Kuchler." He brushes snow off the seat and winks. "Haven't you learned that by now?"

I straddle the SnoMo, arranging my skirt to stay on the safe side of modest. "You would have greater appeal if you lost the arrogance."

His boyish grin turns into a pleased smile. "You think I have appeal?"

"I could have sworn I implied you were arrogant."

He grabs his helmet then settles in behind me. "You like me, Tinsel. Admit it."

My first name slipped in there gives his words a more intimate quality, and my body tingles in response. It doesn't have permission to do that, so I bristle from this internal mutiny. "What's the matter? The adoration of over two thousand elves isn't enough for you? You need the esteem of the one elf who sees through your bluster and bravado to the egotistical core within?"

"Silent night, that's harsh." He rams the helmet on his head. "Just drive, wouldja?"

My mouth falls open. "You're offended? All I did was point out the obvious."

"Drive."

"Fine." I yank on my helmet, start the engine, and take off, making certain it's jerkier than before, but alas, the real jerk stays on the SnoMo. His arms crush me, and he head-butts me with his helmet. I head-butt him back. Of all the Kringles throughout history, I had to get stuck with this one.

Despite—or maybe because of?—my ire, I handle the SnoMo with more skill than I've exhibited in most areas. I swerve around trees and clear small jumps as if I'd been practicing for years. Niklas even lets out an exuberant whoop when I get some decent air. A bubble of laughter escapes me.

By the time I return to our starting point at the Workshop, Niklas has loosened up considerably, his hands no longer gripping my waist, but rather resting there. Though I'm wearing several layers, I'm acutely aware of those hands. Not good, since I'm supposed to be mad at him.

I park beside another human-sized SnoMo near the front

entrance and let it idle as Niklas removes his helmet. He shakes out his hair. "Not bad, Kuchler. You perform like that tomorrow and this trip will be a piece of fruitcake."

"Thank you." I dismount and pull off my helmet to leave it on the vacated seat when Niklas traps my wrist in a gentle hold.

"Did you mean what you said back there? You know, about all that arrogance stuff?" His gaze searches my face, and I want to run a hand through my tangled hair, positive it's flattened against my head.

"There's something to be said about a humble man, Niklas."

"You mean weak."

"A man's strength is found in his humility." Freeing my wrist, I plop the helmet on the seat and attempt a casual smile. "See you tomorrow."

"Please tell me you have a snowmobile suit to wear for our ride." Niklas raises his voice as I walk away toward my snowshoes. "It's ninety minutes to Waldheim, and you'll freeze if you're not properly dressed."

"Kristof gave me an extra suit last year during our lessons," I toss back over my shoulder.

"Kristof, huh? I suppose you think *he's* humble?"

"You could learn a thing or two from your little brother."

It's not until he's driven off and I'm heading home that I realize I had the last word back there.

It doesn't thrill me like I thought it would.

ON OUR WAY

There's a note nailed to the Lower Stables' west entrance when I arrive the next morning. My name is printed on the front in stocky, black Calligraphy. I tug it from the nail and push open the door.

"*Guten Morgen*." I flick on the lights, smile at the reindeer, then unfold the note.

"Mornin'. Ye ready fer the big day?" Peppermint asks.

My hands begin to tremble.

"Tinsel?"

The black lettering blurs, and I swipe my eyes with the back of my mitten. "Has anybody else been in here, either after I left last night or earlier this morning?"

Chip yawns and puts his snout over his stall door. "Kristof came ta say g'night."

"It couldn't have been him. He wouldn't have written this." I hope.

Licorice cocks her head. "Written what?"

With the note in one hand, I unlatch the stalls doors with the other and read aloud.

"'May Christmas Hope be with you today on your errand—'"

"Och, that's nice," Cocoa says as he enters the aisle.

I arch my eyebrow. "'—because if you are anything less than a success, I will not only ensure you have no chance at the internship, I will make your days in Flitterndorf miserable.'"

Cocoa exchanges glances with the other reindeer. "Eh, maybe no' so nice."

I open Chocolate's door. "'Don't think an inept elf like you will ever rise to become Chief Operations Elf. You are a disgrace to the Green Clan, and I will see to it you stay where you belong. Among the animals.'" I meet Chip's gaze and unlatch his door with shaking fingers. Whatever confidence I gained from the SnoMo lesson the note has successfully ground into ice crystals. "Who would write such a thing?"

"Someone who feels threatened, o' course," Cinnamon says from her stall.

"Do you think he—or she—could make good on this threat?" I wring my hands once I've freed all the reindeer, and they crowd around me in the aisle. "These materials Niklas and I are getting…Meister K needs them to make the last batch of Christmas toys. If something goes wrong because of me—"

Chip gives my shoulder a playful whack with an antler tine. "Santa knows what he's doin'. Most o' the time. If he hand-picked ye fer this errand, he has his reasons."

Butterscotch dips his head to look me in the eye. "And ye havna botched everythin', Tinsel. Ye've made some messes, but yer no' incompetent."

I take a deep breath and shove aside my insecurities. "You're right. I can do this. I will do this. And I'll make whoever wrote this note eat his or her words." My shoulders slump again. "Right after dance practice."

Butterscotch noses my head. "Why another long face, lass?"

"Because the Festival Dance is yet another area where I can ruin my chances for the internship with my blunders. Goodness knows what Frau Tanz will do if I damage her flawless record.

Had she paired me with someone my own size, I might have stood a chance."

"Niklas!" Chip exclaims.

"Well, yes, he's the obvious choice, but—"

"Who are you talking to?"

I yelp at the deep voice and spin about. Niklas hovers inside the west entrance, a frown marring his brow.

"N-Niklas." My fingers fist in Cinnamon's guard hairs. "How long have you been standing there?"

"Answer the question." He glances at the reindeer, his grip tightening on the doorjamb. "And what are these guys doing, roaming free?"

Butterscotch angles his head. "Maybe ye should tell him?"

I chew the inside of my cheek. "I don't know."

"You don't know why they're free?"

I scowl at Niklas. "I'm not talking to you."

"If ye tell him"—Chocolate bounces on his hooves—"maybe he'll get jealous. Jealousy paired with the Meisters' ultimatum should do the trick."

"Meisters' ultimatum?" I echo.

"Hey!" The line deepens between Niklas's eyebrows. "Who told you about that?"

"Nobody. The reindeer said—" I clamp my mouth shut. Fruitcake!

Niklas stares until I drop my gaze. I rake my fingers through Cinnamon's coat then give her an awkward pat.

"Are you..." Niklas begins and then stops. "Are they..." He glances from me to the reindeer and back again. "You're not..." Pinching the bridge of his nose, he grumbles, "That's impossible." And he charges back outside.

The door slams shut behind him. I blink. "Sugarplums and figgy pudding. What's got his *lederhosen* in a twist this morning?"

"The Meisters' ultimatum," Eggnog replies in his forlorn way. "We overhaird his father and grandfather talkin' 'bout it yesterday in the FTA. Either Niklas spends more time with us and lairns to communicate, or he forfeits racin'."

I rub my temple. "Learn to communicate? So, I'm not the only one."

"Only one ta communicate?" Butterscotch snorts. "Nay, lass. The Kringles have that ability, too. But *understand* us? Aye, 'tis ye alone."

"But you said—"

"The Kringles canna hear our words. They merely sense our emotions. And even then, it takes years fer a Kringle and his team ta build up their relationship ta that point. Meister K has been workin' with the Big Eight since he was twelve, Meister Nico with the Second String since he was thirteen."

"And Niklas?"

Butterscotch shakes his head. "Kristof visits instead, like we told ye. Which is good. If anythin' happens ta Niklas, the role o' Santa falls ta Kristof, so 'tis important he, too, has fostered a relationship with us."

I make my way through the reindeer to the east entrance. "Why is that important?"

"The Christmas Eve flight depends on it. Reindeer have keen instinct in the air and sometimes 'tis vital fer Santa ta heed our emotions."

"Fer example," Cocoa chimes in, "'tis no' uncommon fer the Big Eight ta encounter wind shears durin' that flight. They ken when one's about and their awareness o' danger warns Meister K ta let up on the reins, allowing them ta steer around the wind shear."

"And if he can't sense their caution?"

"The sleigh could crash."

I squeeze the door latch. "So to be a successful Santa, Niklas needs to bond with you, yet he avoids you."

Licorice drops her head. "And we dinna ken why."

"Nobody does." Hope ignites in Chip's brown eyes as I swing

open the door. "But now that the Meisters have forced the issue, maybe we'll get some answers when he starts comin' ta visit."

MY SECOND ATTEMPT AT DANCING DOESN'T GO ANY BETTER THAN the first. I drop Pix three times, step on her feet twice, trip over some other couples, and at one point bump into Niklas. We stagger from the impact, but he catches me against him before I teeter off my feet. Our gazes collide. My heart accelerates, but I push him away before three dozen elves get the wrong idea—again—about my feelings for the guy.

Frau Tanz's gaze bores a hole in my head as this morning's note burns a hole in my pocket.

When practice ends, I flee the gymnasium, grab my snowshoes, and march toward the parking lot. Kristof waves to me from his perch astride his SnoMo, and I redirect my steps, cradling the snowshoes in my arms. "What are you doing here?" *And did you write me a nasty note?*

"I figured with such a long day ahead, your two left feet could use a lift to the Workshop."

"Mmm. Funny. Aren't you supposed to be on some errand?"

"I leave in an hour."

I bite my lip and study his face. His eyes twinkle, and his smile widens. He looks innocent enough. "Okay, I accept your offer." I tuck my things into his luggage rack, scoot sideways behind him, then slip my arms around his waist. Odd. Our proximity doesn't have strange effects on me like it does with his brother.

Speaking of whom, Niklas stands by his SnoMo surrounded by his fan club as Kristof weaves through the parking lot. I catch his eye and wiggle my mittened fingers in a saucy wave. Why does it please me when his eyes narrow in return?

TWENTY MINUTES LATER, CLOTHED IN KRISTOF'S OLD SNOMO outfit, I join the group behind the Workshop where Meister K, Herr Geier, and a team of elves wait for me and Niklas.

An elf from the Tech Department puts a helmet into my hands and points to the tiny speakers and microphone wired within. "These will allow you to communicate with Niklas during the drive."

I smile my thanks. Astride the SnoMo, I familiarize myself with the instrument panel as Meister K issues last-minute instructions. A soft *thump* jars my body, and I look over my shoulder. Transportation elves hook a cargo sled about the size of my mattress behind the SnoMo.

My chest constricts. I could barely handle a SnoMo on its own, yet I'm to steer with something attached to its back end? The terrain will consist of hills and ravines, steep cliffs and narrow trails. Drop me in the mix of those ingredients and you could have a recipe for disaster.

My breathing turns shallow and labored, and then a hand squeezes my shoulder. I give a tight-lipped grin as Kristof crouches beside me. He waits until his grandfather wraps up with some encouraging words, then whispers, "You look adorable."

I choke on a laugh. "Lying is grounds for the Naughty List."

"But it put the pink back in your cheeks." He gives my shoulder a shake. "Don't panic, Tinsel. You'll be fine. Grandpop wouldn't send you if he thought otherwise."

My gaze flits to Niklas. I hope to receive similar affirmation from him, but rather than an encouraging thumbs up or a smiling nod, he compresses his lips and tugs his helmet over his head.

I lift my chin. So. He still doesn't think I can pull this off, huh? Well, I'll show him *and* whoever wrote that note. I don my own helmet, grip the handlebars, and mumble to myself, "The surprised look on their faces when we return a success will be worth leaving Flitterndorf for the day."

"I can hear you, Kuchler." Niklas's voice emits through the

helmet's speakers as we leave the little group behind the Workshop and travel across the backside of Huff 'n Puff Hill. "You're not going to talk to yourself all the way to Waldheim, are you? That'll give me a headache for sure."

"A little discomfort might do you some good."

We descend the hill and enter Figgy Forest, following a narrow trail southeast toward Waldheim. It's not long before we traverse Candy Floss Stream. I can still see my Fourth Level self clambering from those waters after falling off the now-disintegrated tree trunk. Half a mile later marks the farthest point I've ever traveled outside Flitterndorf.

At first, this new part of Figgy Forest looks much the same as the old part. The same evergreens, the same fallen, decaying trunks, the same broken branches and crusted snow. I'm not familiar with the bends in the trail, though, or the ravines that drop away to my right, and I maneuver through those areas with caution.

"At this speed, it'll take us half a day to get there," Niklas grumbles thirty minutes into our journey.

I clench my teeth. "Would you prefer I arrive safe and intact, or not at all?"

"I'd prefer we arrive earlier."

Snowman, is he ever snarky today. That deserves a little retaliation. "You know, I learned something interesting this morning."

"And what would that be? Five things one should avoid when mucking out stalls? Or maybe five ways to annoy one's dance partner?"

"More like, *eight* ways to spend quality time with your reindeer"—I smile when his SnoMo and sled swerve—"in order to foster relationships and…how did he put it? 'Lairn' to communicate."

"Who told you all that? Herr Stricker? The Minor Flight Team?" Niklas pulls further ahead, so I speed up.

"C'mon, Kringle." I aim to solve this mini-mystery. "How

come you don't visit your reindeer? According to my sources, it's been more than seven years since you've spent any time with them."

"I have my reasons."

"I hope you're prepared to share because I'm told the Third String would like to hear those reasons."

Niklas scoffs. "They're going to be disappointed. I'm not explaining myself to anybody. And I certainly won't be spending quality time with any reindeer, either."

"Niklas!"

"Drop it, Tinsel."

"You're a lump of coal."

"Not the first time you've told me."

"And I guarantee it won't be the last."

BIG

You might wonder how Flitterndorf, given its location in North America, remains undiscovered in an age of satellite imagery and Google Earth. Thanks to ancient magic at work, an invisible field protects Santa and his elves for twenty-five miles in all directions from the Workshop. Though Niklas and I follow a well-worn path leading to Figgy Forest's unprotected side, any human (other than a Kringle) coming from the opposite direction will have the uncanny urge to turn parallel to the invisible barrier. He or she will then either follow its curve around to the other side or make a U-turn right there in the path.

I know exactly when we cross the barrier, for the temperature drops more than thirty degrees. My warm layers notwithstanding, the cold finds every access point and wriggles its way into my skin. I hunch my shoulders, grateful for the windshield that blocks the rushing air. Flitterndorf might lie under a blanket of snow for much of the year, but twenty degrees Fahrenheit is a cakewalk compared to negative twenty degrees.

After countless twists and bumps, the trail winds us past a ranch house tucked among the trees, and my jaw slackens.

Resting on stilts so the permafrost beneath it doesn't melt and make it collapse, the house is easily three times larger than an elf dwelling. With brown siding. Not a spot of green or red anywhere. A moment later, another house on stilts crops up. Then another. By the time we turn onto Waldheim's main road, my mouth hangs fully open. Front doors loom higher than two-elves tall. The windows stand about one elf in height and width. Streetlights tower above me along a sidewalk almost as wide as the streets back home. My parents would need a ladder to climb into some of these parked vehicles. Yes, the Workshop and stables are big, but here, everything is—

"My size," I breathe aloud. An excited tremor rushes through me. No ducking through doorways. No shortening my stride to keep in step with someone. No looking down to meet his or her eyes.

Niklas turns into the back lot of an industrial building, and I follow in a daze. Granted, I knew a human village would reflect its human-sized occupants, but it's hard to appreciate something I've only glimpsed in Great Oma Fay's small photographs.

I park beside Niklas and unbuckle my helmet. To think in a few minutes, I'll meet moving, breathing humans and—

Oh, snowman.

I forgot to pack a hat.

It's times like this I question my IQ and gene pool. I drop my head onto the handlebars with a groan.

Niklas chuckles through the speakers. "What's the matter? I thought you'd be thrilled at the Tinsel-sized setting."

"Yes, but"—I gesture to my helmet—"I don't have a hat to hide my ears. Which means I can't take off my helmet all day, because if anyone saw me, they'd freak out. Yet I'll *look* like a freak if I have to walk around in this thing. A cross between Darth Vader and some wannabe action figure. Can you see me strolling down the sidewalk—"

"Simmer down, Kuchler. I've got you covered." Niklas

removes his helmet, digs around in a saddlebag, and pulls out a colorful knit beanie.

I reach for it as he draws near. “Thank you.” Taking off my helmet, I shrug my braid over my shoulder then jam the beanie onto my head. “A little cramped and a little hot, but it’ll do.”

His mouth quirks at one end. “Your ears might be resilient to cold”—he pushes his gloves into my hands and tucks the wisps of hair away from my face before readjusting the beanie—“but without some protection, they don’t stand a chance in Waldheim’s temps.” He smooths my ears one by one inside the hat, his fingers skimming over my skin. My tummy squirms. He catches my gaze. The green flecks in his eyes glint in the lamplight, and my tummy flips some more.

His fingers linger at the base of my ears, and his clove scent drifts around me. “You wouldn’t think I’m a jerk if you knew why I didn’t want to be around the reindeer.”

“So tell me.”

“Niklas!”

He turns at his name, hands dropping to his sides. A young man bundled in a thick parka approaches us, a broad smile revealing straight, white teeth against olive skin. He holds out his hand to Niklas. “Hey, man, you made it. Good to see you.” The two share a firm handshake before the stranger’s dark brown gaze falls on me. His face brightens even as he asks Niklas, “Nico couldn’t make it? Everything’s okay, I hope.”

Niklas waves off his concern. “Pa’s fine. He couldn’t break away from the shop this time.” He puts a hand at my back. “Logan, I’d like you to meet Tinsel. She’s come in my father’s place.”

“Nice to meet you.” Logan takes my gloved hand, his grip strong and confident, his gaze raking over my face. I grow warm at his scrutiny. “Tinsel, huh? That’s unique.”

I suck in my lower lip. It hadn’t occurred to me how my name might come across to those outside Flitterndorf. "It's…a nickname."

Still holding my hand, Logan leans forward with a disarming grin. "Based on your sparkly personality, no doubt. Or the radiant aura that follows you into a room."

"Um, thank you." I know, it's over the top. But even if his flattery is nothing more than empty words, it's nice to hear for an elf accustomed to criticism. (And coming from a model-worthy guy makes it all the better.)

Logan squeezes my hand. "I've always liked tinsel. Enhances the other decorations, if you ask me."

Niklas huffs. "Amazing then, how many people avoid it because of its static-cling tendencies, its penchant for tangling, and the fact you'll be picking the stuff off the floor well into June." His gaze drops to our hands, and his jaw hardens. "Tinsel is nothing but a distraction that detracts from the other ornaments."

Logan lets out a bark of laughter, releasing my hand to elbow me in the arm. "I guess we know how he feels about *you*."

"Oh, he's never tried to hide it." I glare at Niklas. If it weren't for our shared history, his words might sting worse.

Niklas yanks on his gloves. "That wasn't—" He frowns and shakes his head. "Logan, about that shipment waiting for us?"

"Mmm, yes, Logan," I say with false brightness, "let's finish this errand as fast as possible, so he can be rid of me."

"Nik won't leave before seeing Gina at the Huggamugg Café." Logan slaps Niklas on the back. "But we'll get your order loaded first. Then you can play."

As I accompany them toward the hardware store entrance, one word twirls inside my head: Gina.

Who is Gina?

And what does she mean to Niklas?

…And why do I care?

❄

It takes some time, but with Logan's father helping, we load the cargo sleds with goodies for the Toy Makers back home, strapping everything together with bungee cords. After a round of handshakes, we part ways, and I follow Niklas alongside the building to Main Street. By the spring in his step, I'm guessing we're headed to the Huggamugg Café.

Thoughts of this Gina-chick war with my fascination for the people we pass on the sidewalk. No *dirndls* or *lederhosen* here. No forest greens or cranberry reds. Most wear earth-toned parkas with fur-lined hoods, trekking boots, and cargo pants. The men and women frown at my frank stares, but the children's gazes latch onto Niklas in round-eyed wonder. One boy escapes his mother's hand and fastens himself to Niklas's leg.

"Santa Claus," he whispers in barely-contained excitement.

Niklas chuckles. Detaching himself from the boy, he crouches so they're at eye-level. "Mateo, we've been over this before. I'm not Santa." He puts a finger aside of his nose and winks. "But I do know him." He sends the mother a smile, and her shoulders relax.

I swear he sets out to charm everyone but me.

"Let's do what we did last year." Niklas reaches into a pocket of his SnoMo bib, withdraws a mini candy cane, and holds it out to Mateo. "You tell me what you want for Christmas, and I'll relay the message to Santa."

The boy clambers onto Niklas's knee, cups a hand to Niklas's ear, and begins to whisper. His mother and I exchange knowing glances, but Niklas never takes his focus from the boy. His eyes twinkle brighter than I've ever seen, his smile wide in delight. Like he was made for this job.

Once Mateo and his mother are on their way again, I peek at Niklas. I'm about to tease him for his blissful expression when two grade school girls barrel from a mercantile store as we pass.

They lurch to a stop and stare at Niklas. As he did with Mateo, he puts himself at eye-level with them, a crooked grin on his lips.

"Savannah and Ruby," he says to each one in turn. "How are you lovely ladies today?"

"Am I still on the Nice List, Santa?" Ruby asks, plucking at his sleeve.

Niklas's dimples deepen. "Remember, ladies, I'm Santa's *helper*. And today, I have something he'd like to give you." He pulls out two more mini candy canes. "Now, Savannah, are you sure you want a bow and arrow set for Christmas?"

She nods, her brown curls bouncing beneath her hat. "Pink camo, please."

"And I want a purple princess dress," Ruby exclaims, now pumping Niklas's arm with her tiny hands.

Niklas laughs. "Okay, okay." He taps their noses. "I'll give Santa the message when I see him."

Ruby kisses Niklas on the cheek. "You can't fool us, Mr. Niklas. We know who you are."

Giggling, the girls skip down the sidewalk, candy canes in their mittened grips.

And that's how it goes all along Main Street. Kids stream from shops and emerge from alleyways to clamor around Niklas. He has a smile for everyone and knows each child by name.

When the latest group of children scamper off, I spread my hands. "This is incredible. I had no idea you were a natural with kids."

Niklas hefts a shoulder. "Kids and Santa Claus—even a future Santa Claus—kinda go hand-in-hand."

"Reindeer and Santa Claus *kinda* go hand-in-hand, too, yet you ignore your team to a fault."

Niklas tips his head back and sighs. "Not this again."

"You won't get away with it for much longer, though. Can't exactly ignore your grandfather's ultimatum, can you?"

"I'd like to ignore *you*."

"Nik—"

"Worry about your own problems and leave me to mine."

"I don't have any problems."

Niklas socks me lightly in the shoulder. "It doesn't bother you that your two left elfin booties are going to make you the laughingstock of the entire community in two weeks? Or that the explosion likely killed your chances for the internship? What—"

"Never mind." I kick a clump of snow on the sidewalk.

A crafty twinkle seeps into Niklas's eyes. "I could help you with that interview, you know."

"You're vying for the same internship. You'd be more likely to jinx me than help me."

Taking my hands, he holds them to his chest and offers me a too-cute grin. "Promise me you won't tell Grandpop I'm avoiding the reindeer, and I'll give you pointers on how to rock your interview."

"*Nein, danke.*" I pull from his hold and resume our trek along the sidewalk. "That wouldn't be right."

"How is my helping you not right?"

"Lying to your grandfather isn't right."

"I'm not asking you to lie." Keeping pace at my side, Niklas slings an arm around my shoulders. "I'm asking you not to say anything."

I squirm out from under him. "Niklas, your success as Santa requires you to have a good working relationship with your reindeer. You can't blow them off forever." Up ahead, a circular sign hangs out over the sidewalk. It depicts a cartoon figure squeezing an enormous coffee cup, its steam curling into the shape of a heart. Swirly letters loop beneath the picture to spell Huggamugg Café. "Is this the place—"

"All right, all right." Niklas careens in front of me, stopping me with a grip on my shoulders. "How about I help you prepare for the interview *aaand*"—he squeezes his eyes shut before meeting my gaze—"I give you private dance lessons so you don't look like a fool on Christmas Eve?"

Frosted windowpanes, I dare any girl to resist the pleading look in those eyes plus a promise of extra lessons. "You had to dangle that candy cane, didn't you?"

"Is that a 'yes'?" He searches my face, and my will falters.

I give the tiniest nod. "I won't say anything to your grandfather." *Herr Referat, however, is fair—*

"*Thank* you!" Cupping my face, Niklas gives me a sound kiss on the lips and then turns, rubbing his gloved hands together. "Okay, who's in the mood for some—" He halts with his hand on the café door and looks back where I'm frozen on the sidewalk. The color drains from his face. "Did I just…?"

I swallow. The act of kissing me horrifies him? Heat crawls into my cheeks, but I tamp down the ball of hurt and raise my chin as though offended. "Yes, you did *just*."

Niklas rubs the back of his neck. "I'm…sorry? Guess I was relieved. Or something. I, uh, didn't mean anything by it."

Pride unleashes my tongue. "That's a relief. I'd hate to think affection on your part prompted the kiss. Would have made things awkward, since I don't return the sentiment."

The muscles bulge in his jaw, and Niklas yanks open the door to the café. "Let's forget it ever happened, then, shall we?"

"Done. In fact, I was halfway to forgetting it as soon as it was over. It's refreshing to find Mr. Perfect doesn't excel at everything."

"What's that supposed to mean?"

Taking a chance this once that no bucket of coal awaits me, I precede Niklas into the café with a lofty pat on his arm. "It means your delivery needs a little work, Romeo. In case you're planning to kiss some other unsuspecting victim—I mean, girl."

HUGGAMUGG CAFÉ

The Huggamugg Café is aptly named, for upon entering, I'm wrapped in a hug of luscious smells hinting at yummy things to eat and drink. Plush sofas and armchairs dominate the floor, at-the-ready to envelop customers in cushiony embraces, while stocked bookshelves lining the outer wall offer their own welcoming gesture. Beside the counter, a trio of Christmas trees cluster together, decorated with homemade items like dried fruit, popcorn string, and hand-sewn ornaments. The furnishings would dwarf a normal elf. But I'm not normal.

I'm smitten at once.

"Why don't you find us some seats while I place our order?" Niklas asks over the drone of conversations around us. He makes his way toward the counter. "You sure you want their cocoa?"

I nod, my attention honing in on some stuffed chairs in the front corner. Choosing one, I sink into the luscious seat cushion and grin. My hips fit inside the chair's contours, with room to spare.

I turn to peruse the book titles on the shelf to my left when a squeal brings all conversations to a halt.

"Niklas!" A dark-haired girl behind the counter shoves the

coffeepot she's holding into a co-worker's hands, rushes onto the floor, and flings her arms about Niklas's neck in a polar bear-sized hug. "I didn't believe it when Logan told me you were coming in for another shipment. This is your busy season. What are you doing here?"

"Hey, Gina." Niklas returns her hug with a tight one of his own. His eyes close, and his lips bow in a small grin.

Hmm...maybe *this* is why it's called the Huggamugg Café.

So glad I forgot about that kiss a few minutes ago.

Chatter slowly resumes and by the time this Gina-chick pulls away (it takes forever), I can't hear what they say anymore. But I can *see* perfectly: Niklas's hand resting at her waist; a wine-red tunic top emphasizing her curves; lustrous black hair accented with blue streaks and a few random, beaded dreadlocks; an infectious grin radiating an energetic spirit.

Niklas gives her his cocky smile and says something that makes her laugh and hug his arm.

Ugh. I see them flirting.

They look in my direction, and I want to hide among the books on the shelf. The girl is prettier than her profile lets on, even with the rounded ears. I tug at the unflattering waistline of my SnoMo bib.

Gina smiles and waves before she turns back to Niklas. Does he like rounded ears? Good garland, what a thought. Of course he does.

After some more words and head bobs, the two part ways. Gina returns to her work behind the counter, and Niklas wends around furniture pieces to join me in the front corner.

"That was a touching scene," I say as he settles into the sofa facing me. I hope to make him uncomfortable, since he did flirt with someone right after kissing me.

A kiss I've totally forgotten about, but it's the principle of the thing.

Niklas chuckles. "Yes, Gina gets easily excited. She, Logan, and I go way back, so I make it a point to cross paths with them whenever I'm in town."

"Are you sure she's a friend and not your rumored fiancée?"

"I've told you the truth about those rumors."

"You've told me something, but is it the truth? Or are you secretly engaged and Gina's waiting for the day she's revealed before the elves as your wife?" It takes effort not to curl my lip at the thought.

He slants me an amused look. "If that were the case, and you were in her shoes just now, wouldn't you hope I'd give you a more affectionate greeting than a mere hug after a few months of separation?"

I raise my eyebrows. "First you kiss me, now you ask my opinion as a pseudo fiancée. Is there something you'd like to tell me, Niklas?"

"I'm sorry"—he leans forward, his gaze drilling into mine —"did you say 'kiss'? I don't recall anything about you and me and a kiss. Perhaps there's something you'd like to tell *me*."

His expression is somber, his lips unsmiling, and yet... Yes, there's the faintest twinkle in the depths of his eyes.

A squat, oval-shaped tray table drops into the space between us, followed by two ceramic mugs topped with whipped cream. "Here you are," Gina announces in a cheerful tone. "Two hot chocolates made with real chocolate bits, one with a shot of peppermint for Niklas. You'll have to tell me what you think." She smiles and holds out her hand. "Hi. I'm Gina."

I shake her hand. "Tinsel. Nice to meet you." Released from the handshake, I reach for the mug, wrapping my fingers around its warmth.

"*You're* Tinsel?" She plops onto the sofa beside Niklas, the pompom laces on her knee-high boots bouncing. "Nik failed to mention that little nugget."

Uncertainty flashes in his eyes. "Uh, shouldn't you be getting back to work?"

"Claire said I could take a break for a few minutes." Gina links her fingers together over one legging-clad knee. "So, Tinsel. We finally meet. I've heard much about you over the years." She shoots Niklas a weighty look, and some unspoken communication passes between them.

"I bet you have," I mumble into my whipped cream before taking a sip. *As the butt of his jokes.* I'm positive they just shared another one at my expense, though her dark brown eyes sparkle with kindness—

"Whoa." Eyebrows arching, I peer into my mug. "This tastes fantastic." The cocoa almost matches *Mutti's* drinking chocolate.

"Yeah?" Gina straightens with pride. "I'm glad you like it."

"Niklas warned me it would be weak."

"He's a stinker." She elbows him in the arm. "He didn't think I'd ever get it right. When I first started working here a few years ago, Nik would stop by when he was in town to tease me about our weak cocoa. I've been trying to perfect it ever since, but every visit he tells me the same thing. It doesn't equal Frau Kuchler's Kandi Cup."

"He says that?" Unexpected pleasure spreads through me.

Gina nods. "So to have her daughter exclaim over my cocoa is a good sign I'm on the right track."

I hide a grin behind another sip. Contrary to my original intentions, I find myself liking this girl.

"Now, what are you two really doing in Waldheim? Nik claims you helped him gather some last-minute supplies over at Fix-It Hardware. I hope it's more exciting than that."

"Afraid not." I run my fingers along the outline of my pointy ears squished beneath my hat. "I shouldn't be here at all, but circumstances at home are...unprecedented right now."

"I suspected something unusual about this visit." Gina pats Niklas on the knee. "There's not a lot that can tear him or his dad away from the workshop in December."

My eyes widen. "You know about the Workshop?"

She gives me a funny look. "Of course."

Well, in that case… I reach for my hat to relieve the pressure on my ears, but Niklas lurches forward and grabs my wrist, nearly upending both our drinks. "Don't!"

I frown. "But she knows."

He squeezes my wrist. "She knows I work with my father in his workshop." He stares hard into my eyes, his gaze pleading, and I grasp what he's not saying. Gina doesn't know it's *the* Workshop and that his father is next in line to be Santa Claus.

The hat stays on.

I lower my hand but glare at him. If she doesn't know about Meister Nico, Gina probably doesn't know the truth about Niklas.

"What?" He returns my glare.

"You can't build a relationship based on lies."

He scoffs and says to Gina, "I have no idea what she's talking about."

For the love of marshmallows! If he and Gina are engaged, their marriage is doomed to fall apart right after the wedding. (If it gets that far. Tradition holds that Kringle weddings take place at the Workshop. Think anything will tip her off as to Niklas's heritage on her way through my pint-sized red and green village?) I meet Gina's curious gaze. "Ever get the feeling some men lack a certain amount of common sense?"

Gina laughs. "I have a brother. Say no more." She tucks a dreadlock behind her ear. "Have you met Logan yet? He works at the hardware store."

Logan is her brother? I'm liking this girl more and more. "We have met. He was very charming."

Niklas muffles a snort with a sip of cocoa.

Paying him no mind, Gina leans forward to pull my mangled braid over my shoulder. "Has anyone ever told you, you have amazing hair?"

I suspect this is another joke, but she looks serious. "*Amazing hair* and *Tinsel* never wind up in the same sentence."

Gina studies the ends. "It's somewhat dry, nothing a little product can't cure, but I can tell the copper color is natural. I work most Saturday mornings at A Cut Above the Rest a few doors down, sweeping the floor and working the cash register for now, and women come in wanting to dye their hair like yours." She shakes her head as the chimes jingle above the front door. "Red is hard to pull off if it's not your true color."

I brush a hand along my braid, tiny snarls catching on my skin. "Sometimes I'd like to chop it"—I make a scissor motion at the nape of my neck—"right there."

Gina's face brightens. "I could totally help with that."

"Dude, save me," Niklas calls out, waving someone over. "They're talking about hair.

Logan pulls a spindle chair beside me and sits on it backward as Niklas adds, "Soon they'll be discussing manis and pedis."

I'm about to make some snappy retort when Logan smiles at me, and the thought disperses. All thought disperses.

"I have something better to discuss," he says. "A bunch of us are going skiing on Saturday. It occurred to me after you guys left the store that maybe you'd like to come with us." Though he says it to the group, his focus remains on me.

Gina gives me an enthusiastic nod, but my shoulders slump. "I'm not good at skiing." My gaze drops to my mug, and I finger its rim.

"That's okay," Gina says. "Logan will teach you. Won't you, Logan?" She swats him on the arm. "He's an excellent teacher."

"I don't think even Logan can get Tinsel to stay upright on skis," Niklas says with a laugh. "Thanks for the invite, but she'll have to pass."

Logan puts up a hand. "Hold on a second, bro. Why not give it a shot? She might have tried skiing in the past, but she's never tried with me." He turns to me. "Gotta let me have at least one chance with her."

I bask in the warmth and acceptance in those mahogany eyes. "Sounds fair."

Gina clasps her hands beneath her chin. "Excellent. I'll hammer out the details and be in touch." Someone calls her name from behind the counter, and she makes a face. "Right now, I gotta get back to work." Standing, she pulls me up for a quick hug. "Great to finally meet you, Tinsel. C'mon, Logan, let's get your pumpkin spiced coffee." She gives Niklas a wink.

Not his betrothed, my elfin foot.

Logan taps my back as he passes. "See you Saturday?"

I match his smile. I won't miss it for anything.

BOXING ME IN

With a wave, I exit the café, prodded along by Niklas's hand at my back.

"Can you believe it?" I bounce on my toes. "I'm on my way to making two new friends." And they're my size. "Not once did they look at me like I'm some bizarre anomaly. Not once did they cringe, fearful my presence would result in calamity." A shiver passes through my body. So this is what it feels like to be accepted.

My pace slows the closer we get to the hardware store. The thought of going home doesn't have the same appeal it did when I left Flitterndorf this morning.

Was it just this morning?

"I knew I should have convinced Grandpop to send Kristof instead." Niklas shoves his hands into his pockets and kicks at random ice clumps on the sidewalk.

I turn to him, open-mouthed. "Didn't you hear what I said? I met some incredible people back there—who *smiled* at me. Why would you want to deny me this little bit of happiness? Do you hate me that much?"

"Hate?" His brow wrinkles. "Don't assume you know everything about me when you've seen only one tiny slice of the pie." Then he lengthens his stride and precedes me to Fix-It Hardware in silence.

I let him sulk. It's easier to concentrate on my surroundings when I don't have to ponder the double meaning in his words, and I'd rather take mental snapshots of Waldheim before we leave. Though I hope to return on Saturday, a dark "what if" tarries on the sidelines. One can't predict the future, after all. I don't want to forget what it's like to pass by windows I can see into without bending over; to feel my heart pound in trepidation when a monstrous diesel truck rumbles by; to skirt around a trash bin taller than half my height. Simple things for these people, but for me it's like a dream I never knew I had has come true.

Back at the hardware store, Niklas checks the straps and bindings on the cargo sleds then spends several minutes talking with Mr. Donati. I lean against my SnoMo, my gaze feasting on the mountain peaks in the distance. I've never seen Mount Gnade from this side before. Around its rugged slope lies Flitterndorf. So close, and yet so far away.

I massage my cramped ears through my hat and grudgingly acknowledge that in some ways, it will be good to get back home.

Tangled lights, am I conflicted or what?

Niklas ambles over, blocking my view of the mountain. "We're all set here. Ready to go?"

"Yes. No. I don't know." I shrug a shoulder. "I'm glad we're coming back in a couple of days."

Niklas holds out his hand, his gaze flicking to the hat atop my head. Ahh, now that I'm ready for. After checking to make sure Mr. Donati has gone inside, I pull off the hat and shake my ears free. Blessed cold air sweeps their tips. Thank goodness snowmobile helmets don't have the same suffocating quality as winter hats. I reach for the helmet, but Niklas snatches it away.

"Hey!" I lunge for it, but he holds it out of reach. A bulky man exits the building to throw something in a metal garbage bin, and my heart races. I clap my hands over my ears. "Give me the helmet, Niklas. Somebody might see my ears."

"Exactly." He leans forward, setting the helmet on the seat behind me, but the earnestness in his face keeps me from making a grab for it. "I see the look in your eyes, Kuchler. You're infatuated with Waldheim. And I don't blame you. You're a tall person living in a short world, and the possibilities beyond Flitterndorf have bedazzled you. But you've got to squelch any ideas about fitting in here." There's a tightness in his gaze as he gently pries my hands away from my ears. "You can't be part of this world, Tinsel. You're an elf. And an elf's place is with Santa."

My hands fist within his hold. "Thank you for boxing in my entire existence. Why don't you put an iron chain around my neck and lock me in the Workshop's dungeons?"

"The Workshop has no dungeons."

"It might as well have them." Wrenching away, I press against the ache in my chest. "And I might as well be the one jailed inside. But then, you can't relate to my misery. The elves put you on a pedestal years ago and you haven't come down since. You bear the Kringle name. You're second in line to be Santa Claus. Technically, you're the reason Flitterndorf exists. Out of all the living beings there, you, Meister Nico, and Meister K belong there the most."

It's Niklas's turn to take a furtive glance around, though the bulky man already disappeared. "Keep your voice down."

"My ears will give away your identity faster than my words."

His mouth compresses. "Santa Claus is nothing without the elves. Flitterndorf needs you."

"Not me. I'm a screw-up there. But what if...what if out here"—I spread my arms—"I'm not such a screw-up? And who says I wouldn't fit in? You? Meister K's books? What if this is the reason I was born tall?"

"Yeah, you'd fit in great. Until circumstances dictated you

remove your helmet or hat or whatever you'd use to hide your ears. What then?"

"Then I'd…tape my ears to my head so they wouldn't stick out through my hair." It's a ridiculous suggestion, and Niklas's frown deepens.

He swipes the helmet from the seat and crams it on my head. "We're getting you home right now. Tonight, your mom will placate you with extra shots of dark chocolate in your cocoa and send you to bed, where you'll sleep this off. In the morning, you'll wake up making sense again." He flips up the visor to glare into my eyes. "And after Saturday is over, you're to forget you ever set foot in Waldheim. Understand?"

I snap the visor back down and make a face he can't see. "Yes, *master.*"

IT TAKES EVERY OUNCE OF MY SELF-CONTROL NOT TO SPEED ON our way home, but were it not for the rocky slope that ends in a ravine at my left, I might have found an excuse to push my limits. Niklas rides behind me, supposedly to give me the better view, but I know he wants to be ready in case I mess up. In case this situation goes from bad to worse. After all, there's a lot of money, as well as future time and hard work, represented on the sled behind me. And on the sled behind Niklas, but he's not the one who makes mistakes.

My grip tightens around the handlebars.

"Slow down, Kuchler." His voice pierces through the helmet's speakers.

I grind my teeth. He's that fixated on my sled that he can sense when I've upped the speed a notch? He must have a speedometer rigged somewhere. No doubt he waits in hungry expectation for me to step a toe out of line so he can harp on me to fall back. And it's so like him to automatically assume I'm going to obey.

What would happen if I didn't? I give the SnoMo a little more gas.

"Slow *down*," he barks. "You're going to take a turn too fast."

"You might be my boss in thirty years or so, but right now I don't answer to you. Leave me alone. I'm fine." I am. I have perfect control over this SnoMo. I think I've even got the sled and its wobbles figured out.

"You answer to my grandfather, and I'm speaking for him now. Slow. Down. You're toting precious cargo—"

"Aw, gee, Niklas, I never knew you cared."

He growls. "You've made your point. You're mad. Somehow it would seem I overstepped my boundaries back in Waldheim—"

"*Somehow*? It would *seem*?"

"I'm sorry, okay? Just slow down already."

"There's an empty apology if I ever heard one. And I need one of those from you as much as I need an empty kiss." I grimace and punch the handlebars. Frostbite! I didn't mean to reference that stupid kiss again. Clearly I don't know what it means to forget something.

"Face it, Tinsel," I whisper in dismay, "that kiss is going to haunt you." It doesn't matter Niklas didn't mean anything by it. It doesn't matter the kiss lasted one second before it was over. It was my first kiss. My lips are not about to forget what it felt like to have another set pressed against them.

Because the truth is, they weren't just any set of lips. They were Niklas's lips.

"Sweet little drummer boy"—I punch my thigh this time—"I have a crush on him after all."

"You know I can hear you, right?" Niklas's voice rasps in my ear.

I shriek and swerve on the path. The SnoMo fishtails. Behind me, the sled follows. First one direction then the other. I jerk the handlebars to straighten my rig, but each time I overcompensate.

The ravine yawns at my left.

I bank a hard right, glancing over my shoulder. The rear of the sled swings off the trail and dips out of sight along the grade. The SnoMo snaps backward; I slam forward. It flips on its side, trapping my leg.

Niklas's shout fills my helmet as the cargo sled drags the SnoMo—and me—down the slope.

MISSION IMPOSSIBLE

The sled, SnoMo, and I plummet down the grade, gaining speed. My helmet thwacks against the ground, and stars blur my vision. Snow flies. Rocks gouge at my back and hip. The SnoMo grinds into my leg. A glove tears away.

I'm gonna crash.

I grapple for purchase. If I don't slow down, I'm—

There! A shrub. I fling myself in its direction as the sled whizzes past first. The trunk smacks into my hands, and my fingers snap closed around it. Heat flares in my shoulders at the sudden stop, but I hold on.

Must hold on.

Pain shoots up my leg as the SnoMo snags on my boot before releasing it in a relentless crash down the mountain. Someone calls my name. Sounds of things breaking, creaking, and smashing fill the air. I duck my head, cling to the shrub, and pray no objects strike or crush me as they ricochet off the ravine floor.

At last, silence settles over the area, except for the incessant repetition of my name in my ear. In time, I realize it's Niklas coming through the speaker in my helmet, demanding I give him some response to show I'm still alive. The longer I lay without moving, the more hysterical he grows.

Niklas is concerned? About me? Finding that hysterical in the other sense, I let out a giggle.

He falls silent. Then: "You think this is funny?"

I lift my head. He kneels at the lip of the ravine, his visor raised as he peers down at me, and I giggle some more. "It is now." And I laugh harder. I'm alive. Releasing the shrub, I ease onto my back and guffaw until my sides hurt. "I'm alive!" I made it through that ordeal and came out breathing. Perhaps I can do some things right, after all.

Provided nothing worse happens.

My laughter dissolves. Uh oh. "Where's the sled?"

"About fifty feet below you." Niklas removes his helmet. "Glad to see you can move. Anything broken?"

"Fifty feet?" I lean on an elbow, cringing at the dull ache in my shoulder, and take a peek. All I see is helmet. Sure, it helped save my life, but I yank it off just the same—and gulp at the wreckage below. Lumber, metal, and building materials are strewn along the ravine's base and partway up the slope. The SnoMo and cargo sled lie in a fractured mess amidst it all.

Oh. My. Christmas. Trees. The world tilts at a crazy angle and I collapse onto my back, my chest squeezing as reality clenches its fist. "What have I done?"

"Tinsel!" A length of rope smacks me on the arm. "Grab hold and start climbing. Once you're safe, you can beat yourself up about this."

"Is that supposed to motivate me?" But I comply, snatching my helmet in the process. My climbing looks more like crawling, and Niklas has the harder job pulling me aloft. Every time I put weight on my left leg, an arc of pain shoots through it. And the ache in my shoulders—

Gnashing my teeth, I ignore my agony. I'm alive to experience the pain, right?

When I reach the ravine's edge, Niklas grips my upper arms and hauls me onto the trail. I collapse on the ground, a quaking mass of limbs, and breathe in the scent of stale snow and frozen dirt. Niklas plops down beside me, placing a trembling hand on my head.

"You're all right," he murmurs. "It's all right."

No, it isn't, but I relish his hand raking over my hair in a repetitive motion. I wouldn't feel anything if it were me smashed upon the ravine floor.

Knowing what did end up there, I let out a moan and press my face into the unforgiving ground. Frost stings my skin. "I can't believe this is happening to me. All that wood…all those supplies…all that money…gone." My eyes well with tears and my stomach heaves. "I can't do anything right."

"We'll figure something out, Tinsel. You're safe, that's what matters." Leaning into me, he whispers, "You could have died."

"That's still a possibility once your grandfather finds out what I did."

"He's not—"

"Just bring me home so I can get the Penalty over with." I flounder to my hands and knees, but when I try to stand, the pain strikes and I cry out.

Niklas braces me at the waist. "You *are* hurt. Where? Is it broken?"

"It's my leg. Not broken." I grimace. "Got a bit roughed up when the SnoMo tried to steal my foot."

"All right, come on." Niklas straightens and scoops me into his arms in such a fluid movement that he's taken half a dozen steps before I strain against his shoulder.

"What are you—put me down!"

He grunts. "I'm likely to drop you if you keep pushing like that."

"I told you nothing's broken. I can walk on my own. Put me down."

"I'll put you down when I'm good and ready." He sets his jaw, a sign I can't win this fight, so I give in with a loud, exasperated sigh. In another minute, he sets me astride his SnoMo, but pain lances down my leg and I suck in a sharp breath. His arms tighten about me. "What is it?"

"Hurts this way."

He readjusts my position, settling me sideways. "Better?" I nod and he backtracks to collect the rope and our helmets.

I process the complex dashboard in front of me and frown. "I'm riding with you?" Yeah, I know, dumb question. How else am I to get home?

Niklas coils the rope and shoves it into a saddlebag. "Your SnoMo is out of commission. This way, I can keep tabs on you"—he withdraws an extra glove and levels his gaze as he fits it onto my bare hand—"and keep you from any more trouble."

I lower my head. "I didn't mean to do it."

He squeezes my hand. "Therein lies the irony. Out of all the elves in Flitterndorf, you are the one least likely to do these things on purpose. But they happen anyway." He straddles the seat behind me. "You good?"

"Nothing hurts as long as I don't move."

Niklas nods then hands me my dented helmet. "Put this on. And hold onto me. I don't want you falling off while I steer."

My breath hitches as I don the helmet. I'm sitting sideways in front of him. Slipping an arm about his waist from this direction has a definite hug-like quality to it.

"What's the matter? Not thrilled with putting your arms around me?" A roguish glint reflects in his eye. "You said yourself you have a crush on me."

With no ready comeback, I slap his visor down and turn away. His laughter makes me bristle and to spite him, I decide to keep my hands to myself. But when he starts down the trail once more, my body jostles against his, and I clasp my arms about his waist to keep from being bucked off.

Over the next hour, the wind whips my loose tendrils into a knotted mess and blows its icy breath down my neck. I welcome the discomfort. I deserve it.

Failure.

Failure.

Fail-ure.

The word beats a rhythm behind my temple, and several times I lean my head against Niklas's chest and cry. My body shakes with my sobs. I'm a failure of the worst kind. Meister K entrusted me with immense responsibility, and it ended in complete disaster.

This morning's note comes back to haunt me. Whoever wrote it threatened my chances at the internship...and promised to make my life miserable.

What, exactly, does that look like?

Niklas's arm wraps around me and squeezes. I squeeze back, wondering where his kindness comes from. He should be ranting and raving at me. He should've left me back there on the trail. I'm not worthy of a ride home.

The closer we get to Flitterndorf, the worse my inner turmoil becomes and the louder my desolate thoughts cry out. Finally, I straighten away from Niklas. "Stop the SnoMo."

"No."

"Please, Niklas." Tears stream down my cheeks, and the guilty ache grows so large inside me, I want to rip it out. "I can't face your grandfather right now. Please. Drop me off at Candy Floss Stream and let me walk home from there."

To my relief, Niklas slows, but he doesn't come to a complete stop. "I can't let you do that. Your leg—"

"I'll push through the pain. Mind over matter." I will force my leg into cooperation if it means avoiding the Workshop.

"Look, I know you're upset about what happened. Yes, it's a mess, but Grandpop won't lay into you the way you think he will."

"It's not that." I yank off my helmet and swipe at the tears encrusted on my face. "I can't bear to see the dismay in his eyes. Don't you get it? I let down *Santa Claus*. And I might have ruined Christmas for thousands of kids around the world. This is going to brand me for life. How the elves viewed me this morning is nothing compared to how they'll view me tonight. I'm gonna go down in the history books as—"

"Whoa, whoa." Now Niklas stops the snowmobile. "You're barreling into tomorrow riding the worst-case-scenario. Take a breath and consider the alternative."

"I should consider packing, because if Meister K doesn't kill me, he's going to banish me from Flitterndorf." Maybe that's the note's idea of *miserable*.

"No elf has ever been banished from Flitterndorf. Not even your great Oma Fay."

I send him a withering look. "There's always a first." I attempt to slide off the SnoMo.

Niklas's arm tightens about me. "Okay, you win. I won't take you to the Workshop. But I will drive around and drop you off at your house."

I sag against his chest. "Thank you."

REGRETS

"Knock, knock." *Mutti* pokes her head around my bedroom door. She smiles at me where I sit at my desk and enters the room, my favorite green mug in her tiny hands. "How's your leg?"

"Feeling better." Thanks to the herbal paste she gave me to slather on my muscles and joints.

There was quite the hullabaloo over my injury an hour ago when I limped into our apartment above The Flaky Crust. But while my parents rushed from their dinner to fawn over me, it's my brothers' smirks and their "she goofed again" looks that replay in my mind.

Mutti glances at the tray of barely-touched food *Vati* brought me. "You need to eat more than that if you're working at the stables this evening. Why you won't ask Herr Stricker to fill in for you when you're in no condition to—"

"It's my Penalty. My job." I rub a hand along my outer thigh. "And after what happened, I need to save as much face as I can with the other elves, even if that means limping through my work."

Her mouth tightens. "You called Kristof?"

I nod. "He's giving me a ride to the stables." But not until everyone's gone home for the evening. There's no telling how fast word has spread among the elves about what happened in the ravine, so the fewer of them I run into tonight, the better.

"In that case"—*Mutti* offers me the mug dwarfing her hands—"here you go." She uses a stepstool to hoist herself onto my bed and sits with her legs sticking out in front. "Perhaps that will help the cold food go down easier."

I take a grateful sip, sighing as the creamy richness glides over my tongue. "You put an extra nugget of dark chocolate in this." How did Niklas know she would do that?

A pleased smile travels across her face as she taps her elfin feet together. "I figured you could use the mood-boost."

I turn to my dinner plate and pierce some baked salmon with my fork. "I'm sorry for all the trouble I've caused." I drag the fish through a puddle of congealed saffron cream. "And for ruining Christmas."

"You haven't ruined Christmas. There's time to fix things."

"You think so?" I pop the lukewarm salmon into my mouth and sit a little straighter in my chair. "I promise I'll make everything right."

"Oh, I didn't mean you." She catches my gaze. "I won't allow you to take full responsibility for what happened earlier today."

"But—"

"Meister K had a part in it, too."

"*Mutti!*" I glance about the bedroom, afraid someone is listening in. "You're talking about the boss."

She waves a hand as though batting a fly. "Given your track record, he knew he took a risk when he entrusted you with this errand. If people are going to play the blame game, then some blame should fall on his shoulders. And if he's the man we all believe him to be, he'll recognize that fact." She points a tiny finger at me. "I'm not saying he shouldn't have entrusted you with the task, or that you couldn't have proven yourself capable. And I'm not saying you can't be trusted in the future. Someday, Tinsel, things will all come together for you. I believe that."

She leans back on her hands with a sudden chuckle. "I'll never forget the joy in Madam Anne's eyes the night you were born. She scrubbed you clean with a towel, held you aloft, and said, 'This one's special, Kandi. She has a rare talent, you mark my words. I'll be watching to see how it develops.'"

I snort and lift the cocoa to my lips. "She must be thrilled to have watched me destroy the school's west wing and dump a load of supplies down a ravine."

"That is not your talent." *Mutti* slips from the bed. "No more feeling sorry for yourself. Kristof will be here soon, so finish your food. And when you return, you're to head straight to bed. You need rest." She squeezes my arm. "Things will look different in the morning, *Liebling*. For all we know, the supplies from Niklas's load alone are enough for the Toy Makers to meet quota." Cupping my face, she kisses my cheek then leaves the room.

I slump in the chair, swirling the chocolate in my mug as *Mutti's* words swirl in my head. If it weren't for this morning's note, I might have believed things could've come together for me someday. Now, I'm not so sure.

Things might not get better unless I leave Flitterndorf.

The thought jets out of nowhere and flutters in my mind, shimmering with possibility. Now that I'm acquainted with a town in the outside world, the idea of venturing back into it doesn't daunt me. I could hang with Gina. Work at the Huggamugg Café. Get better acquainted with Logan.

Bending to take a bite of green beans, I tuck some hair behind my ear, and my fingers graze its tip. I freeze.

My ears.

The stringy beans stick at the back of my throat. Who am I kidding? I can't waste time daydreaming about life outside Flitterndorf. If people discovered I'm a Christmas Elf, they'd go nuts.

And until then, I'd be plagued with visions of all the possible ways I could inadvertently expose my secret.

Because given enough time, I would expose it.

I choke down the beans as a shudder drills through me. I can't let that happen.

Niklas is right. After this weekend, I'm going to have to push Waldheim—and any other town—from my head.

I really, *really* hate it when Niklas is right.

With my fork, I move the food around my plate, no longer hungry. Before today, a satisfying future in Flitterndorf was all I craved. So why, when I realize that's all I can ever have, does my future resemble a ball and chain?

Maybe because my prospects here have drastically narrowed if whoever wrote the note makes good on his or her threat.

"Tinsel! Kristof is here."

Kristof. Christmas.

"Forget the future, Tinsel," I mumble, grabbing my scarf and limping to the door. "You have enough problems right here in your present."

"THANKS FOR GIVING ME A RIDE." I NAVIGATE THE BAKERY'S STAIRS behind Kristof, moving like a toddler as I place both feet on one tread before stepping down to the next. "Especially since you just returned from your errand."

Kristof's shoulders lift in a shrug. "I'm glad to do it."

I clutch the railing and take another step. "What did you have to do, anyway?"

"Smooth some ruffled feathers, but I got my own ruffled in return."

"Is that supposed to make sense?"

He chuckles. "Tell me about your trip." He grins over his shoulder. "Aside from losing the supplies, that is."

I search his face for disappointment or anger, but see only concern. "Yes, well, other than that, I had a wonderful time. Still marveling over the bigness of it all. The kids loved Niklas—now there was a shocker—and we stopped at the Huggamugg Café." *And before we entered, your brother kissed me.*

I wince. I must forget about that kiss. Then maybe I can disregard the split-second in time when I wished it reflected Niklas's feelings.

Confessing my crush out loud, on the other hand, is something I can't overlook. I need to fix that blunder before Niklas lords it over me forever.

"So you met Gina?"

I blink at Kristof's question. "Hmm? Oh, yes. She has quite the bubbly personality." Descending the last step, I follow him to his SnoMo. "We're going skiing on Saturday. Want to come?"

"You're skiing with a bruised leg?"

"I have four days to recover. I'm optimistic."

"Or delusional."

I roll my eyes. "Either way, you want to come with us?"

"Can't. Hockey." He offers me a helmet. "Tell Gina I said hi, though."

I fiddle with the chin strap. "Are Niklas and Gina, you know, *together*?"

His right eye twitches. "Why? You into him?"

"Me?" I laugh and don the helmet. "Holly berries, no way. I, um, was...curious. He and Gina acted close, that's all."

"Typical." Kristof scoffs, buckling his own helmet. "No, they're not together."

"But?"

He frowns.

"It sounds like there's a *but* coming."

"But"—Kristof straddles the SnoMo and turns the key in the electric start—"if you *are* into him, you should get over it."

I edge sideways onto the humming SnoMo behind him and

put an arm about his waist. "Romance is *verboten*. I know, I know."

He stiffens. "Riiight."

I lean to peer around him, but his helmet conceals his expression. "There's another reason?"

"Um..." Kristof depresses the throttle. "No."

I shoulder him. "There's another reason."

He chuckles. "Yes, but don't ask."

"Classified?"

"Something like that."

I purse my lips as he pulls away from The Flaky Crust and turns onto the street. First Niklas makes an obscure comment about pie, implying I don't have all the facts, and now Kristof purposely keeps me in the dark. If slices of pie mean more info, I could use half a dozen more on my plate.

When we reach the Lower Stables, Kristof offers to help with my chores, but I decline. I can't easily converse with the reindeer when others are around, and I still question whether sharing my secret ability would have positive consequences or negative ones.

"If you're sure." His forehead puckers, but I nod and limp toward the entrance. "Call me when you're done, then, and I'll come give you a ride home."

"Okay." I wave and enter the stables. Quiet greets me as I cross the empty interior and exit through the east entrance. The reindeer mill about in the nearby corral. I grab a pitchfork leaning against the wall and join them. "Hi, everyone. Sorry I'm late."

Chocolate snorts, pawing the ground. "Eggnog was afeared we'd have ta bed down out here tonight."

Peppermint trots over and eyes me up and down. "Yer all right, then?"

My fingers tense around the pitchfork shaft as I lob hay into the trough. "Why wouldn't I be?"

Chip nudges me on his way to the trough, and a spike of pain grips my leg. "We haird about yer accident. Are ye ever in a wee bit o' trouble!"

"Translation—a heap o' trouble," Chocolate says with a chuckle.

Great. I grab the grooming box and Licorice prances toward me. "Me first! The dust from the FTA has sullied me coat fer too long."

"Too long? I groom you every evening."

"Aye, that's the problem. Should be twice a day."

I smirk and begin brushing her fur in wide, circular sweeps with the currycomb. "So the rumors about what happened are bad, huh?"

Peppermint picks up her head from the trough. "Ye ditched an entire load o' supplies plus a SnoMo down a ravine, which went up in an explosion o' smoke and fire—"

"I haird it looked like New Year's Eve fireworks," Chip says around a mouthful of hay.

"And ye broke half the bones in yer body," Peppermint concludes. "Accordin' ta the elves, ye single-handedly ruined Flitterndorf's plans for a merry Christmas."

I move to Licorice's other side. "Rumors exaggerate the truth, you know."

"Yer limpin'," Cocoa says.

"There were no explosions, no broken bones." It takes effort not to scrub harder with the comb. "Maybe the part about me ruining Christmas is just as exaggerated?"

Butterscotch draws near to blow on my cheek. "What happened in that ravine, lass?"

I switch to the body brush and, prompted by the look in his big, dark eyes, launch into a hushed retelling of my soon-to-be infamous adventure with Niklas. The other reindeer munch through my story, occasionally shaking their heads or wincing. I move on to brush Butterscotch and end my tale with, "Of course

I have to do something to rectify this mess, but I'm afraid my Penalty this time will feature Meister K giving me the boot."

Chip tilts his head, bits of hay hanging from his mouth. "No Kringle has ever banished an elf afore."

"You sound like Niklas." I skim over Butterscotch's shoulder and front leg with the currycomb, his muscles rippling beneath the comb's rubber teeth. Muscles that power him across the sky. "I wish I could fly." My gaze flits from one 'deer to the next. "Do your flying capabilities extend to the things you carry, like a sleigh, or is the sleigh itself enchanted and that's how you tote it through the sky?"

The animals blink at one another. Then Cocoa answers, "A wee bit o' both, I s'pect, though we havna given it much thought."

"If I could fly and had the power to make other things fly, I'd take a SnoMo and cargo sled and zoom into the ravine myself to salvage whatever supplies I could. And I'd do it tonight." I scrub at a patch of dirt clinging to Butterscotch's coat. "That way, when everyone wakes up tomorrow, the reality won't be as bad as they feared. And maybe then, they could forgive me. Maybe then, the warning in this morning's note won't come to pass." I press my lips against an onslaught of tears. "More than that, I need to make this right for the sake of all those children on Christmas Eve. It's my fault, so it falls to me to fix it. I just don't know how to go about doing that."

Chip studies me from across the trough. "Fer the sake o' Christmas."

NEW PLANS

Back home, I fall asleep dreaming about mangled toys crawling up ravine walls, SnoMos flying through clouds, and peppermint kisses stolen from taboo boys. Niklas stands nearby, jeering, taunting. He tilts his head back and laughs. It sounds like cascading rocks pinging against glass. He laughs a second time.

On his third laugh, I wake up.

Something's rattling my window pane.

I leap from the bed, and heat sears my leg. Wincing, I grope in the dark for something with which to arm myself. When my hand connects with my alarm clock, I clutch it like a baseball and face the window. As my eyes adjust, I take in the pinpricks of light from outside, the moonlight reflecting off the snow—

Two skinny poles appear and clatter against the window in rapid succession. No, not poles. Hooves. Connected to forelegs. Followed by a large snout and a blinking eye.

I let out my breath on a whoosh. Setting the clock on my bedside table, I glance at the time. What in the winter wonderland are the reindeer doing out and about at half past midnight? I limp to the window, unlatch it, and swing it open. A reindeer swoops in from the side, narrowly missing my face with its pawing hooves.

I duck. "Watch it, Furball!"

"Sorry." The reindeer banks to the left and hovers in midair. "'Twas a window there a second ago."

"Chip?" I snap on my lamp and squint at him as he angles closer. I know Santa's reindeer fly, but it's unnerving to see one suspended in midair outside my window without his buddies or a sleigh trailing behind him. "What are you doing? How'd you escape the stables?"

Chip waggles his front hooves. "We can open doors, 'member?"

I cock an eyebrow. "How often do you guys sneak out at night?"

"Define *often*." He leans on my windowsill and dangles his forelegs inside my room. "We're goin' ta help ye."

"Help?"

"With yer plan."

"My plan?" I glance over my shoulder, expecting my parents to barge into the room any second.

"I had ta talk the others into it first, o' course. And then Butterball decided t'would be best if we waited 'til everyone was asleep. But I'm here now." Chip nudges the air with his muzzle. "Git dressed, gel. Time's a'wastin'."

I rub my eyes, certain I'm still dreaming. "Dressed for what?"

"We've got somethin' ta show ye in the stables."

"Can't it wait 'till morning?"

"Nay."

"Am I going to get into trouble?"

"No' if we do this right."

"Do what right?"

"Quit the yakkin', git dressed, and ye'll find out."

"Fine." I snap the curtains closed and rummage through my dresser drawers.

"Wear the warmest stuff ye got," Chip adds after a moment.

I frown, pulling a thermal turtleneck and thick, wool sweater over my head. "The stables aren't that cold."

"We're no' stayin' in the stables."

I adjust the waistband of my wooliest leggings beneath my thickest *dirndl* then shove open the curtains to glare at Chip. "I should tell my folks where I'm going, shouldn't I?"

He makes a reindeer-grimace. "Grown-ups will put the kibosh on the whole thing. D'ye want ta change the truth behind these rumors or no'?"

"You're taking me to the ravine?" Hope blooms inside my chest.

Chip tosses his head. "'Twas yer idea."

"My idea involved me flying in on a SnoMo."

"Well, we reindeer want ta help."

"Why?"

"Ye said 'twas fer the sake o' Christmas. Reindeer are duty-bound ta protect and uphold Christmas."

"They are?"

Chip rolls his eyes. "I dinna ken, but it has a noble ring to it. C'mon, let's go!"

I chew my bottom lip and glance around my room. Though I don't know what Chip has planned, there's a chance I won't return before *Vati* rises to make his pastries. In case he peeks in on his children before he heads downstairs, I stuff pillows beneath my comforter and whack them into something that could pass for a sleeping body. On a whim, I grab my headlamp from my desk drawer and slip it around my neck.

Then I yank on a hat, pull on my mittens, and turn to Chip. "Okay. Ready."

"Great. Now hop on me back."

"Whoa. What?"

"Git on me back."

I retreat a step. "No way."

Chip jumps about in a tight circle in the air. "'Tis harmless. Kristof used ta do it all the time."

"No."

"If yer not scared ta imagine flyin' on a SnoMo, what's the big deal about flyin' on a reindeer?"

"It's the difference between imagination and reality, Furball."

Chip flies close enough to put his nose an inch from mine. "Tinsel. D'ye want ta save Christmas or don'cha?"

I squeeze my eyes shut, fist my hands, and take a deep breath. Save Christmas. A noble cause, right? And if it redeems me in the others' eyes, so much the better.

"Okay, okay, okay." I push Chip out of my face and hoist myself onto the wide window ledge, favoring my left leg. Biting my lip, I swing my feet around to hang outside and then arrange the windowpanes behind me to look closed yet unlatched. The breeze tugs on my hair, and I force myself to look out rather than down. Chip seems far away, even though he hovers at my knees. I dig my fingers into the window frame. "I don't think I can do this."

"Maybe if ye stood up, ye could reach a leg over me back?"

Gripping the frame, I tuck my feet beneath me and start to stand. Pain flares. My knee buckles and I pitch forward with flailing arms. On a strangled cry, I make a grab for Chip and catch him around the neck, but my sudden weight throws him off-balance. He plummets a few feet in the air before he steadies himself with a hissed, "Careful!"

I laugh into his thick coat. "What did you expect from me?"

He makes a wobbly descent to the ground, and once my feet touch the snow-packed earth, I release him and massage the ache in my leg. "Thanks for not dropping me. Maybe I'll just limp to the stables."

"Nay. I shoulda met ye down here in the first place." He kneels on his forelegs, which lowers his shoulders to my waist, and prods me with his antlers. "Climb aboard. Time's tickin'."

I wring my mittened hands with a glance along the darkened street. “Chip, this isn’t a good idea.”

“Aw, come now. Ye havna given it a full shot yet.” He lowers his head to look me in the eye. “I thought ye tried somethin’ many a time afore givin’ up.”

I inhale to fling back a nice, cutting remark, then snap my mouth shut, grab a tuft of guard hair at his neck, and hoist myself sideways onto his back. “Onward, my smart-mouthed steed.” I jab his side with my heel for good measure.

He grunts then shoots into the sky.

I squeal, tightening my hold as Chip circles above the Town Square before angling toward Huff ’n Puff Hill. Rooftops and chimneys whiz by below us. Most buildings loom dark, but the streetlights glow a soft yellow. A grid of straight and winding streets weaves among the business district and neighborhoods. Evergreen clusters dot the landscape.

I’ve always admired Flitterndorf from atop Huff ’n Puff Hill, but I’ve never seen it from this vantage point. Amazing. Though the cold swirls about me, Chip keeps me warm, his mighty body moving beneath mine, his legs beating across the air. I lean forward with a smile. “You reindeer are blessed to see this view every day.”

“And one night o’ the year, we’ll get ta see the world. Should we become the Big Eight.”

Too soon we reach the Lower Stables and Chip’s hooves beat to a halt outside the east entrance. He kneels again, allowing me to slide off, and I limp behind him through the doorway.

Seven pairs of eyes peer at me from their respective stalls. I give a weak wave. “Hi, everyone. Long time no see.”

Eggnog tosses his head in nervous agitation. “Are ye sure abou’ this, Chip?”

Chip snorts. “Tinsel disna need all eight, so if ye want ta stay, Fraidy Cat, then stay.”

"*I* need?" I plant a hand on my hip. "This is *your* plan. I wasn't going to rope you into my mess."

"Ye make it our mess when ye threaten Christmas."

"I didn't—"

"Shush." Chip hitches his muzzle at his twin. "Ye comin', Choc'late?"

In answer, Chocolate jumps over his stall door and trots down the aisle toward us. Licorice takes a graceful leap after him, followed by Butterscotch. Peppermint edges her way into the aisle.

"That's five." Chip cranes his neck to glance at the remaining reindeer. "Anyone else?"

Eggnog retreats to the farthest corner of his stall. Cinnamon snorts out a laugh. "Cocoa and I will stay and make sure Eggnog disna have a panic attack. Ye guys go on. And dinna act stupid."

Chocolate blows out a breath. "That takes away the fun."

"And git back here as fast as ye can," Cocoa warns.

"Aye." Chip's eyes have a Kringle-esque twinkle about them. "'Tis the plan."

DISCARDED TREASURE

Stealing along the basement hallways of the Lower Stables while trying to keep up with the long-legged reindeer, I whisper yet again, "This plan is ludicrous." In case they hadn't heard me the first four times.

Chip expels a sigh. "D'ye want ta save Christmas or no'?"

I hug my arms. They continue on, and I can either follow or get lost in the maze of hallways that tunnel inside Huff 'n Puff Hill.

I follow at a limp.

Crumbling plaster overlays the rough stone walls, and exposed timber beams run vertically every three paces. Electric lanterns, anchored to the wall whenever the hallway bends, cast feeble orbs of light. In between the bright patches stretch wide, oppressive shadows and a staleness hovers in the air.

Something scuttles along the floor at my feet.

Heart pumping, I hasten around the next corner—and plow into the hind quarters of a reindeer. I stagger backward, favoring my bad leg as Butterscotch turns and blinks at me in his mild way. The animals have stopped before a heavy oak and iron door.

"Is this it?"

"'Tis behind this door." Chip taps the thick wooden planks with an antler tine. "But first, we need the key."

"Key?" I hold up my hands. "No one said anything about a key. I certainly don't have one." I jerk a thumb over my shoulder. "Let's go back and think up a Plan B."

Butterscotch nudges me with his shoulder. I stumble a few paces and pain shinnies up my leg, but I clamp my lips against an outcry. These beasts don't know their own strength.

"We have the key, Tinsel." Licorice glances up beside the doorframe. "But we canna acquire it ourselves without a pair o' hands."

I follow her gaze to where a hook impales the wall. From it hangs a rusty skeleton key. Not everyone can access that key, and certainly no elf.

Not one of elfin stature, that is.

Balancing on tiptoe, I strain as high as I can and flick the end of the key with my fingertips. It sways, but remains hooked. On my second try, I add a little jump with my good leg and give the key a swat. It clatters to the cement floor.

All five reindeer say, "Shhh."

"Sorry." Stooping to retrieve the key, I frown at them. "Why do we have to be quiet? We're in the basement, in the middle of the night. There's no one else around." My gaze darts from one end of the inky corridor to the other. "Is there?"

The reindeer exchange cryptic glances. "One never knows."

A tremor passes through me. The corroded edges of the key bite into my clenched fingers, and I point to the door. "I'm not going to find the Abominable Snowman in there, am I?"

"No' behind *that* door." Chip arches his neck and peers down a corridor we have yet to explore, his forehead wrinkling with worry.

With quaking fingers, I jam the key into the lock and give it a hasty twist. As the door swings in, muffled snickers rumble behind me. Heat prickles my neck, and I put a hand on my hip.

"There's nothing to fear, is there? That's a dirty trick. No wonder Eggnog didn't want to come with us."

Butterscotch chuckles, his massive body brushing past me as he enters the room I unlocked. "Eggnog disna want ta come cuz he's afraid ta fly."

"A reindeer afraid to fly?" I poke my head in after him, hesitant to walk into such dark quarters. A musty scent hits my nose. Something scrapes to my right, and I reach for my headlamp when fluorescent lighting ignites the area. I blink against the brightness as Butterscotch moves away from a light switch. "But I've watched him fly during your lessons."

"He flies when forced, but he disna like it."

Chocolate tromps in behind me. "Ye should see the bloke run. Faster than we can fly."

"Then why did he try out for the Third String?" Shielding my eyes from the light, I gaze around the cavernous, steel-walled room.

Butterscotch walks among several reindeer-sized forms covered by heavy canvas sheets. "When yer told from birth 'tis only one goal worth attainin', ye work ta attain it. Fer reindeer, 'tis the Big Eight, which requires that we first make the Third String."

And for an elf, the ultimate goal is the Workshop, even though we know it can't employ everyone. My parents were okay with that. I'm not, no matter how many threatening notes I receive.

I lift the corner of a canvas sheet, dust motes puffing in the air, and discover the ragged edge of a large, wooden wheel attached to a planked cart. Antique tools and trappings hang along the wall behind it. Unfamiliar items, once valued and essential yet now junk to my inexperienced eyes, make a scattered trail along the room's perimeter.

There's got to be a better way to fix my mess than sneaking around the bowels of the stables. "Guys, we should rethink Chip's idea. Too many things could go wrong. At the very least, I should get Meister K's permission before taking you with me." I peek beneath another sheet at a Victorian wardrobe, the Kringle crest etched into the brass knob. "Guys?" I glance over my shoulder.

At the back of the room, the reindeer have gathered around a gigantic structure hidden under canvas. I straighten away from the wardrobe and a tingle races through my body as I approach. "Is that what I think it is?"

Heart pounding, I curl my fingers into the dusty folds of the canvas sheet and slowly draw it toward me. One corner drops to reveal an elegant, curved rear runner, and my breath catches. A worn hull slides into view, its top edge at shoulder height. For a few feet, it travels parallel to the floor before dipping low on either side, allowing a person easy access to its interior. It then flares up and over itself to form the dash.

Thoughts of the Workshop fade as I finish whisking aside the sheet from a pair of front runners and stare with wide-eyed wonder.

Santa's sleigh.

"*Honor's* been down here the whole time?" I breathe, calling to mind what I learned about the original sleigh. It was presented to Nikolaus Kringle at the inception of "Santa Claus," but shortly after its retirement around the turn of the twentieth century, it vanished. Much to the Kringles' embarrassment.

Was it just a matter of searching through storage rooms to find—

"*Honor*? Nay, lass." Butterscotch taps his nose against fading, gold-dusted letters on the hull.

With a finger, I trace the name: *Valiant*. The Kringles' second sleigh, retired for over half a century now. It's seen better days, yet its majestic nature presides. Gingerly, I place a foot onto the runner board. Several pops and snaps bounce off the walls. When the ancient relic doesn't crumble beneath my weight, I risk climbing aboard.

Button-tufted, velvet upholstery lines its bench seat and interior walls. The rich, burgundy color has faded to a dull pink, the fabric worn thin where Santa would have sat. A deep, empty compartment takes up the back half of the sleigh, ideal for…oh, I don't know…toting thousands of toys, perhaps?

I settle onto the seat, waving away the dust cloud that billows up, and then skim a hand along the wooden dash with its archaic gears and switches. Two shallow grooves about two feet apart mar the wood, and I rub my index fingers over them. The perfect width for a pair of reins.

It dawns on me then, like an empowering mantle draped across my shoulders: I'm sitting in Meister K's *grandfather's* sleigh.

Oh, the energy and potential that once fueled this contraption. The magic and faith and conviction. Their enduring presence weaves about me as I sit. The sleigh whispers its impatience to slough off the weight of gravity and take to the skies. Too long has it sat here in the darkness of yesterday's memories. It yearns to be free.

Someone needs to set it free.

My fingers splay over the velvet piles.

I need to set it free.

An antlered head pokes around the side, and I catch the spark in Chip's eye. "What d'ye think?"

I grin. "I think you came up with the best idea ever. Tell me how to hook you guys to the sleigh, and let's go rescue some supplies."

RESCUED

According to Chip, a storage compartment beneath the seat might hold my answer. After fumbling around the cushion—pulling, prying, tugging—I discover a metal knob tucked between the edges of the backrest and seat. I twist it, and a dull *click* resounds from the underside of the seat. One half pops open, revealing a recess of coiled ropes and industrial iron hooks dating back to the mid-twentieth century, a vintage first-aid kit, a beat-up picnic basket…and sets of doubletrees and leather traces for the reindeer.

"Bingo."

It takes some trial and error, but between the six of us, we figure out how to attach the reindeer to each other and then to the sleigh. Following Butterscotch's instructions passed down through reindeer lore, I find a lever at chest height along the back wall in the room, its shaft angling toward the ceiling. I give it a yank. It doesn't budge. Gripping it as though I'm doing a pull-up, I lift my feet in the air and jerk on it with my entire body. Nothing. I hang there and—

CRACK.

The lever drops, dumping me on the floor.

Heat blazes up my leg, but a long-winded moan drowns out my own as the back wall shudders and splits down the middle.

Shafts of moonlight spill through the ensuing fissure in the wall. The break widens by the second as each half of the wall, resting on gigantic hinges, opens outward.

Clods of dirt and snow fall along the opening, but since the reindeer don't panic at seeing a wall in motion, I sidle closer to peer beyond the edge. The nighttime breeze fiddles with the wisps of hair around my forehead, and I shiver in my wool sweater. Moonlight graces the snowy landscape outside and a tree line follows the slope. "Where are we?"

Peppermint towers over my right shoulder. "The back side of Huff 'n Puff Hill."

I frown. "I've never seen a wall-sized door on the hillside."

"It disna look like a wall-sized door from the outside."

"Ohhh." I shouldn't be surprised. I mean, I work for a man who uses flying reindeer to pull a sleigh through the sky so he can deliver toys to countless children all over the world in one night. What's a camouflaged door?

"Okay, lads and lassies." Butterscotch paws at the floor. "Time ta git goin' if we want ta be back afore the Kringles awake."

I'm flying. Over a dark tree canopy. Beneath a brilliant, star-packed sky. Behind a team of competent reindeer. In. Santa's. *Sleigh.*

I can't wipe the smile from my face any more than a child could after receiving a puppy for Christmas.

Not many elves can say they've sat in Santa's sleigh. And none can say they've flown it. Though the wind whips at my face, the experience is worth the small discomfort. The reins do fall into the two grooves on the dash, and I grip them in my mittened hands, pretending I'm the one in charge. But let's be honest. The reindeer know exactly what they are doing. I could lie on this bench seat and take a nap, for all the help I give.

"Is this the ravine?" The wind carries Butterscotch's question back to me, and I scooch over to peek through the sleigh's opening. Far below, the snowy landscape passes by, reflecting the moonlight. A wide chasm snakes its way between the mountains, with the trail Niklas and I took to Waldheim meandering alongside it.

I give the reindeer a thumbs up, and they steer the sleigh lower. A moment later, the wreckage comes into view. They make a wobbly U-turn in the air, and I grab the dash. This sleigh could use some seatbelts. Once they come to a stuttered stop on the ravine's floor, I tumble to the ground on jelly legs. "Must tell the Minor Flight Team you guys need to work on your landings."

When the world stops spinning, I strap on my headlamp, and a beam of light illuminates the area directly before me. I turn my head from side to side. Figgy pudding. Carnage from the sled litters a wide area along the ravine. Damaged planks of wood, busted hardware boxes, and hand tools are scattered every which way. Not everything is broken, but as I free the reindeer from their traces, I realize I'm going to need more room than the well of the sleigh to haul this stuff home.

The cart in the storage room would have been perfect. Had I given this more thought, I might not have left it behind.

"Can I not do anything right?" I kick a nearby ice chunk with my good leg. It scatters across the snow several feet away, but not before it's done more damage to my toe than I've done to it.

"What's wrong, lass?" Butterscotch asks. When I explain my lack of foresight, he tilts his head back and lets out a deep-throated chuckle.

I cross my arms. "This is hardly a laughing matter."

He indicates the sleigh with his antlers. "Are ye fergettin' what that is? It's a Kringle sleigh."

My eyes widen. "Bottomless well. But do you think the magic still works? *Valiant* has been retired for decades."

"D'ye have faith, lass? 'Tis all ye need."

Have faith. I can do that.

The reindeer prove crucial in helping me gather the scattered merchandise. They pluck things off the ground with their teeth, heft things with their antlers, and shuffle things along with their hooves. At first, I limp beside them, collecting buckets of nails and bags of screws, but after several minutes, we agree that for the sake of my injury, I'll stay with the sleigh and pack supplies as they bring them over.

Into the rear compartment I cram all manner of wood—planks, 2x4's, dowels, trim—followed by plaster of paris cartons, hardware boxes, wire coils. Little by little the pile grows, but faith and magic do indeed blend together in *Valiant*, for no matter how much goes in, I always have room for more.

Too bad time doesn't work the same way. The passing of it pulsates behind my temple. Cold seeps into my clothes, stiffens my fingers, numbs my nose. Fatigue weighs down my eyelids. Nevertheless, I continue to cram. I must salvage as much as possible on this trip, because I'm not getting another shot at this. Not if I want to keep things clandestine.

Unless I don't mind whatever consequences come from sneaking out with Santa's old sleigh and five members of the Third String.

Hey, if I'm going to get kicked out of Flitterndorf for failing a mission, I might as well do it in style.

We finish around four o'clock. When I put away the last paintbrush, I turn to the reindeer and give a tired smile. "We did it. My hands hurt, my leg throbs, my head is pounding, but we finished what we set out to do. Will it be enough to appease Meister K and whoever wrote the note? I don't know, but I couldn't have managed this much without your help. Thank you. An extra mound of lichen for you all when we get back." I cover a yawn with my soiled mittens. If we leave now, I might have time to squeeze in an hour of sleep before my alarm goes off.

I tether the reindeer to the sleigh and limp back to my place behind the dash. My hands tighten around the reins. "I better not goof this up while trying to make things right."

"A larger-than-life adventure fer a larger-than-life elf," Chip calls back to me.

"Larger-than-your-average-elf, you mean," I retort.

Chip shakes his antlers. "I said exactly what I meant."

A smile works its way across my lips. There will be no mistakes this time. I give the reins a playful snap. "Dash away, my commendable reindeer. To Santa's Workshop!"

NOT SO GREAT

A shrill beeping invades my warm cocoon. Whimpering, I roll over and smack my alarm clock. It clatters across my bedside table then thunks to the floor.

I never want to get out of bed again. Serves me right for crawling under the covers when I only had forty-five minutes to sleep.

I might have gotten more sleep had I left the loaded sleigh behind the Workshop, but the whole point was to do this on the sly. That meant after another wobbly landing, I had to unpack all the supplies I'd spent more than an hour wedging into the sleigh. The reindeer helped where they could, and we left the mound of supplies blocking the productions door so the elves can't miss it when they report to work this morning.

Afterward, we returned *Valiant* to the storage room and made sure the area looked like no one had disturbed a single speck of dust. Then I had the reindeer promise me they'd head directly to their stalls while Chip flew me home. Thank goodness the bakery's kitchens are at the back of the shop, otherwise *Vati* might have noticed the twitching hooves of an erratic reindeer as it helped an inept elf scramble through her bedroom window.

I never felt my head hit the pillow.

With a groan, I fling an arm over my eyes. If I'm this exhausted, how are the reindeer going to fare today during their flying lessons? I can come back to bed after mucking out their stalls, but they—

Great lords a'leaping!

Dance practice.

Another whimper escapes my lips and I roll again, falling out of bed. A dull ache grips my leg.

This is going to be such a good day.

BY THE TIME I LIMP TO THE LOWER STABLES, THE COLD AIR HAS pushed away the fog of sleep, and I'm able to think with a clear mind again.

This is a *great* day. I flew the sleigh without injury to myself or the reindeer, returned it without any new bangs, dings, or dents, and managed to reclaim about sixty percent of the merchandise I'd initially lost yesterday. If someone still wants to make my life miserable, at least I can say I tried to fix my mess.

After propping my snowshoes against the outside wall, I enter the stables (no new note today, whew!) and call out a cheery, "*Guten Morgen*."

Groans and protests issue from all but Eggnog, Cocoa, and Cinnamon, who greet me with bright eyes and quivering rumps (an attempt to wag their stumpy tails), eager for last night's details. Er, this morning's details.

After much prodding, bribery, and a reminder about the extra lichen, my five trusty "steeds" clamber from their stalls and plod outside, where the cold air should revive them as it did me. Mucking out the stalls and breaking the ice in the water trough, however, saps what little energy I regained from my catnap. My head pounds anew, and it takes me an extra half hour to complete my chores. When I finally stand at the top of Huff 'n Puff Hill in my snowshoes, I already know that by the time I return home, change, and eat breakfast, I'll be late for dance practice.

If Meister K doesn't summon me to his office first.

A giant yawn escapes me, and I stare bleakly down the slope. The bottom looks twice as far as normal.

A ROWDY RENDITION OF "CAROL OF THE BELLS" RESONATES FROM the loudspeakers in each corner of the gymnasium. Couples whirl around the floor in time with the beat. Twirl, flip, spin, sashay. Again and again, the elves repeat the moves in a perfect, rhythmic circle as I linger at the side entrance.

Without meaning to, I single out Niklas dancing with Pix on the far side of the circle. He smiles down at her. She laughs in delight. Not once does he step on her toes. Even though I refuse to crush on Niklas, and even though the idea of him and Pix together is preposterous, a twinge of something ugly squirms in my belly.

Making their way around the circle, they're approaching the side entrance when Niklas glances over. His gaze catches mine and he stumbles to a stop. Within seconds, everyone stumbles to a stop. The music stops. Then Frau Tanz's grating voice carries from the bleachers.

"Nice of you to finally join us, Miss Kuchler." She sits on the top row like a queen, thwacking the switch in her palm. Once again, Herr Geier's made an appearance and sits beside her with his usual pinched expression. "As you can see," Frau Tanz continues, "Niklas had to fill in for you while you were out gallivanting who knows where."

"I wasn't—"

"Silence." She stands. "Thanks to you, Niklas might not learn his own steps in time for the Festival Dance in a fortnight."

Laughing, Niklas turns to the instructor. “I think we all know I won’t be the one to mess up that day.”

She inclines her head with a hint of a smile. Thumbs hooked behind his suspenders, Niklas sends me a wink. What’s that supposed to mean? That I’ll fulfill the bungling role just fine on my own? My eyes narrow. Wait ’til our private lessons start. I’ll show him.

Across the gym, Frau Tanz pins me with a look that frosts my cheeks. “I don’t care what you do or where you go during any other hour, Miss Kuchler, but for the next thirteen days between nine and ten o’clock in the morning, you are mine. Understand?”

I clamp my lips together. Following her ominous words with a yawn would *not* be in my best interest right now. “Yes, ma’am.”

“Take your place beside Pix.”

As I limp over, Pix stands with her hands on her hips, blond hair billowing in perfect waves below her red cap. “If it isn’t the little Christmas-wrecker. What’s next? Flitterndorf’s annihilation?”

Too tired to think up a witty comeback, I bend to take her hands, and as the music once again pumps through the speakers, we begin the dance. I grind my teeth against the discomfort in my leg. On the fourth move, I step on her foot.

She glares up at me. “That was cowardly of you to abandon Niklas. Have you no shame?”

“Abandon him?” I falter, lose the order of the dance steps, and twirl her when I should have flipped her.

I can almost see the steam blasting from Pix’s pointy ears in her irritation. “Half the elves in the Workshop witnessed it.”

“Witnessed what?”

“Niklas had to deliver the unfortunate news about your crash to Meister K all by himself. That should have been your job, but you chickened out.”

I have half a mind to punt her and her priggish attitude across the gym. "Is that what he told everyone?" If he said as much to Meister K, my shot at that internship might be...well, shot.

"I don't know. I wasn't there. But as a member of the Elder Council, my mother was. She said Meister K's face got as red as his *lederhosen*, and then he and Niklas went into his office. Alone. They were in there for quite a while."

Niklas twirls about in the middle of the circle, exaggerating his dance moves. This causes several elves to laugh and fudge their own steps. I peek at Frau Tanz. Does she notice his antics? If so, she ignores them.

"Look at him," I say as I prepare to flip Pix. "Does he look like he's suffered much? The worst he received behind closed doors was probably a lone mini marshmallow in his cocoa rather than a handful." I grab Pix by the waist and flip her at my side, but her foot whacks my bad leg.

Pain tunnels toward both hip and ankle, and I crumple to the floor, taking Pix with me. She crashes in an ungainly heap, her legs flying over her head. Laughter erupts from the other elves, and for a moment, the comical sight takes my mind off the pain. As her face grows a mottled red, however, I choke down my mirth. "I'm sorry, Pix. My leg—"

"Frau Tanz!" she wails above the commotion. "I refuse to subject myself to this oaf for one more dance practice. I demand a different partner."

The music stops again, and everyone falls silent. Frau Tanz's switch slices through the quiet as she descends the bleachers and comes toward me. *Slap-slap-slap*. I struggle to my feet. She stops a few paces away and, after glancing back at Herr Geier, tilts her head to look up at me. "Miss Kuchler, after much deliberation I regret to inform you, you are no longer welcome in this assembly. You are dismissed. From this day forth, it would appear all your hours once more belong to you."

My heart skitters inside my chest. "If I don't dance, I don't graduate."

"That is not my problem. Perhaps in the future, the school board will give more thought to elves with your"—she gives me a derisive glare—"disabilities before making the Festival Dance a graduation requirement."

I blink against my tears. How is it possible for a short-someone to make a tall-someone feel so small? Not trusting myself to respond, I turn and stagger from the gym as fast as my bum leg will let me.

This day is not so great, after all. And the morning is only half over.

A SUBTLE SHIFT

The fire pops in the fireplace, and sparks fly behind the mesh screen. The dancing flames mock me with their agility and grace, and I hug the throw pillow tighter to my chest where I sit on the floor, leaning back against the couch. My brothers clank around in the kitchenette, preparing an after-dinner snack to share. Its scents of apples and cinnamon mingle with the burning wood, but I know better than to ask for a bite. Disappointment cloaks this apartment thicker than a wet wool blanket, and my name gets tossed between them as they discuss the dance practice and the missive I received from the Workshop earlier.

If a hole magically opens in the floor, I'll not hesitate to jump in and disappear.

Mashing my face into the pillow, I drop my head to my knees.

A knock sounds on the door leading to the back staircase, followed by the pitter-patter of little feet scurrying to answer it. "Meister Niklas!" My insides scramble about at my brother's exclamation. "What brings you here?"

I bet I know, and if I had opened the door, I'd have slammed it shut again.

"It's just Nik, Chorley." His voice holds pleasant laughter. He knows my brother's name? "How's life in the pastry department?"

"Sweetly rising, as always."

There's a pause in the small talk. I burrow my face further into the pillow and will Niklas away. I don't want to talk to him. He's either going to tease me about dance practice, or tease me about yesterday. Thank goodness, I've come up with a way around the latter.

"If you'll excuse me," he says.

Yes.

His footsteps draw nearer.

No.

He slides down beside me, sitting so close, his movements tug at my sleeve as he gets comfy. "Hi."

"I'm impressed." The pillow muffles my words.

He shifts again, and his knee bumps mine. "By what?"

"You remember my brother's name, *and* you know what he does for work."

Niklas chuckles. "I only pretend to forget that stuff, Tinsel. If I know the name of every child who believes in Santa, then I certainly know the names of all two thousand four hundred and seventy-three elves in the Red and Green Clans. Including their corresponding occupations."

I rotate my head on the pillow to peek at him. "Honest?"

He sits with his arms draped over his knees, his woolen cap dangling from one hand. His gaze switches from the fire to me. "I'm a Kringle, aren't I?"

"But then"—I sit up straighter—"why the pretense?"

"If I can't find ways to have a little fun as future-Santa-Claus, I'll break under the pressure." Niklas elbows me. "I learned it from you, you know. How to find fun in the face of life's drudgery."

"Your life is not the drudgery mine has been."

"No, but I've watched you find pleasure in the things you've attempted to do. You may not have always succeeded, but you kept a positive attitude."

The flames blur through my sudden unshed tears. "I think those days are a thing of the past." I drop my head onto the pillow once more. "What am I going to do about the Festival Dance? If I don't perform, I don't graduate. And if I'm slated to not graduate, I'll never get offered the managerial internship. 'Course, I can't get the internship without an interview—" My head pops up again. "Did you hear about that? I got a letter from the Workshop saying it's now been postponed *indefinitely*." That's one way to make my life miserable. Hmm… Did Frau Tanz write yesterday's note?

Niklas splices a hand through his hair. "I heard. But don't lose hope. I'll figure out a solution for both the dance and the interview." He lowers his voice. "In the meantime, we'll start your private dance lessons as soon as your leg feels better."

I sigh. "The pain had faded to a mild-nuisance until Pix's foot rammed into my leg." Poking at the threads in the embroidered pillow, I recall her words about Niklas. "I'm sorry I didn't go back to the Workshop with you yesterday. It never occurred to me I was leaving you to face your grandfather's wrath alone. Did you get into much trouble?"

Niklas frowns. "What makes you think Grandpop was angry?"

I shrug. "Something Pix said."

"Grandpop rarely gets angry." Niklas shakes his head. "He was stunned and disappointed, but as usual, he put a positive spin on it."

"I'm waiting for him to call me into his office. What do you think my Penalty will be this time?"

"You're not getting a Penalty."

My mouth drops. "How is that possible?"

"I took the blame. It was my fault you went over the cliff. First I antagonized you in Waldheim, I goaded you further on the ride home, and then you freaked after spilling the gumdrops about your crush on"—he flashes a cocky grin—"me."

Oh, am I ready for this. Pinching my brow in mock-confusion, I shake my head. "I don't have a crush on you."

His fingers tense around his cap. "You're denying what you said?"

"Do you even remember what I said?"

"'Sweet little drummer boy,'" he recites in a know-it-all tone, "'I have a crush on him after all.'"

"Yes, I said 'him.'" I bat my eyelashes. "I was talking about Logan Donati."

Niklas snorts. "No, because before that, you said the kiss was going to haunt you."

"What kiss?"

He opens his mouth to reply then snaps it shut again. His jaw muscles bulge and his lips compress. He holds my gaze for a prolonged moment, his green eyes penetrating, but I meet his scrutiny head-on. I will not let him think I like him.

Inclining his head, he turns away to stare at the fire. "So be it. The point is, you're not getting a Penalty. I am."

"Oh." I twist a corner of the pillow. "Thanks. That's…big of you."

He gives me a sidelong glance. "I'm not always a jerk, Tinsel."

"I never said…" My voice trails off, because we both know I thought it. Sometimes that's just as bad.

His gaze roams around the room, and his expression turns introspective. What catches his eye? *Mutti's* blue and white china plates lined up above the windows? *Vati's* display of medals and trophies he's won for his pastry concoctions? Knickknacks and antiques handed down through the generations?

Does he compare our humble apartment to his grandiose home atop the hill? He probably can't wait to escape these cramped quarters.

"I've always liked your home," Niklas says softly.

His comment pops my rising bitterness, and my cheeks sting. This is the second time in sixty seconds I've misjudged him. "You've never been here before."

"Yes, I have." He stretches out his legs, crossing them at the ankles. His feet almost touch the hearth. "We partnered up in Sixth Level for an after-school project, and I came over here to work on it."

My eyebrows lift. "Holly jolly, I forgot about that. I must have blocked it from my memory. Sixth Level? I bet I was forced to be your partner."

"That would explain why you scowled at me the entire time."

I whack him with the pillow. "I did not."

"Says the elf who blocked the memory." Niklas wrestles the pillow from my hands. "Anyway, that was the only time I've ever been able to stand upright in an elf's home. This place is spacious. Comparatively speaking, of course." And he bops me in the face with the pillow.

"Ow." I rub my nose. "It has to be spacious. I might have developed a hunched back otherwise. My parents had the roof raised when we were in Third Level, you remember that?" I shift my body to face him. "By then, I was already as tall as them. But after everything they've done to accommodate my height, I still feel mammoth living here. I don't dare sit on the couch because I know over time, my weight would break down the cushions." I lower my voice in case my brothers are eavesdropping. "You don't know what it's like not to feel comfortable in your own home."

"So, let's go to the Workshop." He stands and tosses the pillow behind me on the couch. "If you think your leg can handle it, we'll start your dance lessons tonight in one of the conference rooms."

Taking his offered hand, I let him pull me up then smile. "This might be the first conversation we've had where we haven't attacked each other."

He gives my hand a squeeze. "Trying to show you another slice of that pie. Disappointed?"

"Refreshed." I slip into my coat and fit a cap over my tousled hair. "Is that why you didn't pick on me about dance practice?"

"I figured I'd cut you some slack after the way Frau Tanz spoke to you."

"She simply spoke what others think in their heads." I step into the stairwell and Niklas follows. "I'm good for *nothing*."

"Not true. And you're going to prove that to everyone during the Festival Dance."

"Supposing you come up with a way for me to perform"—I glance back at him—"I have yet to get through the first segment without falling on my face." Losing my footing, I stumble down the remaining steps. Pain flares in my leg, but Niklas catches my elbow before I can re-injure myself. "Case in point," I mumble, tugging my clothes back into place.

Niklas lets out a deep laugh. "Then we'd better get to work." He ushers me outside where stars wink overhead and our breath comes out in clouds. "By the way, I don't suppose you've heard the rumor going around this afternoon?"

I shake my head.

Niklas straddles his SnoMo. "Apparently, someone left a load of supplies behind the Workshop during the night. Most were in decent shape, although some pieces looked like they might've taken a tumble. Like, down-a-ravine tumble."

"You don't say."

"Mmm." He watches me over his shoulder as I slide behind him sidesaddle. "You know nothing about it, huh?"

"Uh"—I tug at my skirt—"nope."

Niklas laughs. "You're a lousy liar, Kuchler."

Oh, I hope not. Too many current situations are going to require a little white lie here and there. "What makes you think it was me?"

"It's the kind of thing you'd do—try to fix your mistakes." He passes me an extra helmet. "What I'd like to know is why you didn't ask me to come along and help. And how did you get it done so fast all by yourself? The trip alone, on a SnoMo in the dark, would have taken you two hours roundtrip."

With an evasive smile, I snap on my helmet. Niklas raises an eyebrow. "Aren't you the secretive little elf."

"Emphasis on *secretive* rather than *little,* right?"

He chuckles and starts the engine, and I almost enjoy slipping my arms around his waist. His charm is a side I don't see for more than a few seconds at a time. When taken in large doses, it's quite…heady.

"DID YOU EVEN WATCH MY FEET?" NIKLAS'S VOICE ECHOES IN THE secluded conference room.

I let out an exasperated groan. "Yes."

"Then why aren't you over here?" He stands several steps to my right, hands on hips, a frown on his face.

"Because I keep getting mixed up!"

"We've been at this for two days."

I sit with a huff on the elf-sized conference table we've pushed against one wall. "Maybe if we had music, I'd do a better job."

Niklas arches an eyebrow. "I told you. First you learn the individual steps, then we string them together, then we add in the music. So, learn the steps already."

My eyes narrow, but he ignores my attitude, pulls me by my *dirndl* apron, and arranges me into the beginning position. Again. Then he takes his stance with his back to me. "From the top." He pretends to hold the hand of his invisible partner. "One. Two. Three. Go." He shuffles to the right. I attempt to copy his fancy footwork, but my legs get tangled halfway through the move, and my knee bangs into the table.

Sinking to the floor, I roll onto my back and fling an arm over my eyes.

A chuckle issues from somewhere above my head. "What are you doing, Kuchler?"

"Resting. I must be sleep-deprived. Why else haven't I mastered the frostbitten grapevine yet?"

"You want a list?"

I stick out my tongue.

"Fine. We'll take a five-minute break." He nudges my hand with his foot. "Want to hear about today's dance practice?"

"Only if you tell me Pix tripped and fell without my help."

"Sorry, no." There's a grin in his voice. "Want to hear the latest rumor surrounding the mysterious merchandise?"

"Heard it. The elves are crediting you for it."

"What else are they left to conclude when the real hotshot won't expose herself?"

I strike out blindly with my arm and connect with his leg. He laughs. "I could tell you what Gina texted me this morning, but you probably don't want to—"

"Gina texted you?" I sit up, find Niklas leaning back against the conference table, and rise to join him. "What did she say?"

"She can't wait to see you, they're going to hook you up with the best equipment on the market, and she's forbidden Logan to hog you all day."

My eyebrows rise. "Really?"

His jaw hardens. "Guess he's pretty taken with you."

"I mean about the equipment." I'll mull over his Logan-comment later. "To think a brand name might be what keeps me upright on the slopes."

"If it works, I'll have Grandpop make you its equal for Christmas." After spending the next few minutes telling me what I can expect at the ski slope, he stands with a stretch. "Okay, break's over. Back to formation."

But we've barely resumed practice when I fumble another

move, crash into him, and we land in a jumbled mess on the floor. Attempting to get up, I plant my elbow in his stomach, and the air whooshes from him on a groan.

"I'm so sorry." I scramble away before I maim him some more and jam my hands into my hair. "This is ridiculous. I should not be dancing the boys' steps."

"You're right." Niklas winces, massaging his stomach as he struggles to a sitting position. "You're painfully right." And then his expression clears as a mischievous grin lifts the corner of his mouth. "Here's what we'll do instead. I'm going to teach you the girl's steps, and you're going to shock the *lederhosen* off everyone when you dance in the ceremony"—he puts a hand to his chest and makes a seated bow—"as my partner."

My eyes go wide. "We'll never get away with it. Frau Tanz—"

"Won't know what's going on until it's too late because we won't reveal our big surprise until the ceremony. C'mon, Kuchler." Niklas hauls me to my feet and spins me into his arms in one fluid, breathless move. My left hand falls at his shoulder as he takes my right hand and holds it out to the side. "Let's show Flitterndorf how capable you truly are."

Whether it's the encouragement in his words or the warmth in his touch, adrenaline tingles through my bones.

His crazy idea just might work.

HIT THE SLOPES

Gina grins at me, her eyes crinkling behind her ski goggles. "You ready?" Wearing a long stocking cap, a bright pink down jacket, and gray snow pants, she bounces on her skis. On my other side, Logan shifts his skis back and forth over the snow.

I swallow and glance down the slope. It looks steep for a beginner run, but I've nailed the bunny slope. Logan claims this is the logical next step. I grip the ski poles and blow out a breath.

Logan chuckles. "Relax, Tinsel. Gina and I will be with you the whole way down."

My gaze flits to Niklas on Gina's other side. "And where will you be?"

"Waiting for you at the bottom." He winks behind his goggles. "I want a front row seat when you crash." He takes off down the hill with precision and speed.

Logan snorts. "I get the feeling he expects you to fail."

My lips compress into a tight line. "He's mistaken if he thinks I'm gonna give him that satisfaction."

"That's my girl." Logan winks, too, but where Niklas's wink made me stiffen, Logan's makes everything in me go soft. "Now, remember what I taught you." He gestures with his hands and ski poles. "Pizza slice all the way down for this first run. And big S-curves."

I readjust my hands and bend my knees. "Pizzas and S-curves." I track Niklas's progress down the hill and push off.

My skis want to straighten into two parallel lines, but Logan keeps his word and stays with me, instructing me to keep my ski tips pointed toward each other and to match his wide turns. It's a slow, painful process, but Niklas watches me from below, expecting me to take a spill, and I'm determined to disappoint him.

At long last I slide to a stop at the bottom while other skiers zoom past on their way to the lift for another run. I made it. Without falling.

Gina glides in beside me with a delighted squeal. "You did it! That was fantastic."

Logan gives me a high-five followed by a side-arm squeeze. "Nice job, rookie. From here on out, you'll only get better."

Laughing, I bask in their praise. Niklas shuffles over on his skis, and I raise my chin. "Guess I'm not as big of a klutz as you think I am."

His mouth lifts in a lopsided grin. "I knew you could do it."

"You said you wanted a front row seat to watch me fall."

He cocks his head. "I did say that, didn't I?" His smile widens. "Ready for round two?"

My shoulders slump. "Fruitcake. I forgot I'd have to go again."

THE AFTERNOON PROGRESSES WITH MORE SUCCESSES (ME), LOTS OF talking (Logan and me), and some mild flirtations (Logan) (and maybe me). We chat about everything from our favorite music to parental woes, although depending on the subject, I give vague responses to conceal my true identity.

Eventually, Logan instructs me to lessen the width of my pizza slice, and I'm delighted when my speed increases and I stay upright. Encouraged, I relax my stance, which helps absorb the bumps in the runs better than my rigid, unyielding posture. The cold air brushes my face, the ground rushes beneath me, and adrenaline surges through my limbs.

Ninety minutes after I attempted my first run, I come to a smooth stop at the bottom of the hill. Logan, who has been by my side the entire time, pulls up behind me and I smile. "Why don't you take this next run by yourself? Go do some moguls. Or impress the spectators on the jumps. Skiing this beginner trail has got to be boring for you."

"Are you kidding? I've never had a better excuse to keep checking out the hottest girl on the slopes."

I duck my head and poke holes in the snow with my pole. "Thank you, but I'm doing decent now, and you deserve a break from babysitting."

He claps a gloved hand to his chest. "Man, I hope you think of me as more than a babysitter." Then his gaze travels up the neighboring slope where an expert skier zigzags his way down the run. His expression morphs into longing. "Okay. One run." He gives a slow grin, his teeth white against his olive skin. "Or maybe two."

"Or three. Or four." I match his grin. "When you're done, come look for me in the lodge. I'll be taking a much-needed break."

"Thanks, Tinsel." He kisses me on the cheek then skis away in the direction of the black diamond lift. Maybe someday I'll be competent enough to go with him.

"I totally saw that," a female voice singsongs above me on the slope. I turn as Gina and Niklas finish their run before neatly angling to a stop beside me.

Heat creeps up my neck. "Saw what?"

Frowning, Niklas gestures at all the skiers zooming past. "The entire slope saw Logan kiss you."

"It was a friendly kiss. On the cheek."

"So he kisses you then ditches you?"

"I told him to have fun on some harder slopes."

Niklas leans on his poles. "I'm surprised he was persuaded to leave your side."

"It's not like *you've* stuck around."

"And watch you two flirt? *Nein, danke.*"

"Your loss." I shrug. "Might've picked up some pointers."

"I know how to flirt."

"I've never seen it."

"Because I wouldn't waste it on you." He pushes away on his poles and skis toward the lifts.

My jaw clenches at his departing back. "He's such a jerk sometimes."

Gina grins. "He's jealous. Guys are always jerks when they're jealous."

"Jealous?" I let out a laugh. "Of who?"

"Logan. When Nik saw him kiss you, his face turned the same color as his eyes."

GINA AND I DECIDE TO SKI A COUPLE RUNS TOGETHER. ON THE lift, she dishes about her past boyfriends and advises me in the realm of relationships—not that I plan to enter into one anytime soon. Then we get talking about her job and her boss's Christmas decorating attempts at the coffee shop. As I listen to her opinions on what makes for great holiday decor, my gaze falls to the slope below us where a line of children trails behind—hey, that's Niklas. They follow him, curve for curve, movement for movement, while he laughs and shouts encouragement. I point out the spectacle to Gina.

She shakes her head with a chuckle. "He has that effect on children wherever he goes. It's kinda freaky." Her eyebrows pull together. "When I was little, my great-granddad used to tell stories about a man he knew who was like the pied-piper, but without the pipe. The kids would flock to this man like ducks after bread, and he always knew their names, even if he'd never met them before. Niklas reminds me of those stories."

On our third run down the slope, having gained confidence from my progress, I pull ahead of Gina and try for a little more speed. Bending my knees, I prepare for the turn in my S-curve—

"Watch out!"

Wha—? Where? I falter, lose my balance, and plow into the snow, where I skid for several feet. Someone crashes into me from behind, and I throw my arms overhead, squeezing my eyes shut as the body topples over me. For the next several seconds, myriad skis scrape across the snow in different stages of stopping, and children's voices exclaim, "Santa! Santa's hurt!"

Santa? Niklas. Crumbling candy canes, I took out Santa's grandson.

"Santa Claus? Are you okay?" One after another, the kids ask the same question. Then a chuckle comes from above, and I open my eyes. Niklas kneels beside me, a group of children at his back. Gina skirts the crowd as she makes her way toward us. I try to sit up but my skis are tangled.

"I should have known better than to try to slip past you," Niklas says. Eyes twinkling, he bats the snow off his hat, purposefully making the flakes fall into my face. "We should outfit you with blinkers so you can warn other skiers before you make sudden turns."

I grab his arm and force myself into a sitting position. "Give me a wide berth like the good folk in Flitterndorf have learned to do," I say as he manually disengages my skis from my boots, "and we'll both leave here unscathed."

A little boy on skis the length of my arm swerves to a stop beside Niklas and points a gloved hand in my direction. "Who's that, Santa? Are you gonna put her on the Naughty List for making you crash—whoa." His jaw drops. "Hey, guys, lookit her ears!"

I gasp and clap my hands to my head. My hat's gone.

The boy yanks at my arm. "Aw, let's see 'em, huh?"

Another boy jostles the first as he leans in for a closer look. "I wanna see, too."

"See what? What about her ears?" A girl pushes her way between the boys, but she has a domino effect, and they topple into me, forcing me to brace my hands against the ground. A circle of unblinking, inquisitive eyes stare at my exposed, pointy ears.

Suddenly I'm mauled by a dozen kids with two dozen probing mittens and four dozen questions.

"Do they hurt when I pull on them?"

"Do they get stuck in your comb when you brush your hair?"

"I wish *I* had ears like those."

"I wouldn't want 'em."

"How'd you get them to be so pointy?"

"You're pretty."

"You're weird."

In the background, Gina fights a grin and Niklas laughs. "Okay, kids, that's enough. Careful, now." He reaches into the huddle, takes me by the hand, and lifts me to my feet. "We don't want Miss Tinsel hurt."

"Who is she, Santa?" the first boy asks.

Niklas purses his lips, swiping my hat from the snow. "Well, Joel, she's my..." He contemplates the hat before passing it to me, clearly stalling for time. "She's my...elf assistant."

My eyes widen along with the kids. How could he?

One girl scrunches up her face. "She ain't a elf, Mr. Santy Claus. Elves are short."

"You're right, Alana. Most elves are short. But a few elves are taller." He crouches to her level and includes the other kids with his gaze. "Want to know a secret? An elf's height reveals how important that elf is to Santa. The taller the elf, the more important they are. You can imagine how special that makes Tinsel."

"Ooooh," says a chorus of little voices. I compress my lips at the blatant lie. Since when am I special to him?

"She must do some amazin' stuff, then, huh?" a girl pipes up from the back.

Niklas winks at me. "She hasn't accomplished much yet, but I hold out hope that—"

A tug on his sleeve cuts him off, and he looks at Joel. "Is she more 'portant than Mrs. Claus?"

He chuckles. "There is no Mrs. Claus yet."

"Is the *elf* gonna be Mrs. Claus someday?"

"Uh..." Clearing his throat, Niklas sends Gina a look. "No, she won't. Can't. It's against North Pole policy."

Though his words reflect the edicts I already know, my gut twists to hear his rejection in front of a dozen kids—and after he said I was special! And why did he glance at Gina? Are they an item after all?

The sea of pitying, juvenile faces before me begin to blur.

Straightening to my full height, I jerk my hat into place. "I wouldn't want to become Mrs. Claus, anyway. Santa can be bossy and egotistical, and he'll only get fatter from here on out." I shove my boots into my skis as my hurt feelings shove the bitter words from my mouth. "He takes his lofty position for granted, has little respect for the elves that do the grunt work at his shop, and don't get me started on the reindeer. I'll pass on Mrs. Claus, thank-you-very-much." Grabbing my poles, I give the shocked kids a tight smile, add, "Have a nice day," for good measure, and take off down the slope.

Ignoring whoever calls my name, I make my skis less like a pizza and more like French fries and gain speed. It's glorious. It's freedom. It's—out of control. The bottom zooms closer, but my skis are past the point of cooperation.

So, I do what most self-respecting beginner skiers would do. I crash.

Pain flares in my leg, twinges in my shoulder. My skis fly off, and I tumble head over heels over head over…yeah. Meet Tinsel: the elfin hamster wheel.

At last I slide to a stop, spread-eagle on my back.

"Tinsel!" Gina rushes up on her skis and stares at me sprawled in the snow. "Goodness gracious, are you hurt?"

"Nothing broken." Unless you count my pride.

"That was the most spectacular wipeout I've ever seen."

I sit up with a groan. "You should have seen me last week on Huff 'n Puff Hill."

"Huff 'n Puff Hill?" Gina's brow knots as she picks up a ski and hands it to me.

"Oh. It's the name of…a place in town." I avoid her gaze and rock onto my feet.

"Cute name." She drops the second ski beside the first one. "And cute ears. What was all that about just now, with you and Niklas? All that Santa Claus talk? You know those kids are convinced Niklas is, like, the jolly fat man himself, right? I don't get it. He's not fat. He doesn't have a beard. Or wear a red suit. Or —" She frowns at her own logic, then turns her frown on me.

I bite my lip. How am I supposed to explain to Gina what she saw? Tell her it was a trick of the light?

"Can I…" Gina reaches toward my hat, then pulls back. "Do you mind…can I see your ears? From the glimpse I saw before the kids swarmed you, they looked like the ones from the *Lord of the Rings* movies."

"Yes!" I latch onto the perfect cover. "Yes, they're fake ears. Because…because Niklas and I were helping at a Christmas party earlier today."

"This morning?"

"Um…yes, this morning." I wave my hand in the air when I realize how early that would have made the party. "But it was a cameo appearance; we weren't there for the whole thing. Rudolph and Frosty joined us, too." I elbow her in the arm. "People in full-body costumes, you know? Niklas dressed as Santa, and I went as his elf, complete with the bell-topped booties and pointy ears."

"Why are you still wearing them?"

I rub my fingers against their outlines through the hat. "They're, um, hard to remove." I crouch to grab a ski pole when Gina swipes the hat from my head. "Hey!"

Gina grins. "I want a closer look."

I sigh. "Fine." Shutting my eyes, I pray Gina suddenly gets blurry vision or my hair keeps getting in her way or I have wrinkles where the lines of attachment would occur for fake ears. Anything to keep her from seeing the truth.

"Wow." She steps away with an appreciative nod. "That's incredible. Like, I can't tell where your God-given ears stop and your fake ears begin."

I laugh. "Isn't that the point?" I cover the source of interest with my hat. "Let's head to the lodge for a break. I could use some food and hot cocoa. I don't care how weak it tastes, I need some chocolate."

Gina swings an arm about my shoulders. "You are talking my language, girlfriend."

JUDGMENT CALL

Gina and I warm ourselves by the stone fireplace in the lodge, our fingers wrapped around disposable cups of cocoa, our feet liberated from ski boots. Pinecone-stuffed hurricane lamps and festive greenery top the mantel, and Christmas music plays in the background. Pine air freshener mixes with wafts of cheesy fries and burgers cooking in the kitchen.

When Gina opens and closes her mouth for the third time since we've claimed the sofa, I take a fortifying breath. "All right, what is it?"

She angles her body toward me, pulling a foot beneath her opposite leg. An evergreen tree stands in the corner behind her, decorated with handmade ornaments. "You know Niklas wasn't trying to be mean on the slope, right?"

I swirl my cocoa. "He mocked me in front of those kids. What he said about me being special? A complete lie. And then he turns around and rejects me as a potential Mrs. Claus."

Gina blows on her cocoa. "He was pretending to be Santa, so doesn't that make it a pretend rejection?"

"He took away my dignity."

She lowers her cup. "What about you? You gave him a dressing-down out there. We might know it's a farce, but those kids believe he's Santa, and you disgraced him."

Right. To them, I represent a slew of nameless elves, but there's only one Santa Claus. I rest my head against the sofa cushion and glare at the colored lights wrapped around the rafters. "You're saying I should apologize?"

"I think you both should apologize."

"Niklas doesn't give apologies. He doesn't give anything. He takes." Someone should put his picture next to the word *selfish* in the dictionary.

Except, it wasn't selfish to take my Penalty as his own.

"No offense, Tinsel, but you seem to judge him rather harshly."

I lean forward. "You don't understand our history."

"I dare you to give him the benefit of the doubt for twenty-four hours"—a smile works its way across Gina's mouth—"and see what happens."

"Can I choose when those hours occur?"

She laughs. "They must be consecutive."

Cringing, I sink back into the sofa. "That's a tall order."

"According to Niklas, you're a tall elf. Shouldn't be too difficult."

I roll my eyes. "You have no idea."

We gravitate to more light-hearted conversation after that, sharing childhood stories and awkward things we've done (I have a wealth of examples to choose from). Commiserating over school woes and frustrations (she's nineteen and working toward an associate's degree online).

I'm chuckling at the image of her as a kid surrounded by shaven-haired Barbie dolls with hand-painted faces reflecting her stylist skills, when my gaze snags on Logan entering through the side doorway.

He brushes snow off his ski jacket, laughing and nodding to

someone behind him. Removing his helmet, he shakes the hair from his eyes, lips spreading wide over beautiful teeth. Niklas steps into view, helmet in the crook of his arm, merriment twinkling in his eyes. They scan the groups of skiers, calling out greetings to acquaintances, their affable manner inviting strangers and friends alike into their midst.

My heart slams against my chest at the picture of them side by side. Logan, with the dark, dreamy Italian look about him. Niklas, with his German fair hair and pale eyes. Logan's smiles reflect sincerity, while Niklas's grins suggest tomfoolery. Logan encourages me; Niklas challenges me. Logan charms me. Niklas incites me. One makes my heart soar; the other makes my heart sigh. I'm helpless and clueless and—

Someone jostles my arm. Gina smirks when I turn to her. "I didn't want them to catch you staring. My brother already has an over-inflated ego."

I dip my chin, shifting on the cushion. "Thanks. Say, um, I was wondering. Are you and Niklas—"

"Such serious faces," Logan says as he and Niklas shuffle over to the sofa opposite ours. "What are you two talking about?"

"My doll fetish," Gina answers. Niklas cocks an eyebrow, but she grins behind her cup of cocoa. "Did you boys play nice on the black diamonds?"

Logan throws an arm over the back of the couch. "I killed a few moguls, but with no girl to impress, skiing lost its appeal." He taps my foot with his outstretched boot. "How about you and I try a blue run after I get something to eat?"

"Am I ready for that?"

"You won't know if you don't try."

But Niklas shakes his head, unlatching the top buckles of his ski boots. "You've already suffered one bruised leg this week. You don't need to damage the other one."

My cup flexes beneath my clenched fingers. "Why do you automatically assume I'm going to damage something?"

His dimple flashes. "Some of my earliest memories involve you, Tinsel. I know your capabilities as well as your limitations."

"And if you had it your way, you'd keep me limited." Benefit of the doubt, indeed. "Since this isn't your decision to make"—I give Logan my sweetest smile—"I'd love to try a blue run."

Niklas's expression hardens. Gina's earlier comment about his jealousy ricochets in my head, but I blow it off. He'd have to like me before he could be jealous, and his comment on the slopes showed otherwise.

A young boy scoots between the two sofas. "'Bye, Santa Claus. Don't forget me Christmas Eve."

Niklas gives the kid a fist bump. "Hang tight, Austin. I won't forget. Lots of action figures." He winks at the boy as Logan mouths to Gina, *Santa Claus?*

Gina splays her fingers in the air. "It was amazing, Logan. These kids followed Nik's every move down the slope. Kept calling him Santa Claus. But the best part was this." She reaches for my hat, but I'm quicker this time and clamp it down before she can yank it off. "Aw. Let him see. Please?"

"No."

"See what?" Logan's dark gaze studies my face, and my heart thuds. Slowly, I remove my hat.

He lets out a whistle. Gina smiles. I expect Niklas to make some snarky comment, but his focus is on Logan.

"Wow." That's all Logan says. But he keeps staring.

"Aren't they neat?" Gina's hand flits near my ear. "They look so real. Tinsel says she and Niklas were at a Christmas party"—Niklas's gaze cuts to mine at the fib and I feign concern with my hat—"where Nik dressed as Santa, and Tinsel went as an elf. I'm thinking the Huggamugg Café should host their own Christmas party, don't you? We can, like, entice the children with promises of a visit from a slimmed-down Santa Claus and his trusty, red-haired elf. What do you think?"

Logan moves to squeeze between me and Gina and leans

close. Goosebumps prickle along my arms. "They're incredible," he murmurs. "How long can you wear them before you have to take them off?"

"Oh"—I wring my hat—"a while. You'd be surprised."

"You make one attractive elf."

Niklas lets out a snort.

"You disagree?" Gina asks.

Chest tightening, I force myself to look Niklas in the eyes. Their pale hue cuts across the distance between us, and the muscles in his jaw jump. "She's Tinsel. Tinsel is…" He hefts a shoulder.

Logan laughs. "Yeah, we know what you think about Tinsel. Well, *I* think"—he takes my hand—"that if you do come again for a Christmas party, I'd like the chance to take you out to dinner, as well."

"Dinner?" He can't possibly mean what just jumped into my head.

"Yeah. Dinner. You and me."

He does mean a date. Emotions whirl inside, from excitement to panic (he's asked me on a date!), from pleasure to distress (I've never been on a date). I stare at our hands, my light skin against his darker tone. "I don't know what to say."

"Say yes." Logan brushes his thumb across my knuckles, and I lift my eyes. His chocolate gaze melts into mine, inviting me closer.

Niklas growls. "Quit ogling her like she's some entrancing bauble on a Christmas tree, Logan, and show her some respect."

"Respect?" I scoff at Niklas. "You don't even know what that looks like, given what you dish out to me every day."

He stands, knuckles white where he grips his helmet straps. "It sure as frostbite doesn't look like what you dish out, either, Kuchler." And he walks away.

FED UP

Niklas and I don't talk after that. Logan takes me on a few blue runs (I don't break anything and only fall twice), I ski once more with Gina, and then we pack it up around four o'clock.

As Logan drives us back to Waldheim in his well-used Chevy, he and Gina try to convince us to stay for dinner. With Niklas asleep in the front passenger seat, it's up to me to decide, and I decline since he and I have another ninety-minute ride before we reach Flitterndorf. By the time I'll arrive at the stables to do my chores, the Third String will wonder where I've been. Plus, we brought some food for the return trip, so it's not like we'll go hungry.

When we pull up to the Donatis' garage beside Niklas's SnoMo, Logan kills the engine, and Gina hops from the vehicle. While she proceeds to prod Niklas awake, Logan and I remove ski equipment from the bed of his truck. I'm acutely aware of his gaze on me as we haul skis into the garage and prop them against a metal shelving unit. During our second trip, after I tuck some boots on a shelf, Logan takes my hands and holds them to his chest.

"When can I see you again?" He looks at me with puppy-dog eyes. "At least tell me how I can reach you."

"Through me." A rumpled-looking Niklas sets down another set of boots and runs a hand over his face. "You can reach her through me."

Logan chuckles as Gina enters the garage clutching several ski poles. "Can I trust you to relay any messages I might have for her?" He sends me a questioning look. "Don't you have a cell phone?"

I shake my head.

"Email?"

Sighing, I turn to Niklas. "You mind coming up with an explanation as to why I don't have an email account?"

"Her parents are old school," Niklas says without hesitation. "No electronics, no computer." He shrugs and walks toward the SnoMo. "I don't know how they expect their kids to function in society, but there it is."

I cross my arms. "Thanks a lot."

Logan returns to the truck for the remaining equipment, a frown marring his brow. "I can accept the part about no cell phones or computers, but you've gotta have a landline."

Of course, my parents have a landline. It connects them to the other elves in Flitterndorf. Period.

Niklas must think I'm going to disclose our secrets in my frustration, for he says, "You can communicate via my email address, okay, Logan? I promise I'll give her the messages. And I won't read them. I'll print them off and hand them over."

"What about a Christmas party at the café?" Gina links her arm through mine. "Please say you'll come as Santa and his elf."

Niklas tunnels his fingers through his already mussed hair and meets my pleading gaze. Though his eyes soften, he replies, "It's complicated, Gina."

"It doesn't have to be." My chest constricts at the thought I might not see either Logan or Gina again, and I give Gina's arm a squeeze. "We'll come to the Christmas party. Contact Niklas, work out the details, set the date, and we'll be there."

She gives me a hug. "Don't forget about those twenty-four hours."

My mouth curls into an unwilling smile. "I'll try not to." Turning to Logan, I pause, unsure how to say goodbye to him. With a hug? And if so, would that be one-armed or two? Or maybe a slug on the shoulder is more apropos? "Um..."

Logan opens his arms wide, making the decision for me. "It's only fair I get a hug, too." He holds me close, and I inhale his spicy cologne mixed with the outdoors. "And it's also only fair"—his breath tickles my ear—"that if you set a date with my sis for a party, you give an answer about a dinner date with me."

On jelly legs, I pull far enough away to look him in the eye. "I'd like that."

He grins, and I hold my breath as he leans in and presses his lips just to the right of mine. My nerves explode in all directions. Somehow I make it to the SnoMo without my knees buckling. Niklas already wears his helmet, and I'm thankful for small favors because I don't want to see his expression right now.

In both my actions and my words, I have defied my future boss.

And I'm not the least bit sorry.

If I had confidence that I'd stay on the SnoMo and not topple off into a gorge somewhere (not going there again), I would keep my arms to myself rather than around Niklas's waist.

Personally, I don't think he wants my arms there any more than I do.

We remain in stony silence the entire ride home. The closer we get to Flitterndorf, the tenser his back muscles become. As soon as he brakes near the Lower Stables' west entrance, I hop off the SnoMo and unfasten my helmet.

It's late enough that the Minor Flight Team has gone home for the night, yet early enough I won't get into trouble for neglecting my responsibilities. Rubbing an ear with one hand, I give Niklas the helmet with the other. "Thank you for the ride." I turn toward the door.

The *click* of Niklas's chin strap shoots through the silent night. "What do you see in him, anyway?"

I stop and spin on my heel. "What's not to see?" Holding up my gloved hand, I list off Logan's positive attributes one by one with my fingers. "He's handsome. Laid back. Considerate. Flattering. Generous. Helpful. Funny—"

"Never mind."

A steady breeze plays with my hair, and I tuck the flyaways behind an ear. "Logan is your friend. If I weren't an elf, would you still discourage me from liking someone you obviously enjoy hanging out with?"

Niklas drops his gaze. "I don't…" He plucks at the helmet in his lap. "I don't want to see you get your hopes up." He grimaces, as though he knows he sounds lame.

"Logan and Gina have only known me for a few days, yet they've accepted me faster than the elves from my own Green Clan. They're not the ones I'm worried about shattering my hopes." I adjust my scarf against the chill. "And since when are you concerned about my emotional welfare? You didn't care today when you encouraged the kids to laugh at my ears."

Niklas straightens, his eyes flaring wide. "Is that what your silent treatment has been about? Didn't you hear them? They loved your ears."

Who is he kidding? "I heard their laughter and their taunts." And I saw their pity.

"I can't believe this." He flings up his arms and looks at the sky. "I helped you save face out there on the slopes when your hat fell off, gave you the perfect excuse to show the real you in public, and you're mad at me?"

"No." I stalk back and jab a finger at his chest. "You created the perfect excuse to make fun of me." Jab. "Because that's all I am to you." Jab. "Nothing. But. A joke." Jab jab jab.

Good thing I didn't make any promises to Gina about those twenty-four hours, because they aren't happening anytime soon.

I return to the stable's entrance. "Someday you're going to be my boss, and nothing could depress me more." I wrench open the door and march across the stables' interior, venting as I go even though he can't hear me now. "You charm your way into winning everyone's favor but mine. With me, you taunt, insult, make snide comments. I know I'm tall and clumsy and a misfit, but shouldn't the future Santa look past all that?"

The reindeer wait outside in the corral, and I grab the water hose to fill their tank. "I don't know why you started hating me back when we were kids"—the reindeer exchange curious glances at my self-talk—"and I don't know what I did to earn your ridicule, but I wish you'd forgive me already."

"*Me*? Forgive *you*?"

I jump. Niklas followed me?

Drawing near, Niklas shoves his hands into his coat pockets. "Try the other way around, Kuchler. You find fault with everything I do. Every action I take, no matter how impersonal, you think it's aimed against you. I can't say more than five words without you twisting them around to mean something completely different—and harsher—than what I intended."

"Oh, *really*?" I glare at him, but the hurt tightening his features pricks my conscious, and I look away again. The reindeer move closer. "What about when you insulted me in front of Logan when we first met? All those innuendos about tinsel? Or how about when you said I wasn't entirely an elf? And how else was I supposed to take that comment today about you knowing my capabilities—"

"For the love of Christmas, you have it all wrong. See?" He turns his attention to the reindeer that have crowded around us. "She believes the worst—good garland!" Niklas sucks in a breath and leans back as Butterscotch flanks me on my right.

"'Tis what happens when ye sow ridicule," the lead reindeer rumbles, making Niklas…tremble? "Ye reap contempt."

The pulse quickens at Niklas's neck and his Adam's apple bobs. Frowning at his reaction, I pat Butterscotch's shoulder. "*Contempt* might be a bit harsh."

Chip steps forward at my left. "Sounds abou' right ta me."

Niklas flexes his gloved hands. "Those things are dissing me, aren't they?"

"Wow. Thirty seconds in their presence and you're already catching on. You must be a Kringle." And high-handed. And arrogant. And—

"How are you doing it?" He speaks to me though his gaze is fixed on Chip. "How are you able to read their emotions?"

"I'm not." I grab the grooming bucket and enter the corral. Butterscotch and Chip follow. "I'm talking to them."

Licorice prances over, her gaze on the currycomb in my hand. "Me first."

"Nay, ye went first yesterday." Cinnamon shoves her aside. "Tonight, I go first."

Licorice pokes her with an antler tine and I move between them. "Stop or I'll give you gals a time-out. Licorice, it's Cinnamon's turn to go first. I'll get to you after Cocoa."

The reindeer thrusts her nose in the air and stomps away.

From beyond the corral fence, Niklas grips the top railing, his jaw slack. "They talk? And you understand them?"

I pull the comb through Cinnamon's coat. "The way my ears hear it, they use the same language we do." I smirk. "Except, they have an accent."

"Nay, gel," Chip rumbles. "Yer the one with the accent."

Niklas shakes his head. "That's impossible. No elf has ever had this ability. No Kringle, either, as far as I can tell."

"Great." I yank hair from the bristles of the comb. "Now, not only do I stand out as being tall and clumsy, I'm also the only one in Flitterndorf history with a hearing defect."

"Tinsel. Look at me."

Gritting my teeth, I move to Cinnamon's other side. I hold strong for several seconds before giving in to Niklas's penetrating stare.

He leans his arms atop the rail. "This is a *blessing,* not a defect."

His comforting words puncture my irritation, deflating it like a balloon until it collapses into surrender. I purse my lips. "Why can't I ever stay mad at you?"

His mouth curls at one end. "I think the answer lies in what you said. I'm a Kringle."

No. It's because he's *Niklas.*

But I'm not about to tell him that.

SECRETS

Niklas offers to clean out the stalls, which allows me a jump start on grooming, but as I chat with the reindeer, I feel his gaze each time he pushes the wheelbarrow past the corral. He says nothing more about my supposed "blessing," however, and once I finish my task, I join him inside the stables where we work in companionable silence for several minutes.

At length, he looks up from where he fluffs hay in Cocoa's quarters. "This could be your talent, Tinsel."

Across the aisle, I lay out fresh hay for Butterscotch and laugh. "This isn't a talent. This is a quirky abnormality." I toss a handful of hay at him, but it falls short and scatters on the flagstones in the center aisle. "I don't suppose you have any news about a certain interview that's been postponed?"

"Ah, but if conversing with the 'deer is your talent"—he lobs some hay at me with the pitchfork—"what need have you for an interview?"

The hay strikes my boots and I give the mound a kick. "I'm not mucking stalls forever. I have plans."

"I didn't—"

"Despite what you think, the managerial internship is a perfect fit for me."

He stacks his hands on the end of the pitchfork. "Then how does Wednesday at three-thirty sound?"

"Wednesday?" I nod. "I can make that work."

"Good, because Herr Referat will be expecting you." Niklas tosses more hay at me. "And be prompt. He's not an elf that tolerates tardiness."

I stand among falling strands of hay. "You've already arranged it for me?"

Niklas gives a one-shouldered shrug.

Oh. "*Danke.*"

"You're welcome."

Chewing on the inside of my lip, I brush hay from my clothes as Gina's request rolls through my mind. Maybe now is a good time, after all. "I'm sorry for misjudging you."

"I told you I'm not always a jerk." He steps close to pluck hay from my hair. His clove scent, tinged with sweat, hay, and manure, lingers between us. "But I'm sorry if I came off acting like one on the slopes today. You're more than just a joke."

I raise an eyebrow. Did he tag an insult to the end of that apology?

He makes a face. "That came out wrong. Don't read into it."

Smothering a grin, I back away and scan the area. "You made a mess in here, you know."

"Merely following your lead."

My lips twitch. On a whim, I take the pitchfork from him and prop it against the wall. "C'mon, I want to show you something." I open the east entrance, and three reindeer stumble from the doorway, their faces steeped in guilt. Eavesdropping, huh? "I'm taking Niklas on a little excursion for a few minutes. If you want me to keep my job, you'll stay out of mischief while we're gone."

Minutes later, my footing confident and sure, I move along

basement hallways I hadn't known existed last week. Tonight, the lanterns glow brighter and the darkness shrinks away.

Niklas plucks at my sweater. "What are we doing down here?"

"You'll see."

"I haven't walked these hallways since I was a boy. We used to play hide and seek—" Niklas claps a hand on my shoulder and whirls me about. Suspicion narrows his eyes. "How do you know your way around here?"

I offer him an innocent smile then hurry on until we come to the correct door. "This is it."

His eyebrows lift.

"You don't recognize where we are?"

"I told you, I haven't been here since I was a little boy."

I hop to flick the key off the hook. "Then you're in for a surprise." Fitting the key into the lock, I give it a turn and push open the door. I move along the wall to flip on the light switch, then close the door once Niklas enters the room. He surveys our surroundings, everything the way the reindeer and I left it after we returned *Valiant*.

"Frankincense and myrrh, I do know this room." Niklas meanders off to the left and sifts through a pile of rusty tools I have yet to explore. "Pa brought me down here a few times once I turned six." He peeks beneath a canvas sheet at what I think is the wardrobe. "And then I refused to come anymore."

"Why?" I whisk aside the sheet covering the sleigh.

"Because Pa took me for a ride in—" Niklas turns, and his gaze freezes on the sleigh. "In that."

"So you've met *Valiant*." I run my hands over the elegant curve of the runner. "Isn't she a beauty? And you've flown in her, too. Wasn't it amazing?" I expel an excited breath. "And thrilling. And spectacular. And liberating."

"No. No, it wasn't amazing, or thrilling, or anything like that." Niklas cuts me a sharp look from the other side of the sleigh. "Why and how would *you* think it was?"

Aw, fruitcake. "Um. Uh. I meant..." I wince. My secret's out, for better or for worse. "You got me. I was the one who brought back the supplies from the ravine—"

"Yeah, I figured that out already."

"—and I used *Valiant* to do it."

He fists a hand in his hair. "You flew this sleigh? By yourself? Are you crazy?"

"The reindeer knew what they were doing. And I followed Butterscotch's instructions. It was fun."

"This ridiculous excuse for transportation"—Niklas gestures to the sleigh with his hands—"is not fun."

"Why are you acting like a wuss?" I hop in the sleigh and reach for the reins. "Flying it is beyond easy. If I can do it, you can do—"

Niklas yanks my arm. "Get down from there."

"Hey!" I stumble off the runner board and plow into his chest. He catches me by the elbows. It's on my tongue to rebuke him, but his ashen lips and blanched face kill the words unspoken. I clutch his forearms. "Niklas? What's the matter?"

"Nothing." He jerks away as though I've burned him. "It's getting late. We'd better head back upstairs."

"But don't you want to check out *Valiant*? You said it's been years since you rode in her. She was your great-great-grandfather's. That's decades of history pulsing through these wood grains—"

"Tinsel, stop!" He slashes a hand through the air. "I know her history, and I'm not interested."

I stomp my foot. "Why don't you take pride in your heritage? You have an amazing future ahead of you, yet all you think about is the next SnoMo race or creating some other excuse to goof off." I brush past him on my way to the door. "I can't believe Herr Referat is considering you for the managerial internship. You're nothing but a spoiled little Kringle who's—"

"Afraid to fly."

I trip to a halt and whirl about. "What?"

He stuffs his hands into his front pockets. "You heard me."

A laugh sputters from my lips. "You're lying." His expression darkens and I sober instantly. "You're not lying." I draw closer, peering into his face. "You're scared to fly? Like, *scared*-scared?"

"Tinsel." He growls, but I give him my exaggerated doe eyes, and a reluctant smile bends his mouth. He butts my shoulder with his. "Quit saying it out loud."

"If it makes you feel better, one of your reindeer doesn't like to fly, either."

"Not liking to fly and being afraid to fly are two different things."

"Does Meister Nico know?"

"No." Niklas scuffs the floor with his boot. "Pa brought me here to whet my appetite for flying, but after the second time, I kept making excuses so I wouldn't have to go again. After a while, he stopped asking. If he suspects something, he hasn't let on."

"Does Meister K know?"

"Frosted windowpanes, are you kidding?"

"What about Madam Marie?"

He shakes his head.

"Kristof?"

"I haven't told anybody. And you can't, either. If word leaked out, I'd lose everyone's respect." He kneads his neck and paces, giving the sleigh a wide berth. "Don't you see how ironic this is? A Santa Claus who's afraid to fly. When the time comes for me to take my place among the Saint Nicks who have gone before me, I won't be able to do it. And the Elder Council will give the position to Kristof."

I fiddle with my apron strings, tied in a bow at the front. "Would that be so bad? You don't always act like you want the yoke that comes with being Santa. You enjoy the privileges, but when it comes to taking responsibilities, you slough them off faster than the Grinch stole Christmas. You never spend time with the reindeer, you rarely apply yourself, you confuse the elves' names—"

"We've been over that. I know their names. I mess with them to have a little fun. And I've received straight A's since First Level, so how is that not applying myself?"

"You never tried for those A's."

Humor crinkles his eyes. "I can't help it if I'm a genius."

I cross my arms. "Explain the reindeer, then."

He gives me a look like *Duh!* "What do reindeer do best, Kuchler?"

"Fly."

"Exactly."

I shake my head. "*They* fly. They don't fly *you* around. Just because they possess a trait that makes you vomit doesn't give you the right to ignore them."

Niklas continues to pace, periodically kicking random objects in his path (hopefully not rare, priceless antiques). "I still have a hard time being around them. And being in here with that frost-bitten thing leering at me..." He jerks his head in *Valiant*'s direction then holds out his hands. They're trembling.

Seeing his vulnerability chips at the defenses inside me, and I cup his hands between my own before I talk myself out of it. "I'm sorry."

His gaze locks with mine, his eyebrows pinching together. "Whatever you may think about me, I do want to take my place as Santa Claus." He pulls away to run a hand through his hair. "As Santa, I have the unique privilege to point children to the true Light and Hope in this world. Whether I meet them on the street or on the slopes, the joy that floods their eyes gives me a rush not even racing can match. I see their fears scurry away, and for a few moments, faith has an opportunity to take root."

An animated glow infuses his expression, and my heart pounds. Do humility and passion make an attractive combo, or what?

Then Niklas looks at the sleigh and his face dims. "But how am I supposed to chase away their fears when I can't face my own?"

"You do everything else perfectly. Maybe this is an opportunity to lean on someone else's strength for once."

"I don't do everything perfectly. I make mistakes."

"Not like me."

"You're not Santa's scaredy-cat grandson."

I toss the canvas sheet over the sleigh as an idea shoots into my head. "How about in return for teaching me to dance, I help you overcome your fear of flying?"

"I'm teaching you to dance so you won't tell Grandpop about me and the reindeer."

"Oh. Right." I brush out the wrinkles, the canvas rough beneath my fingers. "Okay, how about I keep your fear a secret if you agree to some flying lessons?"

"You're enjoying this, aren't you?" Niklas's eyes narrow. "My one Achilles' heel and you waste no time exploiting it."

"We'll start small. For the first lesson, you'll simply sit in the sleigh. How 'bout that?"

"How about we outfit the SnoMo with turbo jet engines, and Santa can zoom along the ground delivering toys?"

I cock my hip with a hand at my waist. "And what are the reindeer supposed to do while you're out having all the fun?"

He flashes me that dimple. "We'll get them SnoMos, too."

ROMANCE IS VERBOTEN

On Sunday, Niklas greets me in the Workshop's lobby with the announcement he wants to put off both the dance and flying lessons until Monday. "We need a day of rest," he says.

"We had that yesterday." I remove my mittens. "And though you might not care about proficiency in flying, I need to excel in the Festival Dance."

"You don't need to excel. Just don't make a mistake."

"For this elf, that requires practice, so let's go." I pull him down the hallway to an available conference room.

"I hope you know a good doctor," he grumbles, "because today I'm introducing the part where I flip you."

At the close of the lesson, however, it's not a doctor I need after all those falls, it's a masseuse. But though my lesson is nothing to boast about, Niklas's flying lesson is one hundred percent laughable. The Kringle won't even put his foot in the sleigh. How does he expect to fly the thing if he refuses to get inside it?

Getting him to relax around *Valiant* weighs on my mind Monday morning as I muck the stalls. I'm about to vent my frustrations to the reindeer and seek their advice when I remember they're part of the problem. So, I keep silent and give them each a fat, juicy carrot and a scratch behind the ears before heading home for sustenance and a shower.

At ten-fifteen, I make my way back up the hill to meet Niklas at the Workshop.

I enter the lobby, breathing in the pine-scented air. The fluted strains of "O Holy Night" melt away the tension in my back, and the warmth of the stone fireplace envelopes me in a hug. My gaze flits over the decorations as I shrug off my coat with a smile. I was made for Christmas. All elves are made for Christmas, but *I* was made for *this*. The Workshop. And on Wednesday, I'll convince Herr Referat I'm the elf he wants for the internship.

Niklas stands near the gigantic Christmas tree, a trio of female elves beside him. He watches me, his lips hinting at a smile, and then an elf says something to reclaim his attention. He bobs his head at their chatter, his manner encouraging, and gestures between papers anchored to the clipboard in his hand and the mounds of presents under the tree. The number in Assembly still falls short of where it should be, but they're gaining ground. Thank goodness.

Draping my coat over my arm, I draw near as Niklas gives a parting word to the elves. He hands the clipboard to the nearest one with a...well, two days ago I would have said a patronizing pat on her head, but the elf beams at the extra attention. If she's cool with it, maybe I shouldn't give Niklas such a hard time.

He turns to me with that playful grin of his, and my step falters. There's something different about it today. About him. A softening around the edges I haven't noticed before. Or maybe it's the way the lights on the tree reflect in his irises that make his eyes more intense. I don't know. Something's afoot, because my stomach's gone squirrelly, the vein in my neck pulsates like a drum, and I can't get enough air in my lungs.

And I can't wrench my gaze from his.

"Hi," he says.

"Hi." Need. Air.

Niklas's grin widens. "Sorry for staring. You looked so peaceful when you walked in. Like you fit. Like you had come home. I don't know." He chuckles. "It sounds funny when I say it aloud, but..." He waves a hand in the air as though searching for the right words. "You made a picture befitting Currier and Ives. I was mesmerized."

My toes curl inside my boots. "Thanks."

Now that's a compliment you pocket away for later when you're alone and have time to examine it from all angles. And it's a compliment that makes you wonder if any sentiments were supposed to come along with it, but the giver decided to keep them to himself.

Not that I'm looking for sentiments. Not from Niklas, anyway. I don't think.

His gaze wanders over my face. I tug my scarf from around my neck. Did they add too many logs to the fire, or what? Finally, Niklas steps aside and motions toward a hallway. "You ready for another dance lesson?"

As soon as my hands stop sweating.

"It might be hard to find a room this morning." With his hand at my back, Niklas guides me past a closed door. "Many conferences are taking place now that we're eight days out from Christmas Eve." He inclines his head at a group of elves who pass us going the other direction. "Morning, Herr Decker, Herr Biermann, Frau Krüger."

The elves greet him with enthusiastic smiles that snap into frowns when they notice me. I lower my gaze.

"Do you think we'll meet quota?" I murmur as we walk past more elves whispering outside a closed conference door.

"Herr Trommler, Frau Fiedler, good to see you." Niklas waves. "Frau Wirtz, good morning." He guides me around the curve of the hallway. "Santa always meets quota. Herr Ziegler, Herr Nadel,

Frau Schneider," he greets three more elves with a nod before a large group hurries down the hall in our direction.

As they speed by, these elves lift their faces to Niklas and say individual renditions of "Hello," or "Good morning." Niklas responds to each by name, asking one elf in particular, "Is your husband feeling better today, Frau Kaufmann? Did the soup do the trick?" At her fervent nod, he gives a thumbs up. "Glad to hear it."

Once the tide passes, I peek at Niklas. Yep, there's a smirk on his face. I laugh. "Okay, point made."

He affects an innocent air. "I have no idea what you're talking about."

I link my arm through his and spin him around to double back the way we came. "You know the elves' names. I was wrong. I'm sorry. Now let's go to the stables."

"But we haven't practiced the dance yet."

"And we're not going to if we stick around here. As you predicted, all the rooms are being used. Let's..." I pull on his arm until he bends his head closer, and drop my voice. "Let's go to the storage room to practice. No one will bother us there, and we won't have to commute when it's time for your flying lessons."

He makes a face. "I can't dance with that sleigh staring at me the entire time."

"The sleigh is an inanimate object. It doesn't stare at anybody. Do you have any other suggestions?"

Niklas sighs. "No."

We weave our way through the crowd, and the barbed looks from my fellow elves prick me like needles. Frau Betriebs glares at my hand tucked in the crook of Niklas's elbow. I begin to withdraw it, but Niklas presses his arm against his side, trapping my wrist. I throw him a questioning glance.

He looks straight ahead. "My arm is cold. Your hand is warm. Leave it."

"The elves are watching," I whisper.

The dimple appears in his profile. "And jumping to all the wrong conclusions."

"Right. Your pedestal might start to wobble." I try to withdraw again.

Niklas captures my hand with his. "I said leave it. I can handle a few faulty judgments."

The warmth of his fingers travels up my arm on a path dangerously close to my heart. "Your reputation might be able to withstand some soiled gossip, but my rep's stained beyond repair." And I have no idea if another dirt smudge will blend in among its kind, or accentuate the flaws.

We agree to meet again on Tuesday, in the evening this time. Meister K has requested Niklas attend several meetings throughout the day, and my parents need my help at The Flaky Crust during the extended hours after dinner. Before you worry about my aptitude at the shop, let me reassure you I'm competent behind the register. I can also fill boxes with *Mutti's* chocolates and *Vati's* pastries sans disaster. Making the chocolates and pastries—now that's another story.

This Tuesday, however, though I'm physically present behind the shop's counter sitting on a tiny stool that brings me down to the customers' eye level, I'm mentally AWOL. The chocolates remind me of Gina (note to self: fill a box to give her at the Christmas party), and thoughts of Gina shift into thoughts of Logan. His Italian-esque face drifts before me, and my stomach clenches. He asked me on a date. Me. Tinsel Kuchler. I'm going on a date with Logan the next time I'm in Waldheim!

Oh, gingerbread. I'm going on a date.

I've never been on an official date before. How am I supposed to act? Never mind that. How *will* I act? Will I totally botch it and make a fool of myself? Cookie crumbs, what if he wants to go out dancing? And then what if I trip over my own two feet like I kept doing yesterday with Niklas during my dance lesson?

Okay, I didn't trip that many times. In fact, I'd say I'm getting the hang of the steps. As to what Niklas would say, that I don't know. He's acting peculiar. Or maybe I'm the one acting peculiar. I certainly felt peculiar when I was with him yesterday. Light-headed and dizzy. It had nothing to do with the spins we took around the room and everything to do with the way he held me while we spun. And the warmth in his gaze made it difficult to concentrate on the dance steps.

But I did it.

Now to do it again this evening without melting into a besotted slush puddle halfway through the lesson.

Wait. Wasn't I thinking about Logan?

"Tinsel!"

I snap to attention at the annoyed bark. Frau Betriebs drums her fingernails on the countertop, a box filled with chocolates clutched in her other hand. She purses her lips. "I'm waiting for my change."

"Oh. Of course." Two elves stand in line behind her. How long have I been daydreaming? I depress the metal button on the same register Great Oma Fay used to operate, and the cash drawer pops open with an obnoxious *ding*. I count out her change and hand it to her with a smile.

She snatches it from me. "You should be ashamed of yourself."

I blink. "Excuse me?"

"Carrying on with Meister Niklas as though you two are sweethearts. Don't try to deny it, Kandi," she adds to my mother, who has donned her mama bear mien and put a protective arm around my waist. "I saw them yesterday cavorting in the hallways at the Workshop. It's disgraceful. Tongues are wagging, mind you." She shakes her finger in my face. "You're no exception to the ancient edicts because of your height, missy."

"Will that be all, LuLu?" *Mutti* asks, her chin lifted.

Frau Betriebs puffs out her cheeks, her eyes narrowing. "You'll do well to keep your daughter in line."

"*Vielen dank* for your concern." *Mutti* pastes on a false smile. "Have a nice day."

Frau Betriebs leaves with her nose in the air, and *Mutti* squeezes my side. "Don't let her get to you," she murmurs for my ears alone. "She's jealous because Niklas doesn't look twice at Pix."

My fingers linger on the register buttons, their printed numbers worn away with use. "And why should he? Romance between elves and Kringles is *verboten*." I meet her gaze. "No exceptions."

Mutti taps me on the nose. "Oh, *mein Schatz,* there are always exceptions."

SO CLOSE

"Ow!" I rub my elbow and glare at Niklas from where I've landed on the concrete floor after my latest flip. "Go easy on me, wouldja?"

He gives a hapless shrug and helps me back to my feet. "I'm not trying to be difficult. You were better at this yesterday. What's going on?"

"Maybe if you didn't gawk at me, I wouldn't get flustered and mess up."

"You'll have more than two thousand pairs of eyes on you during the performance. I'm trying to get you used to the idea so you can ignore the attention and focus on the dance."

Ignore over two thousand pairs of eyes, maybe. Ignore *Niklas's* eyes? I'm beginning to wonder if I've ever succeeded in that endeavor. More like I deluded myself into believing I had, when all the while the truth quietly mocked me in the background.

Just as Frau Betriebs' words mock me in my head. *You're no exception to the ancient edicts. You're no exception to—*

Yes, I know, thanks.

Perhaps *she* wrote that note the other day. Though why would she care if I'm a disgrace to the Green Clan when she's from the red one?

"Let's try it again from the top." Niklas steers me into the proper position. His fingers curl around mine, their hold gentle yet steady. I bite my lip. His other hand slips along my waist. My mouth goes dry. His eyes invite me to step a little closer…

Romance between elves and Kringles is verboten.

Jingle bells, look at my feet! They certainly have improved at the grapevine. Where'd that scuff mark on my boot come from? Niklas wears his racing boots—

"Don't look down. Look at me."

"I can't. You're unnerving." *Valiant* looks bored. I should convince the Third String to take her out again. Maybe have them work on their landings. What are the chances Niklas might—

My gaze collides with his. Shards of emerald and cuts of crystal glint in his irises. Green always has been my favorite color. Mmm, such long lashes.

He winks.

I trip.

"Niklas!" I yank from his hold and spin away.

He laughs. "I couldn't help myself." He takes a step toward me, but I raise a hand to ward him off.

"I need a break." *From you.*

"Seven days, Kuchler. That's all you have before—"

"I know, I know. We'll practice some more." My gaze lights on the sleigh again. "Right now, it's time for your flying lesson." Although thus far, they've been more like arguing-about-getting-into-the-sleigh lessons.

His head drops back. "Argh!"

"At least you're not twitching anymore, being in the same room with this thing." I climb aboard *Valiant* and sit, grateful for some space between us. "That's an accomplishment compared to where you were on Saturday."

Niklas sticks his thumbs behind the suspenders of his *lederhosen* and pouts.

I spread my arms along the top of the backrest, my hands playing with the soft velvet, back and forth, back and forth. Straight ahead, the secret door masquerading as a wall separates us from the deep twilight outside.

With my boot, I toe the reins where they lay on the carriage floor. Then I bend over, grab a length, and rub my fingers against the crusty, aged leather. I bring it to my nose and inhale its mahogany tones. Another spin in the sky is a must. "Niklas?"

"Hmm?" He sidesteps closer and taps the hull with an index finger.

"Have you ever known me to fly a sleigh before last week?"

His mouth pulls down as he studies *Valiant's* molding. "You've never even flown a model airplane. Why?"

I flick the reins. "Considering all the things I've botched over the years, don't you think it's bizarre that the one time I fly this thing, I do it without messing up?"

"You said you followed the reindeer's instructions."

I snort. "Following instructions has never been my weakness, yet I screw up nonetheless." I stand and imagine the reindeer before me, pawing the ground, anxious to be off. "On Chocolate, on Cocoa, on Eggnog, on Chip. On Butterscotch, Licorice, Cinnamon, and…Peppermint." I laugh. "Doesn't have the same ring to it, does it?"

Niklas's gaze wanders over me. "You look good up there."

I drop the reins. "Oh, no you don't. This is your post. C'mon, Kringle, it's time." Reaching for his arm, I give a tug. He doesn't budge. "We've been at this for three days now and you have yet to get your butt in the sleigh." I heave again. Nothing. "You're safe, Niklas. We're on the ground, we're not going anywhere. The reindeer aren't even here. It's harmless." Using both hands, I grip his wrist and forearm and *p-u-u-u-ll.*

Niklas pulls back.

Bracing my feet against the sleigh's inside wall, I give a ferocious yank, and Niklas stumbles through the opening. He crashes into me, and together we plow into the seat cushion where I end up squashed beneath him, laughing.

"See? That wasn't so bad." I lift my head. My smile falters at his nearness. There's that freckle beneath his right eye. His pupils dilate as he holds my gaze for five heartbeats (I count each pound of my heart against his chest), and I inhale a lungful of…mmm, cinnamon and spice this time.

His gaze wanders to my lips. "I know something that will make it better."

Romance is verboten. Why is that, again? Niklas lowers his head, his eyelids drifting closed. He's about to kiss me—

He blinks, his mouth tightens, and he backs away to a sitting position, the velvet cushion rasping beneath him. "Some emails."

I scramble to sit up. "Emails?" My voice squeaks and I clear my throat. What happened to that almost-kiss? Frau Betriebs laughs in my mind's eye, and I want to kick her.

"From Gina. And Logan."

Oh. Right. Logan. The guy Niklas thinks I'm crushing on. The guy with whom I've accepted a date.

Niklas withdraws two folded sheets of paper from his pocket and holds them out to me. "Gina addressed her email to us both, so I already know what it says."

I scan the contents, a cut-and-paste of several emails from the last two days. In the first, Gina shares some ideas for the Christmas party. I read farther on, then smile at Niklas. "She's wondering if I can join her Friday for a girls' night out. How cool is that?"

Niklas arches an eyebrow.

My hopes dash to the floor. "Of course, I'll have to decline." I smooth a hand over the printed words. Mustn't forget there's to be no fraternizing with the humans.

When I come to Logan's emails, I fidget on the seat. Best to read these when Niklas isn't around. I fold the papers in half and then in half again. "Can I keep these?"

Niklas nods, the muscles in his jaw jumping like popcorn, and I tuck the papers in the pocket of my *dirndl*. Then I clasp my hands together and press them between my knees. An awkward silence settles over us. The keen awareness that ran beneath the surface of our earlier banter dissipated when Niklas mentioned the emails. I should be grateful.

I don't feel grateful.

When I can't take it anymore, I stand up. "Congratulations!"

"For what?"

I exit the sleigh. "You've sat in *Valiant* for several minutes without freaking out. That's excellent progress." I grab the canvas covering, and Niklas helps me spread it over the sleigh. "Tomorrow I'll give you an overview on the tethering system."

"Tomorrow? Couldn't I just sit again?" He meets my look of *Seriously?* over the canvas. "Hey, it took tremendous guts for me not to bail." His brow wrinkles with pleading.

Pursing my lips, I give the canvas one last pat. "Fine. You can sit." Relief loosens his features, and I grin. "What time do you want to meet?"

"Right after Frau Tanz's dance practice. I'm needed in more meetings tomorrow afternoon." He kicks at the doorjamb as we leave the room. "Frosted meetings. My SnoMo feels neglected. It's been days since I escaped into the woods."

"Poor Niklas must work instead of play." I lock the door behind us, then pass him the key.

He returns it to its hook, his forehead puckering again. "I think Grandpop has something up his sleeve, but I'm at a loss as to what it could be."

We travel through the murky hallways, tossing ideas back and forth about Meister K's plans, each one kookier than the last. After I bid the reindeer goodnight, we bundle into our coats and emerge from the stables. Fat snowflakes fall in a white cloud as I toss a knitted scarf about my neck.

Niklas sputters beside me. "Watch where you fling that thing."

"You wouldn't get pelted if you didn't stand so close."

He flicks a tasseled end of the scarf. "May I give you a ride home?"

"Tonight"—I blink away the snowflakes collecting on my eyelashes—"that would be lovely."

With a grin, he stashes my snowshoes in the rack of his SnoMo. "You know, your scarf reminds me of the knitting class we took in Eighth Level."

I groan, tying a loose knot beneath my chin. "That class was torture. I tried to make a simple dishcloth, but it came out with a ragged hole in the middle."

"It made the perfect poncho for my Han Solo doll." Niklas takes a seat on his SnoMo.

I cock my head. "What?"

"You threw the dishcloth away after Frau Häkeln graded it, but I didn't think it looked too bad, so I fished it out and used it for Han. One of Great-Grandpop's masterpieces, that action figure. And for the past five years, mine has worn a one-of-a-kind poncho."

"Wait a minute." I press my fingertips against my temples and squeeze my eyes shut, replaying our recent conversations. "You used my dishcloth for a poncho, my petrified cookies for chew toys, my rock-hard fruitcake for a door stopper, and who knows what else I have yet to discover."

He shrugs. "Yeah. So?"

"So not only do you keep bringing up my mistakes, but you rub it in that you're able to fix my messes. Mr. Perfect has the solution for every blunder I make. Next, you're going to tell me how you've solved the problem of meeting quota by Christmas Eve."

"My point isn't to gloat. It's to encourage you to think outside the box."

Tears press behind my eyes. "I don't remember you telling our teachers to think outside the box every time they announced I had failed at something. You know what I do remember?" I hug my arms to myself as the wind increases. "More than the ribbing that followed once the dismissal bell rang; more than the name-calling; more than the put-downs, I remember *you,* ringed by your fan club, instigating the jokes and insults."

His eyes close briefly and a line forms between his eyebrows. "Tinsel." His tortured gaze finds mine. "Our classmates expected me to. I had to go along with them because someday I'm going to be their boss. I need their respect."

"You don't earn respect by stripping it from someone else." Ducking my head to hide the well of tears, I yank my snowshoes from his luggage rack and shove my feet into their bindings. "Forget the ride. I'll see myself home."

I'M SORRY

When I walk to the stables Wednesday morning, I'm still hurt from Niklas and annoyed with myself for getting emotional. To cry means I care about what he thinks. I don't want to care.

Romance between elves and—

I kick a mound of snow outside the Lower Stables, and my toes encounter several logs buried beneath the crystalized blanket. Screaming into my mittens, I hop around a few minutes before limping inside. "Can this day get any worse?"

"Considerin' it's just begun and 'tis you we're talkin' abou'"—Chip yawns as I switch on the lights—"I'd say the odds are stacked against ye."

I put a hand to my ear. "I'm sorry, what was that? You don't want a carrot this morning? You want Peppermint to have it?" With my hat, I give Chip a light swat on his snout and grin. "How very generous." Scratching him under the chin, I turn to the others. "Morning, everyone. I hear you have a big test during your flight lessons today."

Eggnog tosses his head and backs into the rear wall of his stall.

"Hey, no need to be nervous." I fish an apple from my stash of treats in the corner and offer it to Eggnog. "I've seen you practice. You know the drills." Even if he doesn't execute them accurately. "You'll do fine."

"I prefer all four o' me hooves on the ground." He sniffs the apple then lips it into his mouth.

"Contrary to what you've been told, it's not the end of the world if you don't make it as a Big Eight. If you run as fast as Chocolate claims, I'm sure Meister K could find another place for you outside the FTA."

His light brown gaze cuts to mine. "A reindeer who disna fly is like an elf without a talent. How's that workin' fer ye so far?"

Hours later, coat and sweater draped over my arm, I make my way to the storage room. Eggnog's words drum inside my head. For the love of gingerbread, I was trying to encourage him. He didn't have to flip my logic back on me.

Could I be content without a talent? Doing something, working someplace, other than where I've planned?

Puh-*lease*.

Well…maybe?

I can't think about this right now. Niklas waits for me in the hallway, and who knows which personality I'm going to encounter today. The arrogant one I've known for years, or the more considerate one I've recently glimpsed.

Which one is the true Niklas?

But he doesn't wait in the hallway. Entering the storage room, I find him standing by the wardrobe, its canvas sheet pooled at its base, its mirrored door propped open. Thick folds of burgundy fabric drape across his arms. I draw near, realizing he holds a fur-lined coat as a putrid stench hits my nose. "Silent night!" I press my coat and sweater against my nose. "What is that smell?"

Niklas glances at me with a crooked smile and gestures at the half-dozen or so old coats hanging in the wardrobe. "How many years do you think they've been locked away in here, discarded and forgotten?"

I run my hand over the coat he holds. Rabbit fur. "Who do they belong to?"

"They're part of my heritage. Coats from previous Santas. This one is Great-Grandpop's. Someday mine will hang here, too. Nothing but a memory."

With my free arm, I shift through the coats inside the wardrobe. Some are a dark green in color, others are burgundy. All are trimmed in what used to be white fur, yellowed with time and use. "These are amazing. Smelly, but amazing." My fingers glide along the pelt. "Someone should hang them in the lobby where everyone can admire them and remember our roots."

His face brightens. "Good idea. I'll mention that to Grandpop this afternoon." With reverent hands, he tucks the coat back among the others.

My conscience pricks. "I'm sorry I accused you of not caring about your family history. Just because I've known you since we were five—"

"Four."

"—*four,* doesn't mean I know everything about you." Something winks in his hair as he closes the wardrobe, and I reach to pluck it out. "Case in point. Are you going for a new look or is there a reason you have tinsel in your hair?"

Niklas makes a face. "My mom's gone loopy. In a last-minute decorating frenzy this morning, she draped tinsel all over the tree in the living room *and* the garland above the windows." He brushes a hand back and forth over his hair to dislodge any other stray pieces. "It's the most annoying stuff in the world."

My smile fades. "Yes, you've said that." Pinching the "annoying stuff" between my fingers, I turn toward the sleigh.

"Listen, about last night…" Niklas begins.

"Mmm, last night." I climb into the sleigh and take a seat, tossing my coat and sweater onto the cushion beside me. "Not one of my fonder memories."

"I don't imagine I'm in many of those."

"You're not."

"And I probably owe you an apology or two." He props his arms atop the sleigh on either side of the opening, eyes twinkling. "Or three."

"Probably." I roll the tinsel into a tiny ball between my fingers. "But you needn't bother. An empty apology is worse than no apology. Let's get these lessons over with. The sooner we finish, the sooner we can go our merry ways, and you can be rid of this annoyance for the day."

Niklas gives me a funny look. "Did I miss something? What did I say that has you on edge now?"

"It's not what you said so much as what you implied. Though when it comes to how you feel about *Tinsel*"—I flick the ball of metallic string at his face—"you never beat around the Christmas tree."

"Wow. What makes you think I've ever thought of tinsel-tinsel and you-Tinsel as being one and the same?"

I clench my hands in my lap. "You made it clear the day you introduced me to Logan."

His eyebrows shoot up. "I wasn't talking about you. I was talking about"—with a grimace, he digs inside his shirt collar and pulls out two more strands of tinsel—"this! This incredibly aggravating stuff people call decoration."

"It didn't sound that way from where I was standing."

"You were holding hands with Logan."

"We were shaking hands."

"Longer than necessary." Taking a deep breath, Niklas hops into the sleigh and sits facing me. He braces one hand on the back of the seat as his gaze searches mine, probing, seeking some answer to a question I don't know yet. Then he exhales and rubs a hand along his thigh. "Look, I need to apologize. What you said last night, you were right. In craving the elves' admiration, I've let their opinions influence how I treated you over the years. In seeking their praise, I took cheap shots at you and scored most times."

Hesitantly, he brushes his fingers along my knuckles, then hooks a finger around my pinky and tugs my hand across the seat cushion toward him. "I'll admit there are times I enjoy it up on that pedestal you've mentioned, but in staying there, I've sacrificed our friendship." He turns my hand over and coaxes my fingers open. Electric sprays shoot up my arm. "And that's years of a beautiful thing I've lost out on. I'm sorry, Tinsel. Please forgive me."

My insides swirl like a shaken-up snow globe. I shouldn't read anything romantic in his touch, but then, why touch me at all? I clear my throat as he plays with my fingers, his skin gliding against mine. "Since you can be Kringle enough to admit all that, I can be elf enough to admit I haven't treated you any better. And I'm sorry for constantly jumping to the wrong conclusions." I force myself to draw my hand away. "But don't change too much, or I won't know how to handle you anymore."

"Then, I'm forgiven?"

"You're forgiven." I rub my bare arms. "Nice job getting into the sleigh, by the way. I didn't even have to beg this time."

A slow smile moves across his mouth. "There's this cute elf I know, and she once told me that without the reindeer's help, the sleigh's not going anywhere, so what's the harm in sitting in it?"

I snort. "Laying it on kinda thick, aren't y—" I straighten, my ears tuning into noises coming from the hallway. "Do you hear that?" Tilting my head, I hold my breath. Footsteps. Whistling.

"Hear what?"

I roll my eyes. "Never mind. I forgot which one of us has the better ears."

Niklas smirks. "Do you mean better performing or better looking? Because if we're talking better look—"

I cover my hand over his mouth in time to hear keys jangle. The footsteps and whistling grow louder. "Someone's coming." Niklas's brow furrows, and I let out an exasperated huff. "Someone's coming down the hall. He...she...they could be headed for this room." And the door's ajar. I jump from the sleigh. "I don't know if we're actually allowed to be in here, but if we're not and someone catches us—"

"Great gobs of snow." Niklas scans the room and motions to the wardrobe. "Quick, in there."

SWEET NOTHING

Niklas opens the wardrobe door, and the stench assaults us. Muffling a cough, he pushes the coats to either side, and I scramble into the narrow space he created. He squeezes in after me, facing me, and pulls the door closed as best he can from the inside. A sliver of light filters through the crack outlining the door.

I wish I'd thought to snag my sweater from the sleigh. Then I could've buried my nose in it.

Niklas coughs again. "I should have left this door open to air out the coats. It reeks like something died in here." His breath ruffles the hair at my temple, tickling my skin. My stomach flips at his proximity. "Except for your hair."

The air stalls in my lungs.

He bends forward slightly, his chest expanding. "Is that coconut and vanilla?"

"My shampoo." Like a lens pulling everything into focus, my senses heighten, and the wardrobe's tight confines take on a new and titillating quality. Niklas stands close enough, we might as well be hugging. Today he smells of honey and sandalwood, and I forget about the pungent fur coats. He releases a shaky breath, its warmth caressing my skin, and I fist my hands in my *dirndl* skirt so I don't do something insane like reach out to him.

Someone pounds on the door to the storage room, and I jump. Niklas lays a hand on my arm with a finger to his lips. Perhaps he means to calm me, but his touch on my skin has the opposite effect.

"Anybody in here?" comes a gruff voice. The door hinges squeak, and several footfalls enter the room.

"I don't see anyone," a second voice says.

"The door was open and the lights are on. Someone's been here recently."

"Hey! The sleigh's uncovered. Who's been fiddling with Santa's—"

Niklas's fingers skim down my forearm. Every one of my nerve endings sizzle in hysteria. The narrow ribbon of light bathes one half of Niklas's face, emphasizing its angles and planes, reflecting in his pale irises. His fingers reverse direction.

I lick my lips and whisper, "Niklas."

"Tinsel."

"What are you doing?"

"Setting myself up for another Penalty. And it's going to be totally worth it." His hands slide around my waist.

I swallow. Speaking so low I'm almost mouthing the words, I ask, "There's a Penalty for hiding in a wardrobe?"

"The wardrobe has nothing to do with it." He draws me closer, his heart beating a rapid rhythm against my chest.

One of the elves smacks the side of the wardrobe. "Do you think we should try to cover this up?"

I freeze, eyes wide. Niklas grins.

"Are you kidding?" The other elf sounds familiar. And grumpy. "We'd need a ladder to do that. I'll have to report it to Meister K."

Niklas leans in, the scruff on his jaw tickling my cheek.

"Come help me cover the sleigh as best we can," the elf

continues. "Then we'll make sure nobody's tampered with anything else and get back to the Workshop."

Their footsteps move away.

Niklas's lips brush my ear. "Remember that kiss we were supposed to forget about?"

My eyelids flutter. "The one that horrified you outside the Huggamugg Café? Don't know what you're talking about."

His cheek moves alongside mine until our noses touch. "The kiss didn't horrify me, Tinsel. I was horrified you had guessed how much I liked you."

"Mmm, I can see where that would be a detriment. After all, romance between elves and Kringles is *verboten*."

His fingers tighten at my back. "But you're not entirely an elf, are you?"

The mush inside me congeals. Roasted chestnuts, not those words again. I push against his chest. "So you often like to remind me."

"Tinsel." He grips my hands, holding them still. The ribbon of light plays over his taut features. "That wasn't an insult. I thought you weren't going to jump to the wrong conclusions anymore."

"I apologized for it. I didn't say it would never happen again." It's a struggle to keep to a whisper. "What do you expect? You've conditioned me over the years to read insults into your comments. Yeah, you said you're sorry, but that doesn't rewrite the past." I twist my hands, trying to pull away. "Don't think I'm gonna let you mess with me after—"

"I'm not messing with you." His fingers squeeze mine. "I'm thankful for the twelve-and-a-half percent of you that's human."

I stop struggling. "But…why?"

He shrugs a shoulder. "It's the part that made you tall."

"You're thankful I'm tall?" The one thing that sets me apart from my clan.

"Well…" His gaze drops to my mouth, and the pad of his

thumb grazes my lips. "Kissing you is easier when I don't have to bend over quite so far."

"Oh."

His fingers move along my jaw to trace the curve of my earlobe. "The ancient edict about elves and Kringles had nothing to do with my reaction that day in Waldheim. I wasn't ready to expose my feelings, and I didn't know if you liked me in return."

"I didn't want to like you. Does that count?"

Niklas lifts my hand to press his lips against my fingers. "You said my delivery on that kiss needed work. Will you give me a second chance to get it right?"

I'm melting like a snowman in July, yet I hesitate. Dare I trust him? Do I believe he cares about me? If he speaks the truth, then he certainly excelled in hiding his feelings. But why confess them now?

And if he's lying, what will he gain?

My brain is a muddled mess. Hard to think rationally when his hands trail down my sides to slip around my waist again.

I pluck at his suspenders...and then choose to trust. "The only problem with the other kiss was its length. It ended too soon."

In the fractured light, Niklas's teeth flash white in a smile. "That I can fix." Dipping his head, he molds his lips to mine.

The kiss starts out sweet and tentative; innocent, like *Vati's* plain peasant rolls. I reach up and thread my fingers through the hair at the nape of his neck, the waves indeed as silky to the touch as they look. With a soft moan, Niklas crushes me against him, and the kiss grows bolder and heady, like *Mutti's* succulent, chocolate covered cherries. He kneads the muscles in my lower back as new emotions unfurl within me. A dizzying awareness permeates my body like heat from the sun.

Niklas likes me. The idea is intoxicating.

We ease apart, our breath mingling in the narrow space between, our hearts thwacking. Niklas rests his forehead against mine with a ragged exhale. "How'd I do?" He wraps a lock of my hair around his finger and gives it a playful tug. "I'm game for another round if my timing's still off."

"Your timing is atrocious," I whisper with a quivering smile. "Another round is a must."

Emitting a throaty laugh, he angles in for another kiss. "I knew you didn't like Logan."

His smug tone chills me faster than Jack Frost freezes water, and I pull back within the circle of his arms. "What did you say?"

Something scrapes against the wardrobe, and light bursts into our hideaway as the door swings open. "Ah *ha*!"

I yelp and shove Niklas into the fur coats. An elf stands outside the wardrobe, his finger pointing at our knees. Then his gaze travels up and up, and his jaw drops like a broken nutcracker. "Wha…?"

My face flames, likely mirroring the elf's scarlet cheeks. He manages several awkward bows. "M-m-meister Niklas. It's a pleasure to see you, sir." He glances in my direction. "Y-you, too, Tinsel."

"What's going on?" A second elf stomps over to the wardrobe, my sweater in one hand, my coat and accessories in the other. He stumbles when he sees us. "Meister Niklas? Tinsel?"

"Herr Geier," Niklas says with a calm I don't feel.

The COE gestures wildly with my things. "What are you… How are you… What in the winter wonderland are you two doing in this room?" Our faces must betray some guilt, for his eyes sharpen with suspicion. "What were you two doing in *there*?"

Niklas draws a finger over his bottom lip. "You want the long or short version?"

Red creeps up Herr Geier's neck. "Well, I…! Of course n—Would you please…" He lets out a huff and flails some more. "Get down from there." We clamber from the wardrobe, and he scrutinizes us in silence as we brush fur from our clothes. He thrusts my things at me. "These yours?"

"Yes." I grab them and hold them against my chest.

His lips compress in a tight line. "It's fortunate we found you when we did, Meister Niklas." He slaps the wardrobe door closed and crosses his arms. "They've been looking for you at the Workshop for quite a while now. Something about the arrival of your betrothed and your future father-in-law."

His what?

Hands fisting around my clothes, I turn on Niklas. "Your *betrothed*?"

His face blanches, incriminating him without words. "Tinsel—"

"You *are* engaged. You frostbitten liar!"

Eight years' worth of anger tunnels through my arms and I strike out, shoving him so hard he stumbles backward into the wardrobe and busts through the mirrored door with a sickening *crack*. His momentum rocks the antique, and the whole thing tips over in a resounding cacophony of splintering wood and shattering glass. Niklas ends up on his backside amid the mess as the elves flap about like discombobulated chickens.

This has "Penalty" scribbled all over it in jumbo-sized lettering, but this is one Penalty I'll gladly welcome. Clutching my winter gear, I bolt from the room.

"No, Tinsel. Wait!"

But I don't. I run.

I run through the hallways, run up the stairs, run from the Lower Stables. I run heedless of the ache in my leg and the burning in my lungs and the cold biting my exposed arms. I run to flee Niklas and thoughts of his future wife, the elves and their disapproval, my Penalty, my genetics, my incompetence, my humiliation.

I don't stop running until I slam my bedroom door behind me and collapse onto my bed in an avalanche of tears.

BLIND-SIDED

In thirty-five minutes, I'm supposed to bring out my game face and wow Herr Referat during my managerial interview. Unless Meister K summons me to his office first to talk about the wardrobe debacle.

Hollow eyes and stony features stare back from my reflection in the mirror. Not the best appearance to instill someone's faith in me, but it's better than the red-rimmed eyes and blotchy skin from an hour ago.

That's when my tears dried up. My heart must have dried up along with them, because I don't care about anything right now. I don't care if I get the internship, if I ever find my talent, if I perform in the Festival Dance and graduate, or if I get another Penalty.

I don't care.

And I care even less about Niklas.

Because Niklas never cared a fig about me.

Then why did he kiss me? Good question. I've had a few hours to come up with a reason, and I believe I've nailed it. Niklas had to kiss me. He couldn't stand the thought he did something (in this case, the original, random kiss) that failed to reach the level of perfection he's accustomed to, so he had to try again.

Plus, he needed to prove he was more of a man than Logan. It didn't matter he had a fiancée on the side. His ego couldn't accept that the one elf who never fawned over Santa's grandson would find an average guy like Logan attractive. So, he did what most egotistical males do. He turned on the charm, fed every hungry hole in my heart, and…well, you saw what happened.

Not only did he redeem his first kiss, but he also won the prize (my affection), further suggesting Logan lost.

But in the end, Niklas won't win. I'll make sure of that.

One little leak about his fear of flying should do it.

I rub my fingers over my breastbone. Odd how my emotions have died, yet my heart still beats.

A knock sounds on my door. "Tinsel?"

My brow knits together at Chorley's voice. I open the door a crack. "Yes?"

He fiddles with a piece of paper. "Um, Mash and Tinder… well, all of us, actually, were messing around in your room the other day. And I found this." He holds out the paper. That ugly note someone left for me before my trip to Waldheim. "Do you know who wrote it?"

I shake my head, slipping the note into my skirt pocket.

"Oh. That's too bad. I would have beat him up for you. Or her, if it's a her."

I raise my eyebrows at this uncharacteristic display of brotherly protection, and Chorley's ears turn red. He rubs his foot along one pant leg. "Anyway, I just want to say whoever wrote this is in the wrong. And I hope you kick *lederhosen*-butt at the interview."

"Thank you," I whisper.

"Tinsel?" *Mutti* calls from another room. "*Alles in Ordnung, Liebling?* You've been in there for hours."

I check my reflection one last time—freshly pressed forest-green *dirndl,* white blouse, favorite striped stockings, semi-tamed hair—then cross the apartment to find my mother in the kitchenette. I give her a well-practiced smile. "I'm fine." Today, I'm grateful for our difference in height as it prevents her from studying my face too closely.

"Doesn't your interview start soon? Have something to eat before you go."

Shaking my head, I stuff my feet into my boots. "I don't have time. I need to find my snowshoes and—"

"Snowshoes? Let your father give you a ride." *Mutti's* hopeful gaze beseeches mine. "Save your energy for the interview, *ja?*"

I open my mouth to refuse—I crave solitude, not the squished confines of an elf-sized SnoMo—but then realize how much longer trekking uphill will take me versus flying up on a snowmobile. More minutes equal more opportunities to intercept other elves. Elves who might have already heard about my destruction in the storage room, or heard Niklas boast how he fooled me into kissing him. Into falling for him.

(A momentary defeat, that last one, I promise.)

I fold myself onto a stool and pick at the snack *Mutti* lays out for me until it's time to leave with *Vati.*

I FINGER A GLISTENING ORNAMENT ON THE TOWERING TREE IN THE Workshop lobby, waiting for Frau Bericht to return and bring me to Herr Referat's office. My stomach's in knots, and I rehearse my answers to the questions I hope he'll ask.

"Tinsel Kuchler."

The cutting tone makes me jump, and I turn around. "Frau Betriebs. May I help you?"

She straightens to her full height and raises her chin. "You are to follow me, please. Herr Geier would like a moment of your time."

"But Herr Referat—"

"Knows about the change in plans."

I frown. "Then I'll interview with him after meeting with Herr Geier?"

She tugs at the hem of her burgundy jacket. "Don't fret about the interview. Now, come with me."

Twisting an apron string around my finger, I follow Frau Betriebs up a flight of stairs. Why does he want to see me? To reprimand me for smashing the wardrobe? We travel along an empty hallway to a secluded conference room, where she raps twice on the door, pauses, and raps thrice more.

Like a code. My senses heighten.

The door opens from the inside, and I duck through the doorway to find the other nine members of the Elder Council seated around a conference table. At its head on the far side sits Herr Geier. Herr Chemie sits at his right. Frau Betriebs closes the door behind me and takes her place among the others. With all ten members present, they fix their gazes on me.

My hands clench at my sides. "What's going on?"

Herr Geier stands and cranes his head back so he's peering down his nose at me. "I'll be blunt, Miss Kuchler, as we'd rather not dally over such unsavory business. We might have been able to look past your height, but no longer can we turn a blind eye to this folly."

Uh-oh. "Folly, sir?"

He paces by his chair, hands clasped behind his back. "At almost eighteen years of age, you show more promise for creating disasters than you do in honing a useful talent. In the last twelve days alone, you have destroyed hundreds of Christmas gifts, a SnoMo packed with supplies, and a priceless, irreplaceable wardrobe." My heart thwacks against my ribcage as he drones on. "But the candy that broke the reindeer's back is what went on *inside* the wardrobe. Tell me, Miss Kuchler, what part of 'romance between elves and Kringles is *verboten*' do you not understand?"

Murmurs ripple through the room, and a tingling sensation sweeps across my face.

"You are a disgrace to the Elfin race and a danger to our society. Not even your great grandmother shamed our kind as you have." Each word shooting from Herr Geier's mouth strikes me like the blow of a hammer. "Disrespecting property, ignoring authority, defying ancient edicts. You've put Christmas in jeopardy for the entire world. Since the inception of Santa Claus, this is the first year we might not make quota, risking the happiness of thousands of children on Christmas morning.

"We've been patient, but the time has come to act." He motions around the table, and I hide my trembling hands in the crooks of my elbows. "The Elder Council has spoken with Meister Kringle, and we agree Penalties no longer suffice." He raises his chin. "Tinsel Kuchler, you are hereby banished from Flitterndorf."

My head snaps back as though I've been slapped. "Meister K's never banished an elf before."

"Ah, but then, there's never been an elf quite like you, has there?"

"I don't believe it." My voice trembles, and I press a hand to my churning stomach. "I want to speak with Meister K."

"He's the one who approved this decision." Herr Geier nods to Herr Chemie, who hands me a document with the Kringle seal at the bottom. Meister K's signature is scrawled beside it. I recognize his telltale loops and flourishes from my many Penalty contracts he's signed over the years. At the top, "Banishment" treks across the page in large, block letters, followed by paragraphs of legal jargon specifying the terms of the elf going into exile.

Me.

Bile rises in my throat as pinpricks of light dance in my

peripheral vision. "There must be something I can do. Some promise I can make."

Herr Geier scoffs. "The only thing you can do is choose what the rumor mill churns out. If you proceed quietly and obediently, we will spread the word that you *chose* to leave, thereby sparing your family the shame of your banishment. Raise a ruckus and who knows how this will reflect on your family." He steeples his fingers. "The other elves might look upon them differently. Their business at The Flaky Crust could suffer, maybe to the point they'd have to close their beloved shop. You wouldn't want them mucking reindeer stalls for the sake of a job, would you?"

My throat convulses and my vision blurs.

Planting his fists on the table, Herr Geier leans forward. "Think carefully, Miss Kuchler. Generations from now, when little elves listen to tales of 'The Colossal, Bumbling Elf,' which version would you like them to hear?"

Either way, I lose.

No more family. No more Third String. No future COE.

A tear rolls down my cheek and under my chin. Frau Betriebs was right. I didn't need to fret about my interview, after all.

GONE

My parents' excited smiles falter when I trudge into the bakery's kitchen. No doubt my face looks blotchy again. *Mutti* abandons her chocolate shells at one end of the huge table and rushes over. *Vati* stalls mid-roll on his dough.

"*Schatz, was ist los?* Tell me what's the matter." She leads me to a stool and tugs on my hands. I sit. "Did something happen in the interview?"

My gaze lowers to the worn tabletop. "I didn't ha—" I shake my head and whisper, "I didn't get the internship."

"Oh, *mein Liebling*. My love. I'm so sorry." Pressing her lips together, she turns toward the warm milk on the stove.

I cover my face with my hands. "*Nein, Mutti.* A Kandi Cup can't help me now. It's over. It's done." I hiccup through my tears. "I have to leave."

"Don't retreat to your room yet." *Mutti* picks up her tube of orange filling. "There will be—"

"I have to leave *Flitterndorf*."

Silence follows my statement, then the table vibrates as *Vati* resumes rolling out the dough with a *harrumph*. "That's nonsense. Why, your great Oma Fay—"

I slam my hands on the tabletop, and my parents jump. "I do *not* want to talk about her. *She's* the reason I have to go, the reason I'm tall and can't…can't…" My fingers curl like claws.

"Your height does not define you," *Vati* says.

"How about lack of talent? My penchant for disasters?"

He shakes the rolling pin in my direction. "You are fearfully and wonderfully made, Tinsel. Who you are, how you are, is not an accident. You have purpose. You have worth."

Someone tell that to the Elder Council. "I've lived my entire life trying to please everyone. Trying to figure out where I fit in. Trying to make myself smaller in order to do it. Because I believed that one day I'd make it to COE and prove…" My throat clogs, and I let the sentence die with a swallow. "But what purpose does a mint have among chocolates? If I can't find my value here, what am I left to conclude but that I must look beyond Flitterndorf?"

Mutti blinks rapidly, her cheeks flushed. "Surely you can stay until after Christmas."

"No. I've already put Christmas in jeopardy. Give me a few more days and I might do something to destroy it completely."

"Figgy pudding." *Vati* scowls as he spreads raspberry jam on the dough. "Have you been listening to LuLu Betriebs again?"

As a matter of fact…

"Where will you go?" *Mutti* asks. "When will we see you again?"

"I know some people in Waldheim. Maybe I can stay with them until I get my bearings." I stand and turn toward the back door. "If you'll excuse me, I'm going to pack."

Mutti gasps. "You're leaving now?"

"Herr Geier has been kind enough to offer me a ride." To ensure I leave quietly, obediently, and ASAP. "He'll be here in half an hour." I won't get to say goodbye to the Third String.

Will my heart ever stop hurting?

Vati's knife clatters to the table. "Tinsel, this is rather hasty.

Why don't you sleep on it tonight and talk it over with Meister K tomorrow, *ja?* 'Crying may last for a night, but joy comes in the morning.' I'm sure he—"

"I promise you, Meister K supports this decision."

As I duck under the crossbeam, *Mutti's* forlorn words echo in the kitchen. "You said you'd never leave."

VATI TRIES TO TALK HERR GEIER OUT OF ESCORTING ME TO Waldheim, but the COE comes prepared for my parents' concerns and makes the situation sound like a grand adventure. He ensures they will hear from me often and is himself excited about all the things I'll do and see. "We must support her in this endeavor," he says again and again. "This is, after all, her choice."

Sure it is, because if I don't leave willingly, I get kicked out anyway, and some elf stamps "Exiled" next to my name in the Elfin Book of Births and Deaths. To the forever-shame of my family.

In the end, their faces grave and questioning, my parents relent and send me off with tears, kisses, blessings, several pastries, and a tin heavy with chocolate. My brothers stand on the couch to give me some awkward hugs goodbye. Once outside, I secure my backpack and duffle bag to the elf-sized SnoMo, then squeeze in behind Herr Geier. He takes off without offering me a helmet.

I catch one last glimpse of The Flaky Crust, warm light pooling from its windows, before we turn down another street and neighboring buildings eclipse it from view. An ache forms in my chest. I lost everything today. It'll be a long time before I find happiness in a second-choice life.

When we reach Figgy Forest, four elves riding SnoMos materialize from the trees and join Herr Geier on the path, two in front and two behind. One wears a *dirndl.* Reinforcements? Like I'm going to do anything to endanger my family's future.

The ride to Waldheim passes in silence.

At the outskirts of downtown in a copse of evergreens, my sending-off party comes to a stop.

"You're on your own from here," Herr Geier says. "Can't risk Christmas by letting humans catch sight of us elves, now, can we?"

My feet tingle as I slide from the SnoMo, and my knees creak when I bend to unfasten my bags. Clenching their handles in my fists, I straighten. "Is this when I'm supposed to thank you or curse you? It's a little fuzzy to me."

He lifts his visor to reveal narrowed eyes. "I expect you not to dally long in Waldheim, Miss Kuchler. You have an entire world to explore." He makes a tight U-turn, followed by the others, then pauses to glance back at me. "And just so we're clear. If you ever show yourself in Flitterndorf again, it will be to the detriment of your family's livelihood. Understand?"

"Is that your threat or Meister K's?"

"It's in the terms of banishment. You know the COE doesn't act without Kringle approval." His green outfit looks black in the darkness.

Green. I purse my lips. "Did he approve that nasty note you wrote me last week?"

Nostrils flaring, Herr Geier flips his visor down, and then he and the others speed away into the woods. That elf is as sour as he looks.

And he's left a bitter taste in my mouth.

THE HOUR IS FAR TOO LATE FOR DECENT FOLK TO BE MEANDERING the snow-caked streets by the time I reach Gina's house. Far too late to ring someone's doorbell. But since it's also far too freezing to curl up somewhere and wait until morning, I ascend her porch with shivering limbs and knotted stomach.

Letting the duffle bag drop at my feet, I press the doorbell, then step back and rub my arms, my shoulders quaking from the cold. Chimes go off inside the house, and I hold my breath. What am I going to do if this plan backfires like my chemistry final?

After a moment, the porch light flicks on. I squint against the brightness. The bolt turns, and the door opens about six inches. An older version of Gina peers through the opening. I briefly met Mrs. Donati the day we went skiing, but the frown tightening her mouth and wrinkling her forehead indicates she doesn't remember me. "May I help you?"

"I'm s-sorry to disturb you," I stammer through chattering teeth. *Please don't reject me.* "I kn-know it's late, b-but—"

"Tinsel?" Gina peeks over her mother's shoulder, then smiles and pulls the door free from Mrs. Donati's grip. "It's Tinsel, Mum. Don't be rude. Tins, what are you—" Her eyes grow big as she takes in my appearance. "You're freezing!"

"I'm sorry for sh-showing up unexpectedly, but I d-didn't know where else t-t-to go."

"Come in, come in." Gina opens the door wider as her mother retreats into the house, turning on lights as she goes.

"Are you s-sure?" I bite my lip, but the warmth seeping from the doorway beckons me inside, and I grab my duffle bag. "Your m-mom…?"

Gina glances over her shoulder and grins. "She's about to brew a pot of tea. Looks like you could use several cups' worth." Helping me shrug out of my backpack, she peers past me toward the driveway before shutting the door. "How'd you get here, anyway? You didn't, like, walk all the way from home, did you?"

"A c-co-worker"—I use the term loosely—"gave me a ride t-to the edge of town."

She clicks her tongue. "A nice co-worker would have given you a ride all the way to my house."

A FRESH START

As I defrost over three cups of tea at the kitchen table, I give Gina choice bits of the events leading up to my leaving home, fully admitting I can't divulge all the details. Like kissing Niklas in the wardrobe. And my banishment. She wouldn't understand that part. Instead, I stay consistent with the lie I told my folks about my failed interview.

When I finish my tale, she shakes her head. "But to give up on your goals because you didn't nab the internship you wanted? That seems too dramatic, even for you. I know you can't tell me everything, but I get the feeling you've only given me one piece of the whole pie."

"Pie. You sound like Niklas."

She props her chin in her hand. "What did he say about you leaving?"

I lace my fingers around the teacup. "He doesn't know yet. He'll find out tomorrow." When I don't show up for our secret lessons.

"You didn't tell him?"

"He has nothing to do with the decisions I make."

"I thought you liked him. I know he likes you."

"For a few moments, I thought he liked me, too." I swirl the tea with my spoon, the familiar ache back in my throat. Okay, I'll admit it. "He kissed me, Gina. Because I did what you suggested and gave him the benefit of the doubt. And immediately afterward, I found out he's engaged."

Her eyes and mouth form three perfect O's. "No freakin' way."

"An el—a worker at the shop called him on it, and he didn't deny it."

"So *he's* why you left."

"No, but not having to see his lying face every day will be an added perk."

She spoons more sugar into her tea. "What about the party at the coffee shop on Sunday? Will you still go as an elf?"

"I gave you my word." My insides churn at the thought of seeing Niklas, but I have a few days to convince myself the encounter won't hurt.

Gina drums her fingers against her cup. "Something doesn't add up. As soon as I know he's awake, I'm gonna text him and—"

"Please don't." I grip her wrist. "It's too embarrassing, and the fallout is far too delicate. Let's leave him in the dark for now, okay? I'll deal with him when I have to."

"That's, like, four days away, three days too many to let things fester, but"—she holds up her hands as I open my mouth to object—"it's your life."

"Thank you. And I promise my life won't infringe on your family's for too long."

She grins. "Are you kidding? You're not the first stray we've boarded." Her gaze drifts over my hair and hat, and her grin broadens. "Makeover."

"Excuse me?"

"What you need is a total makeover. New haircut, new clothes—"

"No." I set down my teacup with a groan. "No makeover. I'm not in the mood."

"That's the best time to get one, though I don't mean tonight, of course. Did you bring any makeup with you?"

"I don't own any."

Her eyebrows shoot up, and she rubs her hands together. "I'm going to have such fun introducing you to the world of cosmetics. And fashion." She angles her body around the table to study my *dirndl*. "No offense, but do all your outfits look like that?"

I tug at my wool skirt. "Why?"

"Well, it's cute, but that's not what we're after."

"What are we after?"

"The 'wow' factor." Gina taps her lips. "I might have some outfits that would do the trick."

A makeover. It hadn't occurred to me my *dirndls* would be considered fashion-fails in Waldheim, but the last thing I want is to stand out. And if blending in means I must paint my face, as well, then bring on the mascara. "Okay, fine, we can try a makeover. Except"—I finger my earlobe through my knitted hat —"no haircut."

Gina fakes a pout. "Trust me. You'd look fabulous."

"Really, I don't—"

"Niklas's jaw will hit the floor the next time he sees you." She reaches across the table to squeeze my hand. "And that reaction will be worth every tear you've shed today."

GINA SETS UP AN AIR MATTRESS FOR ME ON HER BEDROOM FLOOR, and my gaze bounces from one massive piece of furniture to another. No worries about bumping my forehead against the doorjamb; no hunching my back to avoid the ceiling; no bruised knees from knocking into tables when seated. No sense of lugging around a towering body since half the furniture is as tall as me, and a good number is taller than me. When I stretch out on the mattress minutes later, my legs don't reach the end.

At last I'm proportionate to my surroundings.

And I can't even rejoice, because the price to attain it cost me my family, my future...my identity.

I DON'T KNOW WHICH OF US IS MORE STARTLED THE NEXT morning: Logan, when he shuffles into the kitchen and sees me sitting at the table eating oatmeal, or me at the sight of him in nothing but boxer shorts and a well-worn tee shirt.

For the record, he fills out both quite nicely.

So why does an image of Niklas in his *lederhosen* lodge in my mind?

Logan's gaze flicks between Gina and me as he yanks open the fridge door. "Did I know Tinsel was coming and somehow forgot? Or is this a new development?"

"New development," Gina says around a bite of toast, studying the newspaper splayed across half the kitchen table. "I'll explain later."

He rummages through shelves and pulls out a milk carton. "How long are you staying?"

I meet Gina's gaze. We haven't exactly discussed that.

"Uh, through the weekend," Gina answers. "Maybe through Christmas."

He frowns. "You're not celebrating with your family?"

I scoop up some oatmeal in my spoon only to dump it out again. "Not this year. We, um… We…" Another scoop.

"They had a falling out." Gina glares at her brother. "I'll. Explain. Later."

"Fine. Meanwhile"—he grabs an apple, closes the fridge door with his foot, then claims the chair beside me—"you look like you could use some cheering up." He winks, setting the milk and apple on the table. "And since you're here now, let's not wait until Sunday for our date."

Gina shakes her head. "Friday night is Girls' Night, and Saturday I'm hoping to take her skiing again."

"All day long?"

"Well, no, but—"

"Saturday night it is, then." Logan's dark gaze latches onto mine, and a lazy smile curls his mouth. I wait for my stomach to flutter, but it must be sleeping. "What do you say? Want to have dinner with me?"

My spoon sinks into the oatmeal again, and I nod. Here's hoping the favorable attentions from a guy in the present can soothe away the painful memories of a guy from the past.

I SPEND THE DAY AT THE HUGGAMUGG CAFÉ DURING GINA'S SHIFT, expecting the shop's activity to keep me too occupied to pine for home. But with the Christmas carols playing over the sound system, the decorations staring at me from the café walls and ceiling, and the patrons offering "Merry Christmas" salutations, thoughts of Flitterndorf stay front and center.

Gina's boss, Claire, saves me from my dire musings after the morning rush when she asks me to revive a beauty-challenged, four-foot, artificial Christmas tree.

"The whole strand of lights quit on me yesterday," she says, "so if you could take everything down, restring the tree with new lights, and put everything back on again, that would be heavenly. Since I'm color blind, it's best if I don't touch it myself."

"I'll try, but I'm no Martha Stewart."

"Are you color blind?"

"No."

"Then you'll do great."

She returns an hour later, Gina at her side, and clasps her hands in delight. "This is magnificent."

Gina nudges my shoulder. "Don't be surprised if I ask you to redecorate my family's tree over the weekend."

The mood boost from their compliments lasts until Claire offers me a hot drink after lunch, "on the house." I choose a peppermint mocha, figuring Gina's drinking chocolate will remind me too much of *Mutti,* but instead the peppermint reminds me of Niklas, who always orders a Kandi Cup laced with the zingy extract.

Thankfully, Claire gives me another opportunity to test my decorating skills with a project involving Deco Mesh and garland to be draped along the front windows, and up my spirits go. When Gina's shift ends and we head back to her house, I bounce along the sidewalk, imbued with a new level of self-confidence. I might lack talent compared to my fellow elves, but it appears I have enough among the humans.

If I can't become the Workshop's COE anymore, maybe I can become an interior designer. Is there such a thing as a Christmas decorator?

I let the thought linger, trying it on for size, and tilt my head back as we pass beneath a plastic display of Santa and his reindeer strung across Main Street. My shoulders droop. I miss The Third String. Do they miss me? Have they heard—fact or fiction—what happened? Do they care?

If I were still in Flitterndorf and couldn't become COE, I think I'd try to work with the reindeer.

Exile stinks like moldy fruitcake.

Back in Gina's bedroom dominated by her doll collection (she wasn't kidding about that fetish), she fiddles with her iPhone and docking station until Christmas rock music blares from the speakers. Then she proceeds to empty her dresser and closet of jeans, dress pants, shirts, blouses, and scarves, tossing them on her floor.

"Start rummaging through," she calls from the closet, "and let me know if you see anything you like."

Gina has clothes galore. So many options, colors, and styles. The growing pile makes my head spin. And given that I've been on an emotional rollercoaster today, it's not a good combo.

"You're not even looking." Emerging from her closet, she holds up a mint green blouse between us and squints one brown eye. Then she tosses the blouse atop the pile.

"I've worn *dirndls* all my life, Gina." Kneeling, I rifle through some shirts. "I don't know what to piece together and what would look good. Can't you choose for me?"

"Look at it like decorating a Christmas tree, except you're ornamenting yourself. You did it at the café"—she chucks a sweater at my head—"so I'm not buying the helpless act now."

Scoffing, I pull the sweater from my head. Whoa. Now that neckline is too low. My gaze shifts beyond the sweater. But those blue jeans have potential.

I hold them up. "I don't suppose you have these in a larger size?" There's no way my colossal frame will fit into her jeans.

She looks at me like I have three heads. "Those should fit you easy-peasy."

"Folk back home say I'm oaf-like."

She snorts. "Compared to what? Pixies?"

Kinda sorta. I flick the button with a fingernail.

Gina crouches beside me, draping her arms over her knees. "Look, how about we pick out a few outfits for now and do something else? You know what always cheers me up?"

"What?"

"A new hairstyle." And she whips off my hat.

TRANSFORMED

"No!" I drop the jeans to cover my ears. "Roasted chestnuts—give it back!"

She laughs. "Chill. I've seen your fake ears, remember? Wait." Her brows furrow. "Why are you still wearing them? Or are these new ones?"

Snowballs and icicles, this is a disaster. "My hat. Please."

"I don't get it. Why are you—" Her brows slowly rise. "They're not fake, are they?"

Dread spirals through me. "Gina." My voice comes out in a whisper. "Please."

She swallows and plunks down on her bed. "Not fake. Okay. So, are we talking a birth defect or *Lord of the Rings*?"

"Birth...defect?" My stomach clenches at my pitiful attempt to sound convincing, and when her face pales, I think I might hyperventilate.

"*LOTR* it is." Gina inhales through her nose and exhales through her mouth. "Does this mean you're, like, immortal? Have magic? Is your whole family like this?" Her hands grip the edge of her mattress. "Or is this why you had to leave home?"

She thinks I'm a freak. I can't stay where I'm not welcome, but what are my options? Where else do I go? With a groan, I snatch my hat from where it dropped on the floor and jam it on my head. Turning in circles, I try to separate my belongings from hers and scoop them into my arms as tears prick my eyes. I knew something like this was going to happen. But did it have to happen so soon?

"What are you doing?" Gina's bewildered gaze follows my frenzied actions. "You can't leave now."

"I can't stay." I grab my woolen stockings. "I've weirded you out more than a normal person could in a lifetime."

"I'm not weirded out." She puts a hand to her temple. "Okay, yes, I am, but give me a minute, wouldja? I just learned my friend's a freakin' elf." She rubs her eyes. "You could have tried harder using the birth defect angle."

I sink to the floor, clothes and all. "I'm emotionally spent, Gina. I don't have the energy to deceive you anymore." My belongings tumble from my arms and I bow my head. "And I need someone to confide in."

Gina sighs and settles opposite me on the floor. Her face is ashen and her forehead creased, but it could be worse. She could be screaming. Her gaze shifts to my hat, and she takes another deep breath.

"So. You're an elf." She clears her throat. "What kind? Light? Dark? Woodland? Urban? Do you live for thousands of years like Lady Galadriel?"

"It's bad enough you know the elf-part. I shouldn't divulge the rest."

"You can't leave me hanging now. With my imagination, the truth could get way warped. Besides, you wanted a confidant."

I draw parallel lines with my hands among the tufted piles in her beige carpet. "You have to promise not to tell anyone, including Logan."

"Promise."

"I'm..." I scrub out the lines and make another set. "I'm a Christmas elf."

There's silence for several seconds. "Christmas. As in...Santa?"

I nod.

Gina bites her bottom lip but keeps the rest of her expression neutral. "Now you're telling me Santa Claus is real?"

"Yes."

Her eyes go out of focus. "And I suppose he has flying reindeer, like in all the stories?"

"Yes. In fact, it was my Pen—my job back home to muck the reindeer stalls. Well, not all of them. Niklas's reindeer."

"His *flying* reindeer."

"Um, right."

Glimpses of skepticism and possible panic break through her neutral façade until she presses the heels of her palms into her eyes. "Never mind. I could have never imagined this freaky twist."

My chest constricts. She doesn't believe me. "Remember your great-grandfather's stories? I bet the man he talked about had been the current Santa Claus." No response. "I'm not crazy, Gina."

She jumps up and paces the room. "Well, no. You certainly haven't acted like a lunatic before now. A-and you've got the ears to prove your story. On the other hand, this has been one killer of a week for you and, you know, stress can do funny things to people." She whirls around and points at me. "Y-you said Niklas just now. Niklas is Santa Claus? That's why the children react whenever he comes to town. He's..." Her eyes narrow and she wrinkles her nose. "*He's* Santa? I thought Santa was, like, old. And fat. And bearded. And always jolly. And—"

"Niklas is Santa's grandson," I interrupt before Gina has an apoplexy. "Someday he'll be Santa, but not yet. And while most Santas have a weakness for cookies, a few here and there stay trim, though it's an understandable generalization."

"And the shimmying up and down chimneys? Working from a Naughty and Nice List? Are those *generalizations*, too? Or just outright lies?"

"Weeell..." I twist my index finger. "The chimney part is true. But the list originated with Thomas Nast's drawings and was propelled along by the song, "Santa Claus is Coming to Town." It doesn't matter how good or bad you are—candy crumbs, where would you draw the line between 'good enough' and 'not-quite-good-enough'?—but whether you believe in Santa Claus."

Gina stares, unamused, and then plops on the floor to cradle her head in her hand, muttering gibberish. I glance at the clothes strewn about. It wouldn't take long to gather mine, shove them in my duffle bag, and be on my way.

"Gina?" I cough around the knot in my throat. "Are you—"

She holds up a hand. "I'm fine. There's...a lot to take in right now. Pointy ears are one thing. Being told Santa and his elves exist is altogether different, no matter how many yarns my relatives might spin."

I pluck at the carpet again, then reach for my clothes and arrange them into folded stacks. My gaze darts to Gina every few seconds. Finally, I force a smile. "I didn't mean to dampen the mood. Maybe you should give yourself a new hairstyle, since that always cheers—"

"Makeover!" She lifts her head. "Yes, absolutely. But not me. You. With those ears, you'd look amazing in a pixie cut. Better than amazing. You'll have Niklas wishing he could trade in his fiancée for you."

I shake my head. "Even if he wanted to—which he doesn't—he couldn't, so forget about Niklas and me. Think, instead, about everyone else. If you cut my hair, my ears will be harder to conceal, hats or no hats."

She purses her lips. "Since I'm not convinced about the Santa-stuff, let's stick with the birth defect line. But"—she wags a finger at me—"if you expect anyone else to buy it, we're going to have to work on your poker face."

GINA MANAGES TO SWAY ME ON THE HAIRCUT. IF I'M FORCED TO get a new life, I might as well choose how to dress and style my hair. I'm already halfway there, sporting a pair of Gina's black skinny jeans and a powder blue, boat neck sweater. We have an hour to complete my transformation before the rest of her family trickles home from their respective jobs.

"I was eight the last time I trusted anyone other than my mother to give me a haircut," I say as she pulls my locks into a low ponytail. "Frau Friseur gave me a bob that might have looked nice on someone with straight hair, but with my unruly waves, I looked like a walking pyramid." Gina snorts, brandishing a pair of scissors, and I take a deep breath. "I've doubted her talent ever since."

"Well, I didn't say anything about a bob. The words were *pixie cut*." She snips the air. "Ready?"

I squeeze my eyes shut. "Yes."

There comes the delicate grate of scissors against hair, and then something falls into my lap. I open my eyes to finger the disheveled, eighteen-inch long ponytail.

"I'll give you an envelope later," Gina says behind me, "and you can donate it. That's going to make some woman a fantabulous wig." She pulls a comb through what's left of my hair, then nudges my shoulder. "What are you thinking about?"

Toying with the scraggly ends that used to hang down near my waist, I refuse to look in the mirror. "Hoping I didn't make a mistake."

"It's hair. It'll grow back." The scissors grate again as she begins to shape my hair. "But you didn't make a mistake."

Still, I don't peek until twenty minutes later when she orders me to.

"I want to see your reaction," she insists over the spray of an aerosol can. The caustic odor makes my nose wrinkle. "I need to know your honest opinion."

I open first one eye, then the other, and stare at Gina's creation in her vanity mirror. I recognize the elfin ears jutting out between locks of hair and angling toward the ceiling, but where'd those high cheekbones come from? Have I always had wide eyes? Who knew what a layered pixie cut and long, wispy bangs could do for my face. I shake my head, and my hair bounces, liberated from so much weight.

Gina leans over my shoulder. "You look fab. The cut is perfect." With a finger, she fixes a curl in front of my ear. "Who's your stylist, again? She must be top-notch."

I laugh and push her hand away. "If your boss at *A Cut Above the Rest* doesn't recognize your talent, she deserves a lifetime supply of coal." I turn my head this way and that, admiring her skill. "You're incredible. Thank you." On a whim, I cover the tips of my ears with my fingers as Gina cleans the mess on her vanity table.

Glancing at me in the mirror, she gasps. "Don't you dare touch those! You're going with the birth defect, remember?"

"Gina, really? I need to think about my future in a world of humans. Who's going to hire me with pointy ears?"

"Someone who looks past the superficial to recognize your potential." She stows her scissors in a drawer and aims a towel toward her laundry basket tucked in her closet. "Like Claire would. Or me, if I open my own beauty salon someday. And you can always milk the elf shtick during the Christmas season."

I sweep stray bits of hair from her vanity into a small trash-can. "You don't think my ears are a big deal? Niklas was adamant people would have strong, negative reactions to seeing them."

"You kidding?" Gina opens her bedroom door a crack, peeks

into the hallway, then opens it wide and ducks out of the room. She returns pushing a vacuum cleaner. "These days, the only thing cooler would be if you said you were, like, a zombie."

The vacuum flares to life, and I sink onto Gina's bed, tucking my feet under my legs as she moves the contraption around her floor. I catch sight of my reflection in the mirror, and a smile creeps into the corners of my lips. First the successes at the café, then Gina's acceptance of my true self, and now her confidence that people won't mind my ears.

This new life I have to settle for might turn out better than I thought.

CONFLICTED

Against Gina's protests, I wear my hat to the café again on Friday. I don't want to deal with people's inevitable stares and questions just yet, although Logan took the revelation Thursday evening with little more than a few bats of the eye.

"Sweet. I'm going on a date with a short-haired version of Tauriel," he joked, referring to Peter Jackson's version of *The Hobbit*. "With one difference." He tugged a lock of hair near my ear. "You're cuter."

Over his shoulder, Gina pretended to gag, but I grinned. If he keeps doling out the charm, I'll forget about Niklas in no time.

Friday evening, Girls' Night Out becomes Girls' Night *In* at Gina's place, with popcorn, cocoa, Christmas cookies, and a basketful of Christmas movies. Gina and I decided beforehand I would appear hat-free, and her friends' expressions run the gamut as she makes the introductions. Surprise, curiosity, wariness, even indifference. Finally, one of them says, "Love your ears. Where'd you buy them?"

"I was born with them." The words sound authentic and sure, leaving people no room for doubt.

She pushes my shoulder with a laugh. "Get out. Wish I'd been born with ears like those."

The four friends rave about the beauty of the elves in *The Hobbit* and *LOTR* movies; speculate how big or small Santa's elves would be if Santa existed; then decide that in honor of my ears, the first movie we'll watch is *Arthur Christmas*.

As we camp out by the TV with our bowls of popcorn, I meet Gina's gaze and she winks.

For the first time since leaving Flitterndorf, I'm eager to see Niklas on Sunday—so I can gloat at his lack of faith in human beings. Freaked out, indeed.

Partway through the movie, Logan invades our female sanctuary.

"Don't mind me," he says over one girl's groan, another girl's pillow-toss to his head, and a third one's glare (I'm sensing some history there). He squeezes between me and Gina on the couch and gives me a lopsided grin. "How's my favorite elf doing?"

"Fine." My gaze flicks back to the movie, and my brow tightens.

He taps my forehead. "If you're 'fine,' what's with the frown?"

"Shh," someone hisses, turning up the volume.

I slink lower on the cushion as Logan gestures to the screen. "Movie not to your liking?"

"It's a fun story line." I shrug. "Cute characters and all that."

Logan shifts closer in a cloud of spicy aftershave. "But?"

"I'm disappointed."

He takes my hand and plays with my fingers. His own feel cool and calloused. "How come?"

Is it wrong to compare my mild reaction to his touch with my wild reaction to Niklas's? "Because whoever wrote the script seems determined to remove the magic from Christmas with some technical explanation of how Santa goes about delivering thousands of toys in one night. The result is a sweet story, but the magic's gone." I angle myself on the couch to meet Logan's gaze. "Why are people so intent on rationalizing everything they don't understand? Can't they accept not all things come with explanations, and that's okay?" I press my lips together and ratchet down the fervor in my voice. "Some areas in life aren't meant to be understood. That's where faith comes in."

Logan curls his finger beneath my chin. "You're adorable when you're passionate about something." His gaze lowers to my mouth.

My heart hammers in my chest. He's going to kiss me. Am I ready for that?

Gina leans over him to shake my leg. "You watching?" she whispers as he drops his hand. "This is the good part."

Ready or not, the moment's broken, and after a few seconds, Logan squeezes my fingers then leaves the room.

We watch three movies and stay up past one in the morning, camped out for the night in the living room, but I still have trouble falling asleep. You'd think exhaustion would overpower a restless mind, but Logan's flirtations keep replaying behind my closed lids.

He might've kissed me had Gina not interrupted. He might try for a goodnight's kiss tomorrow after our date. Would that help snuff out the lingering effects of Niklas's kisses?

I grimace and sit up in the borrowed sleeping bag. It's not right to use Logan to get over Niklas.

I hug my knees to my chest. Soft, contented breathing from five other bodies fills the silence. Outside the window, above the neighbor's roofline, stars cascade across the sky like salt crystals spilled across black satin. In a few days, Meister K will fly among those stars to deliver presents to believing kids all around the world.

Bitterness fills my mouth. I can't believe he banished me like that. My eyes sting, and I finger the tips of my ears. A Christmas elf lives to support the toy-making community, whether working as a Toy Maker, or offering services in the way of groceries, SnoMo repairs…a Kandi cup and pastry. But what purpose does a banished elf have?

"You're worrying about your ears again, aren't you?" comes Gina's groggy whisper beside me.

I twitch, startled, and then relax. "Yes. No. I'm conflicted."

Gina pillows her head with an arm and stares at the ceiling. "If Niklas would come to his senses and ditch his fiancée, half your problems would be solved. There'd be something to lure you home."

I frown. "Why are you so set on seeing me and Niklas together when I need to be convinced of the opposite?"

"Why are you so sure you can't be together?"

For starters, I'm banished. That immediately complicates things. Second: "Romance between elves and Kringles is *verboten*, Gina." I glance at her friends, praying we don't wake them with our chatter.

"Why?"

I open my mouth with a ready reply, except I don't have one. My shoulders sag. "I don't know. Perhaps at the onset, the elves were afraid intermarrying with humans would wipe out their kind, so they put the edict in place to prevent it from happening. Or maybe it was vice versa. My grandfather's descendants are certainly proof the human gene is recessive."

"Change the edict."

"Not that easy when it's become engrained in our culture."

Gina props up on an elbow. "You're not fighting for this very hard."

I drag a hand through my short waves. "What's there to fight for? Niklas is engaged and I'm ban—" I clear my throat. "I'm beyond done talking about this." Scooching into the sleeping bag, I punch my pillow and lay down. Gina stares at me, then sinks onto her back.

After a moment, she whispers, "He's had a crush on you for, like, ever."

I snort. "He has a lousy way of showing it."

"Granted he never came right out and admitted it, but all the signs were there. He found every opportunity to talk about you over the years." Gina laughs softly. "I used to be quite jealous of you. How could some backwoods, clumsy girl bring such light to his eyes in a way I never could?"

So, she *had* crushed on Niklas once upon a time. "Should I be insulted or flattered?"

"I got over him last year. And I was über excited to finally meet you. It was fun watching him squirm when he had to introduce me to his secret heartthrob."

I curl up on my side, wishing I could take comfort in her words. "Are you sure you're not confusing this supposed interest with his bizarre fascination for my mistakes?"

"He kissed you, didn't he?" She huffs. "There's a good explanation for his fiancée, Tinsel, and it has nothing to do with warm fuzzies. I wish you'd let me ask him about it."

"No. If an explanation exists outside the obvious, he should have given it already."

"Did he have a chance? You left without a goodbye."

"We grew up together. He's had opportunities. Of course, there were always rumors floating around"—I grimace at the memories that take on new meaning now—"and Kristof tried to warn me not to waste time on him. But I never paid attention because I had convinced myself I didn't care. I deceived myself, and now my heart has to pay the price."

Gina shifts in her sleeping bag. "Why, again, are you going out with my brother tomorrow night?"

I chew on the inside of my cheek. "It's one date, not a lifetime commitment."

"You're leading him on. Logan likes you. A lot."

"And I like him."

"Not as much as Niklas."

I fling an arm over my eyes. "Niklas is in my past. Logan could be part of my future."

And broken heart or not, I need to focus on where my future will lead me, rather than where my past has dumped me.

A DATE AND A THREAD

Logan takes me to a local diner Saturday evening, choosing a table by the window that overlooks Main Street. I order the arctic char and avoid the hot chocolate, while he orders a musk ox burger with a cup of coffee. Similar to Flitterndorf, everyone here knows everyone else, and patrons pass by our table to greet Logan and cast curious glances my way. They're too polite to remark about my ears, but I have a hunch come Monday morning, some will seek out Logan at the hardware store to pummel him with questions.

"You did a great job skiing today," he says when our food arrives. "You took fewer spills than last week."

"That's some accomplishment, I suppose."

He taps my foot under the table while fixing the burger to his liking. "Every bit of progress is a mini-victory. Focus on how far you've come, not on how far you think you should be."

With a tight smile, I cut into my fish. His words should encourage me, but they lack the challenging punch of Niklas's mockery. I could have used some goading earlier on the slopes.

Can't believe I miss that about Niklas.

Outside, snow crystals dance in the glow of the street lamps.

Today marks the winter solstice. The twilight hours grow shorter from here, and in another two and a half weeks, the sun will make its reappearance along the horizon. That's Niklas's favorite day of the year. He's happier in those twenty minutes when the sun lets us know it hasn't forgotten us than Meister K is after a successful Christmas Eve delivery run.

Today is his second favorite day of the year.

I'm on a date with Logan, thinking about Niklas. Fruitcake.

Resting my forearms on the table edge, I lean forward, determined to refocus. "You must have fun working with your dad every day, huh? I had hoped to follow in my father's footsteps at the bakery, but it's best if I stay far away from ovens, brick or otherwise."

Logan chuckles around a bite of his burger, then reaches for a napkin. "It has its good points, but I'll be leaving for Terrebonne, Quebec after the New Year."

"Oh?" My swallow of char needs extra coaxing before it will go down. "Why?"

"I have a cousin there who owns an auto repair shop. I plan to work for him for a few years, then come back and put Old Man Cheater—sorry, *Skeeter*—out of business by opening my own shop."

The animation in his face reminds me of the thrill I felt dreaming about my future as COE. "I hope it works out for you. Until a few days ago, I thought I had my future tied up in a neat Christmas bow." I pierce another cut of fish. "Now, it looks like something Santa ran over with his sleigh." Or severed with a few strokes of his pen.

Logan sets down his coffee cup and places his hand over mine. "You could come with me, if you want." My shock must register on my face, because he's quick to add, "Nothing scandalous. It's true I like you, ears included, but we'd keep it honorable."

"It would be fun to travel someplace new, but…" Great Oma

Fay's story swims in my mind. She, at least, had a home to return to when her sweetheart ditched her for a new love interest. Whatever decisions I make, whatever their consequences, I'm on my own. "I don't know, Logan. We're still getting to know each other."

His fingers draw lazy circles on the back of my hand. "If you're searching for a change, consider Terrebonne as a possible option. It has more potential than what you'll find around here."

On the drive back to the house, the radio fills the silence. It's not an awkward lapse in conversation, but I've run out of things to say, and I'm too tired for small talk. After cutting the engine, Logan walks around the truck to open my door. He tucks my mittened hand in the crook of his elbow and leads me up the front steps to the porch. I smile at his sweet behavior, a contrast to some *other* people I'd rather not think about.

At the door, he draws me into his arms. "I had a great time this evening." The porch light plays over his perfect features, his perfect lips.

"Me, too." Guessing what is about to come, I find my mind and heart in contention. I don't want to lead Logan on if there are no sustainable feelings, yet heaven forbid I continue to pine after Niklas. A kiss might help me figure this out. Nothing like a little power of suggestion to force something into existence.

His head lowers. I rise on tiptoes—

The front door bursts open, and Gina greets us with an overly bright smile. "Goody, you're back." Her gaze jumps back and forth between us. "Did you have a nice time?"

"It was about to get better." Logan leans past her and grasps the door to pull it closed, but Gina stops it with her foot.

"Do that later. Dad's making *Panforte*, and Mum and I are decorating cookies. Come help us." She grabs my arm and pulls me inside. I give Logan a contrite smile as I slip off my coat, disappointment cloaking me in its place. That kiss could have answered some questions, and Gina thwarted it.

Rather than lead me to the kitchen, however, she drags me in the opposite direction, calling behind her, "We'll be back in a minute!"

I frown as she shuts us in her bedroom. "What's going on?"

"Read this thread." She shoves her cell phone under my nose. "I might have egged him on a little, but I was hoping he'd confess something."

I blink, pulling the phone away to view the screen, but I can't make out any words for several seconds. In a bubble beside each of his texts, Niklas's face smiles at me. I tap on his icon, and his picture expands to fill the screen. My gaze ambles over his features—the disheveled blond hair, the laughing green eyes, the carefree grin—and an ache forms in my chest. It's been three days since I last saw him amidst shards of wardrobe. I've never gone that long without talking (or fighting) with him.

Gina plops on her bed. "I said to read his words, not drool over his face."

I cough and minimize his picture. "Sorry."

"Then again, his texts might cure your drool."

My twitter-pated heart falls flat on its face, and I prepare for the worst.

Niklas: R we still on for a Santa appearance tomorrow?

Gina: Yes! Kids can't wait to see Santa and his elf. :)

Niklas: About the elf. Tinsel left FD a few days ago. I'm told she might hv gone to Waldheim. Don't suppose she's there w/ u?

Gina: Not right this second. She's on a date w/ Logan.

(Seven minutes elapsed before his next text. Dare I speculate what that meant?)

Niklas: Why didn't u tell me?

Gina: U never asked. And ur a jerk for kissing a girl while secretly engaged.

Niklas: Didn't faze her, since she so quickly ditched FD to be w/ Logan.

Gina: Ur still a jerk for deceiving her.

(I agree with Gina on this one.)

Niklas: It's complicated.

Gina: Deception usually is. How IS the fiancée, btw?

Niklas: Great.

Gina: She w/ u right now?

Niklas: Watching a movie.

(My throat begins to burn.)

Gina: R u actually watching it?

Niklas: Ha ha.

Gina: Don't do anything I wouldn't do.

Niklas: Did you tell that to L and T before their date?

Gina: No! *Face palm* Think txting him now will do any good?

Niklas: RME. See u tomorrow, G.

Her eyebrows rise when I meet her keen gaze. "So? What do you think?"

I hand over her phone with a snort. "I think you got it right—he's a jerk. If the Naughty List did exist, he'd deserve a permanent spot at the top." He's a jerk who doesn't care about me. I wrap my arms around my roiling stomach and sink onto the air mattress. "Thanks for making it sound like he didn't emotionally wound me, though. This way I can hold my head up in his presence."

"I'm sorry." Gina swipes her thumb across the phone screen. "I honestly thought he would insist it was all a big misunderstanding."

"This just reaffirms my heart should move on." The tears build behind my eyes. One last cry. I'll allow for one more—then I'm done.

"I should've let you kiss Logan, after all," Gina grumbles.

I shake my head, a lone tear following the curve of my cheek to roll beneath my chin. "He's leaving for Quebec in two weeks. Why start something that can never see completion?"

Wish I'd known to take my own advice with Niklas. I could have spared myself this current heartache.

My shoulders shake with silent sobs. The air mattress dips as Gina kneels beside me and squeezes my arm. "It won't always hurt this bad. I promise."

HERE COMES SANTA CLAUS

Classic Christmas carols issue from overhead speakers at the Huggamugg Café. People mill about the tables, chatting, laughing, sipping cocoa, eating cookies. A line of children snakes among them, ending at the red armchair Claire positioned in the back corner.

For the third time that afternoon, I settle a screaming toddler onto Niklas's rounded lap (he wears a fat-suit beneath his Santa getup). He tries to catch my gaze as I step back, but I've been avoiding eye contact ever since he arrived.

That doesn't mean I haven't enjoyed watching his interactions with the kids. Or, like now, taken guilty pleasure when his efforts to win over a child fails.

So satisfying to realize this Kringle can't charm everyone.

I smother a grin with my hand as he attempts to get the squirming, uncooperative child to smile. It's a good thing his snow-white beard (rather convincing for synthetic facial hair) hides the lower half of his face. If the tight lines about his eyes are any indication, he's frowning under those curls. As a rule, I object to any mother who forces her child to see Santa, but today I find myself thinking *bring it on*. Niklas's perfect life warrants an occasional, uncontrollable disturbance in the form of an innocent babe.

"Oh, isn't that precious?" the mother warbles to anyone who will listen. Right now, that's me. She fishes out her cell phone and motions me closer to Niklas and her son. "Would you mind? I'd love to capture this moment for all time."

I hold up my hands with a shake of my head. "The picture will look much better if you take it with just Santa and little Johnny."

The mother's smile falters. "His name is Hubert. And I'd like both Santa *and* his elf in the picture." She backs me up and forces me deep onto the arm of Santa's chair. Niklas's shoulder, swathed in his father's burgundy coat, presses into my side. "There. Perfect." The mother retreats again and looks at her phone. "Everyone say 'cheese.'"

Hubert's wail picks up ten notches, and Niklas's knee bounces at an alarming rate. Instinctively, I reach for the toddler's hand. He grasps my forefinger, and his cries soften.

"Look! He's smiling," the mother says. I puff with pride at the fact I got him to calm down—until he sticks my finger in his mouth and chomps down with his eight front teeth.

I blink back stars.

"Perfect." The mother stows away her phone and rushes forward to claim her child gnawing on my finger. His teeth scrape along my skin, and I mash my lips to keep from crying out.

"Aren't you a good little boy?" the mother coos as they move away. "Yes, you are. You're Mummy's precious angel."

"Frosted windowpanes." Niklas grabs my hand to peer at my finger, and I almost fall into his lap. "Are you all right?"

His probing makes me grimace as a red dot stains his white glove. This is what I get for enjoying his misery too much—a little misery of my own.

"That brat cut into your skin."

"Niklas." I yank my hand from his and glance at the waiting children. "Santa's not supposed to call kids brats."

"Kids aren't supposed to maim Santa's elves."

I meet his gaze for the first time that day. "Neither is Santa."

WHEN THE LAST CHILD HAS HAD HER CHANCE TO TELL SANTA Claus what she wants for Christmas, I excuse myself to go change. Mindful of my now-bandaged finger, I shimmy out of my *dirndl* and back into jeans and a sweater. As I pack away the *dirndl* with careful folds, my hand lingers on the thick fabric. Gina's clothes are a fun switch, but nothing lends comfort like the familiar drape of a beloved skirt. Who knows when I'll wear it again after the Christmas season passes.

Flinging my bag over my shoulder, I emerge from the bathroom into the main hallway that links the café's back rooms. Niklas pushes himself away from the wall, running a hand through his tousled hair, and gives me a boyish grin. Sweet little drummer boy, does he ever look good.

Mustn't forget how he uses it to his advantage.

Raising my chin, I take in the SnoMo outfit he wears, his riding gloves gripped in one hand, the stuffed backpack sitting at his feet. "Heading out?" I move toward the door that leads to the dining area. "Safe trip. Tell my parents I'll be in touch."

"Tinsel, we need to talk." Niklas puts a hand on my arm but I yank away.

"I have nothing to say to you. I wouldn't have even come today were it not for the promise I made to Gina."

He squeezes his gloves in first one fist then the other. "Why'd you leave Flitterndorf? Everyone's been worried about you."

I let out an incredulous laugh and readjust my bag. "Oh, I bet they are…*not*. Be honest, Niklas. You're relieved you don't have me underfoot, pushing you to fly a sleigh or begging you to teach me to dance. And the elves, no doubt, are rejoicing in the streets that their tangled-up Tinsel has finally 'left' for good."

"What's with the air quotes?"

"Ask your grandfather."

"Look, if this is about Gretel—"

"Who's Gretel?"

Pink blooms in his cheeks, and I could kick myself. I did not need to know *her* name. "Don't flatter yourself. You and your fiancée didn't factor into my decision to leave."

"Your parents said you felt out of place and needed to find your purpose somewhere else. Is that true?"

"More or less."

He waves a glove around. "Is Waldheim that somewhere else, then? Are you happy here?"

"For now." Here I don't have to watch Niklas fawn over some other girl. "But I won't stay for long. There's a whole world to see, after all." At Herr Geier's insistence.

His brow creases. "Where will you go?"

"Don't know. Quebec, maybe. The States. Europe. I'm a free elf. I can go anywhere." If I had an endless supply of money. And a passport. Crumbling candy canes. Leaving Canada might not be easy.

Niklas nods, brow still creased, and slings the backpack over his shoulder. "I guess that's it, then. Enjoy your new life." He starts toward the rear entrance at the end of the hallway, and my chest pounds erratically. Then he stops and turns. "Tinsel?"

"What?"

A smile lifts the corner of his mouth. "I was wrong, you know. About you blending in. I can see you've succeeded. You've got new friends, stylish clothes, and I even hear people have been cool about your ears." He meets and holds my gaze. "My favorite is the haircut, though. You look beau—"

Logan bursts through the doorway, scanning the area. When he sees me, he breaks into a smile. "There you are! I've been looking all over for you." He gives me a peck on the cheek, and my gaze inadvertently flits to Niklas. Do I imagine his jaw hardening? "Leaving already, man?" Logan asks him.

"Yeah, 'fraid so." Niklas gives Logan a fist-bump with his free hand. "Things to do back home. You know how we Kringles get around Christmastime."

Logan laughs. "No kidding. Your dad would rival Santa Claus himself, if the dude was real. Hey, I never congratulated you on your engagement. Did the lucky lady come with you today?"

Niklas's answering smile looks strained. "Ah, no. Busy day for her, too." Retreating down the hall, he raises a hand in farewell. "I'm gonna jet. Take care, you two."

In three seconds, he's gone, the back door closing behind him.

Gone. Should I ever see him again, he'll likely be married.

I think he was about to call me beautiful.

Tears start tumbling from my eyes, and to my horror, I can't stop them.

"Tinsel?" A dubious expression clouds Logan's face. "Geez, are you okay?"

I shake my head...nod...then shake my head again.

"You, uh, want to talk about it?"

Another vehement shake. With a soft laugh, he wraps me in a hug. Grateful for his affection, I drop my bag and slip my arms around his waist, pressing my face into his shoulder.

We stand there for a long moment, not saying anything, just breathing. But he smells like aftershave, not cloves. And his brawny arms don't lend much comfort.

"You're not crying over Niklas, are you?" His words sound hesitant, cagey.

I sniff. "It's been a long day."

With the crook of his finger, Logan lifts my chin and thumbs a tear beneath my eye. "If I may"—his lips hover over mine—"there's something I'd like to try."

Why not? What's a kiss to an already mangled heart?

Then Logan straightens. "Nik. Did you forget something?"

Niklas? I whip around. He stands in the doorway, helmet clutched in his hands, his mouth slightly open.

But he shakes his head and lets out a wry laugh. "Forget something?" He taps the doorjamb with his helmet. "No, no. I mean...I thought I did, but I realize..." The mirth leaves his face, and his gaze falls away. "I was mistaken. Nothing here belongs to me."

When the back door closes on Niklas for the second time, I slump against the wall with the sickening impression I've somehow hurt him. He's the one who betrayed his fiancée, lied to me, and trampled all over my emotions, yet I'm the one left feeling like scum.

REINDEER IN THE YARD

The next morning over breakfast, Gina informs me I said what every guy dreads to hear when I told Logan, "I just want to be friends."

"That's why he hasn't come down from his room yet," she whispers with another glance at her mother scrambling eggs at the stove. Gina scoops up a spoonful of cereal. "He'll avoid you until he either swallows his pride or leaves for Terrebonne. Whichever comes first."

Sure enough, he exits any room I enter that morning until he leaves for work. Knowing I did the right thing, yet burdened with guilt for having hurt Logan, I'm thankful when Mrs. Donati ropes me into helping her ready the house for guests that evening. With Gina gone at the coffee shop until three, dusting and vacuuming keep me busy through the morning, a welcome distraction from my woebegone thoughts.

When I finish, Mrs. Donati calls me into the kitchen for another favor.

More cookies.

As long as she understands I don't do the actual baking. My skills lie in burning chew toys.

My heart twinges at the reminder of the Third String. I long to be with them right now. With my family. The flurry of activity to prepare for Christmas Day here at the Donati residence is nothing compared to the preparations for Christmas Eve in Flitterndorf.

There's the sleigh to wax and polish, the Big Eight to prep, the frenzied rush to transfer presents to the loading dock (did the elves ever make quota?). Atop Huff 'n Puff Hill, they'll set up for the Christmas Eve Festival with food and drinks, games and dances. My parents will arrange their kiosk next to the sack races like they do every year and offer delicious chocolates and pastries. I lick my lips, imagining the rich taste of a triple fudge Kandi Cup.

Christmas Eve in Flitterndorf is *my* favorite day of the year.

And I'm going to miss it.

Aside from Logan's persistent cold-shoulder, dinner at the Donatis' that evening proves a lively affair, with laughter and teasing, rehashing old memories, and speculations on what the New Year will bring. The adults are discreetly told about my "birth defect," though Gina plays up my elf role with the children so well, I'm confident Santa has gained a few more lifetime believers.

After dessert, Logan takes the younger kids outside for a snowball fight while Mr. Donati brings out a deck of cards for the adults. Twenty minutes into an intense Canasta game, however, several screaming kids barrel back inside. Logan hurries after them with a glance over his shoulder, as though something might be chasing him, and slams the door.

"Good gracious, Logan, what's the matter?" Mrs. Donati asks.

All the kids start talking at once, and when no one succeeds in calming them, Logan cups his mouth and hollers, "There's a reindeer in our yard!"

I exchange a glance with Gina, then peek out the front windows. "A reindeer?" Even the Third String shouldn't wander far from the stables this close to Christmas. I head for the coat closet. "I'll see what it wants."

Logan's brow puckers. It's the most emotion he's shown me since yesterday. "You're not going to approach a wild animal, are you?"

"There's a, uh, herd in the woods near where I live. Lived." I hop about trying to shove my feet into my boots. "Maybe the reindeer's from that herd? Anyway, I'll be fine."

Once I'm braced for the cold, I step onto the front porch. Half the guests follow me.

Frosted fruitcake. I could do without the audience. I catch Gina's eye. "Would you mind if—"

"Is tha' ye, lass?" a snort issues from my right.

I whirl about with a squealed, "Butterscotch?" I bound off the porch, stumble through the snow, and hurl myself at his neck. The regal creature blows a gentle puff of air against my hat, and tears bite my eyes. "What are you doing here? How did you know where to find me?"

"I figured it out 'tween Niklas's grumbles o'er the last day and a half, plus me hours studying maps in Flight Training." Butterscotch tosses his head. "Thair's been an accident, lass. 'Tis Niklas."

I raise a mittened hand to my mouth, my stomach churning. "What happened?"

"He took the sleigh out—"

"Big Red?"

"Valiant. And he dragged half o' the Third String with him. Includin' Eggnog."

"Oh, no."

"Oh, aye." Butterscotch stamps a hoof. "I dinna ken why, but the reins went slack, then Eggnog panicked, and the rest o' us couldna right the sleigh. So we crashed."

"Is everyone okay?"

"Niklas was unconscious when I left, and one reindeer's down—"

"What do you mean, down? And unconscious?" I fight the panic rising inside.

Butterscotch butts me in the chest with his head. "Talk on the way. Too much ta explain, and we're wastin' time."

"Tinsel?" Gina calls from the porch, uncertainty in her voice. "What's going on?"

My audience!

I wring my hands and turn to the porch-load of people in different stages of shock. Even Gina's mouth hangs open in a small 'o.' "I don't know all the details, but Niklas is hurt and—"

"What?" Gina clambers down the steps. "Where? How bad?"

"I don't know. I'm headed to check it out now."

Logan raises a hand, a glazed look in his eyes. "I'll go with you. We'll take my truck."

Butterscotch butts me from behind this time, and I shake my head. "Thank you, but I'll take the reindeer." He kneels with his forelegs on the ground, and I move to his side. "He's much faster than a vehicle." Into his ear, I whisper, "Get out of sight before you jump into the sky, okay?"

The color drains from Logan's face as I settle myself onto the reindeer's back, but he manages to choke out, "Should we call for an ambulance?"

"Not yet." It's bad enough several people witnessed me talking to a reindeer. Best to keep the number of people who see Santa's sleigh to zero. Unless absolutely warranted. "I'm sorry, I need to go. I'll try to keep you posted."

Gina grabs my sleeve, worry etched in her brow. "You're coming back, right?"

"Eventually." I give a tight grin. "Half my stuff is here." And I'm wearing her jeans.

"I'm sorry I didn't fully believe you. You know, about all that Santa stuff." She squeezes my arm. "But I do now."

My smile relaxes. "Then you've been a great friend to have accepted me all this time regardless of my quirks."

I wave goodbye, hoping she won't have to do too much explaining, then Butterscotch gallops down the street. Oomph—he's much smoother in the air. After cutting between some houses, crossing another street, and ducking down an alleyway, he finally takes to the sky.

As Gina's neighborhood shrinks from sight, my thoughts turn to Niklas. His deceit still rankles, and I've put my heart under lock and key, but it's Niklas. And he's lying unconscious. I can't *not* care about that. Is it simply a case of being knocked out or is it much worse?

"Where did he get the crazy notion to fly the sleigh?" I ask Butterscotch. "He's afraid to fly."

The reindeer lets out a snort. "And evidently too proud ta admit it. We widna be in this predicament otherwise."

"Have you sent anyone to inform Meister K?"

"He widna understand us. 'Sides"—he turns his head to look at me with one eye—"would *ye* want ta be the one ta give Santa the news he has a busted sleigh, an injured reindeer, and his grandson lies unconscious—on the night afore Christmas Eve, no less?"

My nose wrinkles. "Good point."

"I'm hoping ye can help us."

"I'll do what I can, but I have no talent for—"

He shakes his head, his antlers almost taking me out. "Talent disna equal capability, and yer capable of a great many things. Trouble is, ye've been surrounded by doubtin' elves all yer life. Ye've come ta accept an inferior position among them afore gettin' the chance ta realize yer full potential. This could be yer big break. If yer willin'."

My chest expands at his words. I'm willing. But I'm banished.

Butterscotch veers to the right and starts descending. Among the evergreens pulses the muted glow of a campfire. If Niklas lies unconscious, who made the fire? He comes into view as we draw closer, alert and crouched near the flames. I expel a pent-up breath, relaxing my grip on Butterscotch's antlers. Chip rests opposite him on the ground, and Eggnog and Peppermint mill nearby. Along the forest floor, the sleigh lies in splintered chunks, the fallout from Niklas's reckless behavior. My grip tightens once more.

Should you ever wonder if it's possible to want to throttle and hug a person at the same time, the answer is yes.

Butterscotch alights in the clearing. I hop from his back as Niklas scrambles to his feet and shines his flashlight beam on us. "What are you doing here?"

His sharp tone keeps me from giving him that hug. Probably for the best, since he belongs to another girl.

"Butterscotch found me with the Donatis and told me what happened."

Niklas heaves a relieved sigh. "I thought I'd lost him."

I drop to my knees beside Chip and whisper, "Are you okay?"

"Pure dead brilliant," he says with clenched jaw.

I run a hand over his shoulder and along his back. When I reach his foreleg, his body shudders. His eyes squeeze shut. Scratching under his muzzle, I touch my forehead to his. "You'll be all right, I promise."

"I'm fine, thanks for asking," Niklas grumbles, dropping to the ground to lean against a wood pile. "Nothing but a blow to the head."

"A few more might be in order before the night's out." I take the flashlight from him and move away to rummage through the sleigh's remains.

"What are you doing?"

"There had been an old tin box beneath the seat. A first aid kit. Any antiseptics or medications it held have long since spoiled, but the gauze bandages are still good. If the box didn't get destroyed in the crash."

"I grabbed a new kit before I left."

I spin about and shine the beam in Niklas's face. "What?"

He angles his head away, holding up a hand to shield the light. "I'm afraid to fly, Tinsel. A person like that doesn't ascend thousands of feet in the air without having something on hand in case of an emergency."

"Ribbons and bows. Smart move." I pass the flashlight beam over the debris, now searching for a white steel box instead of a green tin one. "And here I thought you'd lost your mind, putting your reindeer in danger." Something glints several feet to the right. "There it is."

"Not my mind. I lost my heart."

My own heart squeezes as I pull the kit from under a broken board and return to Chip's side. "What do you mean? You did this to impress your betrothed?" I scour the area for two long, sturdy sticks and find them in Niklas's pile of firewood. "I should be thankful you didn't crash *Big Red*, though *Valiant* deserves better than a nondescript glade for a resting place."

Butterscotch makes a guttural noise. "Tinsel—"

"I didn't choose to crash," Niklas says. "Grandpop makes flying look easy."

I sandwich Chip's foreleg between the two sticks then open the kit. "It *is* easy."

"There should be a written warning on the dash not to look down."

"But that's half the fun." I begin to wrap an elastic bandage around Chip's makeshift brace.

"Tinsel, if I may..." Butterscotch tries again.

"I was doing semi-decent up to that point, if you overlook my quaking limbs and queasy stomach. Then one of these guys started flying weird, and I lost whatever nerves I had left. We dropped fast, started crashing through trees...I don't remember landing." Niklas sweeps a hand in Butterscotch's direction.

"When I came to, this big guy was gone, and I had a huge mess on my hands."

I try to keep the bite from my tone. "It wouldn't have happened if you'd spent the last six years learning to communicate with your team." Around and around Chip's leg I wind the bandage. "You would have known to leave Eggnog back at the stables, because he's as skittish to fly as you are. You would have known when to give the reindeer their head and when to use your own. You would have known—"

"—ta wait two more days afore tryin' his hand at flyin'!"

Goosebumps prickle my arms at Butterscotch's uncharacteristic outburst. "And what difference would that have made?"

"The elves discovered stress fractures on *Big Red* and sent it ta the shop fer repairs." He rakes a hoof along the ground. "Meister K planned ta fly *Valiant* tomorrow."

My gaze shoots to the sleigh's shattered remains. "Oh. My. Melting. Snowmen."

WRECKED

"That's why *Valiant* was sitting pretty in the FTA," Niklas says after I relay Butterscotch's news. "The elves must have pulled her from storage to prep her for flight."

I throw Niklas a withering glare from where I pace, keeping the fire between us so I don't do him bodily harm. "If you had taken your job as a future Santa seriously, this wouldn't—ugh." Spinning on my heel, I squeeze my head between my mittened hands. "What are we going to do? What are *you* going to do? You can't fix this mess by tomorrow. All those children. What'll happen when they don't receive a present from Santa Claus? They'll stop believing, that's what will happen."

I swipe off my hat and wring it in my hands, imagining it's Niklas's neck. "Santa only delivers to believing children. If the children stop believing, there won't be a reason to make any toys. What are the elves supposed to do then? That's their purpose in life." I fling my arms out to either side. "You've stripped over two thousand elves of their purpose!"

Niklas sighs. "Would you quit the drama, please? What happened to your optimism?"

"It's smashed to smithereens all around us."

He closes his eyes, leans his head back. "I get it, Tinsel. I screwed up. I'm sorry."

A fresh torrent of words spills into my mouth, but Niklas looks so miserable that I swallow them without uttering a syllable. Taking a deep breath, I count to ten.

And it hits me like a fruitcake shot across the clearing. I've screwed up dozens of times despite my good intentions. If anyone knows how rotten he feels, it's me. Shouldn't I cut him a little slack?

I pull in my bottom lip. He's been sitting in that same spot almost since I arrived. Dark streaks run down one side of his face. Strange. I shine the flashlight on him again.

"Roasted chestnuts, you're bleeding." I grab the first aid kit then crouch before him and yank off my mittens. Searching his face for the source of blood, I remove his fur-lined *Ushanka* with shaky fingers. Blond locks fall over his forehead. I'm not good with my own blood, let alone someone else's, but I manage to keep my mind a blank slate as I angle his face toward the firelight. "Your head must ache like a Toy Maker's taken a mallet to it." I brush aside his hair. There it is. A gash mars his forehead about a half-inch above his right eyebrow. I gulp. Is it deep enough to warrant stitches? "Why didn't you say something?"

"I did," he murmurs. "You were more concerned with the reindeer."

I press my lips together at the truth of his statement. "I'm sorry. I was angry."

"Are you still angry?"

"Does Rudolph have a red nose?" My fingers tremble as I sift through the contents of the first aid kit and pull out an individually wrapped antiseptic wipe. It takes me five tries before I rip open the packaging. Tears blur my vision.

"Hey." Niklas's gloved hand wraps around mine. "It's going to be okay." He jiggles my hand, and I meet his gaze. "Christmas is going to be okay."

I gather courage from the certainty in his eyes. "Promise?"

"Promise." He swipes my cheek with his glove. "Don't be getting emotional on me, Kuchler. We can't risk your eyelashes freezing shut when you might need your sight to sew me up."

I laugh, followed by a sniff. "You don't want me going anywhere near your face with a needle. Remember that quilting square I sewed two years ago?"

Niklas clears his throat. "Maybe just a butterfly bandage, then."

Gripping the antiseptic wipe, I hover over the gash. "This might sting a little." I dab at the blood encrusted on his skin. Though Niklas draws a sharp breath, he doesn't flinch away. He studies my face, his gaze like a flame warming every feature it drifts over and burning the ones it lingers upon too long. I squirm. He probably looks at Gretel with the same degree of intensity.

Right before he's about to kiss her.

Not that he's thinking about kissing me.

And I'm not thinking about kissing him, either, for that matter. Even though his lips aren't far from my own. Nope, I'm moving on.

I tear open a fresh wipe and continue cleaning away the blood. The wound is deep, but a butterfly bandage should suffice until he returns to Flitterndorf. "What convinced you to fly the sleigh, anyway?"

"To prove I could. It's a form of weakness to fear flying. Santa Claus shouldn't have any weaknesses."

"So you jeopardized your life and the lives of your reindeer?" I pat his cut dry with some gauze before placing ointment on it. "Behind the magic, behind the red suit, Santa is but a man." I look him in the eye. "All men have weaknesses."

And when the weakness manifests itself, I should extend compassion, not condemnation, regardless of a bruised heart.

Niklas glances at his hands. "I have too many."

"Startin' with the fact yer a jealous coward," Chip says.

A smile pulls at my lips, and I relay the reindeer's comment to Niklas. "Plus, we've already established you can be pigheaded. And cocky. And proud. And—"

"Before you get too comfy with your nose in the air, Gram says you're as prideful as I am."

I pause with the bandage posed above his eye. "You've talked to Madam Anne about me?"

"My entire family has argued about you."

"Argued? For the love of reindeer." I pull the gash closed with the bandage and shake my head. "Why would you do that?"

Chip snorts. "So's he could later be rejected."

With furrowed brow, I glance between animal and man. "Chip says you argued so you could be rejected?"

Niklas glares at the reindeer. "Thanks a lot."

"Yer welcome," Chip replies with overt smugness.

"Chip says—"

"I got it." Niklas raises a hand. "Came across loud and clear."

"What is he talking about?" With one last antiseptic wipe, I remove the remaining blood along his cheekbone. "Who rejected you?" *Please say Gretel.*

Heaving a sigh, Niklas rests his head against the wood pile. "You, Tinsel. Chip's talking about you." He pinches the bridge of his nose. "This entire situation, our current predicament, it's all because of you."

DO I OR DON'T I?

Niklas's words pour ice over my warming sympathy. "*I* rejected *you*? How hard did you hit your head?"

He raises his hands. "Chip mentioned rejection, not me."

"But you said our current predicament is because of me." I scramble away and toss the wipes and trash from the bandages into the fire. "I am not taking the blame for what happened here tonight."

His mouth lifts at one corner. "You know the saying, 'Behind every man's downfall is a woman.'"

"Why, you frozen-hearted, pompous—" I kick the sole of his boot. "I have half a mind to take off with the reindeer and leave you to freeze to death." Yanking on my mittens, I storm over to the sleigh's remains and scan the area for the biggest plank of wood I can find. "Does your precious fiancée know you avoid taking responsibility for your own actions by blaming the nearest female?"

"I didn't mean it in that sexist way you're thinking."

"If you had any idea what I'm thinking right now, you'd be at my feet, begging for mercy." Gritting my teeth, I crouch to grab what looks like a sizable board, but only half of it comes away in my hand. I shine the flashlight over the debris and move closer to a bulky shape at the clearing's edge.

"What are you doing?"

"Trying to figure out how you and the reindeer are getting back to Flitterndorf." The beam of light slides along a large chunk of the hull. Perfect. I pick my way through the debris. "Someone needs to inform Meister K about *Valiant* and come up with her replacement."

Snaps, pops, and hisses strike the air as a few logs thunk into the fire. "No one is telling Grandpop anything. I made this mess, and I'm going to get myself out of it."

I shoot Niklas a glare over my shoulder. "You can't fix this by yourself."

"With your help I can."

I'm banished. My help is limited. Grunting, I haul the hull remnant toward Chip. Of course, Niklas doesn't know I'm banished. Left up to me, he never will.

Niklas stands with careful movements and meets me halfway. "Let me help."

"You've sustained a head injury. Sit down."

Prying the hull from my hands, he nudges me out of the way.

I scoff. "Stubborn Kringle."

"Where do you want it?"

"Next to Chip." I begin a search for the ropes that would have been in the well beneath the seat.

"What's it for?"

"To pull Chip back to Flitterndorf." With a half-smile, I motion to Eggnog pacing and muttering at the edge of the firelight. "I'm told he's a fast runner. If we can harness him to the plank, he can haul Chip behind him. Butterscotch and Peppermint can fly."

"And how do I get home?"

I extract a coil of rope from under a wedge of cushion. "Walk."

At his shocked expression, I smirk. "If you ask nicely, Eggnog might let you ride on his back."

"Provided he keeps one hoof on the ground at all times."

"Scaredy-cat."

Niklas collects reins and traces into a pile. "And while I'm meowing astride a reindeer, where will you be?"

I untangle a second rope from among splintered boards. "Butterscotch can return me to the Donatis' before heading to Flitterndorf."

All four reindeer swivel their heads to gape at me. Niklas growls. "Would you forget about Logan for one day, please? Christmas is in jeopardy."

"Mmm, why is that, again?"

Niklas's jaw tightens. "Sure, keep rubbing it in."

"I intend to." I flash him a grin. "Opportunities like this don't come around often."

He slaps a harness onto his growing pile. "I need your help, Tinsel. Whether or not you call Flitterndorf home, you're still a Christmas Elf, and it's your duty to protect this holiday."

"It's for the sake of this holiday I can't return with you. Or have you forgotten I only create disasters?" I loop some rope around one half of the wood plank, cinch it tight at the top edge, then repeat for the other half to make two parallel lines. Leaving several feet of rope to extend beyond the top edge, I rummage through Niklas's pile for some reins.

He crouches beside me. "What are you doing now?"

"Making a temporary driving harness for Eggnog."

"I thought you only created disasters."

My hands stall in the pile as his words combine with what Butterscotch said on the way here. I meet his penetrating gaze. "How am I supposed to help, Niklas? What you need is a new sleigh, and—" Eyes widening, I grip his arm. "*Honor.*"

His brow knits. "What?"

"Santa's original sleigh. That's the answer. Find *Honor* and you save Christmas."

"And keep the elves' respect." He nods. "I like it."

Then I slump. "Except, how will you find, in a matter of hours, a sleigh that's been missing for over a hundred years? Some versions of the story say she was destroyed."

"Who in their right mind would destroy Santa's sleigh?"

I stand and look around. "Besides you?"

"That's getting old, Kuchler."

Hiding a smile, I measure Eggnog's girth with some rope. The reindeer noses my head. "*Honor* wasna destroyed, Tinsel. Reindeer lore claims she was packed away in the basement o' the stables."

My eyebrows rise. "And how trustworthy is your reindeer lore?" I begin knotting the rope for the harness. "Do you even know *where* in the basement? Those hallways go on forever. You won't have time to look through all those storage rooms to find her before tomorrow morning."

"We dinna ken that part." Butterscotch ambles over with lowered head as I take another measurement and make more knots. "Lost in the retelling o'er time."

"One or two o' the Big Eight might ken," Peppermint chimes in. "Rocket is a direct descendant o' Blitzen, after all." She blows through her nose. "Though they willna discuss it with the likes o' the Third String."

Butterscotch taps my head with an antler. "They might talk t'an elf with a talent fer communicatin'."

My cheeks burn as I attach Chip's platform to Eggnog's harness via the ropes. Talent? Me?

"And they'd definitely talk to a Kringle," Peppermint adds.

"Aye, now what a fine team that would make," Chip pipes up from where he lies on the ground. "A Kringle with the command and an elf with the means. Shame they're too stubborn and proud ta work together."

Finished hitching the platform to the harness, I kneel beside Chip. "Okay, Furball, I don't suppose you could shimmy onto this board, could you?"

Chip's eyes narrow. "I'm part o' the Third String. I could fly home if I had ta."

I grin. "Two feet will do it." Then I lean down to whisper, "And I'm not proud."

"Prove it. Come back ta Flitterndorf and help us save Christmas."

I peek at Niklas. His face reflects the light from his phone before he switches it off and tucks it away. My brow tightens. "What are you doing?"

"That was your boyfriend, texting to see if I was okay." He crosses his arms. "So, what are you and your antlered peeps concocting?"

"My 'peeps' say *Honor* exists, but it requires talking to the Big Eight to find out where she is." I stand and wipe my hands on my jean-clad thighs. "I think you need to tell Meister K—"

"No. Weren't you the one who went to a ravine without telling anyone so you could bring back supplies and right your wrong? You should understand my need to fix this without Grandpop's help."

"We're hours away from Christmas Eve—"

"And you can talk to the Big Eight." Niklas steps forward to grip my upper arms. "Tinsel, if you help me, we can both come out looking like heroes."

I chew the inside of my mouth. "Unless it backfires."

"There you go with the negativity again. What has Waldheim done to you?"

I turn away with a huff. "Anyone know what time it is?"

Butterscotch searches the sky. "Judgin' by the angle o' the stars, abou' ten-thirty."

Aside from me and Niklas, no elf or Kringle will be tromping around the stables at this hour of night. If we managed to pull this off, and everyone knew I had a hand in saving Christmas, Meister K might retract my banishment. Hope flutters inside my chest. "Okay, I'll come. But I can't be seen."

Niklas nods. "Neither of us can. Not right away."

We make plans to reunite at the forest's edge behind Huff 'n Puff Hill. Whoever gets there first will wait for the others, at which point we'll head for the hidden door to the storage room. Before we part ways, I double-check Niklas's bandage and reassure myself Chip can't tumble off the platform. Eggnog kneels to allow Niklas access to his back, and I hug my arms across my middle.

"Maybe you should lie on the plank with Chip." I study Niklas's face in the waning firelight. Is he pale, or is it the trick of the light? "You've lost blood, you might have a concussion, you could pass out again. If you fall off Eggnog, you could break your neck, or worse."

"Why, Kuchler"—Niklas chuckles for the first time since I found him—"is that concern in your voice?"

And is that swagger in his? "Just wondering how you'll carry out the role of Santa Claus from a wheelchair, that's all." I cock my head as Eggnog stands, Niklas astride his back. "But then, for all we know, Gretel might make a great backup Santa."

"Gretel?" He shudders. "She'd certainly fit the suit better than me."

My jaw drops. "That's a rude thing to say about the girl you love."

"I wasn't talking about her."

"You said—"

"I know what I said."

I stomp my foot. "You don't make any sense."

"If you saw the whole pie, you'd understand."

"Give me a whole pie, and I'll smush it in your face."

"It was my parents' idea, Tinsel. Not mine." He leans down. "Ever heard of an arranged marriage?"

CHANGE OF PLANS

By the time my mind catches up with his words, Eggnog has already taken off in a burst of speed and disappeared into the night.

"...Parents' idea, not mine. Ever heard of an arranged marriage?"

I have no clue how to decipher that.

As Peppermint and Butterscotch pound across the sky, I lean into Butterscotch's neck and shout, "Does he mean a literal arranged marriage? Like, he doesn't want to marry her, but has to?"

"The gel's name is Gretel Brunner. Relations 'tween the Kringles and Brunners go back fer centuries, but the alliance has turned rocky o'er the years." Butterscotch snorts. "Seems Meister Nico and Madame Marie believed a union between the families would help smooth things out, and they've been pushing it on Niklas fer a while."

I scowl as we approach Mount Freude. "And no one's ever heard about this? Word never leaked out?"

"Put the pieces together meself this past week. 'Tis no' the last o' the Kringles' secrets, lass." Butterscotch suddenly swerves to the right, and I clutch his neck as we descend below the tree canopy.

"What's the matter?"

"Activity near the stables." He dodges around tree trunks, his speed slowing. Peppermint follows. "Somebody must've realized *Valiant's* missin' and alerted everyone else. Imagine the panic that could lead ta."

I squeeze my eyes shut. "What are we going to do? I can't be seen. And until we talk to the Big Eight, Niklas can't be discovered, either." After that, I don't care how much trouble he gets into.

It's what I tell myself, anyway.

"We'll keep ta the trees so as ta go undetected." Butterscotch dips and soars among the branches. "Eggnog should be fine, since he's approachin' from behind the hill."

"But if there's activity outside the stables, there could be activity inside the stables. And in the basement. Maybe in a certain storage room." My head begins to pound. "We can't chance entering through the hidden door. What are we going to do?"

"Meet up with Niklas an' see if he's got any bright ideas."

Niklas. And his arranged marriage.

Does he want to marry Gretel?

Not that his answer matters. I'm banished.

When we arrive at the edge of the forest, Niklas already waits with Eggnog and Chip. He wears a satisfied smile. "Took you long enough to get here. Don't tell me Eggnog runs faster than those guys can fly."

"'Twas amazin'." Chip shakes his head as I dismount Butterscotch. "I'll never make fun o' Eggy again. Smoothest ride ever. Would've thought we were flyin', save fer the passin' trees."

I hug Eggnog and catch the spark in his eye. "If I had to guess, I'd say you no longer scorn your gift for running"—I hazard a glance at Niklas—"and you just had the ride of your life."

Niklas props an arm on Eggnog's back. "That was better than racing a SnoMo. You'll have to try it sometime."

My smile slips. "I'm here to help find *Honor*." And maybe redeem myself. But if not… "Once that's done, I'm going back to Waldheim."

"Sure, sure. Wouldn't want to keep your boyfriend waiting too long now, would we?" Niklas winks, and my stomach turns over.

"You know, don't you?"

"That Logan's not your boyfriend? Oh, yeah."

Muddy snowballs. Not the way I wanted this conversation to go. "How'd you find out?"

Niklas pulls out his cell phone and jiggles it in the air. "Logan, himself, actually. While we waited for you guys to show up, I texted him with an update, letting him know I'd return his girlfriend in one piece after she helped me out of a little pickle." He taps the phone against his thigh. "Imagine my surprise at his response."

"What'd he say?"

Niklas affects Logan's voice as he reads the text thread. "'Dude, she's not my girlfriend. Totally blew me off after you left the Christmas party. But good luck, 'cuz I think she's in love with you.'"

My hand goes to my throat. "Great lords a'leaping—he's totally lying."

"About not being his girlfriend or your feelings for me?"

"The latter, of course."

Niklas's dimples appear in his cheeks. "But if he's not lying about the former, why assume he's lying about the latter?"

"He hasn't a clue how I feel about you."

Niklas bends forward. "He's not the one who needs to know."

Butterscotch blows into my hat. “Can ye two lovebirds sort this out after we save Christmas?”

“We’re not lovebirds.”

Niklas’s grin widens. “He called us ‘lovebirds’?”

“No, he didn’t. I mean, yes, he did, but—” I cover my eyes with a mittened hand. Why’s he flirting with me? His engagement might be forced, but it still counts. “Let’s focus on Christmas, please, and talk later.”

“Fine. But there will be a later.” Niklas turns his attention to the hillside. “Now, the hidden door to the storage room. Do you know how to access it from the outside?”

“Yeah, about that. We have a problem.” I brief him on what Butterscotch saw from the sky. “If anyone’s inside the stables, it’s possible they know some of the Third String are missing. And if word has reached your family, it’s possible—”

“—they know *I’m* missing.” Niklas rubs the back of his neck. “Snowman. I’m going to receive the biggest Penalty for this stunt.”

My gaze drifts to where I can make out the peak of the Lower Stables’ roof atop the hill. “We can’t go in through the front entrance. But maybe under the cover of darkness we can make it to the back doors via the corral.” I glance at the reindeer. “Unless anyone knows of another secret entrance?”

They don’t. At Chip’s insistence, we leave him with Peppermint and Eggnog at the base of the hill behind the tree line. They’ll wait there until we either open the storage room doors, or they receive word to rendezvous in the stables. I don’t want Chip going much longer without medical attention, but according to him, “My leg’s no’ broken, so tend ta me later. ’Tis more important ta find the sleigh and git it ta Meister K.”

Given the time crunch, Butterscotch suggests he fly Niklas and me as close as he can to the stables without being seen. I concur, then spend several precious minutes convincing Niklas to join me astride the reindeer’s back.

"Climbing the hill will take too long," I repeat for the umpteenth time. I extend my hand but Niklas scowls at it. "Butterscotch won't fly high. He'll skim above the surface. Please, Niklas. For Christmas."

The muscles in his jaw work. Beads of sweat dot his upper lip, and his face turns gray. Nevertheless, he pulls himself up behind me and wraps his arms around my waist. "Go," he rasps.

We reach the corral in seconds. I'm about to dismount when the back door opens, and Butterscotch jets into the sky at a near-vertical angle. Niklas squeezes the breath from me as the reindeer performs a tight, jerky spiral before alighting in the center of the stables' rooftop where it's flat.

Niklas scrambles from the reindeer's back. "What the fruitcake was that?"

"Avoiding elf foot-traffic." I look to Butterscotch. "What do we do now?"

The reindeer hitches his muzzle to our left. "The top windows in the Lower Stables are always unlocked. If we time it right, I'll swoop down, and ye can shinny through the window and drop into a stall undetected."

"And what will you do?"

His eyes glint. "Time it right and sneak into me stall undetected from the back door. That'll frazzle the elves' minds, no mistake."

Niklas scowls when I relay the new plan, but there is no alternative.

"Butterscotch could deliver you to the front door, if you'd like. I'm sure the elves would love an explanation as to why *Valiant* has disappeared."

His expression darkens. "Fine, we go through the windows."

After some false starts and several swoops (and some Christmas-colored cursing from Niklas), we manage to kick open the window. After another few swoops (during which I may have issued a death threat or two), Niklas shifts from clinging to

Butterscotch to clinging to the windowsill. Once he drops out of sight inside the stables, Butterscotch makes one more swoop, and I leap to the windowsill—where I hang, grunting and straining (you try doing a pull-up outside a second-story window). At last, I wedge my boot onto the sill and hoist myself up until I can see into the stables' interior.

Where is Niklas?

I'm straddling the sill when two elves barge through the west entrance. I freeze. *Please don't look up.* Digging my mittened fingers into the sill, I make eye contact with Cocoa and Licorice across the aisle below. They each nod, then begin to jump and buck in their stalls.

"Roasted chestnuts, what's gotten into them?" one of the elves exclaims.

"If one more thing goes wrong tonight…" They hurry to calm the animals, their backs to me, and I drop into Eggnog's stall in a cloud of hay.

"Next time, warn me," a voice whispers nearby, "and I'll be happy to catch you."

Swiping bits of hay from my face, I glance at Niklas pressed against the stall wall and murmur, "I won't be here next time."

His eyebrows snap together, the color returning to his cheeks. "You're still going back to Waldheim?"

I move to his side, tugging off my hat and mittens and stuffing them in my coat pockets. "I can't stay here."

"Why not?"

The door opens and more elves trek inside. We flatten ourselves against the wall. Eggnog's stall is at the far end of the stables, across the aisle from Chip's. What if the elves poke around back here and find us?

"All right, everybody, listen up." Herr Geier's voice cuts across the stables, and Niklas's face hardens. "Meister K says pack it up for the night. We have a team out looking for the missing Third

String, and the Big Eight need to get some shuteye. Everyone else is to report to the Workshop."

"Is it true we'll be working through the night on a new sleigh?" an elf whines.

"We'll never get it done in time," another elf says. "*Big Red* took two months to build and another three weeks to—"

A door clicks shut, and silence echoes in the stables. Niklas and I remain immobile for a minute before I peek over the top of the stall. The coast is clear. "C'mon, let's go." Hurrying into the aisle, I brush off my jeans then give Cocoa and Licorice a thumbs up. "Great job, you two."

They wriggle their rumps. "Yer back! They said ye left fer good. What happened? Why're ye sneakin' around?"

I shake my head. "Later. Niklas, you must tell Meister K about *Honor*. If the Big Eight don't have the answer, you'll need everyone searching for that sleigh. You can't afford to be prideful at this late hour."

The east entrance door opens, and my heart trips. Not again! I whirl in a circle, hunting for a place to hide. Then antlers poke into view, and I blow out a breath as in walks Butterscotch, followed by Peppermint and Eggnog.

And Chip!

"Och—why's me bruider limpin'?" Chocolate hops about in his stall. "What've they done to ye, lad?"

"Chocolate, hush." I hurry to Chip's side as he limps down the aisle. "What are you doing on your hooves? You need to get clearance from the Med Team before you go traipsing about."

"Eggy hauled me all the way up the hill." Chip noses my forehead. "The last few feet I can manage on me own."

"But—"

"Have ye located *Honor* yet?"

"No."

"Then get crackin'," Chip orders. "Christmas has a time limit, gel."

Licorice pushes her nose into the aisle from her stall. "What's all this fuss about findin' *Honor*?"

I open Chip's stall door as the others jump over theirs. "Niklas ruined Christmas, so I'm trying to save it."

Niklas cocks an eyebrow. "Way to throw me under the sleigh, Kuchler."

"My pleasure."

Licorice puffs out a breath. "If it's *Honor* ye seek, I can tell ye where ta find her."

The other reindeer stare at her. "Ye ken where she's at?" Butterscotch asks.

"Aye."

"And ye've been holdin' out on us?"

Licorice tosses her head. "When was the last time any of ye mentioned that old sleigh?"

I hold up my hands. "Children, simmer down. Licorice, start talking."

'FESS UP

My mouth drops open. "She's *where?*"

Niklas nudges me. "Translation, please."

"*Honor* sits in the Workshop's western tower, accessible only by a Kringle and his team's lead reindeer."

"That's what's in the tower?" Niklas scowls. "Whose idea was it to wall it off?"

I frown at Licorice. "If it's walled off, how is it accessible?"

"I dinna ken, but Nik'll figure it out."

"How come you know *Honor's* location but no one else does?"

"Reindeer lore." She raises her head. "Plus I'm a direct descendant o' Vixen herself."

"I'm directly related ta Dasher." Cocoa puffs out his chest. "How is that any diff'rent?"

"'Cuz the male species are no good with details."

Niklas rubs his chin. "A Kringle and his team's lead 'deer, huh? No wonder why I could never get into that room. Are those two arguing?"

"Yes, they are. And you want to tell me how you plan to get into that tower room?" I slap my hands to my sides. "Between you and the Workshop stand two thousand elves."

"Give or take a few hundred." Niklas contemplates the reindeer. "Which one's the leader?"

I point to Butterscotch. "You'll need more than him, though, or haven't you considered what you'll do once you locate the sleigh? You can't pull her yourself."

"I'm winging this as I go." Niklas drags a hand over his face. "How many reindeer do I need?"

"Two can manage an unloaded sleigh fer a short distance," Butterscotch says.

I relay his words and pat Licorice on the neck. "Take her, too."

Niklas nods and rummages through the supply closet. He arranges leather traces and reins into a coil, then ducks his head through the center to wear it cross-body. "Remind me later to bring them an extra bunch of carrots for their help."

"Remind yourself. I'm leaving now."

"You can't leave!" Checking his flashlight, he switches it on and shines it in my face. "We need you."

Cringing from the beam, I jam on my hat to prepare for the cold outside. "I located *Honor*. The rest is up to you."

"We don't know what the rest is." Niklas tries to catch my eye. "Please don't go."

Don't look at him. Adjusting the scarf about my neck, I study the buckles on his boots.

"Who's going to help me communicate with my reindeer? What if I have a concussion and pass out again?"

Don't look. I withdraw the mittens from my coat pockets while examining the traces across his chest.

"Please, Tins." He cups my elbow. His chin hovers at the top of my peripheral vision. "I need your help."

Don't look don't look don't—argh! His gaze traps mine in a sea of green, and it seeps into the cracks of my resistance. With a sigh, I stuff the mittens away again.

"Thank you." He squeezes my arm before releasing it.

Peppermint snickers. "He didna have ta try hard ta convince ye."

My eyes narrow. "No comments from the peanut gallery, thank-you-very-much."

Niklas tilts his head. "Why is Peppermint laughing at you?"

"Oh, caught that, did you?"

A lazy smile curls his lips as he heads for the basement door. "That she likes me is coming across loud and clear. She thinks you and I have potential."

I scoff. "Then she's the only one in Flitterndorf who hasn't heard about your engagement."

"Arranged marriage." He starts down the basement steps.

The west entrance whooshes open, and Niklas ducks out of sight in the stairwell. I whirl about, my stomach tanking as Jangles enters. When he sees me, his mouth drops open like an exaggerated cartoon. "Tinsel? You're back! Where have you—" He glances at the reindeer in the aisle. "What are you—" Eyes bulging, he whirls about and races back out the door.

I wince. "Not what I needed right now."

"Thank goodness he didn't see me."

I glare at Niklas. "You're not the one who's—" *Supposed to be in exile*. This is bad. I should find Meister K. Maybe if I plead my case and inform him of our plan—even though I'd be empty-handed—he'd retract the banishment. "Do you think Jangles is going to tell everyone?"

"Don't know, and I don't want to be here to find out." Niklas waves a hand. "C'mon. Before he comes back."

I glance at Cocoa. "Shut the door behind us." Then I hurry after Niklas, feeling my way down the stairs in the wan glow from his flashlight. "Where are we going?" Butterscotch and Licorice clomp behind me. "Licorice said the sleigh's at the Workshop."

"That's where we're headed."

"We're headed to the basement."

"*Nein,* we're headed to the secret passageway."

"A secret—" I trip down the last two steps and stumble against Niklas's back. "I asked earlier if anybody knew of another secret entrance. I took your silence for a 'no.'"

Niklas peers into the dark hallway before venturing in the opposite direction of the storage room. "The passageway isn't another outside entrance to the stables. It's an underground link between the stables and the Workshop. There's a difference." He touches each vertical timber brace on the wall as we pass it, counting under his breath until he gets to number seven. He shines the flashlight on the brace at shoulder height. "Should be around here somewhere." He presses his thumb against a knot. Nothing happens. "Hmm. This one?"

I pace behind him as he tries each knot on the brace. "This is wrong. I shouldn't be here. I should be talking to Meister K. What's going to happen to my family? D'you think if no one finds me, they'll assume Jangles saw an apparition?"

Niklas grabs me by the upper arms. "Tinsel, stop." He squeezes my arms. "I don't know what you're going on about, but whatever it is, things will work out."

"You don't know that."

"I'm a Kringle. I'll *make* it work out." He resumes searching the knots.

"You don't always get what you want."

He stretches up on tiptoe, pressing every knot he encounters. "True. One thing keeps eluding me—ah ha!"

A dull scraping echoes through the hallway, and my eyes widen as the entire section of wall between brace seven and eight sinks into the floor. Inch by inch, it reveals a gaping, black tunnel behind it, big enough for antlered reindeer to walk through, single file. Stale air wafts across my face, and Niklas motions us to follow him inside.

I trail my fingers along the curved wall. Little flecks of dirt fall away at my touch. "How many secrets do the Workshop and stables have, anyway?"

"How many Santas have there been?"

The scraping begins anew and I yelp, whirling around as the wall rises back into place behind Licorice. It seals with a *whump*. I edge closer to Niklas and his flashlight as we move through the tunnel, the reindeer's hooves clacking in the background. "So what secret are you planning to add when you're Santa?"

He grins. "Can't tell, it's a secret." He shines the light ahead, but darkness devours the beam after a few yards. His fingers brush against my wrist. "Take my hand."

I inch closer still. "Why?"

"I haven't been through here in almost a decade, but Kristof claims the ground has crumbled away in places, leaving behind bottomless holes. Plus, he's convinced a yeti calls this tunnel 'home.'"

"A *yeti*?" With a squeak, I grab his hand *and* clutch his sleeve. "Are you serious?"

"Totally joking. Just wanted the excuse to do this." Niklas threads his fingers through mine, and a tingle races up my arm.

Butterscotch snorts.

I clear my throat. "You know, the reindeer gave me more details about your upcoming nuptials."

"Oh, yeah?"

"Yeah. About Gretel Brunner. The unrest between the two families, a marriage meant to smooth things over." I work to free my fingers, but his grip tightens. "Niklas, I get that you might be forced into this, but you can't hold my—"

"I'm not engaged."

I stumble and he catches me. "What?"

"Remember when Grandpop sent Kristof on that errand? He had gone to see the Brunners about this marriage stuff and try to soothe their offended nerves—admittedly I wasn't my most charming self the last time I saw Gretel—but his visit turned out to be in vain, because last Tuesday I made it clear to my family why I would never marry her." He spirals the beam of light ahead of us. "That didn't go over well. Grandpop might be a jolly old soul, but when you oppose family obligations, out comes the Abominable Snowman."

"Then…you're not engaged."

"Officially, I never was."

"Why didn't you correct Herr Geier on Wednesday when he said your fiancée had arrived?"

"Because he took me by surprise. And you ran off before I could defend myself. I would have gone after you, but Geier insisted I had a responsibility to speak with Gretel and her father, who had shown up hoping to change my mind. It didn't work." He moves the beam back and forth. "And thanks to Gram and Mum, Grandpop was on board with me by then, so the Brunners returned home disappointed."

"But your text to Gina indicated—"

"Gretel was with me? Yeah, because I'd just found out you were on a date with Logan. It stung, and I wanted to sting back." He moves the beam up and down. "Besides, as far as I was concerned, Gretel *was* great, since she wasn't pestering me anymore and—"

"You said you were watching a movie."

"I was. All by myself." He twirls the beam.

I clap my hand over the flashlight. "You're giving me a headache."

"Talking about the Brunners is giving *me* a headache."

"And bringin' up the rear is givin' me a headache," Licorice grumbles.

I puff out my cheeks. Emotionally, I'm soaring like a reindeer, but technically, nothing's changed. He's still a Kringle, and I'm still an elf. An exiled elf.

"If refusing to marry this Brunner girl will cause major problems for the families, maybe you should reconsider." I wriggle my fingers from his. "As a Kringle, you've got familial duties. For the sake of Flitterndorf, an arranged marriage could—"

Niklas pulls me to a stop, the beam of the flashlight reflecting off the arched ceiling. "You think I should marry someone I don't love?"

"I don't know. Did you give her a fair chance? Maybe in time you'd learn to love her." *What am I saying?*

"Did I give her…?" A dimple appears in his cheek. "No, Gretel never got a fair chance. Something was already in the way."

My brow knits together. "Something?"

"Some…one." He runs a finger along my jawbone. "An elf, to be exact."

"Oh."

Butterscotch nudges us against the wall with his antlers and squeezes past. "We'll mosey on ahead. Catch up when yer done, but dinna take long."

The reindeer click into the darkness as my gaze roams over Niklas's shadowed yet familiar features. The perfect chin. His broad lips, fuller on the bottom than the top. The freckle under his right eye I can't see, but know is there. I tuck these features away in my heart. "What about the ancient edict prohibiting—"

"I defied flesh and blood last week. You think I'm going to let a leather binding and some paper pages stand in my way?" He recaptures my hand, and we once again move along the tunnel.

"Why didn't you ever say anything?"

He shrugs, adjusting the reins and traces on his shoulder. "I couldn't. Chip's right. When it comes to you, I'm a jealous coward. You accuse me of being arrogant and overly confident, but"—he swipes his forehead with an arm—"in truth, you can empower or cripple me with nothing more than a trite word or offhand gesture."

"I can do that?"

"You have more talent than you know." Niklas blinks, then shakes his head. "But it wasn't until I left the Christmas party that

I realized I couldn't let Logan have you without first fighting for you. That's why I took *Valiant* out last night. I'd hoped that in conquering my fear, I'd earn your respect, and...win your affections." Slowing our pace, he blinks again. "And there you have it. The whole pie."

He stumbles sideways into the tunnel wall.

"Good garland!" I wrestle the flashlight from him to examine the bandage above his eye. Blood seeps through and smudges his brow.

"I'm fine." Sagging against the wall, Niklas holds up a hand. "Just a little lightheaded."

"You've reopened the wound. You need medical attention. I'll finish looking for *Honor* and—"

"You're crazier than Santa during a Christmas Eve blizzard if you think that's going to happen. I'm helping you every step of the way. Finding *Honor,* sprucing her up, presenting her to Grandpop." He expels a breath and shoves away from the wall. "If I'm there for the big unveiling, maybe I won't get into as much trouble."

As he marches after the reindeer, I pick up one of the traces that fell to the ground. "And you're as stubborn as Santa during a Christmas Eve blizzard. Serving an occasional Penalty might do you some good."

A WAY IN

The tunnel deposits us at the back corner of the Workshop in a deserted, dusty hallway. Christmas carols filter in from another area of the building, Bing Crosby's baritone reverberating beneath my feet, and the clamor from inside the Productions Wing echoes along the corridor.

"What time do you think it is now?" I ask Butterscotch.

"I dinna ken. Half-past midnight, perhaps."

Niklas motions me across the hallway to a ratty wooden door. Pressing a shoulder against it, he turns and jiggles the knob. The door shudders open, swinging inward to reveal a wide stone staircase that follows the curve of the interior wall and spirals out of sight.

"We have a little over four hours before the Packing elves need a sleigh," I tell him, preceding the reindeer into the enclosed area.

Niklas pushes the door shut with his hip. "Less than that before Grandpop has a stress attack." He claims my hand again and ascends the stairs.

I glance at our linked fingers. *Exile. Ancient edicts.* It doesn't matter where our hearts might lie, circumstances will keep us apart. I should pull away, but I don't. If I'm still banished at the end of the day, I'm taking these memories with me. "He wouldn't stress if you told him about *Honor*. With the elves on board, they'd have her primed for flight long before we ever would."

"*Nein*. I want to surprise him."

Niklas walks with set shoulders, his head lifted in determination, and a realization begins to dawn. All these years, I've been so focused on trying to prove my worth to the clans, I never stopped to think what it must be like for Niklas to prove he's worthy of the mantle that will one day be his responsibility. I'm but an elf. He's going to be Santa Claus. The weight from the elves' expectations must be excruciating. For all I know, their pedestal could feel more like a prison.

No wonder he goofs off when he can.

After three rotations on the spiral staircase, my legs are burning and Niklas braces one hand against the wall as we climb. I glance at the reindeer behind us. They fly six inches above the steps. "Cheaters."

Butterscotch winks.

I squeeze Niklas's hand. "Any thoughts on what we're going to do once we locate the sleigh?"

"Fix her up."

"Yes, but how are we going to get her out of the tower? She won't fit through the door. She might not stay in the air. Do you realize how old she is? What happens to wood after one-hundred-plus years? How easily can we smuggle gallons of epoxy, paint, stain, etcetera, from Productions?"

Niklas pauses to catch his breath, hands on his knees. "Relax, Kuchler. Magic runs through her veins."

"Fat lot of good that did *Valiant*."

His dimple reappears. "Watch it, or I might make you perform the boy's part in the Festival Dance after all."

A chill sluices over me like water from an early spring stream, and I hasten up the stairs, away from his playful gaze. "I'm not performing."

Niklas follows after me. "At all? But it's required for graduation."

"Can't graduate from a school I'm no longer attending." Will this tower never end?

"You're not..." Niklas grumbles something incoherent. "You're *still* going back to Waldheim? After everything I've confessed?"

"I can't stay here, Niklas."

Rounding the bend, I come to a halt as the floor levels off before a broad stone door, its engraved, marble frame angling up to a peak in the center. I splay my fingers against the door's cold, sleek surface. No handle to turn or depress. No keyhole to pick. No hinge pin to pop. Licorice pokes her nose over my shoulder.

I trace a dark vein in the marble. "You figure the sleigh's behind this door?" She nods. "Accessible by a Kringle and his team's lead reindeer." Another nod. "But you don't know the key to opening it." Her third nod has me frowning at the door. "So now what?"

"Start lookin' fer the key."

Four square flagstones are centered in a row before the threshold. The middle two each bear an indentation that looks like a kidney bean. Indicative of boots, perhaps. But when I suggest Niklas stand there, nothing happens.

Only a Kringle and his team's lead reindeer. I suggest Butterscotch stand behind him. Nothing. Beside him? Nothing. Other side? Still nothing.

I poke at the curlicue engravings in the doorframe, frustration knotting my back. "Is there a secret button? Like the one that exposed the tunnel?"

Niklas sets the traces and reins on the ground, and we start examining and pushing every crevice on both the door and its frame. We slide our fingers along the slits between the stones in the wall. The reindeer hop on the floor, pounding each square, pawing at the walls.

Absolutely nothing. I slap my palms against the door before turning away. "What good is reindeer lore if you lose the most important piece in the retelling?"

"I could try to ram it," Niklas offers. "Or Butterscotch could."

"And break a shoulder or antler tine in the attempt." I plop onto the top step. "Christmas is ruined."

Niklas sinks down beside me. "No, it's not. There's still time."

"We need to tell Meister K."

"No." Niklas clears his throat at my glare. "Tinsel, you don't understand. That pedestal you joke about…if the elves realize how royally I've failed, I'll fall off. And the landing won't be pretty."

I lay a hand on his arm. "You don't have to be perfect to make the perfect Santa."

He looks at my hand and weaves our fingers together. "Please. Stay. Don't leave again."

"Niklas, I—"

His grip tightens when I try to pull away. "Is it because of the elves? Where you fit among them?"

I shake my head. "My time in Waldheim is teaching me to accept who I am, talent or no talent." 'Course, who I am now involves exile. When will I learn to accept that part of me?

"Then why can't you stay?"

I wrap my free arm across my middle. "We don't have time to talk about this." Every minute I remain in Flitterndorf, I put my family in jeopardy.

But Niklas cups my chin, makes me look at him. "If you're leaving, I deserve to know why."

The lines about his eyes deepen as he searches my face, and my heart clenches. Perhaps he does deserve an explanation. Or perhaps I don't want to leave him thinking the worst about me, and any conclusion he jumps to on his own will paint me in a more selfish light than exile. "Your grandfather banished me. That's why I can't stay. Why I shouldn't have even come back to help."

Seconds pass before Niklas says, "What are you talking about? You left of your own free will."

"That's what everyone was told, because I agreed to go quietly. I didn't want to shame my family with news of my banishment."

Niklas hops up and begins to pace. "Grandpop's all about mercy and umpteen chances. He's never banished anyone. No Santa has ever banished an elf."

"Lucky me, I get to be the first." Leaning back on my elbows, I glare at the ceiling, a mass of timber and mortar and rock.

"Maybe you misunderstood him. What did he say? What were his exact words?"

Nooks and crannies ripple across the rocks' surface. "He didn't say anything. He used Herr Geier to do his dirty work."

Niklas scoffs. "Grandpop wouldn't send someone else to deliver news like that. The COE overstepped his position."

"Along with the entire Elder Council?" Mortar crumbles away in places. Some patterns repeat. Huh. No, wait.

"You went before the Elder Council?"

"Mmm-hmm." Only one repeats. Four times. A grouping of two elongated tear drops and two small circles.

"This can't be right." Niklas squeezes my shoulder. "I'm going to talk to him as soon as we deal with *Honor*."

No, not tear drops and circles. Those look like…hoof prints.

Reindeer hoof prints.

I wonder…

"Niklas." I jump up, giddy as a child on Christmas morning, and point to the ceiling. "I've got it. Butterscotch, see those four sets of indents? Fly up there and place your hooves in them. Niklas, you stand at the threshold, your feet inside the kidney beans." I nod at their perplexed faces. This has got to work. *Please let this work.*

Butterscotch hovers in the air then flips upside down and plants his hooves in the larger prints on the ceiling. Licorice snickers. "Och, if Chip could see ye now, *Butterball.*"

"Ye better pray I dinna lose me dinner," he replies with dark undertones.

Niklas steps up to the threshold and—

Nothing.

"No!" I stomp a foot. "I don't understand. What else can it be?"

"'Twas a good idea."

"Hold on." Niklas hops on the square. "Maybe it's me. After all, I'm not your typical fat Santa." A wolfish grin spreads across his mouth as he snags me about the middle and hoists me into his arms.

"Hey! What are y—"

With a groan, the heavy door begins to slide into the wall. My mouth drops, then I laugh and turn in Niklas's arms to hug him around the neck.

"For once, I'm glad I'm not your typical small elf."

TOWER ROOM

Niklas sets me on my feet and approaches a rickety sleigh centered in the room. A hodgepodge of area rugs lies scattered across the floor and ancient tapestries hang from the windowless walls.

"So this is *Honor.*" He rubs his neck with a grimace. "We're in trouble."

The sleigh sits in woebegone dejection, her hull faded to a dingy green, traces of rosemaling swirled across the peeling paint. The cushion is but threadbare fabric pockmarked with holes from mice over the years, and the runners jut at odd angles. I won't be climbing into her any time soon.

Licorice twitches her nose. "Call me an eejit, but she needs more'n the two of ye ta fix her up if she's ta fly in a few, wee hours."

"Licorice is right, Niklas." I spread my arms. "This job is too big for us."

He closes his eyes, runs a hand through his hair, heaves a sigh. His brow wrinkles, but in the end, he nods. "Okay, I give up. *Honor* needs to get to Grandpop. He'll be down in Productions with the elves."

"Great. Let's find a way to get her out of here." I gaze around the room, its stone walls solid except for the doorway. "Well, we can rule out a window."

"And we can rule out the stairs." Niklas runs his hands over the walls. "They could've lowered *Honor* down through the roof. Knowing what I do about the Workshop and stables, I have a hunch there must be something." He raises his eyebrows at me and the reindeer. "Help me look. A button. A switch. A pull. Anything."

We peek behind tapestries and framed portraits, run hooves and the toes of our boots along the seams between wall and floor, test the wall sconces, even examine the sleigh for this elusive "something." But twenty minutes later we're retracing our steps, and the weight of every passing second presses upon my shoulders.

"How in the winter wonderland are we supposed to find our way out of this fix?" I follow a crack along the outer wall with my fingers, poking here, prodding there. "What good is legend and lore and secrets if they're not—*oompf*." I trip on an area rug and grasp the nearby wall sconce to keep from falling. It breaks off in my hand, and I land on the floor, the sconce clanging beside me. The glass hurricane shade shatters.

"Typical," I mutter, rubbing my bruised knees.

"Look." Niklas points to where the corner of the rug folded back on itself when I tripped. The oak floor has scratches on its surface perpendicular to the wall, as though something sharp was dragged over it. I scramble to my feet, and Niklas casts the rug aside. Another set of scratches parallel the first, and I track them with my gaze. If the marks continue in a straight line under the other rugs, they would join up with...the sleigh's runners.

I crouch again to examine the wall where the scuff marks meet it. Here and there, faint white lines mar the stone surface. "The wall. The sleigh came through this wall. But how?"

"Maybe by this?" Niklas presses his thumb into the cavity where the sconce had been. I back away when the wall groans and begins to descend toward the outside via cables buried within the adjoining walls. He grins as frosty air whooshes into the room. "And you think your blunders never produce anything good."

I rub my arms, the corner of my mouth lifting. The wall lowers until it looks like an extension of the floor then stops. "We better work quickly. Someone's bound to notice a wall's missing in the western tower, and I don't want to be found out until I'm standing in front of Meister K with this sleigh in tow."

Niklas ducks into the stairwell, returning with the traces and reins. "I thought I was taking it to him."

"You? Look what happened the last time you flew a sleigh."

His gaze flicks over *Honor,* but though his face pales, his jaw sets and his eyes narrow. "I'm not going to crash again."

"But if I take it, he might reverse my banishment."

"I still say that's a misunderstanding—"

"The signed document left no room for error."

"—but just in case, I want to talk to Grandpop about it before you reveal yourself." His brow knits as we harness the reindeer. "Though it doesn't make sense. What did you do to deserve exile?"

"You want the list Herr Geier gave me?"

Niklas scowls. "Whoever said perfection is a requirement for an elf? Even Herr Geier would fail at that." He meets my gaze over Licorice's back and stalls my movements with a hand on my wrist. "I'd rather have you and all your imperfections than somebody else's idea of perfect."

My insides smolder at the fire in his eyes. "Really? But the ancient edict—"

"If I hear that excuse one more time"—he drags a hand over his face before tossing the reins over the sleigh's dash—"I'm going to kiss you in front of the whole assembly at the festival."

"I might not be there." I frown at the gray pallor of his skin and shift around Licorice toward him.

"I'm going to fix this, Tins. Trust me." Niklas blinks, puts a hand on my shoulder. "In the meantime, hide with the Third String. There shouldn't be much activity in the Lower Stables, only the Upper Stables. I'll find you after I—"

His eyes drift closed as he slumps against me. "Niklas!" I catch him under the arms, but he's dead weight, and we crumple to the floor. "Niklas?" Passed out cold. I glance up at the reindeer, my chest squeezing. "What do I do?"

"He needs ta see the doc."

"The doctor. He'd be with the others in Productions, wouldn't he?" I snap my fingers. "Two for one. We deliver the sleigh, and the doc can examine Niklas." I readjust my hold on him and try to stand. "Quick, Butterscotch, let's get him onto your back."

"Yer not goin' ta hide?" he asks, kneeling.

"No. Yes. Maybe." I drape Niklas onto Butterscotch's back, then walk around and pull his arms until his body is centered over the reindeer. He doesn't stir. I bite my lip. "Snowman, he better be okay." Mounting behind his listless form, I curl a protective arm around his waist so he won't fall off and exchange glances with Licorice. "You ready? Let's go."

At Butterscotch's nod, the reindeer trot forward, *Honor*'s runners scraping behind us, and leap into the sky. I bend over Niklas as we veer around the tower wall. *Please don't fall off, please don't fall off.*

Around the Workshop we zoom, past darkened windows and timber and stucco, until we touch down in the rear lot, crunching across the frozen snow. We stop mere inches from Productions' door, and I release my breath as I slip from Butterscotch's back. Niklas's pasty countenance keeps me from knocking on the door, however. I smooth a lock of hair from his forehead, recalling his determination to set things right with the elves, and my heart constricts. Were his intentions honorable in telling me to hide, or was he hoping to take full credit for finding the sleigh? I could leave him here for the elves to find...or show myself. He told me to trust him.

Do I?

Licorice turns her head in my direction. "What're ye thinkin', lass?"

I press a kiss to Niklas's cheek and whisper, "Please be okay." Then I give the reindeer a tremulous smile. "I'm gonna hide. See you back at the stables." I turn, pound on the door with a fist, then dash along the length of the Workshop and disappear around the corner.

Behind me, the door squeals open and a high-pitched voice calls out, "Who's th—hey! Hey, everyone, look. It's some of the reindeer. And...and a *sleigh*. But how...? Roasted chestnuts—Meister Niklas? Someone, quick. We need Meister K!"

Praying Niklas will regain consciousness soon, I slink away before a swarm of elves floods the back lot and possibly spot me.

INSIDE LOOKING OUT

The cold seeps through my mitten pressed against the windowpane. Outside along the hilltop, the Red and Green Clans partake in the Christmas Eve Festival with its kiosk vendors and seasonal games. An immense stage, flanked by spotlights, stands between the Workshop and the stables where the Letztes Niveau students will perform the Festival Dance and Santa will deliver his congratulatory speech to the community before taking to the skies.

But there's one glaring difference in this year's Festival as opposed to all other years. (Besides the fact I'm stuck watching the festivities from a window at the rear of the Lower Stables.)

This year, a subdued atmosphere blankets the party, because this year, the stage is empty. *Big Red* should be front and center, its bottomless well bulging with toys, waiting for the elves to bring out the Big Eight. But at T-minus forty-five minutes, I've caught grumbled snippets (when I'm forced to hide under a hay pile in Chip's empty stall) that the Assembly elves are at-the-ready with the gifts but the Construction crew hasn't finished the minute details of *Honor's* makeover.

Leif from the Minor Flight Team emerges through the crowd

now, leading a limping Chip toward the west entrance. They must have released him from the clinic. Abandoning my post at the window, I dive under the pile of hay as the stable door opens.

"Look who's back," Butterscotch says from the front stall.

"Tinsel's hidin' in yer stall," Peppermint adds. "Watch yer step."

"In me stall?"

"Aye. Dinna squash her."

A piece of hay tickles my nose. I'd better not sneeze.

Leif chuckles as his footsteps move down the aisle, Chip's hooves clipping on the flagstones at an irregular gait. "Look how interested your friends are in your return," he says. "They must've missed you."

"Missed him?" Cinnamon snorts. "'Twas right dandy and quiet without the lad."

"Aye," Cocoa agrees, "but borin'."

Leif's footsteps stop at Chip's stall. I lie still, holding my breath. My nose tingles. *Don't sneeze.*

"And it looks like either Jangles or Skelly put extra hay in here for your comfort. Now, you stay put until it's time for Meister K's send-off."

My eyes water. Hay shifts by my feet as Chip clops inside.

"No unnecessary activity, understand?" Leif's footsteps move away.

"Ah-*choo*!"

Fruitcake.

The footsteps stop…backtrack. "Who was that?"

My heart thumps against my ribcage. I can't be found.

"Is someone there?" The steps draw near Chip's stall when one of the reindeer makes a noise much like my sneeze. Leif chuckles. "Ah. It's you, Eggnog. *Gesundheit,* then."

I wait until the west entrance door shuts before springing from under the hay and smiling across the aisle. "Thanks, Eggy." Then I hug Chip around the neck. "Well? What'd they say?"

He wears a cast on his foreleg from hoof to shoulder. "'Tis fractured, but I should regain full use o' me leg in time."

"That's great news." I peer into his eyes. "Why aren't you happy?"

"'Cuz they're givin' Niklas the credit fer gettin' me home."

My stomach churns, something it's been doing ever since I left Niklas sprawled across Butterscotch. "Licorice said the elves think Niklas found the sleigh, too, since he was with it." The fact he was unconscious doesn't seem to matter.

An abrupt cheer rises from the crowd, and I return to the window, brushing hay from my clothes.

Circling above the stage, eight dignified reindeer, sleek and fancy with glistening fur and shiny bell collars, pull a glossy, green sleigh behind them. *Honor?* My breath fogs the glass. Frowning, I rub it away with my mitten. It is *Honor,* barely recognizable in a fresh coat of deep, olive green paint. Bright red and gold rosemaling trail along the hull, and brand-new runners flare behind her in elegant swoops and curves. Meister K sits atop a cherry-red tufted cushion. The elves responsible for this miraculous restoration deserve an extra fully-loaded stocking tonight.

The sleigh glides to a stop onstage, and Meister K disembarks with a mighty, "Ho Ho Ho." Elves from all over the hilltop rush toward the bench seating. I scan the crowd for my family, but most elves have their backs to me, and many look alike from this distance. Do my parents miss me? I second-guess the wisdom in remaining hidden.

It's true what Niklas said: no elf is perfect. So why am *I* the one singled out and exiled? I'm not a lost cause. I get some things right. And let's be honest, no one would have found *Honor* if it weren't for the reindeer and my…talent for communicating.

Talent.

A smile tugs at my lips as the stage fills with Kringles and about a dozen elves. Pressing my forehead against the glass, I search for Niklas. Why didn't he come find me like he promised? Either he forgot, or he's still unconscious at the clinic.

I count the elves on stage. Ten. Interesting. "I think the Elder Council is up there with the Kringles this year. That's new. Why do you suppose Meister K did that?"

"Och, don't get me started on the Elder Council." Chip shakes his antlers.

Peppermint hops in her stall. "Why? What happened?"

"So, Effie from the Second String was at the clinic with a bruised shoulder. We got ta talkin' and—"

I tune out Chip's rambling as the elves settle in and Meister K begins his yearly send-off speech. My gaze drifts to the Letztes Niveau students waiting in twitchy anticipation at the base of the stage stairs. They pace and shuffle, decked out in their costumes, their caps set at perfect angles atop their heads, their faces shiny and bright and…and one towers above the rest.

Niklas.

"Gaun yersel." Cinnamon lets out an offended huff. "The Big Eight said that? Then what?"

"Ye listenin', Tinsel?" Chip asks.

"Mmm." If my thoughts could fly, I'd send them in Niklas's direction, where he grips the metal stair railing, his head bowed as his grandfather recaps the community's success over the last year. What's he doing? Did he forget about me, after all?

An ache forms in my throat.

Trust me, Niklas said.

Give him the benefit of the doubt, Gina said.

I'm trying.

"…Christmas that almost wasn't," Meister K says into a microphone to a sea of bobbing heads and exclamations. "You have outdone yourselves these last few weeks in an effort to bring joy to the hearts of believing girls and boys all around the world. Tonight, as I deliver the gifts you've painstakingly toiled over, may you find peace in the knowledge your work was not in vain."

Applause rises from the crowd but Meister K holds up a hand, and it dies away. "Credit must be given, as well, to our unsung hero, without whom my Christmas Eve flight would not have been possible. And for that, I give you Niklas, who—"

Thunderous applause and thousands of stomping feet drown out Meister K's words as Niklas jogs across the floorboards. A gasp flies from my mouth. He motions to the crowd, hollering something, but no one can hear him above the cheers and shouts. I wrap an arm about my roiling stomach. Niklas is taking the credit? But he crashed the sleigh. He neglected his reindeer.

Trust him.

He accepts the mic from his grandfather. I clench my teeth. Enough is enough. I might be banished, but the elves need to know the truth. What's more shameful to my family, anyway? To know I'm banished, yet helped save Christmas, or to think I abandoned my responsibilities just to find my "place" in the world?

My place is here. I might make mistakes, but *I'm* not a mistake.

Meister K has some explaining to do. I whirl away from the window and edge around Chip.

"...switched the chemicals on a student's exam. I reckon 'twas yers, Tins."

"What? Huh?" I move into the aisle, Chip's words hovering in my brain, trying to find a place to land.

He rolls his eyes. "Tinsel-gel! I told ye ta listen."

"Sorry. What about switching chemicals?" I halt. "Did you say *exam?*"

"'Tis what Effie said one o' the Big Eight said Herr Geier said he did."

My chest starts to burn. "Herr Geier? He switched... On my exam? But why? Are you sure?"

"Ye really weren't payin' attention."

"Chip."

"Effie said somethin' about him wantin' ta get rid of a student, and she mentioned the explosion. Sounds clear 'nuff."

Another round of applause escalates outside as my suspicions escalate within. Herr Geier wouldn't have dared.

The heat inside me intensifies, and I pace the aisle. I should expose him. But what if the reindeer are wrong? I'm getting this info fourth-hand, so some details could be mixed up.

On the other hand, if Herr Geier did sabotage my chemistry final to get me in trouble, then it's possible… My pacing slows. It's possible he went even further.

What if I'm not officially banished?

My body quakes, and my hands fist. If I were a nugget of coal, I'd be combusting. I charge down the aisle toward the west entrance. "Wish me luck, team. I owe it to myself—and my family—to get to the bottom of this."

And should it end poorly, reflecting badly on my family, they can follow me back to Waldheim.

THE TRUTH SPILLS OUT

I burst outside, the door slamming against the exterior stable wall. On stage, Niklas breaks off mid-sentence as the whole assembly turns in their seats, craning their necks to see what caused the interruption. Gasps and shrieks rise among them.

"It's Tinsel!"

"I told you I saw her!"

"What's she doing here?"

I race across the crusty snow toward the stage and point a finger at Herr Geier standing in the front row of the Elder Council. "Did you sabotage my chemistry final?"

Protests and outrage travel through the audience. Herr Geier's face reddens. "Ex*cuse* me?"

"Tinsel, what is the meaning of this?" Meister K plants his hands on his hips, bushy brows drawn over his eyes.

I wend my way through the Letztes Niveau students and Niklas meets me as I bound up the stairs. He sports a new bandage above his eye. "Are you okay?" His voice carries over the microphone.

"Chip told me Herr Geier might have switched the chemicals

on my final exam the other week." I storm past Niklas, past *Honor* and the Big Eight and Meister K. My hands shake as I face Herr Geier. "Did you do it?"

He puffs out his chest. "I most certainly did not."

"The bloke's lying," one of the reindeer mutters. I spin in their direction.

"Tinsel, this is a grave accusation." Meister K pulls on his beard. "I insist we—"

"Excuse me." I skirt around him to approach the reindeer. "I mean no disrespect, sir, but"—I confront the Big Eight—"which one of you spoke just now?"

They stand three human-sized hands taller than any of the Third String with hooves the size of dinner plates, their smallest antler tines as thick as my wrist. A few of them perk up at my question, and the one closest to me in the second row narrows an eye.

"Wot's this, then?" he says in a clipped, British accent. "A miss that understands reindeer speech?"

"An elf. Tinsel Kuchler."

He bobs his head. "Rocket, at your service."

"Nice to meet you." I'd curtsey, except I'm in jeans. Awkward. "Were you the one who said Herr Geier is lying about switching the chemicals? Could you please clarify?"

Meister K huffs. "This is ridiculous. What—"

"Wait, Grandpop." Niklas steps between us. "Leave her be."

Rocket lifts his chin. "Certainly I can, miss. Heard it from the old chap hisself. Taking pride in it, he was. Gushing to himself how he swapped the chemicals on someone's final exam. Just the one student, see, as he was set on ousting her from town. Tired of her bungling, he said. So, he swapped... Wot was it, again, Jiffy?" he asks his partner.

"Said 'e put potassium chlor*ide* 'stead of potassium chlor*ate* at 'er lab bench," says Jiffy in her thick, cockney words. "Takes longer to melt, see?"

I whip about and stare at Herr Geier. "You *did* do it."

"Of all the holly, jolly, merry Christmases, Tinsel, I demand to know what's going on." Meister K's gaze jumps between me, the reindeer, and Herr Geier. "What has got you so upset, and what's this"—he waves a hand at the Big Eight—"interaction with my reindeer?"

"I'm getting the truth, sir."

"You're telling me Rocket's grunts mean something to you?"

Niklas puts a hand at my back. "Believe it or not, Tinsel has one of the most unique abilities Flitterndorf has ever known."

"You mean she…" Meister K blinks at me. "You can understand the reindeer's emotions?"

I throw my shoulders back. "No, sir. I know what they're saying. That's my talent."

Exclamations undulate through the crowd at this, and Meister K's eyebrows rise toward his hairline. "Your talent. Fascinating. What did they tell you?"

"Rocket and Jiffy heard Herr Geier say he switched the chemicals on my exam. Potassium chloride for potassium chlorate."

Every one of the Big Eight nods his or her head, drawing Meister K's attention.

"Utter nonsense." Herr Geier's mouth twists in a sneer. "Don't believe her. She's making this up to shift the blame from herself."

"Did 'e call us liars?" Jiffy snarls.

Rocket bares his teeth. "Implied it, yeah."

Meister K pulls at his beard again.

"She's not making this up!" Herr Chemie charges from the back row of the Elder Council. "Tinsel's not lying. This explains why that cabinet was open and the chloride and chlorate were out of place on the shelves. I noticed when the students were taking their exams and should have questioned it then, but I didn't." He shakes his fist at Herr Geier. "*You* did it! *You* sabotaged her final, damaged the school, and almost destroyed Christmas."

The veins protrude in Herr Geier's forehead. "How was I to

know the test tube would break? I simply wanted her to fail." He glares at me. "Failure doesn't reflect well when you're gunning for internships you have no business attaining."

A bench creaks. A reindeer's bell jangles. The words he didn't say swirl among us on a hilltop quieter than a house anticipating Santa.

I'm not solely to blame for damaging the school.

True, it was me who accidentally knocked the Bunsen burner into the cabinet when the glass shattered, but now I know why my solution wouldn't melt.

A half-laugh, half-sob escapes my lips, and Niklas squeezes the back of my neck. But before I'm fully free of the mental two-ton weight, there's one more thing I need to address.

I turn to Herr Geier. "Meister K never banished me, did he?"

He sucks in his cheeks as Meister K's eyes widen.

"Banish?" Meister K puts a hand to his chest. "Why would I banish one of my elves?"

"That's what I've been wondering for the last several days." I dig my fingers into my biceps. "But I stood before the Elder Council as the COE made the announcement himself. He had a document with what looked like your signature, and was adamant he doesn't act without Kringle approval."

"Is that so?" Crossing his arms, Meister K frowns at Herr Geier. Crimson travels up the elf's neck. "The Chief Operations Elf is not *supposed* to act without my approval. What document is she talking about?"

"We went along with a phony document?" Frau Betriebs screeches, her hands to her throat, her face white like snow.

Chaos erupts then, the kind that happens when you release a group of children to grab a present—any present—from a pile of gifts at the other end of the room, but there's one less present than child. Shouts burst from the audience, yelling emanates from the Elder Council, and quarrels break out among the clans.

"She's a menace to society and the bane of the Green Clan!"

Spit flies from Herr Geier's mouth, and he flails his arms. "A filthy mint among chocolates. Mark my words, one day she'll destroy Christmas if left unchecked. She's no elf—"

Niklas shoves his face into Herr Geier's comfort zone. "She's more elf than her father." He glances toward the audience. "No offense, Herr Kuchler!"

Herr Geier wags his finger at Niklas. "And you, defying every law your ancestors created. Why, I—"

"Siii-LENCE!"

UNSUNG HERO

Meister K's voice booms over the crowd via the microphone. A high-pitched ringing follows and all chatter halts. Meister K thumps back and forth across the stage in his thick, black boots, one hand holding the mic, the other fisted behind his back.

"It appears someone has taken liberties right under my beard. Herr Geier?" He stops in front of the COE, who stares at a spot on the stage floor. "Did you, in fact, sign my name to some document that exiled Tinsel from Flitterndorf?"

Herr Geier's lips mash together, but he gives a little nod.

Meister K scratches his cheek. "This is a grievous offense, indeed. Never has an elf acted in such a duplicitous manner. One worthy of banishment, *nicht wahr?*" Hushed exclamations ripple through the crowd, and Meister K clears his throat. "Yet I will extend mercy, where you withheld it from Miss Kuchler. Every action, however, comes with a consequence—good or bad—and this situation is no different." He bends to grip the elf's shoulder, his eyes lacking their customary twinkle. "Herr Geier, it pains me to do this, but you are hereby stripped of your position as COE and head of the Elder Council. Herr Referat will be your replacement, and you shall return to rug hooking after the Sunrise Festival. We'll discuss your Penalty later."

Herr Geier hangs his head, and once Meister K releases him, he runs from the stage, disappearing beyond the reach of the spotlights. My heart wrenches, and I press a hand against my chest. It's not easy eating humble pie in front of the entire community.

Meister K clasps my shoulder now, but this time his eyes crinkle. "As for you, Tinsel, I cringe to think what you've gone through this past week, what you must have thought about me. I am truly sorry. Please know, child, I would never banish you from your home." He leans forward, his mustache lifting in a smile. "No matter how many chemistry labs you might or might not explode."

My eyes clog with tears. "Thank you, sir."

"I think we all owe Tinsel an apology." Niklas takes the mic from his grandfather and turns to the audience. "We owe her an apology for our faulty assumptions in the past, our hasty judgments, our condemnation. You want to judge someone? Judge me. I'm the one who crashed *Valiant* when I panicked at the reins." The muscles in his jaw bunch. "Because I'm afraid to fly."

I cover my mouth at his admittance. Agitated chatter rises and falls among the elves, but Niklas continues.

"Until recently, I didn't even acknowledge my own reindeer, simply because they could fly. But guess who loves my reindeer. And guess who has quite a knack for flying." He gestures to me, and all gazes follow. Moisture collects in my lashes as he recaps my actions during the last two weeks, from using *Valiant* as a way to salvage the supplies to discovering *Honor's* existence and location.

The blood pounds in my ears. He's spilling his weaknesses in front of everyone. For me.

"So if you want someone to thank for saving Christmas, thank Tinsel. She's the unsung hero in our midst tonight, not me."

He never intended to take credit for himself, after all. And I was so close to doubting him. The tears roll down my cheeks, and I dash them away with a mitten. In the words of Licorice, I can be such an *eejit*.

With a crooked grin, Niklas walks across the stage toward me. "Does anyone here remember what *flitterndorf* means?"

No one answers. Who bothers to ponder the translation of a commonplace name, centuries old? Like reindeer lore, it gets lost over time.

"It means *tinsel town*." He closes the distance between us, his gaze locked with mine. "And when Tinsel wasn't here, life wasn't the same. There was no spark. No energy. No excitement."

I angle the microphone toward me. "No blunders."

My comment ignites some laughter, but Niklas scowls. "That's not who you are. You're not a blunder. You're not a mistake. All one has to do is think outside the box to see you have purpose, you have worth." The fervor in his gaze has my heart doing cartwheels. "You're one of the hardest-working elves I've ever met, and I find your level of determination and optimism admirable, gratifying. And extremely attractive."

"Attractive?" a voice shouts from somewhere in the back. "Romance between elves and Kringles is *verboten*. It's one of the edicts!"

A sly grin pulling at his lips, Niklas slips an arm around my waist. "Here's what I think about some half-baked, ancient edict." And he covers my mouth with his, kissing me in such a way that leaves no doubt as to his opinions on the matter.

Silence stifles the crowd. Long. Oppressive.

Until someone's hand-clapping pierces the stillness. A second one follows. Then a third and fourth. Soon, a good portion of the crowd is applauding. Even as I fist my hands in his coat lapels to keep Niklas close, I break away to smile into his face. "That doesn't sound like a Kringle falling off his pedestal. Not the way I imagined it, anyway."

His eyes sparkle. "That's the sound of a Kringle *jumping* off his pedestal, because his mint among chocolates is worth more to him than some lonely pier." Lifting the mic, he motions to our peers standing at the base of the stairs. "I'm in the mood to dance before my grandfather dashes away. Anyone else?"

Meister K takes his place in the sleigh as my classmates form a circle onstage. Niklas pulls me among them, and I wobble on legs turned to rope candy. "Are you sure this is a good idea? I'm not wearing my *dirndl*—"

"So? You're beautiful."

"And I haven't practiced in a week. What if I mess up? What if Frau Tanz—"

"She's no longer a threat." He spins me into his arms for the beginning stance. "Besides, you won't mess up."

"How can you be sure?"

"Because you'll do what you've always done. What tinsel does best."

I arch an eyebrow as the first notes to a lively rendition of "Carol of the Bells" chime across the hill. "And what's that?"

He winks. "You'll shine."

A tingle rushes through me, and I smile through blurry vision. As the key notes signal the dancers to begin, I allow myself to trust Niklas's lead and perform the steps as best I remember. He guides, I twirl. He lifts, I flip. He moves, I follow.

While I'm not the perfect dancer, I do wear the biggest grin.

When the last of the musical notes melts away, the crowd whoops and cheers, and Niklas crushes me in a hug. "You were fantastic."

I laugh into his shoulder. "I don't know about *fantastic,* but you do tend to bring out the best in me."

His arms tighten. "I've waited a long time for you to figure that out."

"Tinsel Kuchler," Meister K bellows above the commotion. "A word, please."

I gulp and approach the sleigh. Surely he knows it was Niklas's idea to kiss me. "Yes, sir?"

He leans toward me, an elbow on his knee. When I catch the twinkle in his eye, I breathe easier. "Herr Referat has informed me you missed an interview due to Herr Geier's schemes. Would next Thursday at nine o'clock work for you?"

I bounce on my toes. I get another chance! Now maybe I can finally prove—

Hold the mistletoe.

There will always be someone questioning my abilities, someone undermining my worth. When do I stop striving to please the unappeasable and accept myself as I am? A tall, clumsy elf who can talk to reindeer. Meister K has faith in me. Niklas likes me. My parents love me. In the end, there's nothing to prove.

I smile up at Meister K. "Next Thursday would work just fine, sir, but"—I glance at the Lower Stables, where the Third String has lined up to watch Santa's departure, and my smile broadens—"it's time I follow where both my heart *and* talent lie."

IT'S THE MOST WONDERFUL TIME OF THE YEAR

Two Weeks Later

"CINNAMON, LET ME SEE A PEPPERMINT TWIST." CLAD ONCE AGAIN in a *dirndl* (jeans are comfy, but there's nothing quite like a cherished outfit), I lean back against the split-rail fence in the Flight Training Arena. Cinnamon makes a tight spiral in the air, useful for descending into narrow spaces, and I clap. "Way better than two days ago. Okay, Cocoa, your turn."

Nearby, Jangles works with Licorice, who performs a combination of Spilled Milk and Molasses, shooting across the arena before coming to a halt. Butterscotch, meanwhile, perfects his Candy Canes (U-turns) with Leif. Outside the fence, Eggnog hovers three feet above the wide walkway that surrounds the arena.

I give him a thumb's up. "Nice job, Eggy."

Another muted *BOOM* of a firecracker shudders the air, and I grin. The Sunrise Festival is in full swing on Huff 'n Puff Hill, the anticipation infectious as everyone waits for the sun's return in roughly twenty minutes.

"Hey there, Hotshot."

A shiver passes through my body, and I turn as Niklas enters the FTA carrying two paper cups, steam curling above their lids. He greets me with a sound kiss on the lips and holds out a gloved hand. "One caramel Kandi Cup with extra whipped cream."

"Thank you." Tucking my mittens around its warmth, I glance at his cup. "And would that be peppermint?"

"Yep."

I snort. "You always get peppermint."

He rubs his nose against my cheek. "I like mint." Leaning his arms atop the railing, he inclines his head toward Eggnog. "How's he doing?"

"Better. He doesn't have the same petrified look in his eyes as last week."

"Yesterday I got the sense he's looking forward to the race this weekend. Am I wrong?"

I chuckle and take a sip of cocoa. "You read him right. He can't stop talking about it. Doesn't seem fair that he's going to blast by all the other reindeer, though."

Niklas grins. "It gives the others a goal to work toward." He scuffs a boot in the soft dirt. "You ready to go?"

"Don't know. Jangles calls the shots around here."

"Oh, you think so? Hey, Jangles! Sunrise in fifteen minutes. I'm taking Tinsel for a bit." Niklas tugs my arm with a wink. "What's the use in being a Kringle if you can't leverage it once in a while?"

Shaking my head, I duck through the railing. "How did it go at the Workshop this morning?" Behind me, Jangles calls for the others to take an hour-long break and join the festivities.

"I've hung all but two Santa coats in the lobby, so one Penalty is almost complete. Wish the other was that easy."

I feign shock. "You don't find peeling potatoes in the Workshop kitchens absolutely enthralling?" I search his gloves. "Got any blisters yet?"

"Ha ha." He opens the door for me, and I trip across the threshold. As in times past, his hand is the one thing that keeps me from falling on my face. He chuckles. "Clumsy elf."

Cupping my elbow, he weaves me through the animated crowd mingling on the snow-blanketed hilltop. Elves both left and right greet us as we pass. Learning to overlook my shortcomings isn't easy for some, but a surprising number have expressed gladness that I'm back. And at least the Minor Flight Team has accepted—appreciates, even—my talents with the reindeer.

Meister K belts out an occasional "ho, ho, ho" as he feeds an enormous bonfire off to the side. Beyond the range of the undulating plume of smoke, a band plays German folk music while students clap to the beat, stomp their feet, or dance a jig. Other elves laugh in conversation, cuddle on blankets spread over the snow, or chase little ones in a game of tag.

Whatever the activity, everyone exudes a sense of exhilaration.

And for good reason. Christmas witnessed the delight of a successful round of deliveries (Niklas gave me an IOU for a pair of handmade skis). New Year's came with sweet kisses and hopeful resolutions (and a visit to the Donati family before Logan left for Quebec). And now, almost a week later, Flitterndorf is about to see the sun again.

Phone in hand, Kristof greets us from the spot he claimed with a blanket near my family, and we settle beside him on the edge of Huff 'n Puff Hill. *Mutti* catches my gaze and winks, a proud smile pushing at her cheeks. Beside me, Kristof's phone chirps. I glance at the screen as it flashes a text from—

He flips the phone over, looking at me askance. His ears turn red and I smile. Interesting.

Niklas motions across the Flitterndorf valley to the crimson hollow between Mount Trost and Mount Freude. "Here it comes." He presses the back of my mittened hand to his mouth. "You watching?"

"Yeah." My gaze wanders a lazy path over his face. He still owns a perfect chin, but the features I once thought steeped in arrogance I now know bear the shades of responsibility and concern. And a drive to excellence, not for excellence's sake but out of a love for those whom he'll one day serve. (In case you're wondering, he turned down the managerial internship in favor of hobnobbing with the Third String.)

(Who did get the internship? Apparently, Pix has major managerial skills. Who knew?)

Niklas grins now, his gaze fastened on the horizon. "You're looking in the wrong direction."

"Am I?"

He blows warm air into my mitten. "Though I can't say I'm not flattered."

I cock my head. "You haven't asked why I'm looking at you. There's this strange—"

"Careful, Kuchler." He nudges me with his shoulder. "Remember the power of your words."

I laugh and snuggle against him. "Sorry. Old habits and all that."

The hollow in the mountains changes from crimson to pink to orange to—

"There it is." Niklas throws up his arms like a spectator cheering his team's winning play. "Sun, O glorious sun!"

As its life-giving rays spill over the occupants of Huff 'n Puff Hill and stretch toward the valley below, a multitude of fireworks explode in the sky. Reds, blues, greens. Elves and Kringles erupt in animated glee, and tinsel rains down from huge sacks strung across the hill.

Niklas makes a face and bats at the strands clinging to his hat and scarf. "It had to be tinsel."

Grinning, I stuff a wad of it down his coat collar. "And we all know how you feel about tinsel."

"Do you, now?" A naughty twinkle sparks in his eyes. "In case Christmas Eve wasn't clear, and somebody needs a little reminder..." Slipping his hand behind my neck, Niklas slants his lips across mine and lavishes me with a very thorough, very memorable kiss.

I'm all a-tangle. And I rather like it that way.

Since I had a little fun with this story and sprinkled some German phrases throughout, below is a list of those words as they appear in the story. In the brackets, I wrote them the way a young American student might write them when trying to sound out new words, rather than with phonetic symbols...because I'm not sure many of us know what those symbols mean anymore.

Depending on where you visit/live in Germany, the "ch" can sound like a hard "k," or softer, like when you pretend you're a cat hissing from the back of your throat. :) Because the latter is how *I* learned it and heard it pronounced, I will reflect that below with an "x."

As for the names of elves and places you'll find when reading, each one is intentional, but I'll leave it to you to do the research, if you're interested in their meanings. Hint: the elves' last names indicate their line of work.

German words as they appear:

Herr—[hair] Mister

Lederhosen—[LAY-der-hoh-zen] Leather breeches, traditionally worn either short or knee-length. In Flitterndorf, they're long, down to the ankles. Hey, it's cold!

Dirndl—[DURN-dl] Traditional work dress

Mein—[mine] My (masculine and neutral form)

Schatz—[shahts] An endearment, like sweetheart, treasure

Vati—[FAH-tee] Dad

Meister—[MY-ster] Master

Ja—[yah] Yes

Oma—[OH-mah] Grandmother

Frau—[frow] Missus/Mrs.

Danke—[DAHNG-keh] Thank you

Lebkuchen—[LAYB-koo-xuhn] A type of cookie with a cake-like texture, typically frosted and containing spices and honey.

Verboten—[fair-BOAT-n] Forbidden

Mutti—[MUH-tee] Mom

Hallo—[HA-low] Hello/Hi

Nein—[nine] No

Opa—[OH-pah] Grandfather

Guten Morgen—[GOO-ten MORE-gen] Good morning

Was geht hier vor?—[vahs gait here fohr] What's going on?

Alles in Ordnung?—[ah-less in ohrd-nung] Everything all right?

Nicht wahr?—[nixt vahr] Isn't that so?

Liebling—[LEEB-ling] An endearment, like darling, honey, sweetheart

Vielen dank—[fee-len dahnk] Thank you very much

Was ist los?—[vahs ist lohs] What's the matter?

The few Scottish words that might confound you:

Gel—girl, with the 'g' pronounced the same way

Shut yer geggy—shut your mouth

Gaun yersel—you're joking

Any other Scottish words are either self-explanatory or understood in context.

ACKNOWLEDGMENTS

I've often heard it takes the help of many to write a book, but I never experienced this with my manuscripts until *Tinsel,* and I have a lot of people to thank for making her shine.

First, thank you to Stephanie Taylor at Clean Reads, for taking a chance on a Christmas-themed debut novel and allowing Tinsel and Niklas to see the world beyond my laptop.

Thank you to my local writers group, in particular Ashley Martin, Leah Schwabauer, Rebecca Mildren, and Lea Freitas, who each played a different role in helping me through the ups and downs of crafting *Tinsel,* and who suffered through endless versions of query blurbs. ;)

Thank you to my fellow ACFW writers who critiqued this story in the Scribes loop, especially Samantha Wooten (I still "hear" your voice in my head as I write and ask myself which words you would cut), Robyn Hook (I'm so thankful for the friendship that developed through the many exchanges of our crits), Kathy McKinsey and Jael Ray (your initial interest in *Tinsel* buoyed my spirits and introduced me to Scribes), and Daisy Townsend (so blessed by your sweet encouragement at exactly those times I needed it). Lastly, thank you, Ane Mulligan, for teaching the online course back in March, 2013. It helped breathe life into characters that had drifted aimlessly in my mind for too long.

I'm grateful for my parents who didn't squash my crazy enthusiasm for Christmas (or Santa Claus), and for my daughters who endure my inattentiveness on the days I'm more wrapped up in my characters' lives than their own. Thank you, Kreh, for your countless prayers on my behalf and bearing with all my writing mood swings over the past sixteen years.

Most importantly, I praise my Heavenly Father for this book. Some feel Santa and God should have nothing to do with each other, but the Lord blessed me not only with a love for the fantasy side of Christmas, but also the creativity to pen these words. Without Him, Tinsel and Niklas would not exist.

ABOUT THE AUTHOR

Though **Laurie Germaine** has been crafting stories from a young age, she found renewed joy when she combined her year-round love for Christmas with an unused BA in German, and the seed was sown for *Tinsel in a Tangle*. A New England native who once dreamed of raising her family in Europe, Laurie now lives in Montana with her husband, two daughters, and their mellow Alaskan Malamute. When she's not immersed in her latest WIP, you can find her knitting or creating dioramas for her 16-inch poseable dolls. Visit her on Facebook, Twitter, or on her blog, Scattered Whimsy.

www.scatteredwhimsy.com

Clean Reads
GREAT STORIES. NO GUILT.

CPSIA information can be obtained
at www.ICGtesting.com
Printed in the USA
FSOW02n0122141117
40950FS